WINNETOU

By Karl May

D0915738

Unabridged 2008 translation of
Karl May's "Winnetou I"

George A. Alexander, Translator

Preposterous Press
Media, Pennsylvania

Acknowledgements

I want to thank my daughter, Becky, for her outstanding cover art; and my sister, Margaret, for insightful suggestions and endless hours of copyediting.

And most of all, I want to thank my wife Jan, without whose help, interest, and encouragement over many years this book would never have been published.

G. A. A.

Although we have done our best to proofread this book and make sure it is free of typographic errors, we imagine there are still a few we missed. If you find one, or if you want to provide any other feedback on this book, please send us an email at:

george@changingoutlook.com

We look forward to hearing from you.

Contents

Foreword

If you spend enough time with Germans, you'll eventually learn about Karl May. He is as much a part of German cultural history as Mark Twain is of US cultural history. His books, and especially the ones about Old Shatterhand and Winnetou (Winnetou volumes I, II, and III, published in 1893) created a sensation. It is no exaggeration to say that Winnetou was the Harry Potter of the time, eventually selling millions of copies in many languages; and the Winnetou books continue to be among the all-time best-selling German books.

Hearing about the Winnetou stories, the movies based on them, and the outdoor re-enactments that still take place every summer in Germany, I became curious and read the books myself. They are wonderful adventure stories, but I was astonished to learn that no good translations were available in English. So I set out to correct that situation, and the book you are holding is the result. It is a new, unabridged translation of Winnetou I.

The main factors that made the books such a hit with readers back in the 1890s still make them interesting reading today. The adventures of Old Shatterhand (stronger and smarter than any of the villains he encounters) and Winnetou (the wise and noble Indian who becomes his blood-brother) are still exciting. And the concept of the American West—wide open, natural, wild and unsettled—appeals to the imagination of modern urban dwellers just as it did to turn-of-the-century Europeans who were dealing with the fallout from the industrial revolution.

Although the story is timeless, it is set in a specific historical time and place (the American West sometime after the Civil War). I have tried to make this translation true to the period, while still making it understandable to today's readers. For that reason, you may find the language old-fashioned at times (but, I hope, still readable).

When I started working on this translation several years ago, I had no idea that there would suddenly be a flurry of other Karl May translations. But that is exactly what is happening at the moment. Michael Michalak, through his publishing company, Nemsi Books (www.nemsi-books.net), and Marlies Bugmann, through her organization, the Australian Friends of Karl May (www.karl-may-friends.net) are publishing several new translations a year.

I hope that all these newly-translated books, including this one, will draw a new generation of readers to the work of Karl May.

George Alexander
August, 2008

Chapter 1

Dear reader, do you know what the word "greenhorn" means? Getting called a "greenhorn" is a highly annoying and disrespectful slur.

A greenhorn is a person who is still "green" (that is, new and without experience in the West) and who must feel his way carefully if he wants to avoid making a fool of himself. Like a calf whose horns are still immature, he has a lot to learn before his comrades take him seriously.

A greenhorn is a person who doesn't get up from his chair when a woman wants to sit there; who greets the man of the house before tipping his hat to the Mrs. and Miss; who shoves the cartridge in the barrel backwards when loading his rifle, or who puts the wadding down the muzzle first, then the ball, and finally the gunpowder. A greenhorn speaks either no English at all, or else a very pure and affected English. To him, Yankee English or backwoods English is an atrocity; he can't make heads or tails of it, much less express himself in it.

A greenhorn mistakes a raccoon for an opossum and a Mulatto for a Quadroon. A greenhorn smokes cigarettes and loathes the tobacco-chewing man. When he gets his ears boxed by an Irishman, a greenhorn runs off and takes his case to a judge, instead of just shooting the fellow on the spot like a real Yankee would. A greenhorn mistakes the footprints of a turkey for the trail of a bear and a sleek yacht for a Mississippi steamer.

A greenhorn is reluctant to lay his dirty boots on the knees of his fellow passengers or to slurp his soup with a panting noise like a buffalo in its death throes. For the sake of cleanliness, a greenhorn packs a sponge the size of a giant pumpkin and ten pounds of soap across the prairie, along with a compass that, within three or four days, points every possible direction but North.

A greenhorn notes down 800 Indian expressions and then notices, as soon as he encounters his first Indian, that he has mistakenly sent the notes home by the last mail and kept the letter he wanted to send instead. A greenhorn buys gunpowder and then realizes, when he is ready to fire his first shot, that he was given ground up charcoal instead. A greenhorn has studied astronomy for ten years without being able to look at the stars and tell what time it is. A greenhorn sticks his Bowie knife in his belt so that it stabs him in the thigh when he bends over. Out in the wild, a greenhorn makes his campfire so big that it blazes as high as the treetops, and then, when he gets shot by Indians, he wonders how they found him.

That's what a greenhorn is, and back then I was just such a greenhorn myself.

But don't believe for a moment that I was ever persuaded (or that I even had a clue) that this hurtful name applied to me! Oh no, for this is the most outstanding characteristic of a greenhorn—you believe that other people are greenhorns, but not you yourself.

Quite to the contrary, I thought of myself as an exceptionally clever and experienced person. Hadn't I always studied hard and never feared an exam? It never entered my young brain that life was the real school, that its students are tested every hour of every day and that they must justify themselves before Providence.

Some unfortunate experiences at home and, I must admit, an inborn need for action drove me to cross the ocean to the United States, where conditions for the advancement of an industrious young man were much better than they are today. I could have made a good living on the East Coast, but I felt driven westward. Working first at one job, then another, never at any of them for very long, I was able to earn enough to finally arrive at St. Louis, well-clothed on the outside and in high spirits on the inside. There, I had the good fortune to find a German family that gave me a temporary place as family tutor.

A certain Mr. Henry came to visit this family. He was quite a character, a gun-maker who conducted his trade with the dedication of an artist. He called himself, with old-fashioned pride, "Mr. Henry, the Gunsmith." This man was exceptionally warm-hearted and generous, although he appeared to be the opposite. Aside from the German family I worked for, he had no personal relationships, and even with his customers he was so short and gruff that they would not have come back except for the quality of his goods. He had lost his wife and children due to a terrible event that he never spoke of; but based on some of his comments I suspected that they had been killed in an ambush. This had given him his rough exterior. He may not even have realized that he behaved like a perfect brute, but at the core he was mild and good. I often saw his eyes get misty as I spoke of my homeland and my family, to which my whole heart was devoted, as it still is today.

Why this old man should take such a liking to me, a young foreigner, was a mystery until he explained it one day. From the time I arrived, he was a frequent visitor at the house where I stayed. He listened as I taught, and when I was finished he monopolized my attention and even invited me to visit him. He had never given anyone else that distinction, and I was therefore hesitant to take him up on it. But he was not happy about my reluctance. I still remember his angry expression one evening when I arrived at his house and the tone with which he received me, not even bothering to answer my "good evening."

"Where were you hiding yesterday, Sir?"

"At home."

"And the day before?"

"At home."

"Don't kid with me."

"It's true, Mr. Henry."

"Pshaw! Fledglings like you don't stay in the nest. They go around sticking their beaks into all kinds of places where they don't belong!"

"And would you care to tell me where you think I belong?"

"Right here, of course. I've been waiting a long time to ask you something."

"Why didn't you?"

"I didn't feel like it."

"So when will you?"

"Maybe today."

"Well, go ahead. Ask away," I invited, and I sat down on the edge of the workbench where he was working.

He gazed at me quizzically, shook his head disapprovingly, and exclaimed:

" 'Go ahead'? As if I should have to get the permission of a greenhorn when I want a word with him!"

"Greenhorn?" I replied, my wrinkled forehead betraying my wounded pride. "I have to assume, Mr. Henry, that you didn't intend to use that word and it just slipped out."

"Don't kid yourself, young man. I meant what I said. You're a first-rate greenhorn. Sure, you have a head full of book learning. It's astounding what you foreigners have to learn! You young fellows know exactly how far the stars are from here, what King Nebuchadnezzar wrote on clay tablets, and how much the air weighs, in spite of the fact that it's invisible. And just because you know all this stuff, you think you're pretty smart. Well, try living a little—take it from me, I've got fifty years behind me—and maybe, just maybe, you'll discover what real knowledge is. What you know now is nothing, absolutely nothing. And your skills are even less. Why, I bet you can't even shoot!"

He said this in an extraordinarily scornful tone of voice, and with an air of certainty that suggested he was completely sure of his facts.

"So you think I can't shoot?" I answered, smiling. "Hmm. Is that what you wanted to ask me about?"

"Well, yes, that's it. How do you answer?"

"I'll show you my answer when you hand me a good rifle."

At that, he put aside the rifle barrel that he had been working on, stood up, walked over to me, gazed at me a moment in amusement, and then announced:

"Hand you a good rifle, Sir? Absolutely not. I wouldn't think of it. I only put my guns into the hands of those who are worthy of them."

"Then you can hand one to me."

He looked at me again, from the side, sat down again, resumed his work on the barrel, and muttered to himself:

"What a greenhorn! His audacity is driving me crazy!"

I knew his ways, so I let him grumble, pulled out a cigar, and lit it. Neither of us said a word for a quarter of an hour. At last, he could stand it no longer. He held the barrel up to the light, squinted through it, and remarked:

"Shooting is harder than stargazing or reading Nebuchadnezzar's old clay tablets. Understand? Have you ever had a gun in your hands?"

"I sure have."

"When?"

"Frequently, over many years."

"You've actually fired one?"

"Yes."

"Ever hit anything?"

"Of course!"

He set down the barrel he had checked, looked at me again, and said:

"All right, but could you hit what you were aiming at?"

"Obviously."

"What? Do you expect me to believe that?"

"I'm not putting anything over on you. It's the truth."

"The devil take you, Sir! You're a hopeless case. I'll bet you couldn't hit the broad side of a barn if it was 20 yards high and 50 yards long. You try to look so serious and honest when you make such claims that it just makes me livid. Don't treat me like one of those kids you tutor, understand? You want me to believe that a greenhorn and bookworm like you can shoot? That you have rummaged around in Turkish, Arabic, and Lord knows what other tattered old books and still had time to learn to shoot? Well, we'll see. Take that old gun down from the nail back there, and hold it as if you were aiming it. It's a bear-killer, the best I ever had in my hands."

I went and got down the rifle and sighted down the barrel.

"Whoa!" he cried, jumping up. "Hold on there! You're handling that gun like it was a light rifle, and it's the heaviest gun I know! You're stronger than I figured."

Instead of answering, I grabbed him by the jacket and belt and lifted him off the floor with my right arm.

"Thunderstorm!" he cried. "Let me down! You're a darn sight stronger than my Bill."

"Your Bill? Who is that?"

"He was my son. We won't talk about that. He's dead, like the others. He had a lot of promise, but he was killed with the rest while I was gone. You look a little like him. Your eyes are almost the same, and you have the same look around the mouth. That's why I . . . oh, forget it, it doesn't concern you."

An expression of deep sadness had spread over his features. He ran his hand across his face and then resumed, in a more cheerful tone:

"But, Sir, with muscles like yours, it's a crying shame you spend so much time with your books. You should have been getting exercise."

"Actually, I did."

"Really?"

"Yes."

"Boxing?"

"We didn't have boxing back home. But I did a good bit of wrestling and gymnastics."

"Riding?"

"Yes."

"Fencing?"

"I took lessons."

"Stop making things up!"

"Care to take me on?"

"Thanks, I had enough a minute ago. Anyway, I have work to do. Have a seat."

He returned to his workbench, and I sat down. The conversation that followed was mostly just single syllables. Henry seemed to be thinking hard about something important. Suddenly, he looked up from his work and asked:

"Did you ever study math?"

"It was one of my favorite subjects."

"Arithmetic, geometry?"

"Naturally."

"Surveying?"

"A particular favorite. I often went out to practice with the transit, even when I didn't have to."

"And you can really do a survey?"

"Yes. I've often done surveying and leveling, although I don't claim to be a trained surveyor."

"Well, that's good, excellent!"

"Why do you say so, Mr. Henry?"

"I've got my reasons, understand? You don't need to know just yet. You'll find out soon enough. But first we need to see if you can really shoot."

"All right, put me to the test!"

"Oh, I will, I will. You can depend on it. When do you start teaching in the morning?"

"Eight o'clock."

"All right, come here at six tomorrow morning. We'll go over to the firing range where I test my guns."

"Why so early?"

"Because I don't want to wait any longer. I'm in a hurry to show you what a greenhorn you are. But enough of that. I have other work to do that is much more important."

He seemed to be finished with the gun barrel, and he took a many-sided piece of iron out of a box and began to file its corners. I saw that each surface had a hole in it.

He was so lost in his work that he seemed to have forgotten my presence. His eyes gleamed, and I observed what I would almost call an expression of love on his face when he examined his work from time to time. I saw that this piece of iron must mean a great deal to him. I was curious to learn why, so I asked him:

"Is that part of a gun too, Mr. Henry?"

"Yes," he answered, as though startled by my presence.

"But I'm not familiar with any kind of gun that has a piece like that in it."

"I can believe that. It doesn't exist yet. It will be the 'Henry Repeater.'"

"Oh, a new invention?"

"Yes."

"Then I apologize for asking. It must be a secret."

He scrutinized all the holes for a while, turned the piece of iron in various ways, held it up to the back end of the barrel that he had previously been working on, and finally said:

"Yes, it's a secret, but I'll trust you with it because I know you can keep quiet, even if you are a complete and utter greenhorn. So I'll tell you what it's going to be. It will be a carbine, a repeating carbine that can fire 25 shots."

"Impossible!"

"Hush up! I'm not so dumb that I would undertake something impossible."

"But it would have to have chambers to hold 25 rounds."

"It will."

"Surely that would make it so big and bulky that it would be too cumbersome."

"There's only one chamber; it is not awkward and it isn't cumbersome. This piece of iron is the chamber."

"Hmm. I don't know anything about your trade, but what about heat? Won't the barrel get too hot?"

"Not a chance. The material and construction of the barrel are my secret. Besides, is it ever necessary to fire 25 shots one after the other?"

"Hardly."

"There you have it. This piece of iron is roughly a sphere which is allowed to move eccentrically. There are 25 holes, each with a cartridge. With each shot, the sphere moves to the next position, with a new cartridge facing the barrel. I've been working on this idea for years and couldn't get it to work, but now I think I've got it. I already have a good name as a gunsmith, but soon I'll be famous, and I'll make a pile of money."

"And a guilty conscience as well."

He glanced up at me, bewildered.

"A guilty conscience? Why?"

"Don't you think a murderer should have a guilty conscience?"

"Zounds! Are you calling me a murderer?"

"Not yet."

"You think I will be one?"

"Yes. Aiding in murder is almost as bad as the killing itself."

"The devil take you! I'd never participate in murder."

"A single one, perhaps not. But I'm talking about mass murder."

"What are you talking about?"

"If you create a gun that shoots 25 shots, and allow any old low-life to get his hands on one, you'll see a horrible slaughter on the prairies and in the mountain passes. They'll be shooting down Indians like coyotes, and in a few years there won't be an Indian left. Do you want that on your conscience?"

"And," I continued, "if anyone with the money can buy this dangerous weapon, I have no doubt you'll unload thousands of them in no time. But the mustangs and the buffalo will be killed off, along with all the other wild animals that the red man needs. Hundreds and thousands of claim jumpers will equip themselves with your carbine and head west. The blood of men and animals will flow in the streams and it won't be long until there is nothing living left on either side of the Rockies."

"Good Lord!" he cried. "Did you really just come over from Germany?"

"Yes."

"And you were never here before?"

"Never."

"Nowhere in the West?"

"No."

"A complete greenhorn, then. And yet this greenhorn tries to talk like he's the grandfather of all the Indians, living here for a thousand years! Young man, don't you get me angry! And even if everything were as you say, I would never consider building a gun factory. I'm a loner, and I'll stay a loner. I have no interest in dealing with dozens or even hundreds of workers."

"But couldn't you patent your invention and make money selling rights to it?"

"No rush about that, Sir. Up to now I've always had enough money to get by, and I think I can continue to manage just fine without a patent. And now get out of here! I'm in no mood to listen to the cheeping of a bird that isn't even ready to fly yet, let alone sing."

I wasn't inclined to take offence at this. It was just his way of expressing himself, and I knew what he meant. He had taken a liking to me, and he was obviously ready to help me out any way he could. I held out my hand, he shook it heartily, and I left.

I had no idea how important this evening would turn out to be for me. Nor did I imagine the role that both the heavy bear-killer ("that old gun," as Henry called it) and the unfinished "Henry Repeater" would play in my life. But I was excited about the next morning. I really had done a lot of shooting, and I was a good shot. I was certain that I would fare well in the eyes of this odd old man.

Chapter 2

I arrived promptly at six the next morning. He was already waiting for me. He shook my hand, and a fleeting ironic smile passed over his coarse features:

"Welcome, Sir! You look pretty self-confident. You think you'll be able to hit the side of the barn I mentioned last night?"

"I hope so."

"Well, we'll find out soon enough. I'll take this light rifle, and you bring the old bear-killer. I don't feel like dragging that much weight around."

He slung a light double-barreled rifle around his neck, and I took the "old gun" that he didn't want to carry. When we arrived at his shooting range, he loaded both guns and fired two shots himself with the rifle. Then it was my turn with the bear-killer. I wasn't yet familiar with the gun and so my first shot just hit the edge of the black bulls-eye. The second was better, and the third was exactly in the middle. The rest of my shots went right into the hole created by the third. Mr. Henry's astonishment increased with each shot. Then I had to try the rifle, and when I had the same success with it, he cried:

"Either you're in league with the devil, Sir, or you were born to be a frontiersman. I never saw a greenhorn shoot like that!"

"I stay clear of the devil, Mr. Henry," I laughed. "I don't want any part of that kind of a deal."

"Then it's your task, your duty even, to become a frontiersman. Do you think you'd enjoy that?"

"Why not!"

"Well, we'll have to see what we can make out of this greenhorn. You know how to ride?"

"If I have to."

"If you have to? You don't ride as well as you shoot, then?"

"Pshaw! What's riding anyway! The hard part is getting on. Once I'm in the saddle, there's no horse that can get me off."

Again he gave me a questioning look, trying to tell if I was serious or joking. I kept my expression noncommittal, and so he said:

"You really think so? You figure on holding onto the mane? You're mistaken there. You got it right when you said getting on was the hardest part: you have to do that yourself. The horse takes care of the getting-off part, and it goes a heck of a lot faster."

"No horse will do that to me!"

"Really? We'll see. Are you up for a test?"

"Sure."

"All right, come with me. It's just seven o'clock and you still have an hour left. We'll go visit Jim Korner, the horse trader. He's got a chestnut stallion that will give you some trouble."

We headed back into town to the horse trader's lot. He had a big corral with lots of stalls around it. Korner himself appeared and asked what he could do for us.

"This young fellow claims that no horse can get him out of the saddle," Mr. Henry replied. "What's your opinion on the matter, Mr. Korner? Would you let him give your chestnut stallion a try?"

Korner looked me over, then nodded and said:

"His frame looks good and flexible. Anyway, a young fellow isn't nearly as likely to break his neck as an older one. If this gentleman wants to give the chestnut a try, it's all right by me."

He called back into the stable, and presently two boys brought the saddled horse out of the stall. It was very unruly and tried to break loose. Mr. Henry started getting worried about me and suggested I forget about the test, but I wasn't particularly scared and I was now beginning to view the matter as a point of honor. I asked for a whip and spurs and, after several failed attempts, managed to swing myself into the saddle. The moment I was on the horse's back, the two boys took off running. Instantly, the mare jumped once straight into the air, and then a second time off to the side. I held on to the saddle, trying desperately to get my feet in the stirrups. I had hardly managed to do this when the horse started to buck; when that didn't work, he headed for the wall, to try to scrape me off on it, but I was able to turn him away with the whip. Then began a tough and dangerous battle between horse and rider. I used everything I had: my limited abilities, the insufficient training I that I'd had, and the power of my thighs, and in the end, I won. When I got off, my legs were trembling from the exertion, but the horse was covered with sweat and big, heavy globs of foam hung around its mouth. Now it obeyed every command.

The horse trader had become anxious about his horse. He had a helper cover it in blankets and lead it slowly back and forth. Then he turned to me:

"Young man, I never would have believed it. I thought sure you'd be thrown the first time the horse jumped. You don't owe me anything, and if you want to do me a favor, you can come back later and finish breaking in this beast. I wouldn't mind putting ten dollars into it. This horse cost me a lot, and if it can learn to obey, I'll make some money on it yet."

"It would be my pleasure, if it's all right with you," I replied.

Mr. Henry hadn't said anything since I had dismounted. He was just looking at me and shaking his head. Now he clapped his hands together and cried:

"This greenhorn is an extraordinary and unusual greenhorn! He half squeezes the horse to death instead of being thrown in the dirt. Who taught you that, Sir?"

"I learned by accident, through finding myself on the back of a half-wild Hungarian stallion that no one wanted to try riding. I gradually brought him under control, but I just about risked my life doing it."

"Thank goodness for such creatures! But I'm fond of my old armchair that doesn't object when I sit on it. Come on then, let's go. Watching you nearly made me dizzy. But you'll be glad that I saw how you shoot and ride. You can count on it."

He went off to his house, and I went off to mine. He didn't come around that day or the next, and I didn't get a chance to go looking for him. But on the following day, he came over in the afternoon. He knew I had some free time.

"Want to go for a walk?" he asked.

"Where to?"

"To visit a gentleman who wants to meet you."

"Why me?"

"Good question: because he's never met a greenhorn."

"All right, I'll come. It's high time he met one."

Mr. Henry had a cunning and conspiratorial look on his face. I knew from previous experience that he was planning some kind of surprise. We strolled several blocks, and then he ushered me into an office with a large glass door facing the street. We entered so quickly that I didn't get a chance to read the gold lettering on the glass, but I thought I saw the words "Office" and "Surveying." I soon learned that I was right.

The three men in the office gave Mr. Henry a friendly welcome. They greeted me politely and with barely-concealed curiosity. Maps and plans lay on the table, along with various measuring instruments. We were in a land office.

It wasn't clear to me exactly what my friend had in mind in making this visit. He had no message to pass along, no inquiry to make. He seemed to have come purely for the sake of friendly conversation. This quickly became very animated, and although it wasn't initially obvious, it eventually extended to the materials that were spread out on the table. That was fine with me. I could participate better in a conversation about those than in one about American subjects that I wasn't yet familiar with.

On this particular day, Mr. Henry seemed especially interested in surveying. He wanted to know everything. I gradually became involved in the conversation and by the end I was answering one question after another, explaining the use of the various instruments, and describing the process of mapping. I was certainly a real greenhorn, because I completely failed to notice their true intent. It was only when I started talking about the use of coordinates, the polar and diagonal methods, the measurement of perimeters, the use of repeated measurements for checking, and the trigonometry of triangulation, and when I noticed that the three men were making hidden signs to Mr. Henry, that I finally realized what was going on. I stood up from my chair to indicate to Mr. Henry that I wanted to leave. He agreed, and we were sent off in an even friendlier a manner than we had been welcomed.

As soon as we were around the corner from the office, Mr. Henry stopped, laid his hand on my shoulder and said, with a satisfied look on his face:

"Sir, Mister, young man, greenhorn, or whatever, I'm delighted with your performance. Why, I'm positively proud of you!"

"Why?"

"Because you exceeded even my recommendation and the expectations of these men."

"Recommendation? Expectation? I don't know what you're talking about."

"It's very simple. Earlier, you told me you knew a little about surveying. In order to see if you were just making it up, I took you to see these gentlemen, who are good friends of mine, to put you to the test. You passed with flying colors."

"Making it up? Mr. Henry, if you really think I'd do a thing like that, I'm not going to have anything to do with you any more."

"Don't be silly! You wouldn't rob an old fellow like me of the joy of watching you. You know, because of the similarity to my son. Have you been back to see the horse trader?"

"Every morning."

"And you've been riding the chestnut stallion?"

"Yes."

"Can anything be done with that horse?"

"I think so. But I doubt that the man that buys him will have as good a time of it as me. The horse has gotten used to me, but he still throws everyone else."

"Wonderful. That pleases me no end. So it appears the horse will only tolerate greenhorns! Come on down this side street. There's a boarding-house down here where you can get great food and even better drink. We have to celebrate the examination that you passed so well today."

I couldn't understand Mr. Henry's behavior. He seemed completely transformed. Why did he, a lonely and withdrawn soul, want to eat in a boarding-house? His face looked different too, and his speech sounded brighter and happier than usual. I was struck by his use of the word "examination," but for all I knew it was just a local expression.

From that day on, he came to see me daily and treated me as if I were a close friend that he feared he might soon lose. But he saw to it that this preferential treatment never went to my head. He was always ready to put me back in my place with that fatal word "greenhorn."

Strangely enough, the family I worked for began to treat me differently as well. The parents paid me noticeably more attention, and the children were more affectionate. I would sometimes notice them secretly casting glances at me whose meaning I didn't understand. I would describe them as both loving and regretful.

About three weeks after our odd visit to the land office, the lady of the family asked me if I would join them for supper, although it was my evening off. The reason she gave for the invitation was that Mr. Henry was coming, and she had also invited two other gentlemen, one of whom was named Sam Hawkens, a well-known frontiersman. Greenhorn that I was, I hadn't yet heard of him, but I was delighted to be able to meet a real frontiersman, and a famous one at that.

As a member of the household, I didn't have to wait until the clock struck the dinner hour; instead, I came down to the dining room a few minutes earlier. To my astonishment, the room was decorated as if for a party. The little 5-year-old Emmy was alone in the room and had stuck her finger in the jam jar. She saw me coming, pulled her finger out of the jam, and wiped it off in her blond hair. As I raised my finger to scold her, she ran up to me and whispered a few words. To make up for her transgression, she shared with me the secret of the last few days, which had practically broken her poor little heart. I thought I had misunderstood, but she repeated for me: "Your farewell party."

My farewell party? Impossible! What strange misunderstanding could have led the child to this crazy conclusion? I had to smile. Then I heard voices in the parlor. The guests had arrived, and I went to greet them. All three came at the same time (intentionally, as I later learned). Mr. Henry introduced me to Mr. Black, a somewhat blunt and awkward-looking man, and then to Sam Hawkens, the frontiersman.

The frontiersman! In my astonishment, I must have looked pretty silly when I first set my eyes on him. I had never seen anyone like him. (Later, though, I met lots of others.) While his appearance itself was remarkable enough, the impression he made was increased by the fact that he stood in the parlor just as if he were out in the wilderness, with his hat on and his gun in his hand. Just consider his appearance:

Under the sadly drooping brim of a felt hat (the original age, color, and shape of which would have defied the sharpest observer), a nose of shocking dimensions appeared amid a forest of tangled black beard. The only other part of the face that could be glimpsed within the extravagant growth of beard were two tiny, bright, lively eyes. They rested on me with an expression of mischievous cunning. The man observed me with as much interest as I observed him. I later learned the reason for his interest.

This head rested on a body which seemed invisible down to the knees. It was wrapped in an old leather hunting jacket that had apparently been made for a much larger person. It gave him the appearance of a child who was trying on his grandfather's nightshirt for fun. Below this overly long garment two skinny, sickle-shaped legs appeared. They were enclosed in fringed leggings that were so short that they must have been outgrown two decades earlier, and this provided a clear view of the Indian boots which were so large that they could have provided shelter for the man's whole body in an emergency.

This famous "frontiersman" carried a rifle in his hand that I would have touched only with the greatest caution. It looked a lot more like a club than a rifle. In that moment, I couldn't have imagined a greater caricature of a prairie scout. But before long, I would come to fully recognize the value of this odd little man.

After he had a good look at me, he asked Mr. Henry in a thin voice like that of a child:

"Is this the young greenhorn you told me about, Mr. Henry?"

"Yes," he nodded.

"Well! He's not particularly impressive. I hope Sam Hawkens will impress him equally, hee-hee-hee!"

With this strange, high-pitched laugh, which I would later hear thousands of times, he turned toward the door, which was just opening. The father and mother of the family came in and greeted the scout in a way that indicated they had met previously. My back was to them as this happened. They then invited us into the dining room.

We followed this invitation, and still, to my astonishment, Sam Hawkens kept his gun with him. Once we had been shown our places at the table, he pointed to his old weapon and said:

"A real frontiersman never lets his gun out of his sight, and I certainly wouldn't leave my good old Liddy where I couldn't see her. I'll hang her here on the end of the curtain rod."

So "Liddy" was what he called his gun! Later, I would learn that many frontiersmen treat their guns like living beings and give them names. He hung it up, and then hung his remarkable hat in the same spot. But to my astonishment, when he took it off all his hair went with it.

It was really frightening to see his hairless, blood-red head. The mother cried out, and the children squealed at the top of their lungs. But he turned to us and said evenly:

"Don't be frightened, ladies and gentlemen, it's really nothing. I had my own hair from childhood and no one disputed my right to wear it until one or two dozen Pawnees attacked me and removed the hair and half the skin from my scalp. It was a hell of a disturbing experience, but fortunately I survived it, hee-hee-hee! Then I went to Tekama and bought myself a new scalp, if I'm not mistaken. It was called a wig and cost me three big bundles of beaver pelts. No harm done, though: this new hair is much more practical than what I used to have. It can take it off when I sweat, hee-hee-hee!"

He hung the hat on top of his gun, retrieved the wig and put it on his head. Then he took off his jacket and laid it over a chair. The jacket had been mended many times over, with each set of leather patches stitched on top of the last, making this piece of clothing so stiff and thick that an Indian arrow would penetrate it only with difficulty.

Now we could see the whole length of his thin, crooked legs. Above them he wore a leather hunting vest. He had a knife and two pistols stuck in his belt. As he returned to the table, he looked first at me and then at the lady of the house:

"Wouldn't my lady like to tell this greenhorn what this is all about before we eat, if I'm not mistaken?"

The expression "if I'm not mistaken" was a constant phrase of his. The mother nodded, turned to me, pointed to the younger guest and said:

"Perhaps you already know that Mr. Black will be your successor, Sir."

"My successor?" I said, stunned.

"Indeed. Since we are celebrating your departure today, we felt it necessary to find a new tutor."

"My departure?"

I'm grateful to this day that no one photographed me at that moment. I must have looked like astonishment personified.

"Yes, your departure, Sir," she nodded with a well-meaning smile. But I myself was in no mood to smile. She added: "You really should have given notice, but we didn't want to keep you from immediately exploiting your good fortune. We're awfully sad to see you go, but we send our best wishes with you. Tomorrow you leave, with our blessing!"

"Departure? Tomorrow? Where to?" I cried, with some difficulty.

At that Sam Hawkens, who was standing near me, slapped me on shoulder and answered with a laugh:

"Where? To the Wild West with me. You passed your exam with flying colors, hee-hee-hee! The other surveyors are riding out tomorrow and can't wait around for you; you'll have to go with them immediately. Me and Dick Stone and Will Parker, we're engaged as guides. We're headed up the Cañada River and into New Mexico. I don't think you really want to stick around here and remain a greenhorn!"

Then the scales fell from my eyes. The whole business had been rigged! A surveyor, perhaps for one of the great railways that were being planned. What a happy thought! I didn't have to ask any more questions; my good friend Mr. Henry came over to me, shook my hand and said:

"I've already told you why I like you. You're among good people here, but tutoring is not for you, Sir, absolutely not. You need to go west. So I turned to the Atlantic and Pacific Company and had you checked out, without your knowing it. You did well. Here's your commission."

He gave me the document. I glanced at it, and when I saw what my income was to be, I couldn't believe my eyes. But he continued:

"There's a lot of riding ahead. You need a good horse. I bought that chestnut stallion that you yourself broke in, and he'll be yours. And you'll need a weapon too; I'm giving you the bear-killer, that heavy old gun that I can't handle, but you hit the bulls-eye with. What do you say to that, Sir?"

At first I could say nothing. Then, once I could speak again, I tried to refuse the gifts, but without success. These good people had decided to make me happy, and it would have hurt them deeply if I had insisted. To avoid any further discussion, at least for the time being, the lady of the house took her place at the table and the rest of us had to follow her example. We ate, and the topic could not be brought up again until later.

It wasn't until after dinner that I learned what I needed to know. The railway was to run from St. Louis through the Indian Territory, New Mexico, Arizona, and California to the Pacific Ocean. The plan was to research and survey this long route in individual sections. The section that the three other surveyors and I were to survey, under the supervision of an engineer, lay between the headwaters of the Rio Pecos and the Cañada River. The three guides (Sam Hawkens, Dick Stone, and Will Parker) would take us there, where we would meet up with a whole band of upright frontiersmen, whose job would be to protect us. Naturally, we were also assured the protection of the fort garrisons. To surprise me, they had waited until today to tell me all this, a bit late to be sure. But I was reassured that everything I needed, down to the last detail, had been assembled for me. There was nothing more I needed to do except go to meet my new colleagues, who were waiting for me at the engineer's house. Mr. Henry and Sam Hawkens took me there, and I was greeted very cordially. They knew about the plan to surprise me, and so they didn't hold my last-minute arrival against me.

The next morning, after I had said goodbye to the German family, I walked over to Mr. Henry's place. I tried to thank him, but he cut me off, shaking my hand heartily and interrupting me in his coarse way:

"Shut your mouth, Sir! I only got you involved in this expedition so my old gun would have some company. When you come back, look me up and tell me about your experiences. Then we'll see whether you still remain what you are today, no matter what you think: a prize example of a greenhorn."

Then he shoved me out the door, but before it closed I could see that his eyes were moist.

Chapter 3

After three months on the job, we were nearing the end of a glorious fall but had still not completed our task, even though the teams working on the other sections had mostly finished and gone home. There were two reasons for this.

The first reason concerned the difficult terrain that we had to work in. The railway was to follow the Cañada River valley through the plains. Its route towards the river's headwaters was already set, and the sections from New Mexico westwards through the valleys and passes had been similarly determined. But our section lay between the Cañada River headwaters and New Mexico and it was up to us to find a suitable route. This required time-consuming rides, strenuous hikes, and many comparative measurements before we could even begin the actual work. This was all made harder because we were in dangerous territory. The Kiowas, Comanches, and Apaches were all in the area, and they didn't take kindly to the idea of a railroad through land they thought of as their own. We had to be constantly on the lookout, which naturally made our work extraordinarily difficult and slow.

Concerns about the Indians meant that we couldn't feed ourselves by hunting—they would have spotted us too easily. So we had to get everything we needed by wagon from Santa Fe. But this method of transport was very unreliable and we often had to hold up our work while we waited for the wagon to arrive.

The second reason had to do with the makeup of our group. I mentioned that the engineer and the three surveyors greeted me warmly in St. Louis. This led me to expect a good working relationship with them, but it didn't work out that way.

My colleagues were all American-born, and they looked on me as a greenhorn, an inexperienced "Dutchman" (a word which they used as a slur). They wanted to collect their salary without worrying too much about whether they really fulfilled the requirements of the job. As an honest German, I was a hindrance from whom they quickly withdrew the goodwill they had shown at first. I didn't let this affect me and I went about my work. Before too long, I began to notice that they were a little short on expertise. They gave me the hardest tasks and made their own lives as easy as possible. I didn't object: I always say that the more you tackle, the stronger you get.

Mr. Bancroft, the engineer, was the most competent of them, but unfortunately he had a weakness for brandy. A few kegs of this pernicious drink were brought up from Santa Fe, and after that he paid more attention to the brandy than to his surveying instruments. Sometimes he ended up in a heap on the ground, dead drunk, for half the day. Riggs, Marcy, and Wheeler, the three surveyors, had had to pay for their share for the liquor (as had I) and they drank as much as Bancroft, to make sure they got their money's worth. You can imagine that these three were not always in the best shape either. Since I didn't drink a drop, I ended up with all the work while they alternated between drinking and sleeping off their intoxication. I liked Wheeler the best, since he at least understood that I slaved away for them without really having any obligation to do it. Of course our work suffered.

The rest of the company was just as bad. Twelve "frontiersmen" were waiting for us when we arrived at our section. When I first arrived, I had held them in the greatest respect, but I soon perceived that they were a pathetic bunch.

They were supposed to protect us and help us with our work. Fortunately, for the first three months nothing happened that required me to turn to them for their supposed protection, and as for helping us, I can say without fear of contradiction that the twelve laziest men in the USA had somehow arranged to rendezvous on this project.

I found it very tough to work under those conditions.

According to our contract, Bancroft was in charge, and he behaved as if he was, but no one paid any attention to him. When he gave a command, the others laughed at him, and then he cursed as I have rarely heard a man curse, and headed for the brandy to compensate for this effort. Riggs, Marcy, and Wheeler behaved much the same way. I had grounds enough to take over the project, and so I did, but in a way that the others wouldn't notice. A young and inexperienced person like me would never be taken seriously. If I had been dumb enough to speak in a domineering tone, the result would most certainly have been peals of laughter. No, I had to work carefully and quietly, the way a clever wife with a quarrelsome husband learns to direct and lead him without his knowing it. And I was called "greenhorn" ten times a day by these half-wild, rowdy frontiersmen, and yet they gradually began to follow my direction while still thinking they were doing what they wanted.

In this process I had great assistance from Sam Hawkens and his two companions, Dick Stone and Will Parker. These three men were honest through and through. Not only that—and I had no idea of this when I first encountered Sam in St. Louis—they were experienced, smart, and bold scouts, and were held in high esteem all over the West. They stuck with me for the most part, staying away from the others, but not so much that they took offence. Sam, in spite of his peculiarities, was especially good at getting the unruly company to pay attention, and when he asserted himself in his half-strained, half-comical voice, he always did it to help me achieve some goal of mine.

A relationship had quietly developed between us that was a bit like that between a feudal lord and one of his subjects. He had taken me under his wing, and done it without being asked. I was the greenhorn, he the experienced frontiersman whose words and deeds had to be seen as infallible. Whenever he had the time and opportunity, he taught me about all the things you need to be able to do and know in the wild west. Looking back, I'd have to say that if I got my higher education at Winnetou's side, it was Sam Hawkens that taught me grade school. He made me a lasso with his own hands and he let me practice roping him and roping his horse. When I got good enough to lasso my target every time, he was very pleased, and he cried:

"That's right, young man, well done! But don't let the compliment go to your head. A teacher has to praise even the dumbest student sometimes. I've taught many a young frontiersman, and they learned it all quicker and easier than you. But if you keep at it, maybe in six or eight years we won't have to call you a greenhorn any more. Until then, take comfort in the old observation that sometimes a fool gets just as far as a wise man, if I'm not mistaken!"

He pretended to be totally in earnest when he said this, and I accepted it in a similar vein, but actually I knew how completely different his real meaning was.

Of this instruction, it was the practical part that I most welcomed. My job required so much of me that I don't think I would have taken the time to perfect my wilderness skills if Sam Hawkens hadn't been there. Furthermore, we did this training secretly, always at a distance from camp where we couldn't be observed. Sam wanted it that way, and when I asked him why, he answered:

"I'm doing it for your sake, Sir. You have so little talent for this kind of thing, I'd feel utterly ashamed for you if those boys were to see you. So now you know. Hee-hee-hee!"

The result was that the none of the company trusted my ability with weapons or with anything that needed physical coordination. But it didn't bother me.

In spite of all the obstacles mentioned earlier, we finally got far enough that in perhaps one more week we would be able to link up with the next section. Bancroft announced that he would ride ahead to give this message to the next team, taking one of the frontiersmen with him as a guide. This was not the first time such a message had been sent. We had to constantly stay in contact with the section behind us as well as the one ahead. Because of this, I had learned that the engineer in charge of the group ahead of us was a very capable man.

Bancroft decided to leave early on a Sunday morning. He wanted to have a farewell drink the night before, and everyone else was to participate. I was the only one not invited, and Hawkens, Stone, and Parker turned down the opportunity. The festivities went on so long that Bancroft could barely mumble by the time it ended. His companions had kept pace with him and were just as drunk. The planned departure was out of the question. They all did what they usually did: crawl behind a bush to sleep it off.

I mulled over what should be done. The word had to be sent, and these men would be sleeping at least until late afternoon. It would be best if I made the ride, but could I? I was convinced that during the four days I was gone, no one would consider doing any work. As I discussed this with Sam, he pointed toward the west and said:

"No need to ride now, Sir. See those two riders coming? You can give the information to them."

I looked where he pointed and saw two riders approaching. They were white men, and I recognized one as an old scout who had come over several times in the past, bringing information from the next section. Next to him was a younger man, not dressed like a frontiersman. I hadn't seen him previously. I went out toward them, and when I reached them, they stopped their horses and the stranger asked me my name. When I told him, he gave me a friendly look and said:

"So you're the young German gentleman that does all the work here, while the other lazy bums just lie around. You've probably heard my name, Sir. It's White."

So this was the engineer in charge of the next section west, to whom the message was supposed to be sent. There must have been a good reason for him to come in person. He got down from his horse, shook my hand, and looked over our camp. He smiled slightly when he noticed the sleeping men behind the bushes and the brandy keg, but it wasn't a friendly smile.

"Drunk?" he asked.

I nodded.

"All of them?"

"Yes. Mr. Bancroft wanted to ride over to your section, and he gave a little going-away party. I'll go wake him up and. . ."

"Stop!" he interrupted me. "Let them sleep. I want to talk to you without them hearing. Don't wake them up! Who are the three men standing over there?"

"Sam Hawkens, Will Parker, and Dick Stone, our three dependable scouts."

"Ah, Hawkens, the strange little hunter. Capable man. I've heard about him. Let's have the three of them join us."

I waved for them to come, and then asked:

"You came yourself, Mr. White. Is it something important that brings you here?"

"Just checking to see that we're getting what we paid for here. And I wanted to speak with you—with you specifically. We're finished with our section, but you're not finished yet."

"The difficulty of the terrain is the problem, and I'm going to. . ."

"I know, I know," he interrupted me. "Unfortunately, I know everything. If you hadn't worked triple-time, Bancroft would still be back where he started."

"That's not the situation at all, Mr. White. I don't know where you got the idea that I'm the only one working hard. I'm just doing my job."

"Be quiet, Sir, be quiet! Messengers have been going back and forth between our camps, and I've been listening to them without their noticing. It's very charitable of you to protect these drunks, but I want the truth. And since I can tell you're too loyal to tell it to me, I'm going to have to ask Sam Hawkens. Let's sit down."

We went over to our tent. He sat down in front of it in the grass and motioned to us to do the same. We did so, and he began to question Sam Hawkens, Stone, and Parker intently. They told him everything, mincing no words. I added a comment here and there, to soften their observations and to defend my colleagues, but it didn't seem to make an impression on Mr. White. On the contrary, he told me to stop trying to defend them, that it was a lost cause.

Then, once he had heard everything, he asked me to show him our drawings and our record book. I didn't want to do this, but I did it anyway. Otherwise, I would have angered him, and I saw that he meant well by me. He looked through them carefully, and when he asked me about it, I couldn't lie: I was the only one who had made the drawings and records. None of the others had drawn a single line or written a single figure.

"But from this record book you can't tell how much or how little work each person has done," he said. "You have been laudable in your loyalty to your colleagues, but you've gone much too far."

Then Hawkens, a sly look on his face, said:

"Check his shirt pocket, Mr. White! He's got a sardine tin there. No sardines, but he's got paper in there. Probably his private record book, if I'm not mistaken. It'll probably tell a different story than the official book does, hiding the laziness of his colleagues."

Sam knew that I had made private drawings and put them in the sardine tin that I carried. It made me uncomfortable to hear him talk about it. White asked to see it. I considered what I should do. Was I under any obligation to my colleagues to slave away for them thanklessly, and then be quiet about it? I certainly didn't want to hurt them, but I also couldn't be impolite to White. So finally I gave him my record book, but with the condition that he would speak to no one about its contents. He read through it, gave it back, and said:

"I ought to take these pages with me and give them to the proper authorities. Your colleagues are incompetent and they shouldn't be paid a single additional dollar, while you should receive triple pay. Well, as you like. But let me emphasize that it would be good for you to preserve these private notes. They may be of great value to you later. And now, let's wake the splendid gentlemen."

He stood up and raised the alarm. The "gentlemen" arrived with vacant eyes and distraught faces from behind their bushes. Bancroft was angry that someone had disturbed his sleep, but put on a polite appearance when someone told him that Mr. White from the next section had arrived. The two had never met. Bancroft offered White a glass of brandy, but that was a bad idea. White used this offer as the starting point for an angry tirade, the like of which Bancroft had certainly never experienced before. He listened in astonished silence for a while, then he came up to White, grabbed his arm, and snarled:

"Mister, you want to tell me what your name is?"

"My name is White, you've already been told that."

"And what is your position?"

"Engineer in charge of the next section."

"Did any of us try to tell anyone in your section what to do?"

"No, I think not."

"All right, then! My name is Bancroft and I'm the engineer in charge of this section. No one tells me what to do, and you least of all, Mr. White."

"True enough, we're equals," answered White quietly. "Neither of us has to take orders from the other. But if one of us sees that the other is damaging the enterprise that both are working on, he has a duty to make the other aware of his error. Your life's work appears to be in that brandy keg. I count sixteen men here, all of whom lay drunk when we arrived two hours ago. . ."

"Two hours ago?" Bancroft broke in. "You've been here that long?"

"Indeed. I checked the records and drawings and made note of who did them. You've been living the life of milk and honey here, while only one of you, and the youngest at that, has been doing all the work."

At this Bancroft turned and hissed at me:

"You told him this, you and no other! Go ahead and deny it, you despicable liar, you malicious traitor!"

"No," White answered him. "Your young colleague acted like a gentleman and only said good things about you. He tried to protect you, and I advise you to apologize to him for calling him a liar and a traitor."

"Apologize? I'll do no such thing!" laughed Bancroft scornfully. "This greenhorn doesn't know a triangle from a square, and still makes himself out to be a surveyor. We couldn't make progress because he did everything wrong and held us up. And now, instead of admitting it, he's libeling us and running us down like this. . ."

He didn't get any farther. I had been patient for months and let these people think whatever they wanted about me. The moment had arrived to show them that they had been mistaken about me. I grabbed Bancroft by the arm, pressed it so hard that he left his sentence uncompleted. I told him:

"Mr. Bancroft, you had too much to drink and haven't slept it off yet. I'm going to assume you're still drunk and so we'll just pretend you didn't say anything."

"Me, drunk? You're crazy!" he answered.

"Yes, drunk! Because if I thought you were sober and you made these slanderous statements intentionally, I'd have to knock you to the ground like a child. Do you still feel like denying your intoxication?"

I still held his arm tight in my grip. He had certainly never felt the need to fear me before, but now he feared me—I could see it in his face. He was by no means a weak man, but the expression on my face seemed to shock him. He didn't want to admit that he was still drunk, but also didn't dare maintain his accusations. So he turned for help to the twelve frontiersmen that were supposed to protect us:

"Mr. Rattler, why do you permit this man to attack me? Aren't you here to protect us?"

This Rattler was a tall and heavy-built fellow who appeared to have the strength of three or four men, a tough character and at the same time Bancroft's favorite drinking partner. He couldn't stand me, and was delighted to take this opportunity to air the grudge he bore against me. He came forward quickly, grabbed my arm as I had grabbed Bancroft's, and replied:

"No, I won't allow it, Mr. Bancroft. This kid hasn't outgrown his first pair of socks and here he wants to threaten a grown man, to slander you. Let go of Mr. Bancroft, kid, or I'll show you what a greenhorn you are."

This was directed at me, and he shook my arm as he said it. I liked this even better, since he was a stronger opponent than the engineer. If I taught him some manners, it would be more impressive than if I showed Mr. Bancroft that I wasn't a coward. I jerked my arm out of his hand and responded:

"You're calling me a kid and a greenhorn? Take that back right now, Mr. Rattler, or I'll knock you flat on your back!"

"You'll do what?" he laughed. "Is a greenhorn like you really stupid enough to believe that. . ."

He couldn't continue, because I hit him so hard on the temple that he collapsed like an empty sack and lay stunned. For a few seconds there was silence, then one of Rattler's partners cried:

"The devil! Are we going to sit around and watch while this Dutchman attacks our leader? Get the scoundrel!"

He sprang towards me. I welcomed him with a kick to the stomach. This is a sure way to bring down an opponent as long as you have solid footing for the other foot. He fell to the ground. Instantly, I kneeled on his chest and gave him a knockout punch to the chin. Then I jumped up, pulled out my two revolvers, and cried:

"Who's next? Come on!"

Nobody in Rattler's band seemed to have an interest in avenging the defeat of their two colleagues. One looked questioningly at the others. But I warned them:

"Listen to me, you people: anyone who takes a step toward me or reaches for a weapon gets a bullet in the head. You can think what you like about greenhorns in general, but I'm warning you that this particular German greenhorn can take on twelve frontiersmen the like of you."

Sam Hawkens came and stood next to me and said:

"And I, Sam Hawkens, second that warning, if I'm not mistaken. This young German greenhorn is under my particular protection. If any of you even tries to bend a hair on his head, I'll put a bullet through your brain. Mark me well, I mean it, hee-hee-hee!"

Dick Stone and Will Parker decided it was appropriate to stand by me as well, to show that they agreed with Sam Hawkens. This impressed my attackers. They turned away from me, murmuring threats and curses in their beards, and turned their attention to bringing their two fallen comrades back to consciousness.

Bancroft headed back to his tent, where he disappeared. White gave me a wide-eyed astonished look. He shook his head and said in a voice of pure wonderment:

"But, Sir, that was incredible! I sure wouldn't want to fall into your hands. They should really call you 'shatterhand,' the way you laid out those big, tough men with a single punch. I never saw anything like it."

This suggestion seemed to please little Hawkens. He giggled happily:

"Shatterhand, hee-hee-hee! A greenhorn, and already with a frontiersman's nickname, and what a name! Yes, when Sam Hawkens sets his eyes on a greenhorn, something's going to come of it, if I'm not mistaken. Shatterhand, Old Shatterhand! A bit like Old Firehand, who is a great frontiersman, strong as a bear. What do you think, Dick? Will? Do you like the name?"

I didn't hear their answer, since my attention was directed toward White, who had come up to shake my hand. He took me aside and said:

"I like you immensely, Sir. How about joining me?"

"Whether I'd like to or not, Mr. White, I can't."

"Why not?"

"I have to fulfill my obligations here."

"Pshaw! I can take responsibility for hiring you away."

"That doesn't help, if I can't fulfill them myself. I was sent here to help survey this section, and I can't leave until we are done."

"Let Bancroft and the other three finish it."

"Sure, but how soon will that happen? No, I have to stay."

"But consider how dangerous it will be for you."

"Why?"

"You have to ask? Surely you understand that you've made deadly enemies of these people."

"Not me. I've done nothing to them."

"True, or it was true until a few minutes ago. But now that you've knocked out two of them, it's over between you and them."

"Could be. But I'm not afraid of them. And those two punches have earned me some respect. They will think twice before attacking me. Anyway, Hawkens, Stone, and Parker are on my side."

"As you like. You have to make your own decision, for better or worse. But I could really use you. In any case, how about riding along with me for a few minutes?"

"Now?"

"Yes, now."

"You're leaving already, Mr. White?"

"Yes. Given the state things are in here, I don't want to stay any longer than necessary."

"But you'll at least need to eat something before you go, won't you, Sir?"

"It's not necessary. We have what we need in our saddle bags."

"Won't you say goodbye to Bancroft?"

"I won't bother."

"But surely you came to talk business with him!"

"Indeed. But I can give my message to you. In fact, you'll understand it better than he would. My main mission was to warn you about the Indians."

"Did you see any?"

"Not directly, but we found their tracks. This is the time of year when the wild mustangs and the buffalo migrate southward. The Indians leave their villages to hunt them. I'm not worried about the Kiowas—we've made a deal with them about the railroad. But the Comanche and the Apache don't know about it yet, so we can't allow them to see what we're doing. Over in our section, we finished our surveying and we're getting out of the area as quick as we can. Make sure you get done soon! It will get more dangerous by the day around here. Get your horse, and ask Sam Hawkens if he wants to come along."

Naturally, Sam wanted to come.

Actually, I had wanted to work that day, but it was Sunday, the Lord's day, the day which Christ himself, even in the wilderness, gave to thought and spiritual duties. Anyway, I had certainly earned a day off. So I went to Bancroft's tent and told him that I would not be working but would instead accompany White for a bit, with Sam Hawkens.

"Go, and let the devil take you. I hope he breaks your neck!" he answered. Though I didn't realize it, it wouldn't be long until this grim wish would very nearly be fulfilled.

Chapter 4

It had been several days since I had ridden, and my chestnut whinnied joyfully as I saddled him. He had shown himself to be a superb horse, and I was already looking forward to telling my old gunsmith, Mr. Henry, about him.

We rode along at a lively pace through the beautiful fall morning, talking about the planned railroad and whatever else was on our minds. White gave me his suggestions concerning the connection from our section to his, and at noon we stopped by a creek for a bite to eat. Then, White and his scout rode on. We stayed a bit longer and talked about religion.

Hawkens was actually a devout man, even though he didn't show it in front of others.

As we were getting up to leave, I bent down by the stream to get a drink of water from my cupped hand. Through the crystal water I saw what appeared to be a footprint on the bottom. I showed it to Sam. He looked carefully at the print and then said:

"That fellow White was absolutely right when he warned us about Indians."

"Sam, do you mean this is the track of an Indian?"

"Yes, it was made by an Indian's moccasin. How do you feel about that, Sir?"

"I don't feel anything one way or the other."

"Fie! You must be thinking or feeling something."

"What am I supposed to think, except that an Indian was here?"

"You're not afraid?"

"It would never occur to me."

"Well, worried at least?"

"Not that either."

"I see you don't know these red men yet!"

"But I'm hoping to get to know them. I imagine they're about like other people—friends of those who befriend them, enemies of those who fight them. And since I don't intend to be hostile to them, I figure I don't have anything to fear from them."

"You're a total greenhorn and you always will be. Don't be so sure about how you'll deal with the Indians. It won't happen that way. You won't have a choice in the matter. You'll find out I'm right, and I hope the experience won't end up costing you a big chunk of flesh or maybe even your life."

"When do you think the Indian was here?"

"About two days ago. We would be able to see his tracks here in the grass if it hadn't had time to grow upright again."

"Probably a scout?"

"Scouting for buffalo, yes. The tribes around here aren't at war, so he wouldn't have been a war scout. He was unusually careless—probably young, I bet."

"How do you know?"

"An experienced warrior doesn't step in a stream like this, where the print will last a long time in the shallow bottom. Only someone stupid would do that—it has to be a red greenhorn, same as you're a white one, hee-hee-hee! And white greenhorns can be even dumber than red ones. Mark my words, Sir!"

He chuckled softly to himself and got up to climb onto his horse. Good old Sam loved to convey his affection by telling me I was dumb.

We could have gone back by the same route that we had come, but as a surveyor it was my job to get to know our section, so we turned off the trail a bit and then rode parallel to it.

Presently we came to a fairly wide valley full of lush prairie grass. The slopes that enclosed it on both sides were full of bushes at the bottom and led into forests above. The valley was perhaps a half-hour's ride in length, and so straight that you could see from one end to the other. We had only gone a few steps down into this peaceful valley when Sam drew his horse to a halt and squinted ahead.

"Whoa!" he cried. "There they come! Yup, that's them, the very first ones!"

"What?" I asked.

I could see, off in the distance, perhaps eighteen or twenty slowly-moving dark spots.

"What?" he repeated my question, rocking back and forth in the saddle. "You should be ashamed of yourself, asking that question! Oh well, you're a greenhorn, and a champion one at that. Your kind can look at a thing and not see it. Do me the favor, Sir, of advising me what sort of things those are that you see before you."

"Advising? Hmm. Well, I would say they were deer if I didn't know that they never live in groups of more than ten. I'd also have to say that, although they look small from here, they must be a good bit bigger than deer."

"Deer, hee-hee-hee!" he laughed. "Deer up here in the headwaters of the Cañada River? That's a good one! But the other thing you said was closer to the mark. Yes, they are bigger than deer—much bigger."

"Sam, you don't mean buffalo?"

"Naturally buffalo. They're bison, real bison on the move, the first I've seen around here. Now we know Mr. White was right: bison and Indians. We only saw the Indian's tracks, but the buffalo are here before our eyes. What do you think of that, if I'm not mistaken?"

"We must go down there!"

"Naturally."

"And observe them."

"Observe them? Really?" he asked, giving me a sidelong glance.

"Yes. I've never seen a bison before, and I'd love to take a look at these."

My interest was that of a biologist, and Sam just couldn't grasp that idea. He slapped his leg in amusement.

"Observe them? Sure. The way a curious kid looks through a crack in a rabbit hutch, to watch the bunnies! Oh, greenhorn, do I have to tell you everything? I'm not interested in observing. I'm going to shoot one."

"Today, on Sunday?" I said without thinking. He responded angrily:

"I'd appreciate it if you'd shut up, Sir. What does a frontiersman care about Sundays when he sees the season's first buffalo before him? This is meat, understand? And what meat, if I'm not mistaken! A piece of bison steak is more glorious than the heavenly ambrosius—or ambrosiana or whatever it's called—that the Greek gods lived on. I have to have a buffalo steak if it costs me my life! The wind is blowing toward us, that's good. It's sunny here on the north side of the valley, but the south side is in the shadow. If we keep to that side, the buffalo won't see us coming. Let's go!"

He checked his "Liddy" to make sure both barrels were in working order, and rode off toward the south wall of the canyon. Following his example, I checked out my bear-killer. He noticed this, stopped his horse and asked:

"You're thinking of participating, Sir?"

"Of course!"

"Forget it, unless you want to be trampled into pulp in the next ten minutes. A bison is no canary that will sit on your finger and sing. You need a few good summers and winters under your belt before you take on an animal this dangerous."

"But it's what I want to do."

"Shut up and listen!" he interrupted, in a tone of voice he had never previously used with me. "I don't want to have your life on my conscience. You'd be riding into the jaws of certain death. Some other time, you can do what you want. But right now, I won't tolerate insubordination."

If we hadn't had such a good relationship, he wouldn't have gotten away with talking to me like that. But I decided to keep quiet as I rode behind him in the shade of the forest's edge. Then he explained, in a milder tone:

"It looks to me like about 20 of them. But you should see it when thousands graze together on the plains! In the past, I've seen herds of ten thousand and more. It was the staff of life to the Indians, and the white man took it away. The red man protects the wild things that give him food. He kills only what he needs. But the white man? He decimates the vast herds like some hell-bent predator that continues killing even after its hunger is satisfied, just for the sight of blood. How much longer will it be until there are no more buffalo? And not too long after, no more Indians either? Lord have mercy! And it's just the same with the wild horses. There used to be herds of thousands of mustangs. Now you're absolutely delighted when you happen on a group of a hundred."

By this time, we had come to within about four hundred paces from the buffalo, and they still had not noticed us. Hawkens reined his horse to a stop. The buffalo were moving slowly up the valley as they grazed. At the head of the group was an old bull whose vast bulk I observed in astonishment. He had to be close to seven feet high and ten feet from nose to tail. Back then, I didn't know how to judge a bison's weight, but today I would say that this one must have weighed around 1,500 pounds, a remarkable mass of flesh and bones. He had found a muddy pool and wallowed in it contentedly.

"That's the leader," Sam whispered, "the most dangerous one in the whole group. If you pick a fight with him, you better have an up-to-date will. I'm going to get the cow over to the right. Watch where I place the bullet: behind the shoulder blade, diagonally into the heart. That's the best way, and it's the only sure shot except right through the eye, but you'd crazy to take on a bison from the front in order to get a shot at the eye! Wait here, and get yourself and your horse back into the bushes. When they see me and they start running, the stampede will come right by here. But don't leave this spot until I return or call for you!"

He waited until I had worked my way back between two big bushes, and then he rode slowly and quietly ahead. I was feeling very strange. I had often read about how you hunt bison, and you couldn't have told me anything about it I didn't already know. But there's a difference between what's written on a piece of paper and the actual experience of a hunt in the wilderness. Today, I was seeing buffalo for the first time in my life. What wild animals had I hunted before? Nothing that compared to these gigantic, dangerous creatures. So I really did intend to abide by Sam's command not to participate, but that isn't how it worked out. Initially, I wanted only to observe, listen. But now I felt an irresistible urge to get involved. Sam was only going after a young cow. Big deal, I thought, that doesn't take much courage. A real man would choose the strongest bull!

My horse had grown unusually restless and pawed with its hooves. It, too, was seeing buffalo for the first time, and it wanted to flee. I was barely able to restrain it. Wouldn't it be better if I forced it to face the bull? I was not excited; in an inner state of calm I debated what to do. But in the end the decision was made in the blink of an eye.

Sam had moved to within 300 paces of the bison, then he spurred his horse and galloped toward the herd, right by the big bull and toward the cow he had pointed out earlier. She stopped short, missing her chance to flee. He reached her, and I saw him shoot as he rode by her. She staggered and lowered her head. I didn't see whether she collapsed, because my attention was focused on something else.

The great bull jumped up and started heading for Sam Hawkens. What a powerful beast! The thick head with the domed skull, the wide forehead and the short but powerful horns, the thick, shaggy mane around the neck and chest! The image of base, raw power was made complete by the high withers. Yes, this was a highly dangerous beast, but seeing him led to the urge to measure human abilities against his animal power.

Did I choose to do it? Or did my chestnut stallion make the choice and just take me along? I don't know. He shot out of the bushes and wanted to go to the left, but I pulled him to the right and flew toward the bull. He heard me coming and turned toward me. When he saw me, he lowered his head, to greet horse and rider with his horns. I heard Sam yelling with all his might, but I had no time to glance toward him. It was impossible to shoot the bison. First, he was not positioned where I could get a shot in;

and second, my horse had stopped obeying me—in its fright it was running straight toward the threatening horns. To gore it, the buffalo spread its back legs and tossed its mighty head in the air. Using all my strength, I managed to get the chestnut to rear up; he flew in a great arc over the back of the bull, while at the same time his horns passed close by my legs. Our leap ended right in the muddy pool in which the buffalo had been wallowing. I saw it coming and took my feet out of the stirrups, which was fortunate, because the horse slid and we fell. How it could happen so fast I still don't know, but in the next instant I was standing up next to the pool with my gun still tight in my hand. The buffalo had turned toward us and it sprang in a series of awkward bounds toward the horse, which had also stood up and was at the point of fleeing. I would be able to get a shot at the buffalo's flank. I brought the gun to my shoulder. Now the heavy bear-killer would get its first chance to prove itself in earnest. One more step, and the bison would have reached the stallion. I fired. He stopped in mid-stride, whether from fright or because I had made a good shot, I don't know. I immediately fired the second bullet. He slowly lifted his head, gave a roar that shook my bones, swayed from side to side, and then collapsed where he stood.

I would have liked to celebrate this victory, but there were more important things to do. My horse had taken off down the valley, and I saw Sam Hawkens galloping along the valley's edge, pursued by a bull that was almost as big as mine.

It's important to realize that a bison, once aroused, does not let his enemy alone, and takes on the speed of a horse. The bison shows a level of courage, cunning, and endurance that you would not believe without having seen it.

That's the way this steer was pursuing Sam. To avoid him, Hawkens had to make a series of risky maneuvers, which tired the horse. The buffalo was clearly going to outlast the horse, so help was urgently needed. I had no time to check whether my bull was really dead or not. I quickly reloaded both barrels of the bear-killer and ran toward Sam. Sam saw this. He wanted to meet me half way and turned his horse in my direction. This was a big mistake. The steer, which was right behind him, was able to reach the horse as it turned. I saw him sink his horns into the horse's flank. With a toss of his head, he sent horse and rider flying through the air, and then began charging them where they lay. Sam cried for help as best he could. I was still 150 paces away and couldn't waste an instant. I could certainly have shot more accurately if I had been closer, but if I hesitated Sam could be lost. Even if I didn't kill the buffalo, I might be able to get the beast's attention away from my friend. I stopped, aimed at a spot behind the buffalo's shoulder blade, and shot. The buffalo raise his head as if to listen, and slowly turned. Then he saw me and charged, though with somewhat reduced speed. Fortunately, I was able to feverishly reload the spent chamber by the time the animal was no more than 30 paces from me. It couldn't run anymore. Its movements were more like a slow walk, but with its head down, staring forward and with blood running from under its eyes, it came toward me, nearer and nearer, like an unstoppable impending disaster. I kneeled and lifted the gun. This movement caused the bison to stop and raise his head slightly, in order to see me better. This brought the malicious eyes into my sights, and I sent one bullet into the right and the other into the left. A brief shudder went through his body, then he fell.

I sprang up to run to Sam, but it wasn't necessary: he was running towards me.

"Hello!" I called. "You're still alive? Weren't you seriously injured?"

"Not at all," he answered. "I bumped my right hip when I hit the ground—or was it the left, if I'm not mistaken. I can't exactly work it out."

"And your horse?"

"A goner. He's still alive, but the buffalo ripped him right open. We'll have to put him out of his misery. Is the bison dead?"

"I hope so. I'll check."

We checked; there was no life left in the bison. Then Hawkens said with a deep sigh:

"That vicious old ox was toying with me! A cow would have been nicer about it. You just can't count on bulls to be ladylike, hee-hee-hee!"

"What gave him the dumb idea to get involved with you?"

"You didn't see?"

"No."

"Well, after I killed the cow, I just about ran into this bull. My horse was at full gallop, and I managed to stop him just in the nick of time. The bison took offence and came after me. I gave him the second barrel of my Liddy, but it didn't make him any more reasonable. He showed me a level of affection that I couldn't return. He kept after me so much that I couldn't reload my gun; I threw it down because it was useless to me and I could use both hands to handle the horse, if I'm not mistaken. The poor nag did his best, but couldn't save himself."

"Because you made that disastrous last sharp turn. You should have made a wide arc. That would have saved the horse."

"Saved it? You're talking like a wise man. I wouldn't expect it from a greenhorn."

"Pshaw! Even greenhorns can have a good side."

"Yes, if you hadn't been there, I'd be lying there gored and ripped open like my horse. Let's go see to him."

The horse was in sad shape. His entrails were hanging from his shredded chest. He snorted with pain. Sam found his Liddy, loaded it, and put the horse out of its misery. While he was unbuckling the reins and saddle, he said:

"Now I can be my own horse and wear the saddle on my back. That's what you get when you run into a buffalo."

"Yes, and where will you get another horse?" I asked.

"That's the least of my problems. I'll catch me one, if I'm not mistaken."

"A mustang?"

"Yes. The buffalo are here; they've begun their migration

southward. We'll see the mustangs soon. I'm sure of it."

"Can I be there when you catch one?"

"Naturally. It's something you need to learn to do. Come on, though, let's take a look at the old bull. Maybe he's still alive. A Methuselah like that can have an unusually tough life."

We went over to the animal, and it was clearly dead. Now, lying still, its colossal size was even more evident. Sam looked back and forth between the bull and me, shook his head with an indescribable expression on his face and said:

"It's inconceivable, just inconceivable! Do you know where you hit him?"

"Well, where?"

"In exactly the right spot. He's an ancient fellow, and I would have certainly thought it over ten times before I would have been so venturesome as to take him on. Do you know what you are, Sir?"

"What?"

"The most foolish man in existence."

"Whoa!"

"Yes, the most foolish man that ever set foot on this earth."

"Foolishness was never my problem."

"Well, it is now, understand? Didn't I tell you to keep your hands off the buffalo and stay in the bushes? Why didn't you do as I said?"

"I don't know myself."

"So! Doing something without knowing why. Wouldn't you call that foolishness?"

"I don't think so. There must have been a more substantial reason."

"If there was, you'd know it."

"Maybe it was that you gave me a command, and I don't take commands from anyone."

"So! When someone gives you well-meaning advice about avoiding danger, you're so obstinate that you throw yourself right into it."

"I didn't come to the West to avoid its dangers."

"Fine. But you're still a greenhorn and you need to be careful. And when you decided not to follow my advice, why did you choose this huge beast and not a cow?"

"Because it was more honorable."

"Honorable! This greenhorn wants to play the knight, if I'm not mistaken, hee-hee-hee!"

He laughed until he had to hold his stomach. Then, still laughing, he continued:

"If you really have it in your head to play a knight, then play Don Quixote, but none other. You don't have the stuff for King George or King Arthur. You can just fall in love with a buffalo cow and sit in the afternoon sun every day waiting for your love to come wandering by. And that way you can even sit there some evening and be eaten by the coyotes and the buzzards. When a real frontiersman does something, he doesn't care whether it is honorable, just whether it is useful to him."

"But that was the case here."

"How so?"

"I chose the buffalo because he had far more meat than a cow."

He looked at me for a moment in disbelief, then cried:

"Far more meat? This young man here shot the bull for its meat, hee-hee-hee! Why bless my soul, you figured me for a coward because I only went after a cow?"

"Not really, but I did think it was more courageous to choose a more powerful animal."

"So you could eat bull meat? You really are an exceptionally clever fellow, Sir! This bull has eighteen or twenty years on him; he's mostly bones, tendons, and ligaments. And his meat, such as he has, is really not worthy of the name. It's as tough as leather.

You can cook it for days and still not be able to chew it. Any frontiersman chooses a cow over a bull—the meat is more tender and juicy. So you see what a greenhorn you are. I had no time to pay attention to you. So how did your crazy attack on the buffalo go?"

I told him about it. When I was finished, he stared at me, shook his head once again, and then demanded:

"Go find your horse! We'll need it to carry the meat we're going to bring back."

I followed this request. In truth, I felt disappointed in his behavior. He had listened to my story without saying a word. I thought he would give me some kind of acknowledgement, even if it wasn't much. Instead, he said nothing and sent me off to find my horse. All the same, I wasn't really mad at him. I've never been the kind of person who does something merely to get praise.

When I came back with the horse, Sam was kneeling by the buffalo cow he had shot. He had skillfully cut away the hide from the back of the thigh and was cutting out a steak.

"So," he said, "tonight we'll have a feast like we haven't had in a long time. We'll load this steak and my saddle and reins onto your horse. The meat is just for you, me, Will, and Dick. If the others want some, they can ride over here and get it themselves."

"If it hasn't been eaten in the meantime by buzzards and other wild animals."

"Well, aren't you the clever one! Obviously we'll have to cover it with branches and put stones on top of them. Then only a bear or some other large animal would be able to get at it."

So I cut branches from nearby bushes and brought some heavy stones over. We covered the cow and loaded up my horse. Then I asked:

"What happens to the bulls?"

"The bulls? Why worry about them?"

"Isn't there something we can use them for?"

"Nothing."

"Not even the hides?"

"Are you a tanner? I'm not!"

"But I read that the hides of dead buffalos can be hidden in so-called 'caches' and preserved."

"So, you read that, did you? Well, if you read it, it must be true, because everything you read about the Wild West is true, exceptionally true, completely, incontrovertibly true, hee-hee-hee! There are indeed frontiersmen that shoot these animals for their hides. I've done it in my time. But that's not what we're here for, and we don't want to be carrying these heavy hides around."

We started out and within half an hour we were back in camp, in spite of having to walk. The valley where I had killed my first—and second—buffalo wasn't far from our camp site.

Everyone wanted to know why we were on foot and why Sam's horse was not with us.

"We were out hunting buffalo, and my horse was gored by a bull," answered Sam Hawkens.

"Hunting buffalo?" they exclaimed. "Where? Tell us where!"

"Barely half an hour from here. We brought a steak back for us; you can go get the rest."

"That's what we'll do," cried Rattler, who was behaving as if nothing had ever happened between him and me. "Where is it, exactly?"

"Just follow our trail and you'll find it. You can manage that, if I'm not mistaken."

"How many were there?"

"Twenty."

"And how many did you kill?"

"A cow."

"Is that all? What happened to the rest of them?"

"They left. You can go find them. I didn't worry about where they were headed, and I didn't bother asking them, hee-hee-hee!"

"But just one cow. Two hunters and twenty buffalo, and you only shot one?" one of them said in a disparaging voice.

"Do better if you can, Sir! No doubt you would have shot all twenty and several more besides. You will also find two twenty-year-old bulls that this young gentleman shot."

"Bulls? Old bulls? Shooting at twenty-year-old bulls, now that's so dumb that only a greenhorn would do it!"

"Laugh at him if you like. But make sure you take a look at the bulls! I have to tell you that his marksmanship saved my life."

"Your life? How so?"

They were anxious to hear the story, but he declined:

"I'm not interested in talking about it right now. You can let him tell you himself, if you don't mind going to get the meat in the dark."

He was right. The sun was setting, and it would soon be evening. Furthermore, they could see that I wasn't really interested telling the story either, so they got on their horses and they all rode off. I say "all" because none of them wanted to remain behind. They didn't trust each other. Among respectable hunters and in groups of friends, any game that one person kills belongs to all. But these people didn't have that kind of friendly relationship. Later, when they came back, I heard how they had thrown themselves on the cow like wild men, and each had tried, amid the bickering and swearing, to hack off the biggest and best piece of meat for himself.

Once they were gone, we unloaded the buffalo steak and the saddle from my horse, and I led it away to unsaddle it and stake it out. I took my time, and it gave Sam the chance to tell Parker and Stone about our adventure. From where I stood, the tent was between me and them, so they didn't see me coming as I returned. I was almost up to the tent when I heard Sam say:

"Believe me, I'm telling it like it is. This fellow took on the oldest and strongest bull and dropped him like an old, experienced buffalo hunter. I made out like it was foolishness, and I chewed him out properly, but I'm telling you, he's going to be something special."

"You're right," Stone agreed. "He'll make a competent frontiersman."

"And soon, too," I heard Parker say.

"Yes," Hawkens concurred. "You know, gents, he was born to it, truly and absolutely born to it. And his strength! Didn't he move our heavy wagon yesterday, without any help from anyone? Where this fellow hoes, no grass grows for years! But promise me one thing."

"What?" asked Parker.

"Don't let him know what we think about him."

"Why not?"

"It could go to his head."

"I don't think so."

"Oh, yes! He's a modest fellow and not inclined to arrogance. But it is always a mistake to praise a man. You can ruin the best character that way. So go ahead and call him 'greenhorn,' and he really is one. He's got all the characteristics a decent frontiersman needs, but they aren't developed yet. He needs a lot of experience and a lot of practice."

"Well, did you thank him for saving your life?"

"It never occurred to me."

"No? What do you suppose he thinks of you?"

"I don't care what he thinks, not a bit, if I'm not mistaken. I imagine he figures I'm an insensitive and ungrateful scoundrel. But that's beside the point. The point is that he doesn't get a swelled head. He needs to stay like he is. I would have liked to hug him and give him a kiss!"

"Fie!" cried Stone. "A kiss from you? A hug would be risky enough, but a kiss? Never."

"No? Why not?" asked Sam.

"Why not? Haven't you ever looked at yourself in a mirror, or seen your noble likeness in a pool of water? That face, that beard, that nose! Anyone who would consider putting their lips in the vicinity of yours is either sun-struck or stark raving mad."

"So! Aha! That's a right friendly thing to say. So I'm that ugly, huh? And what about you? A beauty, right? Forget it! By my word, if the two us were in a beauty contest, I'd get the prize and you'd draw a blank, hee-hee-hee! But enough of that. We're talking about our greenhorn. I didn't thank him, and I'm not going to. But later, when we roast our buffalo steak, he'll get the best and juiciest piece. I'll cut it for him myself; he's earned it. And you know what else I'm planning?"

"What?" asked Stone.

"I'm going to give him a nice surprise."

"What will it be?"

"I'll let him catch a mustang."

"You're going after mustangs?"

"Yes. After all, I need a new horse. I'd like to borrow yours for the hunt. We saw buffalo today, so the mustangs will show up soon. I figure I just have to ride down to the prairie, where we were setting stakes and surveying the day before yesterday. The mustangs are sure to be there, if they've made it this far south."

I didn't eavesdrop any longer, but went back through the bushes and approached the three hunters from the other side. It was better that they didn't know I had heard their conversation.

A big fire was lit, and two forked branches were driven into the ground on either side of it. They supported the roasting spit, which was made from a strong, straight branch. The three hunters attached the entire steak to it, and then Sam Hawkens began rotating it slowly over the fire. I took private delight at the blissful expression on his face as he did this.

When the others returned with the rest of the meat, they built a fire like ours. But things weren't so quiet and peaceful around their fire. Each wanted to roast his own piece of meat, but there wasn't enough room. The result was that they ended up eating theirs half raw.

I really did get the best piece. It must have weighed three pounds, and I ate it all. But don't count me a big eater just because of that. On the contrary, I generally ate less than most others in my situation. But it would be impossible for someone who wasn't there to imagine the massive amounts of meat that frontiersmen can eat, and that they must eat to survive.

For their nourishment, people require (in addition to vitamins and minerals) a certain amount of protein and carbohydrate. When you're in a civilized place, you can get these in the right proportions. The frontiersman, who may not see civilization for months at a time, lives on meat. Meat is low on carbohydrate, so he has to eat large amounts to give his body enough calories. He must ignore the fact that he takes in too much protein, which does not make for a good diet. I once saw an old trapper eat eight pounds of meat at one sitting, and when I asked him about it, he replied with a smirk:

"What I had, I ate. And if you want to give me a chunk of yours, I can save you from having to keep track of it."

While we ate, the "frontiersmen" discussed our buffalo hunt. They had gotten a different perspective on the "foolishness" they accused me of, once they saw the two dead bulls.

Chapter 5

The next morning, I got ready to resume my work. Sam came to me and said:

"Leave your instruments here, Sir, there's something more interesting to do."

"What?"

"You'll find out. Get your horse ready and let's ride."

"A ride? Work takes priority over that."

"Pshaw! You've labored enough. Anyway, I bet we'll be home by noon. You can spend the afternoon measuring and calculating as much as you like."

I let Bancroft know we were going, and then we headed out. Sam was very secretive, and I didn't bother him since I knew what he had in mind. We rode back through the area we had been surveying until we reached the patch of prairie that Sam had pointed out the day before.

It was probably two miles wide and twice that in length, surrounded by forested hills. A good-sized stream flowed through it, and that provided enough moisture for a rich growth of grass. At the north end, you could enter the prairie from between two mountains. At the south, it ended in a valley that continued southwards. Once we reached the prairie, Sam drew his horse to a stop and surveyed the plain. Then we resumed riding, heading north and following the stream. Suddenly he gave a yell, reined in his horse (which was not really his, but borrowed), got down, jumped over the stream, and went to a spot where the grass had been trampled. He investigated the area, came back, climbed back into the saddle. He resumed riding, but not northwards as before. He turned sharply and headed for the western edge of the prairie, which we soon reached. Here, he got down again, tied his horse to a tree and let it graze. Since examining the tracks, he hadn't said a word, but a contented expression played across his bearded face like sunshine on a forest. Now he turned to me:

"Get off and tie your horse well, Sir. We'll wait here."

"Why tie him so well?" I asked, though I knew exactly why.

"Because you could easily lose him otherwise. I have often seen horses bolt under these circumstances."

"What circumstances?"

"Don't you have any idea?"

"Maybe."

"Take a guess."

"Mustangs?"

"What makes you say that?" he asked, looking at me with some amazement.

"I read about it."

"What?"

"That tame horses, if they aren't well tied, like to bolt to join the wild mustangs."

"The devil take you! You've read so much that it's practically impossible to surprise you. That's why I like people who don't read at all!"

"You wanted to surprise me?"

"Naturally."

"With a mustang?"

"Yes."

"That would hardly have been possible. To be surprised, you can't be warned ahead of time. But you would have had to tell me what was happening before the mustangs arrived."

"I guess you're right. But the mustangs have already been here."

"That was their tracks earlier?"

"Yes, they came through yesterday. Those were the advance guard, the 'scouts' you might call them. I must say these animals are remarkably clever. They always send small groups out ahead and to the sides. They have their officers, just like the military, and the leader is always an experienced, strong, courageous stallion. If they are grazing or if they are moving, the stallions always make up the outer part of the herd. The mares are inside that ring, and the young horses are right in the middle. That way, the stallions can defend the mares and the colts. I've shown you many times how to lasso a mustang. Were you paying attention?"

"Absolutely."

"Do you want to catch one?"

"Yes."

"Well, you'll get your chance this morning, Sir."

"Thanks! But I won't use it."

"No? What the devil! Why not?"

"I don't need a horse."

"A frontiersman doesn't ask whether he needs a horse or not."

"That's not how I picture a good frontiersman behaving."

"Why, what do you think he should do?"

"Yesterday, you told me about the carrion hunters, about the white men who kill large numbers of buffalo even though they don't need the meat. I consider this a sin against the animals and against the red men that need them for food. Do you agree?"

"Sure!"

"Well, it's the same with horses. I don't want to rob any of these magnificent mustangs of their freedom unless I have the excuse that I need a horse."

"Well said, Sir, very good. Every man and Christian must speak and act just as you have said. But who said you were going to rob a mustang of its freedom? You've practiced roping, and I want to test you to see whether you pass muster. Understand?"

"That's different. Yes, I'll go along with that."

"Excellent. With me, though, it's in earnest. I need a horse, and I'll get myself one. I've told you before, and I'm reminding you now: stay firmly in the saddle, and stop your horse just at the moment when the lasso comes taut and the mustang will fall with a jerk. If you don't do that, you'll be pulled off, the mustang will run off with your horse on the other end of the lasso. Then you won't have a horse any more, and you'll become a common foot-soldier like I am at the moment."

He was about to continue, but did not. Instead, he pointed toward the two mountains at the north end of the prairie. A horse appeared there, a single, lone horse. It walked slowly and without grazing, turning its head to one side and the other, sniffing the air.

"See that?" whispered Sam. In his excitement he spoke quietly, though it would have been impossible for the horse to hear us at that distance. "Didn't I tell you they would come? This is the spy they've sent out to see if the area is safe. Sly stallion! The way he peers and smells in every direction! He won't catch wind of us because we're upwind from him. That's why I chose this spot."

Now the mustang broke into a trot. He ran forwards, then to the right, then to the left, and finally wheeled about and disappeared where he had come from.

"Did you see what he did?" asked Sam. "He's a clever one. Used every available bush for cover, so as not to be spotted. An Indian spy would have a hard time doing a better job."

"You're right. It's really amazing."

"Now he's gone back to tell his four-legged General that all is clear. He's wrong, though, hee-hee-hee! I bet they'll be here in ten minutes at the most, you watch. Do you know how we're going to do it?"

"Well?"

"You make a quick trip back to the other end of the prairie and wait there. I'll ride up to where the herd will enter, and I'll hide in the woods. When they come, I'll let them start down toward you and then I'll chase them. They'll run in your direction. When you show yourself, they'll turn and run back. We'll drive them back and forth between the two of us until we've picked out the two best horses. We'll catch them both. I'll choose the better of the two and we'll let the other one go. Agreed?"

"Why even ask? I don't know anything about catching horses, and you're a master of it. I'll do whatever you say."

"Well, you're right. I've broken a few wild mustangs in my day, and I'd have to allow that what you say about 'master' isn't entirely wrong. OK, get going, or you won't be ready when the time comes."

We got back on our horses and rode off in opposite directions, he to the north and I to the south, where we first came out onto the prairie. My heavy bear-killer was a hindrance, especially given the riding we planned to do, and I would gladly have left it behind somewhere, but I had read and heard that a careful frontiersman doesn't part with his gun unless he is absolutely sure that there is nothing around to fear and that he won't need it. But here, an Indian or a wild animal could appear at any time, so I made sure my "old gun" was secured to my saddle so it wouldn't get in my way.

Now came a period of tense waiting for the horses to appear. I hid among the trees on the edge of the prairie, tied one end of my lasso securely to the horn of my saddle, and looped the rest of the rope loosely in front of me where it would be easy to grab.

The other end of the grassy plain was so far from me that I couldn't see the mustangs when they arrived. It was only when Sam drove them toward me that they became visible. I hadn't waited more than 15 minutes when I noticed a lot of dark dots which quickly grew larger as they moved up the valley. At first they looked like sparrows, then cats, then dogs, then calves, and then finally they were close enough for me to see their true size. It was the mustangs, coming toward me in full flight.

What an impression these noble animals made! Their manes waved around their necks, their tails flew in the wind. There were at most three hundred of them, and yet the earth seemed to tremble under their hooves. A white stallion led the way, the kind of splendid animal you would love to catch—but no frontiersman would consider riding a white horse. Such a conspicuous horse would let his enemies spot him from far away.

The time had come to show myself to the mustangs. I headed out from under the trees and into the open, and the effect was immediate: the white mustang jumped back as if he had been hit by a bullet. The herd came to a stop and whinnied, a loud and anxious snort, and then the whole group turned. The white mustang quickly took up his leading position on the far side of the herd and led the animals off in the direction from which they had come.

I followed slowly. I was in no hurry, for I was sure that Sam Hawkens would drive them all back to me. Meantime, I tried to figure out something that I had just noticed. Although I had only observed the horses briefly, it had appeared to me that one of the animals was a mule, not a horse. I could have been mistaken, of course. I planned to look more carefully the second time. The mule had been in the front row, right behind the white mustang, so it was not only accepted by the horses but even seemed to occupy an important position among them.

After a while, the herd came towards me again, and then turned back again once it saw me. I saw that my first impression was correct: there was a mule among them, a light brown mule with dark stripes on his back. I was impressed. Despite the large head and long ears, it was a beautiful animal. Mules need less attention than horses; they are more sure of foot and less afraid of drop-offs. These advantages are one side of the coin. On the other side, they are certainly stubborn. I have seen mules that would rather be beaten to death than take a single step forward, even when they were not loaded down or on difficult terrain. They just didn't feel like moving.

It was clear to me that this mule showed a lot of spirit. Its eyes seemed brighter and more intelligent than those of the horses, and I resolved to catch it. It must have broken away and joined the herd when its owner was hunting the wild mustangs.

Sam drove the herd toward me again. We had now come close enough together that I could see him. The mustangs couldn't go forward or backward, so they had to try to escape toward the sides. We followed them. The herd divided, and I saw that the mule stayed with the main group. It was running at the white mustang's side. It was an exceptionally quick and persistent animal. I decided to stay with the main group, and Sam appeared to have made the same choice.

"Head into the middle! You go left, I'll go right!" he yelled.

We spurred our horses until we were not only keeping pace with the mustangs but would have caught up with them before they reached the forest. They stayed away from the trees. Instead, they turned back toward us and attempted to run between us. To prevent this, we galloped toward each other, causing them to scatter in all directions like a flock of chickens from a hawk. The white mustang and the mule shot between us, separately from the others, and we took off after them. Sam called out to me as he swung his lasso over his head:

"Greenhorn again! You'll never change!"

"Why?"

"Because you picked out the white horse, and only a greenhorn would do that, hee-hee-hee!"

I answered him, but he was laughing too hard to hear me. So he thought I had the white mustang in mind. Let him! I left the mule to him and headed off to the side, where the mustangs were now anxiously and aimlessly milling around, snorting and whinnying. Sam got close enough to the mule to throw his lasso. The throw was accurate and the loop hung around the mule's neck. Now Sam had to stop and get his horse moving backwards, as he had so carefully taught me, in order to withstand the shock when the mule reached the end of the rope and it came tight. He was able to do this, but not quite quickly enough. His horse hadn't turned around or braced itself and was yanked forward by the powerful shock. Sam Hawkens flew through the air, executing a perfect somersault, and crashed to the ground. The horse immediately gathered itself together and started running. The lasso went slack and the mule, which had held its ground and had not been pulled down, recovered its breath and galloped away, dragging the horse, with the lasso still secured to the saddle, after it across the prairie.

I rushed over to Sam, to see if he was injured. He stood up and called to me in shock:

"I'll be jiggered! There goes Dick Stone's nag and that mule, without even bidding me adieu, if I'm not mistaken!"

"Are you hurt?"

"No. Get down quick and give me your horse. I need it!"

"Why?"

"I have to chase them, of course. Quick, get off!"

"I wouldn't think of it! You might do another somersault and then both horses would be gone for good."

As I said this, I spurred my horse after the mule. It had already covered a lot of ground, but it was having trouble with the horse. Each wanted to go a different direction, and neither could, because of the lasso that joined them. That made it easy to catch up with them. I didn't even consider using my lasso. Rather, I grabbed Sam's, which bound the two animals, and wrapped it around my hand. Now I was confident I could restrain the mule. I let the two animals run for a while, galloping along behind them. I gradually began to pull harder and harder on the lasso, so that the loop got tighter and tighter. That way it was possible to control the animals quite readily. By pretending to give in I was eventually able to get them to swing around in an arc until we were back where Sam Hawkens was waiting. Then I suddenly pulled so hard on the lasso that the mule's neck was constricted. It couldn't breathe and fell to the ground.

"Hold on until I have a grip on the varmint, then let go!" cried Sam.

He ran right up to the mule, which was flailing around on the ground.

"Now!" he yelled.

I let go of the lasso. The mule caught its breath and jumped up.

Just as quickly, Sam was up on his back. For a few moments, the mule stood motionless, as if petrified with fear. But then it jumped into the air, first forward, then backward, then off to the side. It arched its back, but little Sam held on tight.

"It won't get me off!" Sam called to me. "Now it will try its last trick and run off with me. Wait for me here. I'll bring it back broken."

But he was wrong about that. It didn't try to bolt, but suddenly threw itself on the ground and started to roll around. It might have broken all the poor fellow's ribs, so he had to dismount. I jumped out of the saddle, grabbed the lasso (which was sliding across the ground) and wrapped it twice around the base of a nearby sturdy bush.

The mule, having gotten rid of its rider, jumped up. It tried to escape, but the bush held, the lasso went taut, and the loop suddenly tightened again. Once again, the mule went down.

Sam Hawkens had retreated to the side, inspected his ribs and thigh, made a face as if he had been eating sauerkraut with strawberry jam, and said:

"Let the beast go. No man will tame him, if I'm not mistaken."

"Are you kidding? I don't like to be shown up by a mule. It must learn to obey. Watch!"

I unwrapped the lasso from the bush and positioned myself on the animal's back. As soon as it caught its breath, it jumped up. Next, I applied the most intense thigh pressure I could manage, and there I had an advantage over little Sam. A horse's ribs must bend under the rider's thighs. This presses the internal organs together and produces deathly fear in the animal. The mule tried the same tricks to get me off that it had tried with Sam, but I gathered up the lasso, which was dragging on the ground, and pulled it up tight around the mule's neck. I pulled on this whenever I saw that the animal wanted to throw itself down. By manipulating the lasso and by using thigh pressure, I managed to keep it on its feet. It was quite a battle, I must say, strength against strength. I began to sweat from all my pores, but the mule was sweating more. Sweat ran down its sides, and foam poured from its mouth. Its movements became weaker and more mechanical. Its snorting, which had been furious at first, gave over to a shallow cough. In the end, it collapsed beneath me, not on purpose, but because it had used up its last ounce of energy. It lay there with its eyes rolled up, not moving. I was breathing very, very heavily. It felt as if every sinew and ligament in my body had been torn apart.

"Heavens, what a man you are!" Sam cried. "You had more strength than this animal! If you could see your face, you'd be shocked."

"I can believe it."

"Your eyes are bugged out, your lips are swollen, and your cheeks are positively blue!"

"That's because a greenhorn like me doesn't want to be thrown, while someone else, a master at hunting mustangs, is smarter and lets himself be peeled off when his own horse is tied to the mule, so that they both run free."

He made a doubly pitiable face and asked beseechingly:

"Keep quiet about that, Sir! I tell you, something like this can occasionally happen to even the most competent hunter. And you've had two fortunate days, yesterday and today."

"I hope to have more days like these. But they weren't so great for you. How are your ribs and your other bits and pieces?"

"I don't know. I'll gather them up and count them, as soon as I'm feeling a little better. Right now, they're just flopping around inside my body. I've never had such a beast between my legs! Hopefully, it will now learn to obey!"

"It has already learned. Look how feebly it's lying there; you almost feel like pitying it. Put the saddle and bridle on it and ride it home."

"It will start bucking again!"

"Not a chance! It's had enough. It's a clever animal and you'll be very glad to have caught it."

"Yes, I think so. I had my eye on it from the start. You were after the white mustang, which was really dumb."

"You thought so?"

"Of course it was dumb."

"No, I mean are you sure I was after the white mustang?"

"What else would you have been chasing?"

"The mule."

"Really?"

"Yes. Even if I am a greenhorn, at least I know that a white horse is useless to a frontiersman. I liked the mule as soon as I saw it."

"Yes, you do have good horse sense, I grant you that."

"I wish you had equally good people sense, Sam! Now come help me get this animal back up off the ground."

We managed to get the mule to stand up. It stood still with legs trembling. It did not resist when we put on the saddle and bridle. And once Sam was mounted, it obeyed the reins as willingly and as sensitively as a well-trained horse.

"It must have had a previous owner who was a good rider, I can already see that." Sam observed. "Must have run away from him. Do you know what I'm going to name it?"

"Well?"

"Mary. I had another mule named Mary once. This saves me the trouble of thinking up another name."

"So your mule is Mary and your gun is Liddy!"

"Yes indeed. Two terrific names, don't you think? And now I want to ask a favor of you."

"Sure. What is it?"

"Don't tell a soul about what happened here! I'd be greatly indebted to you."

"Nonsense. Of course I wouldn't speak of it. That's understood.

You don't owe me a thing."

"Oh, I sure do. If that band of rascals in camp ever heard tell of the way Sam Hawkens got his new, graceful Mary! I would never hear the end of it. If you keep quiet about this, I'll. . ."

"Please, Sam, be quiet!" I interrupted. "Don't waste another word on this subject. You are my teacher and my friend. Nothing more needs to be said."

At this, his sly little eyes became moist, and he responded with feeling:

"Yes, I'm your friend, Sir, and if I knew that you also felt a touch of affection for me, that would be a genuine joy and delight for this old heart of mine."

I reached over, took his hand, and answered:

"Well then, your heart will have that joy. Rest assured, you're as dear to me as, well, as if you were my good, brave, and honest uncle. Is that enough?"

"Enough and more, Sir, enough and more. I'm so delighted that you were willing to express the strength of your friendship here on the spot. Tell me what I should do! I'd eat this new Mary right before your eyes, skin and all. Or maybe you'd like it better if I marinated, fricasseed, and devoured myself. Or perhaps. . ."

"Hold on!" I laughed. "If you did either of these, I'd lose you: in the one case you'd burst and in the other you'd die of indigestion, since you'd have to eat your wig and I know your stomach couldn't handle that. You've already done enough for me, and I know you'll do me some good turns in the future. Everyone is better off if you and Mary both stay alive. Let's head back to camp. I want to get some work done."

"Work! You haven't done any work here? If this wasn't work, I don't know what work is."

I tied Dick Stone's horse to mine with the lasso, and we rode off. The mustangs had long since disappeared. The mule obeyed its rider willingly, and Sam called out cheerfully as we rode along:

"This Mary, she's been to school, and a good school too! I have a feeling, and it gets stronger with every step, that I'll have an outstanding mount from now on. She's starting to remember everything she once learned and then forgot when she was with the mustangs. Hopefully, she has character and not just spirit."

"If she doesn't, you can teach it to her. She's not too old for that."

"How old do you figure she is?"

"No more than five years."

"I agree. I'll take a closer look later and check on it. I have no one but you to thank for this animal. These last two days were bad for me, very bad, but you did yourself proud. Did you imagine you would get to try buffalo hunting and mustang hunting right on the heels of each other?"

"Why not? Out here in the West, you have to be ready for anything. I'm looking forward to experiencing other kinds of hunting as well."

"Aha. Yes. I hope you do as well at them as you did yesterday and today. Yesterday especially, your life hung by a thread. You tried to do too much. Don't ever forget that you're a greenhorn. You don't just let a bison come at you and shoot him in the eyes! Did you ever hear of such a thing? You're still green, and you underestimated that bison. From now on, be a little more careful and don't take on too much. Hunting buffalo is extremely dangerous. There's only one thing more dangerous."

"What's that?"

"Hunting bear."

"You mean those black bears with the yellowish muzzle?"

"Black bears? Heck no. That's a very good-tempered and peaceful type of animal. Why, you could practically teach one to knit and iron clothes. No, I mean the grizzly, the gray bear of the Rockies. You've read everything—did you ever read about the grizzly?"

"Yes."

"Well, just be glad if you never see one. When a grizzly rears up, he's a good two feet taller than you. He could turn your head into a pulp with one bite. Once he's been attacked and enraged, he doesn't rest until he has torn his enemy to bits."

"Or until his enemy has vauquished him."

"Oh ho! See, there's that crazy streak of yours showing again! You're talking about this enormously powerful, invincible bear as lightly as if you were talking about a harmless little raccoon."

"No I'm not. I would never underestimate a grizzly. But they are not 'invincible.' No beast of prey is invincible, and that includes the grizzly."

"I suppose you read that somewhere?"

"Yes."

"Hmm. I think the books you've been reading are to blame for your craziness. In other respects, you're a reasonable fellow, if I'm not mistaken. You could, and would, take on a grizzly bear as readily as you took on that bison yesterday?"

"If I had no other choice, sure."

"No other choice! That's crazy! What on earth do you mean? Anyone can choose differently, if he feels like it."

"He can run away if he's scared. Is that what you mean?"

"Yes, but we're not talking about being 'scared.' It's not cowardly to get out of a grizzly's way. On the contrary, it's practically suicide to pick a fight with one."

"That's where my opinion differs from yours. If a grizzly surprises me and leaves me no time to run, I have to protect myself. If a grizzly attacks one of my comrades, I have to come to his aid. In both these cases, I cannot run and I must not run. And furthermore, I have to think that a plucky frontiersman might take on a grizzly even without these reasons, as a test of courage or just to get rid of such a dangerous beast. And while he's at it, he could make a great meal of the ham and the paws."

"You are absolutely hopeless. I'm extremely concerned about you. You should thank the Lord if you never have a chance to taste those hams and paws. Even if I do allow that no greater delicacy exists on this earth. It's far better than the very best buffalo steak."

"Perhaps you don't need to worry about me just yet. Or are we likely to encounter grizzlies in this area?"

"Why not? The grizzly ranges throughout the mountains, and sometimes he'll follow a river right out into the prairie. Woe to him that crosses his path! Let's talk no more about it."

He suspected as little as I did that this topic would crop up again the following day, in a very different context, and that we would indeed cross paths with this fearsome animal. There was no time to continue the conversation, for we had arrived at camp. It had been moved forward a fair distance, which had been surveyed in our absence. Bancroft had put in an extraordinary effort with the three surveyors, in order to show what he was capable of. We attracted attention.

"A mule! A mule!" they cried. "Where did you get it, Hawkens?"

"It was shipped to me direct," he answered, with a straight face.

"Impossible. Who sent it?"

"By express mail, nicely wrapped, for two cents. Want to see the envelope?"

A few laughed; the others cursed at him. But he had made his point. No one asked any more questions. Whether he was more forthcoming with Dick Stone and Will Parker, I couldn't tell—I started in immediately with my surveying work. By evening, I had gotten far enough with it that it would be possible to resume the next morning in the very valley where we'd encountered the buffalo the previous day. As we talked about this in the evening, I asked Sam if our work might be interrupted by more buffalo. It seemed as if their route to the south lay through the valley. And the group we had encountered was just a vanguard. Perhaps we might run into the main herd. He answered:

"Don't you believe it, Sir! The bison are just as smart as the mustangs. The ones we hunted have returned and warned the herd, and now they'll strike out in a different direction. They'll avoid this valley."

Chapter 6

As morning broke, we moved our camp to the upper part of the valley. Hawkens, Stone and Parker didn't participate: Hawkens wanted to break in his new "Mary," and the other two accompanied him down to the patch of prairie where we had caught the mule. There was enough space there for what he had in mind.

We surveyors occupied ourselves with placing our stakes. Some of Rattler's men helped with this, while Rattler himself loafed with the rest of the slackers. We came fairly close to the spot where I had shot the two buffalo. To my astonishment, I noticed that the old bull wasn't there any more. We went over and saw that the buffalo had disappeared into the bushes. A trail of compressed grass about 8 feet wide showed where it had gone.

"Sakes alive! What's going on here?" cried Rattler. "When we came here for the meat, I checked both bulls carefully. They were dead as can be, and yet this one must have still had some life in him."

"You really mean that?" I asked him.

"Yes indeed. Or do you think a dead buffalo can move?"

"Does it have to move on its own? Maybe it got moved."

"Oh yeah? Who moved it?"

"Indians, for example. A little farther up, we found the footprint of an Indian."

"So! What a clever greenhorn you are. If Indians moved it, where do you suppose these Indians came from?"

"Could be from anywhere."

"How true! Perhaps they came down from heaven! Because if they didn't, we would have seen their trail. No, that buffalo must have still had some life in him. He must have managed to drag himself over into the bushes, where he most likely died. I'll go take a look."

He and his men followed the trail into the bushes. Maybe he thought I would go along, but I didn't. I had no use for the scornful way he spoke to me, and I had work to do. Besides, I didn't care where the corpse of the buffalo was. I turned to my work, but I had hardly reached for the stakes when cries of fear erupted from the bushes. There were two or three shots, and then I heard Rattler cry:

"Into the trees, quick, or we're dead! He can't climb a tree!"

Who did he mean, that couldn't climb a tree? One of his men came sprinting out of the bushes at a pace that could only have been prompted by the fear of death.

"What's going on, what is it?" I called to him.

"A huge bear, a grizzly!" he gasped as he ran by me.

At the same time, a frantic voice cried out:

"Help me, help me! He's got a grip on me!"

It was the kind of cry a man can make only when he sees the open jaws of death gaping before him. I could tell he must be in extreme danger, he had to be helped. But how? I had left my rifle by the tent, since it hindered my work. This was not really carelessness on my part, since we surveyors always had the frontiersmen nearby for our protection. But if I ran back to the tent, the man would be torn apart by the grizzly before I could return. I had to make do with what I had: just my knife and the two revolvers in my belt. But what were these weapons to a grizzly! The grizzly is a close cousin of the cave bears, which are now extinct, and it belongs more to prehistoric times than to the present. It can be as big as nine feet long, and I have spotted specimens that weigh 900 pounds. The grizzly is so strong, it can easily carry away a deer, a foal, or a heifer in its jaws. A rider can only escape a grizzly if he has a strong horse with a will to survive. Otherwise, the bear will run him down. Given the great strength, the total lack of fear, and the remarkable endurance of the grizzly, killing one is considered a formidable deed by the Indians.

So, I sprang into the bushes. The trail led up to the edge of the forest, where the bear had dragged the bull. He had originally come from there, which is why we hadn't seen his tracks—they had been covered up when the bull was dragged back over them.

It was an awful scene. Behind me, the surveyors, who had run back to the tents for their weapons, were crying out. In front of me, the frontiersmen were yelling. And in the middle, the indescribable cries of anguish of one of them who had been caught by the bear.

With every stride, I came closer. I could now hear the growl of the bear itself. Well, not really the growl—the grizzly is different from other bears in that it doesn't growl like them, but rather has a single sound that it makes whether in anger or pain. It is a peculiar sound with rapid snorting and hissing.

I burst onto the scene. In front of me lay the carcass of the bison, completely stripped of flesh. To the right and left, the frontiersmen had retreated to the comparative safety of trees (grizzlies have almost never been seen to climb a tree) and were calling out to me. Straight ahead, beyond the remains of the buffalo, one of the frontiersmen had tried to climb a tree but had been caught by the bear. He was clinging for dear life to the limb of a tree while the grizzly, standing on his hind legs, dug into his thighs and lower body with its paws. The man was doomed to death, with no hope of rescue. I couldn't help him, and no one could have held it against me if I had turned and run. But that scene had an irresistible effect on me. I grabbed a rifle that had been dropped on the ground, but it had already been fired. I took it by the barrel, ran up to the bear, and swung the stock with all my might, striking the bear's skull with the rifle butt. Laughable! The gun splintered like glass in my hands. A skull like that is impervious even to an axe. But I did succeed in distracting the grizzly from its victim. It turned its head toward me, not quickly the way a relative of a cat or a dog might, but slowly as if amazed by the stupidity of my attack. Looking me over with his small eyes, it seemed to be considering whether to return to its current victim or to tackle me. These few moments saved my life, for the plan which now occurred to me which was the only one that could possibly help me in the situation. I pulled out one of my revolvers and came up to the bear, whose head was turned toward me though the rest of his body was not. I shot it once, twice, thrice, four times right in the eyes, just the way I had shot the buffalo in the eyes. I did this as quickly as I could, then jumped off to one side, pulled out my Bowie knife, and waited to see what the bear would do.

If I had stayed where I was when I shot, I would have paid with my life. The huge beast turned from the tree and threw itself on the spot where I had been a moment earlier. But I wasn't there, and now the bear began searching for me with venomous snarls and furious swipes of its paws. It flailed around like a madman, spun around on all fours, ripped up handfuls of dirt, flailed about in all directions with its front paws, and sprang this way and that trying to find me. But it couldn't locate me, for I had been fortunate in my aim. Perhaps it might have found me by smell, but it was so enraged that it couldn't use its senses and instincts.

Finally, it began to turn its attention to its injuries. It sat down on the ground, upper body erect, and ran its front paws, snorting and snarling, over its eyes. Instantly, I was next to it, and I stuck my knife twice deep between its ribs. It swiftly reached for me, but I was already gone. I hadn't hit the heart, and the bear began searching for me again with doubled intensity. This lasted another ten minutes, during which time the bear lost a lot of blood and was beginning to look feeble. Then it sat down again and slapped at its eyes. This gave me the opportunity for two more quick stabs, and this time I was on target. As I jumped to the side, the bear slowly dropped to all fours and stumbled a few steps forward, then to the side, and then back, snarling all the while. Then it tried to raise itself up again but didn't have the strength and instead fell down and rocked back and forth in vain attempts to regain its feet. Finally, it stretched out and lay motionless.

"Thank God!" cried Rattler from his tree. "The beast is dead. We were in terrible danger."

"I can't see how it was so terrible for you," I answered. "You managed to find yourself a pretty safe spot. You can come down now."

"No, not yet. You better check first, to be sure the grizzly is really dead."

"It's dead."

"Don't be so sure. You have no idea how tenaciously an animal like that clings to life. Better check."

"For your sake? If you want to find out if it's dead or not, check it yourself. After all, you're the famous frontiersman; I'm just a greenhorn."

I turned to his colleague, who was still hanging from the limb as before. He had stopped screaming and was no longer moving. His face was contorted and his glazed eyes stared down at me. His flesh had been ripped off his thighs down to the bone, and his guts dangled from his lower body. I controlled my horror and called to him:

"Let go, Sir! I'll lift you down."

He didn't answer, and there was not the slightest movement to indicate that he had understood me. I called to his comrades to climb down and help me. These famous "frontiersmen" weren't about to move until I had poked at the bear a few times to show them that it really was dead. Only then did they dare come down to help me get the horribly dismembered man down to the ground. This was difficult: his arms were wrapped so tightly around the branch that it required considerable force to get them loose. He was dead.

His horrible fate seemed not to affect his comrades in the least. They turned away from him and toward the bear, and their leader said:

"Now the tables are turned. Before, the bear wanted to eat us, and now we'll eat him. Quick, men, get the skin off so we can get at the ham and the paws!"

He pulled out his knife and got ready to skin the bear, but I told him:

"It would have been more commendable if you had used your knife on him when he was alive. Now it's too late for that. Leave him alone."

"What?" he cried. "Are you planning to stop me from cutting myself a roast?"

"Indeed I am, Mr. Rattler."

"What gives you the right?"

"I have the undisputable right to this bear. I killed it."

"That's not true. You're not claiming that a greenhorn with a knife can kill a grizzly, are you? We shot it as soon as we spotted it."

"And then you ran for the trees. Yes, that's exactly right."

"But it was our bullets that did it. They are what ultimately killed him, not the pokes in the ribs that you gave him when he was already half dead. The bear is ours, and we'll do as we like with him. Understand?"

He wanted to start in on the bear, but I warned him: "Stop right now, Mr. Rattler. Otherwise, I'll teach you to pay attention to me. Do you understand that?"

He ignored me and, kneeling, stuck his knife into the bear's fur. I grabbed him around the hips from behind, lifted him into the air, and hurled him into the nearest tree. In that moment of anger, I didn't care if he broke every bone in his body. While he was still in the air, I drew my second revolver in order to forestall any possible attack. He got to his feet, glared at me with fury-filled eyes, took out his knife and cried:

"You'll pay for this! You hit me once before, and I'll not let you get your hands on me a third time."

He started toward me. I pointed my revolver at him and threatened:

"One more step, and I'll send a bullet through your brain! Get rid of that knife! I'll shoot you on 'three' if it's still in your hand. One, two, .. "

He held the knife fast, and I really would have shot him (if not his head, then two or three bullets through the hand—enough to make him show some respect) but fortunately it didn't come to that, for at this critical moment a loud voice rang out:

"People, be nice! What possible reason can two white men have to break each other's necks? Stop it!"

Chapter 7

We looked in the direction from which these words came, and saw a man emerge from behind a tree. He was small, gaunt, and doubled over, and his clothing and weapon were almost like those of a red man. You couldn't really tell if he was a white man or an Indian. His angular face suggested the latter, but the color of his skin, though darkened by the sun, had apparently once been white. His head was uncovered, and his dark hair hung down to his shoulders. His outfit consisted of Indian-style leather pants, a leather hunting jacket, and simple moccasins. His only weapons were a rifle and a knife. He had exceptionally intelligent eyes, and, in spite of his deformity the impression he made was a serious one. You have to be crude and feeble-minded to turn up your nose at a person whose physical deficiencies are not his fault. This, apparently, is exactly the group Rattler belonged to, for he called out to the approaching figure with a laugh:

"Halloo, what kind of a dwarf do we have here? I didn't know they existed out here in the West."

The stranger looked him over from top to bottom and answered in a calm and thoughtful voice:

"You should thank God that you have sound limbs! Anyway, it's the heart and the spirit that counts, not the body, and in those respects I can survive a comparison with you."

He made a dismissive movement with his hand and turned to me:

"You've got some strength in your bones, Sir! There's not many that could duplicate your experiment in making such a heavy man fly through the air. It was really a pleasure to watch."

Then he nudged the grizzly with his foot and continued in a regretful tone:

"So here's the fellow we wanted. We came to late. Too bad!"

"You wanted to kill him?" I asked.

"Yes. We found his tracks yesterday and followed them, here and there through thick and thin, and now that we've arrived we find, unfortunately, that the work has already been done."

"You speak of 'we,' Sir. Are you not alone?"

"No. There are two gentlemen with me."

"Who?"

"I'll tell you once I learn who you are. As you know, you can't be too careful in this region. You run into more bad men than good men around here."

He glanced at Rattler and his men, and then continued in a friendly voice:

"Anyway, with a gentlemen you can tell right away that you can trust him. I overheard the last part of your conversation, so I have a pretty good idea who I'm dealing with."

"We're surveyors, Sir." I explained. "One engineer, four surveyors, three scouts, and twelve frontiersmen to protect us from possible attacks."

"Hmm. As far as this lot is concerned, I'd say you seem to be a man that doesn't need other people's protection. So you're surveyors. You're working around here?"

"Yes."

"What are you surveying?"

"A rail line."

"Is it supposed to pass through here?"

"Yes."

"You've purchased the property, then?"

During these questions his eyes had become penetrating and his face more serious. He seemed to have some basis for wanting this information, so I answered:

"I was hired to do the surveying, and I'm doing it, but I don't concern myself with the rest of it."

"Hmm. But I think you know very well what you're doing. The land you're standing on belongs to the Indians, the Mescalero branch of the Apache tribe, to be precise. I can assure you that this land has not been sold. Nor has it been transferred to anyone else in any other way."

"What difference does it make to you?" Rattler interrupted. "Don't worry about other people's business. Stick to your own."

"That's what I am doing, Sir. I'm an Apache, a Mescalero in fact."

"You? Don't make me laugh! I'd have to be blind not to see that you're a white man."

"But you're wrong! Ignore my skin and listen to my name. I'm called Kleki-petra."

In the Apache language, which I didn't yet understand at the time, this name means "white father." Rattler seemed to have heard the name before. He took a step backward in ironic astonishment and said:

"Ah, Kleki-petra, the famous school-teacher of the Apache! Too bad you're a hunchback. It must be tough for you not to be made fun of by those red idiots."

"Oh, it doesn't bother me, Sir. I'm used to being made fun of by idiots, for anyone with half a brain won't do it. And now that I know who you are and what you are doing here, I can tell you who my companions are. It's best if I show them to you."

He called back into the woods, some Indian words that I didn't understand, and two exceptionally interesting figures appeared and approached with a slow and dignified step. They were Indians, and it was obvious at a glance that they were father and son.

The older was a bit more than average height and powerfully built. His bearing had a touch of true nobility, and you could see his nimbleness in his movements. His face was pure Indian, but not so angular as is common among red men. His eyes had a calm, almost mild expression, the external sign of a quiet inner gatheredness that must have placed him above the more ordinary members of his tribe. His head was uncovered. He had bound up his dark hair in a ponytail from which protruded an eagle's feather, the sign of a chief. He wore moccasins, fringed leggings, and a leather hunting jacket, all made for simplicity and durability. In his belt, he had a knife and several small pouches containing all the necessities of life on the plains. A medicine pouch hung around his neck, and next to it, a peace pipe with a bowl made from sacred clay. He carried a double-barreled rifle, the stock of which was thickly covered with silver nails. This was the gun that his son Winnetou would later make famous as the "silver rifle."

The younger man was dressed in exactly the same way as his father, except that his clothing was not as coarse. His moccasins were decorated with porcupine quills, and the seams of his leggings and hunting jacket were decorated with fine red thread. He, too, carried a medicine pouch and peace pipe around his neck. Like his father, he carried a knife and a double-barreled rifle. His hair was also drawn together at the back of his neck, but without the eagle's feather. It was so long that it fell, heavy and thick, down his back. Many a woman must have envied him this wonderful, dark hair. His face was perhaps even nobler than his father's, and its color was a light brown with a touch of bronze. He was, as I guessed at the time and later confirmed, about my age. He made a deep impression on me from the moment I saw him. I sensed that he was a good person and that he must possess extraordinary gifts. We looked each other over for a while, and for a moment I thought I saw in his dark, serious eyes a friendly flicker, like a greeting that the sun sends through a gap in the clouds.

"These are my friends and companions," said Kleki-petra, indicating first the father and then the son. "This is Inchu-chuna, the great chief of the Mescaleros, also recognized by all other Apaches as chief. And here is his son, Winnetou. In spite of his youth, he has already performed more bold deeds than ten old warriors might do in their whole lifetimes. Someday, his name will be famous throughout the plains and the rocky mountains."

This sounded like an exaggeration, but in the end it turned out to be accurate. Rattler laughed scornfully and cried out:

"A young guy like that, and you're telling me he committed all these 'deeds'? I say 'committed,' since I'm pretty sure it must have been mostly thievery, juvenile tricks, and robbery. We know all about that. Red men just steal and rob."

This was a grave accusation. The three strangers behaved as if they had not heard it. They walked over to look at the bear. Kleki-petra bent down and examined it.

"It died of stab wounds, not bullets," he said, turning to me. He had secretly eavesdropped on my quarrel with Rattler, and now he wanted to confirm that I had been right.

"We'll see about that," said Rattler. "What would a hunch-back school-teacher know about hunting bears? Once we skin that bear, we'll see for sure which wound it was that killed him. I'm not going to let a greenhorn deprive me of me rights."

Winnetou leaned over the bear, felt the wounds, and asked me, as he stood up again:

"Who fought this bear with a knife?"

He spoke excellent English.

"I did," I answered.

"Why didn't my young white brother shoot him?"

"I had no gun with me."

"But there are several guns on the ground."

"They aren't mine. Their owners threw them down and climbed up into the trees."

"As we were following the bear's tracks, we heard shouting in the distance. Where was that?"

"Right here."

"Ugh! The squirrels and the skunks can run to the trees when their enemies come. But a man should fight. If he has courage, then he has the power to overcome even the strongest animal. My young white brother has such courage. Why is he called a 'greenhorn'?"

"Because I recently arrived in the West for the first time."

"Palefaces are strange people. A young man who has just killed the terrible grizzly with only a knife, they call a 'greenhorn.' But those who ran to the trees in fear and cried out from the branches, they are allowed to call themselves expert frontiersmen. Red men are more fair. They never call a brave man a coward, and they never call a coward a brave man."

"My son has spoken well," his father agreed, in English that was not quite as good as his son's. "This young paleface is no longer a greenhorn. One who kills a grizzly in this way should be called a great hero. And one who does it to save others who have gone to the trees, he should get thanks from them, not scolding words. How! Let's go back out to the prairie, to see why the palefaces have come to this place."

What a difference between my white companions and these Indians they despised! Their sense of justice compelled them to speak out on my behalf, although they could easily have remained silent. It was at some risk that they spoke. There were only three of them, and they didn't know how many we were. They certainly put themselves in danger by alienating our frontiersmen. But they seemed not to be concerned with that at all. They walked slowly and proudly past us and out of the bushes. We followed them. Then Inchu-chuna saw the surveyor's stakes, stopped, turned to me and asked:

"What is this? Do the palefaces want to measure this land?"

"Yes."

"Why?"

"To build a road for the fire-horse."

His eyes lost their calm, thoughtful look. An angry light appeared, and he enquired almost hastily:

"Do you belong to these people?"

"Yes."

"And you have measured land with them?"

"Yes."

"You are paid for this?"

"Yes."

He gave me a suspicious contemptuous glance, and his tone was equally contemptuous as he said to Kleki-petra:

"Your teachings sound very good, but they often are not correct. Finally I find a young paleface with a brave heart, an open face, and honest eyes. But I ask him what he does here, and find he has come to steal our land in exchange for money. The white men's faces can be good or evil, but inside they are all the same!"

To be honest, I must say that I could find no words to defend myself. I felt ashamed. The chief was right; what he said was true. Could I really be proud of my work? Me, a moral, God-fearing surveyor?

The engineer and the three surveyors had hidden in the tent, where they had watched for the fearsome bear through a hole. When they saw us coming, they emerged, astonished to see the Indians with us. Naturally, they asked us how we had fended off the bear. To this, Rattler quickly answered:

"We shot him, and we'll have bear paws for lunch and bear ham for dinner."

Our three guests looked at me, to see if I would accept this. So I said:

"And I claim that I stabbed him to death. Here are three experts who say I'm right, but let's not decide on that basis. When Hawkens, Stone, and Parker get back, they can pass judgment. Until then, the bear lies untouched."

"Like hell I'll let those three settle this!" growled Rattler. "I'm taking my men back there to carve up that bear, and anyone who tries to stop us gets half a dozen bullets in his chest!"

"Shut your mouth or I'll shut it for you, Mr. Rattler! I'm not half as afraid of your bullets as you were of that bear. You won't chase me up a tree. You can go back there—I have nothing against that, as long as it is to give your dead comrade a decent burial. You shouldn't leave him lying like that."

"Is someone dead?" asked Bancroft, shocked.

"Yes, Rollins," answered Rattler. "The poor devil lost his life because of someone else's stupidity. Otherwise he would have saved himself."

"How so? Whose stupidity?"

"Well, he did just like the rest of us and jumped into a tree. He would have gotten up out of reach, but this greenhorn foolishly ran up and annoyed the bear, and it attacked Rollins and ripped him right open."

This was evil taken too far. I stood practically speechless in astonishment. To present the situation in this way, in my presence, was more than I could stand. I quickly turned to him with the question:

"Are you convinced of this, Mr. Rattler?"

"Yes," he nodded affirmatively. He took out his revolver, anticipating an attack from me.

"Rollins could have saved himself and I hindered him from doing so?"

"Yes."

"But I say the bear already had hold of him before I arrived!"

"That's a lie!"

"Well, here's a taste of the truth."

With these words, I ripped the revolver from his hand with my left hand, and with the right I hit him so hard that he flew six or eight paces through the air before hitting the ground. He jumped back up, pulled out his knife, and came at me, growling like an enraged animal. I parried his knife thrust with my left hand and knocked him down with my right. He lay unconscious at my feet.

"Ugh! Ugh!" cried Inchu-chuna in astonishment, forgetting his normal Indian reserve in his wonder at this blow. In the next moment, though, you could see that he regretted this lapse.

"Shatterhand again," said the surveyor Wheeler.

I didn't pay attention to these words, for I was watching Rattlers comrades. They were obviously furious, but none of them was ready to take me on. They grumbled and cursed among themselves, but that was all they did.

"It's time you had a serious talk with Rattler, Mr. Bancroft," I told the engineer. "I didn't do anything to him, and yet he persists in rubbing me the wrong way. I'm worried it will come to manslaughter here in the camp. Give him his pay and send him off, or if you don't want to, I can just leave."

"Oh ho, Sir, this matter isn't all that bad!"

"Oh yes it is. Here is his knife and his revolver. Don't give them back to him until he's calmed down. I'm telling you, I value my skin and if he comes after me again with a weapon, I'll kill him. You call me a greenhorn, but I know the law of the plains. If anyone threatens my life, I have the right to kill him on the spot."

This applied to the rest of the "frontiersmen" as well as to Rattler, and none of them had a word to say. Now, Chief Inchu-chuna turned to the engineer:

"I think I heard that you are the paleface who is the leader of these men. Is this so?"

"Yes," he answered.

"Then I must speak with you."

"What about?"

"You will hear. You are standing up, but men should sit when they meet together."

"Will you be our guest?"

"No, that is not possible. How can I be your guest, when you are on my ground, in my forest, my valley, my prairie? Let the white men sit. Who are the other palefaces that are coming now?"

"They're with us."

"Let them sit with us also."

Sam, Dick, and Will were just returning from their ride. As experienced frontiersmen, they weren't surprised to find Indians with us, but they were worried when they heard who the two were.

"And who's the third one?" Sam asked me.

"His name is Kleki-petra, and Rattler calls him the school-teacher."

"Kleki-petra the school-teacher? Oh, I've heard of him, if I'm not mistaken. He's quite a secretive fellow, a white who has lived with the Apaches for quite some time. Seems to be some kind of missionary, maybe a priest. I'm looking forward to meeting him. I'd like to get a feel for him, hee-hee-hee!"

"If he lets you!"

"Think he'd bite my finger? Anything else happen?"

"Yes."

"What?"

"Something important."

"Out with it!"

"I did something you warned me against yesterday."

"I don't know what you're talking about. I warned you about a lot of things."

"Grizzly bear."

"Whoa! A grizzly's been around here?"

"And what a bear it was!"

"Where? You're just kidding me."

"Not a chance. Down there among the trees just beyond those bushes. It carried the old bull back there."

"Really? Really? Well, I'll be jiggered! Everything has to happen while I'm away! Did anyone die?"

"One: Rollins."

"And you? What did you do? Stayed away, I hope?"

"Yes."

"And rightly so! But I find it hard to believe."

"Believe it. I kept myself far enough away that he couldn't do anything to me, but close enough that I could stick my knife between his ribs four times."

"You're crazy! Went after him with a knife?"

"Yes. I didn't have my rifle with me."

"What a fellow! A real, true greenhorn. Brings his heavy bear-killer all this way, and as soon as a bear shows up, he shoots it with his knife instead of his gun. Would you believe it? What happened then?"

"Rattler claimed he had killed it, not me."

I described how the situation had played out, and how Rattler and I had come to blows.

"Boy, I can't believe how dumb you are!" he cried. "Never seen a grizzly before, and marched right up to it like it was a poodle! I have to see this animal, right now. Come on, Dick and Will. You have to see this greenhorn's latest craziness." He was about to leave, but just then Rattler came to, and Sam turned to him:

"Listen, Mr. Rattler, I have something to say to you. You got mixed up with my young friend again. If that happens one more time, I'll see to it that it's the last time. I'm running out of patience. Is that clear?"

He left with Stone and Parker. Rattler made a grim face and gave me a poisonous glance but said nothing. But you could see that that he was like a bomb that might explode at any moment.

The two Indians and Kleki-petra sat down on the ground. The engineer sat opposite them, but they had not yet started their discussion. They were waiting for Sam's return, to see what decision he would make. He came back almost immediately and while he was still some distance away, he called out:

"What idiocy it was to shoot the grizzly and then run away. If you're not going to stand up to a grizzly, don't shoot at him.

Just leave him alone and he won't harm you. That Rollins looks horrible! And who killed the bear?"

"I did," said Rattler quickly.

"You? How?"

"With a bullet from my rifle."

"Well, that's true enough."

"I thought so!"

"Yes, a rifle bullet killed the bear."

"Well, that was my bullet. You hear that, people? Sam Hawkens is backing me up," he cried triumphantly.

"Yes, indeed. Your bullet went by his head and took the tip off his ear. And of course, a grizzly dies on the spot when he loses the tip of his ear, hee-hee-hee! And if it's really true that several of you shot, you must have been so scared that you clean missed him. There's no trace of any other rifle bullets except the one that clipped his ear. But there are pistol wounds to the eyes, and four skillful knife wounds, two near the heart and two directly into it. Who stabbed him?"

"I did," I answered.

"Just you?"

"Nobody else."

"Well then, the bear belongs to you. Actually, since we're working together, the pelt is yours and the meat is for everyone, but you get to say how it is divided up. That's the way it is in the West. What do you say to that, Mr. Rattler?"

"The devil take you!"

He spewed out a few more virulent oaths and then went to the wagon where the brandy keg was. I watched him fill the pitcher with brandy, and I knew he would drink until he could drink no more.

Chapter 8

The matter was now settled, so Bancroft turned to the Apache chief and asked him to make his request.

"I do not make a request. I make a command," answered Inchu-chuna.

"We don't take commands here," the engineer answered.

An expression of anger flitted across the chief's face, but he controlled himself and said calmly:

"Let my white brother answer a few questions, and let him speak the truth. Does he have a house where he lives?"

"Yes."

"And a yard around it?"

"Yes."

"And if a neighbor wants to make a path through this yard, would my brother tolerate it?"

"No."

"The land on the other side of the Rocky Mountains and east of the Mississippi belong to the palefaces. What would they say if the Indians came and wanted to build an iron road there?"

"They would be chased away."

"My brother speaks the truth. But now the palefaces are coming into this land, which belongs to us. They catch the mustangs, they kill the buffalo, they search for gold and precious stones. Now they want to build a long, long road for the fire horse. It will bring more and more palefaces here, and they will attack us and take away what little we have left. And what will we have to say about that?"

Bancroft was silent.

"Do we have less rights than you? You say you are Christians and always talk about love. But then you say you can steal from us, while we must be honest with you. Is that love? You say your God is the good father of all red men and all white men. Is he our stepfather, but your true father? Didn't this whole land belong to the red man? It was taken from us. And what did we get? Suffering, suffering, and more suffering! You chase us further and further and crowd us closer and closer together, so we will soon be suffocating. Why do you do this? Because you don't have enough land for yourselves? No, it is greed, for there is still room for many millions in your lands. Each of you wants to own a whole country. But the red man, the real owner, does not have a place to rest his body. Kleki-petra, who sits here next to me, has told me of your holy book. There, you can read that the first man had two sons, and one of them struck the other dead, so that his blood cried to heaven. How is it now between the red and the white brothers? Are you not the Cain, and we are the Abel whose blood cries to heaven? And now you want us to be killed without resisting? No, we will resist! We have been chased from place to place, always farther away. Now we live here. We thought we would live in peace and breathe easily, but now you are here again, to build an iron road. Don't we have the same right that you have in your house, in your yard? If we applied our laws, we would kill you all. But all we ask is that your laws apply equally to us. But do they? No! Your laws have two faces, and you choose which one you turn toward us. You want to build this road. Have you asked us for permission?"

"No, I don't need to."

"Why not? Is this your land?"

"I think it is."

"No. It belongs to us. Did you buy it from us?"

"No."

"Did we give it to you?"

"No, not to me."

"And not to anyone else. If you were an honest man and were sent here to build a road for the fire horse, you would first ask the man that sent you if he had the right to do that. And if he said yes, you would ask for proof. But you didn't do that. I forbid you to do any more measuring here!"

This last was spoken with an emphasis that echoed with bitterness. I was astonished at this Indian. I had read many books about the red man, and many speeches that Indians had made, but never one like this. Inchu-chuna spoke a clear, understandable English. His logic and his ways of expressing himself seemed those of an educated man. Was this due to the work of Kleki-petra, the "school master"?

The engineer was in an embarrassing situation. If he were to be honest, he could hardy dispute any of the accusations that had been made. To be sure, he brought up a few points in his defense, but they were hair-splitting, diversions, and fallacies. When the chief responded to them and cornered him, he turned to me:

"But Sir, you've heard what we're talking about! Can you help explain our situation?"

"Thanks, Mr. Bancroft, but I was hired as a surveyor, not a lawyer. You can make of the situation what you wish. My job is surveying, not talking."

Then the chief spoke decisively:

"It is not necessary to talk any more. I have said that I will not tolerate you. I want you to leave here today, and go back where you came from. You can decide whether to obey or not. Now I go with Winnetou, my son, and I will return after the time that palefaces call an hour. Then you will give me your answer. If you leave then, we are brothers. If you do not leave, we dig up the war hatchet between us and you. I am Inchu-chuna, Chief of the Apaches. I have spoken. How!"

"How" is an Indian word of affirmation and means roughly "Amen" or "So be it." He stood up, and Winnetou did too. They left, walking slowly up the valley until they disappeared around a bend. Kleki-petra remained sitting. The engineer turned to him and asked him for advice. He answered:

"Do what you like, Sir! I agree completely with the chief. A great, on-going crime is being perpetrated on the red man. But as a white, I also know that it is useless for the Indians to resist. If you leave here today, others will come tomorrow and finish your work. But I do want to warn you: the chief is serious."

"Where did he go?"

"He's gone to get our horses."

"You brought horses?"

"Of course. We hid them when we saw that we were getting close to the bear. You don't go after a grizzly in his lair on horseback."

He stood up and walked away, probably to avoid more questions and arguments. All the same, I followed him and asked:

"Sir, may I walk with you? I promise I won't do or say anything that would make you uncomfortable. It's just that I'm fascinated by Inchu-chuna and just as much by Winnetou."

I didn't want to tell him that he himself evoked great interest.

"Sure, come along for a bit, Sir," he answered. "I've drawn away from the whites and their desires, and I don't anything more to do with them. But I like you. So let's walk together a bit. You look like the most sensible of all these men. Am I right?"

"I'm the youngest, and not particularly smart yet—and perhaps I never will be. That probably just gives me the look of a fairly good-hearted person."

"Not smart? Every American is smart, more or less."

"I'm not an American."

"Where are you from, if you don't mind the question?"

"Not at all. I have no reason to hide my homeland, which I love dearly. I'm a German."

"A German?" he turned sharply toward me. "Then welcome, fellow countryman! That's probably what drew me to you. We Germans are peculiar people. Our hearts recognize each other even before we say anything. Are you surprised to find a German who has become completely Apache?"

"Not particularly. God's ways often seem miraculous, but are still very natural."

"God's ways! Why do you speak of God and not of fate, of Providence?"

"Because I'm a Christian and I don't let my God be taken away from me."

"Rightly so. Then you're a happy man! God's ways often seem miraculous, but they are still very natural. The greatest wonders are the results of natural laws, and ordinary daily occurrences in nature are great wonders. A German, an educated man, a well-known intellectual, and now a real Apache: that sounds miraculous, but the path that led me to this point was a very natural one."

He may have taken me along half-heartedly, but now he was glad to be able to talk. I immediately saw that he was a remarkable character, but I avoided asking anything whatsoever about his past. He did not place this restriction on himself, however. He examined me quite thoroughly about my circumstances. I told him everything, in as much detail as he seemed to want.

We sat down under a tree not far from camp. I could watch his face and observe his facial expressions closely. Life had left deep marks in his face, the long furrows sorrow, the diagonal lines of doubt, the zigzags of desperation, care, and sacrifice. How often his eyes must have looked somber, threatening, angry, fearful, and perhaps doubting as well. But now they were as clear and calm as a lake in the woods, unrippled by any wind, but too deep to see what lies on the bottom. Once he had heard everything worth knowing that I had to say, he nodded slightly and said:

"You are at the beginning of your battles, while I am at the end. But yours will be external, not internal. You have the Lord God with you, and He will not forsake you. I had lost God when I left my home, and instead of the riches that a strong faith brings, I took along the worst thing a man can have: a bad conscience."

He gave me a searching look, and when he saw that I was taking his words calmly, he asked:

"Doesn't that shock you?"

"No."

"But a bad conscience—think about it!"

"Nonsense! You weren't a thief or a murderer. You could never be capable of low-mindedness."

He pressed my hand and spoke:

"Thank you for saying so! And yet you are wrong. I was indeed a thief—I stole a great deal! And such valuable goods! And I was a murderer. How many souls I killed! I was a teacher in a college—the exact location is not important. I took pride in being a free spirit, in having pushed God aside, in being able to demonstrate incontrovertibly that belief in God was nonsense. I was a good speaker and entranced my listeners. These weeds, which I spread with both hands, grew quickly. Not a seed was lost. That made me a thief of the people, a robber of the people, who stole their faith in God. And then came the revolution. Those who know no God do not honor any king or any other authority. I appeared in public as the leader of the dissatisfied, and they almost drank the words from my lips, that intoxicating poison that I took for healing medicine. They flocked together and took to their weapons. How many, many battles! I was their murderer, and these were not the only ones that dies because of me. Others died behind prison walls. Naturally, they started hunting me down, and I fled. I left my country, and no one grieved about it. No living soul cried for me—my mother and father were both dead, and I had no brothers, sisters, or other relatives. No eye shed a tear for me, but many tears were shed because of me!

But I didn't think about that at all until one day the realization hit me like a mighty blow that practically knocked me to the ground. Just a day away from the border (and safety) I was being chased by the police, who were hot on my trail. I was passing through a small factory town. By accident, if there is such a thing, I ran through the yard of a run-down house and entrusted myself, without saying who I was, to an old mother and her daughter who I found inside. They hid me because they took me to be a comrade of the family's father. Then they sat near me in a dark corner and told me, with bitter tears, about their sufferings. They had been poor but contented. The daughter had married just a year earlier. Her husband had heard one of my speeches and was seduced by it. He took his father-in-law along to the next meeting, and the poison worked on him as well. I had snuffed out all the good fortune of these four good people. The young man died on the battlefield, and the old father was sentenced to several years of hard labor. This was told me by the women who had rescued me, the person responsible for their misfortune. They named my name as the one who had lured the men away. That was the blow that struck me deep inside. God's mill began grinding. I still had my freedom, but inside I was suffering a kind of pain that no judge could have sentenced me to. I wandered from one city to the next, tried this and that, but found no rest. My conscience plagued me unmercifully. Many times, I was close to taking my own life, but God's invisible hand always held me back. It led me, through years of suffering and regret, to a German preacher in Kansas who guessed the state of my soul and urged me to share it with him. I did so happily. After long years of doubt, forgiveness and consolation. I finally found a firm belief and inner peace. Lord God, how I thank you for that!"

He stopped talking, folded his hands, and gazed upward with shining eyes. Then he continued:

"To strengthen my soul, I fled from the world and from people. I went into the wilderness. But faith alone is not enough to make you holy. The tree of faith must bear the fruit of works. I wanted my works to be as different as possible from what they had previously been. And then I saw how the red man struggled, full of doubt, against extinction; I saw the murderers rummaging around in dead Indians' carcasses, and my heart overflowed with anger, sympathy, and pity. The red man's fate was sealed. I couldn't save him. But there was one thing I could do: make his death easier, give the brightness of love to his last hours, let the reconciliation come. I went to the Apache and learned to adapt my works to their needs. I was able to gain their confidence and achieve some success. I wish you could get to know Winnetou; he is actually my greatest accomplishment. This young man is destined for great things. If he were the son of a European ruler, he would be a great general and an even greater leader in peacetime. But as the son of an Indian chief he will die, as all his race will die. If only I could live to see the day he declares himself a Christian! If not, at least I will stay by him until I die, in every challenge, danger, and hardship. He is the child of my soul. I love him more than I love myself, and if I ever had the good fortune to step between him and a bullet that was meant to kill him, I would gladly die for him. My death would be a last atonement for my earlier sins!"

He stopped talking and lowered his head. I was deeply moved and said nothing. I had the feeling that anything I might say would sound trivial. But I took his hand in mine and pressed it hard. He understood. He nodded slightly and pressed my hand in return. After a while he asked quietly:

"Why in the world have I told you all this? This is the first time I've ever laid eyes on you, and I may never see you again. Or is it God's providence that I have encountered you here and now? You see that I, who once denied God, now seek to trace everything back to His higher power. Suddenly I feel so strange, so weak, such a hurt feeling in my heart — though the 'hurt' isn't really painful. It's like the feeling you sometimes get in the fall, when the leaves start to fall. How will the leaf of my life be released from the tree? Softly, lightly, peacefully? Or will it be plucked before its natural time has come?"

He stared off into the valley as if in quiet longing. I saw that Inchu-chuna and Winnetou were coming from there, riding their horses and leading Kleki-petra's. We stood up to go back to the camp, and arrived at the same time as they did. Rattler was leaning on the wagon, his face red and bloated, staring at us. He had already drunk so much he couldn't drink any more — a terrible, brutish man! His gaze was malicious like that of a wild steer, pawing the ground, ready to attack. I planned to keep an eye on him.

The chief and Winnetou dismounted and came over to us. We stood together in a rough, wide circle.

"Well, have my white brothers decided whether they will stay or go?" asked Inchu-chuna.

The engineer had thought of a compromise. He answered:

"We'd like to go, but we must stay here in order to obey the orders we have been given. I will send a messenger to Santa Fe and inquire, then I can give you an answer."

This was a clever strategy, since we would be done with our work before the messenger could return. But the chief said, in a decisive voice:

"I won't wait that long. My white brothers must tell me now what they will do."

Rattler had filled a pitcher with brandy and had come over to us. I thought he had his eye me, but he went over to the two Indians and said thickly:

"If you Indians will drink with me, we'll do as you like and leave now. Otherwise, we won't. Let the young one start. Here's the fire-water, Winnetou."

He held out the pitcher. Winnetou stepped back with a gesture of refusal.

"What, you don't want to drink with me? That's a damn insult. Here's brandy in your face, you cursed redskin. Lick it off if you won't drink it!"

Before any of us could prevent it, he flung the pitcher and its contents into the young Apache's face. According to Indian concepts that would be an insult punishable by death. It was punished immediately, if not so strictly: Winnetou slugged the brute in the face hard enough to knock him to the ground. He pulled himself up again with some difficulty. I made up my mind to intervene because I believed he would in fact attack. But it didn't happen. He just stared menacingly at the young Apache and staggered, cursing, back to the wagon.

Winnetou dried himself off and maintained his rigid, unchanging expression, just as his father did. He showed no sign of what was happening inside.

"I ask once more, and this is the last time," said the chief. Will the palefaces leave this valley today?"

"We're not allowed to," was the answer.

"Then that is how we will leave it. There is no peace between us."

I made one more attempt at intervention, but without success. The three went over to their horses. Then Rattler's voice rang out from the wagon:

"Get out of here, you red dogs! But first the young one will pay for having hit me!"

Ten times faster than you could believe for a man in his condition, Rattler had grabbed his rifle from the wagon and aimed it at Winnetou. Winnetou was in the open and without protection. The bullet had to hit him—everything happened so quickly that no evasive movement was possible. Kleki-petra cried out, "Look out, Winnetou, get away quick!"

At the same time, he sprang over to place himself in front of the young Apache. The shot rang out. Kleki-petra, half spun around by the force of the bullet, grabbed at his chest, staggered for a moment, and then fell to the ground. At the same moment, Rattler fell to the ground, felled by the force of my fist. I had tried to grab him, to prevent the shot, but I was too late. Everyone was shouting in horror. Only the two Apaches were silent. They kneeled by their friend, who had offered himself for his protégé, and silently inspected his wound. He had been hit in the chest quite close to the heart, and blood was spurting from the wound. I ran over. Kleki-petra's eyes were closed. His face was rapidly becoming pale and hollow.

"Take his head in your lap," I requested of Winnetou. "If he opens his eyes and sees you, his death will be a happy one."

He followed this suggestion without saying a word. He never blinked, and his eyes never once left the face of the dying man. Kleki-petra slowly opened his eyes. He saw Winnetou bent over him. A blissful smile flickered across his haggard features, and he whispered:

"Winnetou, schi ya Winnetou—Winnetou, oh my son Winnetou!"

Then it looked as if his brimming eyes were looking for someone else. He spotted me, and said, in German:

"Stay with him and carry on my work!"

"I will do it, yes, rest assured I will do it!"

Then his face took on an almost otherworldly expression, and he prayed in a steadily weakening voice:

"So my leaf is plucked, not quietly or lightly. It is the final atonement. I die as I wished to die. Lord God, forgive me, forgive me! Mercy, mercy! I'm coming. . .coming. . . mercy."

He folded his hands. One more convulsive spurt of blood from the wound, his head sank back, and he was dead.

Now I knew what had driven him to unburden his heart to me. God's providence, he had said. He had wished to die for Winnetou, and how quickly that wish was fulfilled! And the last atonement he had longed for had been achieved. God is love, compassion, He doesn't spurn the penitent forever.

Winnetou laid the dead man's head on the grass, slowly stood up, and looked questioningly at his father.

"There's the murderer. I knocked him out," I said. "He's yours."

"Fire-water!"

This short answer was all the chief had to say, but he said it in a grimly contemptuous voice.

"I want to be your friend, your brother. I will go with you!" were the words that escaped from my lips.

He spit in my face and said:

"Mangy dog! Stealing land for money! Stinking coyote! If you try to follow us, I will crush you!"

If anyone else had done and said this to me, I would have answered with my fists. Why didn't I respond? Perhaps, as an intruder in someone else's land, I had earned it. It was really just instinct that I let it go. But, in spite of the promise I had made to the dead man, I could not attempt to go with them.

The whites were standing around wordlessly, waiting to see what the two Apaches would do. The two didn't waste a glance on us. They lifted the corpse onto the horse and tied it in place, then they mounted their own horses, lifted Kleki-petra's collapsing body back upright, and rode off slowly. They spoke not a word of threat or revenge and didn't give a single glance back in our direction. And that was worse, far worse, than if they had openly vowed to deal us the most fearsome death.

"That was awful, and it may soon get worse!" said Sam Hawkens. "There lies the rogue, still unconscious from your blow and from brandy. What'll we do with him?"

I didn't answer. I saddled my horse and rode off. I had to be alone, to escape this horrible half hour, at least externally. It was late in the evening when I finally returned to the camp, tired and weak, shattered in body and soul.

Chapter 9

While I was gone, the camp was moved close to the spot where I had killed the bear. This was done to avoid having to carry the bear. It was so heavy that it took the efforts of ten men just to move it from under the trees, through the bushes, and into the open where a fire could be made.

In spite of the late hour of my return, everyone but Rattler was still awake. Rattler was sleeping off his brandy. He had been carried from the previous campsite and dumped onto the ground like a log. Sam had skinned the bear but had left the meat untouched. Once I had dismounted, taken care of my horse, and walked over to the fire, the little man said:

"Where have you been off to, Sir? It's been painful waiting for you. We couldn't cut open this teddy bear or try the meat without you. But I did take his shirt off in the meantime. The tailor sewed it so well, it didn't have a single wrinkle in it, hee-hee-hee! I hope you don't mind. And now, tell us how the meat should be divided! We'd like to roast a bit of it before we sleep."

"Divide it as you like," I replied. "The meat belongs to every-one."

"Well, let me tell you something. The best part is the paws. Nothing beats roast bear paws. But they have to lie uncooked for a long time before they get the proper ripe taste. They're most delicious when the worms have already gotten a good start on them. But we can't wait that long. I'm worried that the Apaches will arrive soon and spoil our meal. So we'd better do it now and have the paws right away, so that we will at least enjoy them before the Apaches wipe us out. Any objection, Sir?"

"No."

"Well, then, let the work begin. We've got the appetite, if I'm not mistaken."

He cut the paws from the bone and divided them in pieces, one for each man. I got the best piece from a front paw, wrapped it up, and set it aside while the others hurried to get their pieces to the fire. I felt hungry, but still had no appetite, as contradictory as that may sound. Because of the long, strenuous ride, I felt the need for nourishment, but I found it impossible to eat. I couldn't shake my thoughts of the scene of Kleki-petra's death. In my mind, I saw myself sitting with Kleki-petra, heard his confession (which now seemed to me like a death-bed confession), and heard again his concluding words, which foreshadowed his impending death. No, the leaf of his life did not fall easily and quietly from the tree. It was ripped off forcefully, and by such a pathetic man, for such a pathetic reason, and in such a pathetic way! There on the ground lay the murderer, still in a drunken stupor. I might have simply shot him as he lay, but I found him repulsive. This feeling of disgust was no doubt the reason that the two Apaches hadn't punished him on the spot. "Fire-water!" Inchu-chuna had said in the most contemptuous possible tone. What accusations, what reproaches lay in that one word!

If there was anything reassuring about the whole gruesome event, it was that Kleki-petra had died in Winnetou's arms, that it was his heart that had stopped the bullet intended for Winnetou, and that this had been his greatest wish. But what of his plea for me to stick with Winnetou and finish the work he had begun? Why had he directed it at me? Only a few minutes earlier he had suggested that we probably would never see each other again, meaning that my life's course would probably not lead me to the Apaches again, and then suddenly he had assigned me a task that could only be done if I were intimately involved with the tribe. Was his request a random, empty, throw-away phrase? Or is a dying man granted, in his last moments as he parts from his body, a glimpse into the future? It almost seemed so, for later it would indeed prove possible to fulfill his dying wish, even though an encounter with Winnetou seemed likely to bring only disaster at the time.

And why had I so readily given the dying man my promise? Out of pity? Yes, probably. But there was another reason, even though I was not aware of it: Winnetou had made a deep impression on me, unlike the impression anyone had ever made before. He was as young as I was, but so far superior! I sensed that from the first moment I saw him. The serious, proud clarity of his eyes, the calm certainty of his bearing and all his movements, and the melancholy breath of a deep and hidden sorrow that I thought I saw in his young, handsome features, gripped me immediately. How imposing his behavior was, and his father's too! Other men — white or red — would have instantly turned on the murderer and killed him; these two hadn't deemed him worthy of a glance, and not a muscle in their faces had revealed what was going on inside them. What kind of men were we in comparison? There I sat quietly by the fire, mulling things over, while the others enjoyed their meat, until finally Sam Hawkens woke me from my thoughts:

"What's the matter with you, Sir? Aren't you hungry?"

"I can't eat."

"So? You'd rather exercise your brain in thinking? I'm telling you, don't let it get to you. I'm angry at what happened today too, really angry, but the frontiersman has to get used to this kind of scene. That's why they call the West the 'dark and bloody grounds.' Take it from me, every step you take out here, you're walking on ground that is drenched in blood. Anyone whose nose is too sensitive to stand the smell had better stay home and drink lemonade. Don't take it too hard. And give me that paw meat — I'll roast it for you."

"Thanks, Sam, but I really can't eat. Have you all decided what to do with Rattler?"

"Well, we've talked about it."

"So what will his punishment be?"

"Punishment? You mean we should punish him?"

"Of course that's what I mean."

"Ah ha! And just how might we do that? Should we ship him to San Francisco, New York, or Washington to stand trial for murder?"

"Ridiculous! We have the authority to judge his case. He has violated the laws of the West."

"Just look at how this greenhorn knows all about the laws of the Wild West! Did you come over from Germany to play the Lord Judge? Was this Kleki-petra a relative or a friend of yours?"

"Well, no."

"There you have the key point. Yes, the Wild West has its definite and peculiar laws. It's an eye for an eye, a tooth for a tooth, blood for blood, just like the Bible says. If a person is killed, those with a stake in the matter can kill the murderer on the spot, or a jury can be assembled to come up with a verdict and then immediately carry it out. That's how the bad elements are weeded out that would otherwise overwhelm the honest hunters."

"OK, so let's assemble a jury."

"You'd need a plaintiff for that."

"I'm the plaintiff."

"What right do you have to bring charges?"

"My right as a person who can't accept that such a crime goes unpunished."

"Pshaw! You're talking like a greenhorn. There are only two situations where you'd have rights as a plaintiff. First, if the dead man was a relative or a close friend and comrade; but you agreed that's not the case here. Second, you'd have a case if you yourself had been murdered, hee-hee-hee! You haven't been, have you?"

"Sam, this isn't a laughing matter!"

"I know, I know. Anyway, you have no grounds for a case against Rattler, and the same goes for the rest of us. Without a case, we can't assemble a jury."

"So Rattler goes unpunished?"

"On the contrary. Don't get so excited! I give you my word, he'll get his comeuppance as surely as a bullet from my Liddy hits its target. The Apaches will take care of that."

"And we'll get the same punishment!"

"Quite possible. But do you think we'd avoid that by killing Rattler? The Apaches see all of us as murderers, not just him, and that's the way they'll treat us if they get their hands on us."

"Even if we get rid of him?"

"Even then. They'll kill us all, without stopping to ask if he's with us. But just how would we get rid of him?"

"By kicking him out."

"Yes, we did talk about doing that. But we decided we didn't have the right to kick him out, and it wouldn't be smart anyway."

"But Sam! That makes no sense! If I can't get along with someone, I part ways with him. And we're talking about a murderer here! Are we forced to tolerate this villain, who is a drunkard besides? He'll just get us into more trouble."

"Unfortunately, we have to tolerate him. Rattler is under contract to stay and protect you, just like Stone, Parker, and me, and only his employer can fire him. We have to stick to the letter of the law on this one."

"The letter of the law! This is a man who tramples on all the laws of men and God every day!'

"And what if he does? That's all fine, what you're saying, but we can't do the wrong thing just because someone else has done wrong. I'm telling you, whoever is in authority has to be especially careful to follow the rules, and since we frontiersmen have to act as the authority in this case, we have every reason to keep our reputation from being sullied. But putting that aside, what do you think Rattler would do if we kicked him out?"

"That's his problem."

"And ours too! We'd be constantly in danger, since he would almost certainly try to take revenge on us. It's better to keep him here, where we can keep an eye on him, than to chase him out and have him sneaking around looking for a chance to put a bullet through one of our heads. I hope you see my point."

He gave a meaningful glance in the direction of Rattler's friends. If we went against them, they might well team up with Rattler in some nefarious plan. I had to agree with his logic—they were not to be trusted. So I answered:

"Yes, now that you've put it that way, I see that we'll have to let things take their course. I'm just worried about the Apaches—

there's no doubt they will be coming to take their revenge."

"They're coming, and it's all the more certain since they didn't utter a single threat. Not only did they show pride, they were very clever too. If they had taken revenge at the time, it would only have affected Rattler. And that's if we had even supported their accusations, which was anything but certain. But they have designs on all of us, since he is one of us and our surveying makes us all enemies in their minds, enemies that want to steal their land and property. That's why they exercised such extraordinary control and rode away without lifting a finder against us. But it makes it all the more certain that they'll be back to capture us all. If they get us, we can figure on a terrible death. The respect they gave this Kleki-petra requires revenge that is twice or three times as severe."

"And all this because of one drunkard! But they'll surely want to bring plenty of men."

"Naturally! So everything depends on when they come. We have enough time to escape, but we'd have to drop everything and not finish up the surveying."

"Let's not do that, if there's even half a chance."

"When do you think you could be finished, if you did it as quick as you could?"

"In five days."

"Hmm! As far as I know, there are no Apache villages here in the area. I figure the nearest Mescalero settlement is three days' hard riding from here. If I'm not mistaken, Inchu-chuna and Winnetou will take four days before they can get reinforcements, since they have a body to carry. Then it'll take three days to get back here— that makes seven days. Since you think you can finish in five days, I'd say we can risk finishing up the surveying."

"And if your reckoning is wrong? The two Apaches might leave the body in a safe place and then come back to shoot us down. Or it's just as likely that they might encounter a group of their own people. They may even have friends already in the area—I'd be surprised if two Indians, particularly chiefs, traveled this far from their village without anyone accompanying them. It's time for the buffalo hunt, so it is even possible that Inchu-chuna and Winnetou are part of a nearby hunting party that they left to make a side trip. We have to take these possibilities into account if we really want to make a careful decision."

Sam Hawkens closed one of his two small eyes, made an incredulous face, and cried:

"Oh boy, aren't you the smart and clever one. I guess the little chicks are smarter than the old hens these days, if I'm not mistaken. But, to be honest, what you just said wasn't all that dumb. I'll grant you the points you made. Any of those things could happen, and we'll have to keep a sharp eye out. That's why it's important to find out where those two Apaches were headed. At dawn tomorrow, I'm going to follow their trail."

"And I'm coming too," said Will Parker.

"Me too," Dick Stone chimed in.

Sam Hawkens pondered a little while and then answered them:

"You two sit tight right where you are. You'll be needed here. Understand?"

As he said this, he glanced over at Rattler's friends, and he was right. If these unreliable men were left alone with us, there could be a bad scene once their leader came to. It was better for Stone and Parker to stay.

"But you can't ride alone!" said Parker.

"Sure I could, if I wanted to—but I don't want to," Sam replied. "I'll take a companion."

"Who?"

"This greenhorn here."

He pointed at me.

"No, he can't go," responded the engineer.

"Why not, Mr. Bancroft?"

"Because I need him."

"What for?"

"To work, of course. If we want to be done in five days, we'll need everyone working flat out. I can't spare anyone."

"Yes, everyone working flat out. That's a joke. Up to now, it's been one man doing the work of all. And now all of a sudden they'll all start working?"

"Mr. Hawkens, are you giving the orders around here? I won't stand for that."

"I wouldn't think of it. An observation is far from being an order."

"It sounded like one."

"Could be, I wouldn't deny it. As far as your surveying is concerned, it won't make much of a difference whether you have four or five people doing it tomorrow. I have a particular reason to take this greenhorn along with me."

"Do you might if I ask the reason?"

"Why not? He needs to learn how to trail Indians. It'll probably be useful for him to learn how to read tracks."

"That's not important to me."

"I know. But there's a second reason. This mission is going to be a dangerous one. It's an advantage to me and to you if I have a companion that's as strong and as good a shot as this greenhorn."

"I really don't see what advantage that is to me."

"No? I'm surprised. You are generally an extraordinarily clever and insightful gentleman," Sam answered with a touch of irony. "What happens if I run into Indians who are headed here, and they kill me? Nobody would be able to warn you of the danger, and you'd be overwhelmed and slaughtered. But if I have with me this greenhorn, who knocks down the sturdiest fellow with one blow of his cute little hand, then it's pretty likely that we'll come back in one piece. Do you follow me?"

"Hmm. Yes."

"And here's the main thing: he needs to leave with me tomorrow so that no friction occurs. That could end badly. You know that Rattler has it in for him. If he starts in on the brandy tomorrow, it's very probable that he'll head straight for the person who laid him out today. We need to keep the two of them apart at least for one day after the killing. So I'll leave the one I can't use with you, and take the other one with me. Are you still opposed?"

"No. Take him with you."

"Well, then, we're agreed." And, turning to me, he added, "You just heard what a strenuous day you have ahead of you tomorrow. It could be we won't have a moment to eat or rest. So I ask you: don't you want to try a bit of your bear paw?"

"OK, under these circumstances, I'll at least attempt it."

"Yes, give it a try! I know about these attempts, hee-hee-hee! You just take a bite, and then you can't stop until it's gone. Give me that paw and I'll roast it for you. A greenhorn just can't do it right. Now watch, so the next time you'll know how it's done. If I had to do this more than once for you, you wouldn't get a bit—I'd eat it all myself."

Good old Sam was right. I had hardly taken one bite of his culinary masterpiece before my appetite suddenly reappeared. I forgot all about the thoughts that had occupied me and ate. I really didn't stop until there was no meat left.

"Look at you!" he said, laughing. "It's a lot more fun to eat a grizzly bear than to kill one—you've learned that by now. Now we'll cut a couple of substantial chunks from the steak that we can roast yet tonight. We'll take them along as provisions. On this kind of a reconnoitering trip you always have to be prepared. You may not have time to hunt, and you may not be able to build a cooking fire. So why don't you hit the hay and get a good night's sleep. We'll be leaving at the crack of dawn, and you'll need all your strength tomorrow."

Chapter 10

We needed to rest, but I wanted to talk a bit more. I said, "OK, I'll get some sleep. But first tell me what horse you'll be riding."

"Horse? I won't be riding one."

"How so?"

"What a question! You think I'll be riding a crocodile or some other kind of beast? Of course I'll be riding my mule, my new Mary."

"I wouldn't do that."

"Why not?"

"You don't know her well enough yet."

"But she knows me perfectly well. She holds me in high respect, hee-hee-hee!"

"But on a spying mission like the one we're undertaking, you have to be very careful and plan everything in advance. A horse that you're not sure of could ruin everything."

"Is that so? Really?" he asked with amusement.

"Yes," I answered eagerly. "I know that the snort of a horse can cost its rider his life."

"Oh, you know that, do you? Wise fellow that you are! Did you read that somewhere, sir?"

"Yes."

"Thought so! It must be pretty darn interesting, reading books like that. If I weren't a frontiersman myself, I'd move back East, set myself up comfortably on a sofa and read these pretty Indian stories. I figure you can get big and fat that way, even if the only bear paws you get are on paper. I'd be interested in knowing how many of the good gentlemen that write such things ever make it west of the Mississippi."

"Most of them do, I imagine."

"Do you think so?"

"Yes."

"Don't believe it. I have good grounds to doubt it."

"And what are these grounds?"

"I'll tell you, sir. I once knew how to write myself, but it's been so long I'd hardly be able to write my own name on a piece of paper or a slate. A hand that's bridled a horse, handled a gun and a knife, and swung a lasso just isn't suited to scribbling on a piece of paper. Anybody who's really a frontiersman has long since forgotten how to write, and anybody who's not should stay away from writing about something he doesn't understand."

"Hmm! I don't imagine you have to stay in the West so long that your hand can't hold a pencil before you can write about it."

"Wrong, sir! Like I just said, only a veteran frontiersman can describe the West like it really is. But that's exactly the kind of man that'll never do such a thing."

"Why not?"

"Because it would never occur to him to leave the West, where we don't have inkwells. The prairie is like the sea: anyone that knows and loves it never leaves it. No, all these writers don't know the West. If they did, they'd never leave it just to be able make black marks on a stack of paper. That's the way I see it, and I suspect I'm right."

"No. I know of someone who has learned to love the West and who wants to be a competent hunter. But he'll still go back to civilization from time to time, to write about the West."

"Oh yeah? And who would that be?" he asked, looking at me with curiosity.

"You figure it out."

"Me? Figure it out? Are you trying to tell me you're talking about yourself?"

"Yes."

"Ridiculous! So you want to join up with those useless people that write books?"

"Probably."

"Get that notion out of your head, Sir, just let go of it, I beg of you! You would die a miserable death, that's what I think."

"I doubt it."

"And I believe it. I'd even swear to it. Do you have any idea what kind of a life would await you if you did that?"

"Yes."

"Well?"

"I'd travel to distant lands, learn about people and places, and return home now and then to write down my perspectives and experiences."

"But what's the point, for God's sake? I can't see the point of it."

"To instruct my readers and to make a little money."

"If that don't beat all! To instruct your readers? And make money? Sir, you're drunk, if I'm not mistaken. Your readers won't learn a thing from you, because you don't know a darn thing yourself. How can a greenhorn like you, a complete and utter greenhorn, teach your readers anything? I assure you, you won't find any readers, not a single one! And for heaven's sake, why does it have to be you in particular that wants to teach, and furthermore, to teach readers that you won't have? Aren't there enough teachers in the world already? Does anybody need another one?"

"Listen, Sam, being a teacher is a valuable and noble calling!"

"Pshaw! A frontiersman is far more important—thousands of times more! I know, because I am one, whereas you've hardly dipped your toe in the water. In all seriousness, I forbid you to become a writer. And to earn money by it! What an idea, what a completely bizarre idea! What does one of those books cost, like the one you want to write?"

"One dollar, maybe two or three dollars, depending on the size, I think."

"Right. And what does a beaver pelt cost? Do you have any idea? If you became a trapper, you'd earn far more, far more, than if you were a writer, trying to teach your readers something—and even if you found some readers, which would be a shame for both you and them, they'd learn nothing but foolishness. You want to earn money? This is the place to do it. Why, it's practically lying there on the prairie, in the woods, between the cliffs, in the river bottoms. You'd live a tragic life as a writer. You'd end up drinking thick black ink instead of the wonderful spring water of the West, and you'd be chewing on the end of a goose quill instead of a bear paw or a buffalo steak. You'd have a crumbling plaster ceiling over you instead of the blue sky, and under you would be an old wooden bedstead that you'd get lumbago from, instead of the green grass. Here you've got a horse to sit on, not a tattered armchair. Here you can enjoy God's rain and thunder first hand, there you have to put up a red and green umbrella at the first drop. Here, you're a free, happy man with a gun in his hand, there you're stuck at a writing desk and wasting your strength on a quill or a pencil—enough! I need to stop before I really get upset. But if you're really set on this writing business, you're the sorriest man on God's green earth!"

He had worked himself up into quite a state. His eyes blazed and his cheeks were flushed (as much of his cheeks as you could see through his beard) to a bright crimson. The tip of his nose was likewise red. I sensed what was making him so wild, and since I really wanted to hear it from his own mouth, I added a bit more fuel to the fire by saying:

"But, my dear Sam, I assure you that you yourself would be very happy with my book, once it's done."

"Happy? Me? Please don't give me any of that foolishness. You know by now that I don't like that kind of joke."

"It's not a joke. I mean it."

"Really? Well strike me down, if I'm not mistaken! You mean it? What on earth about it would make me happy?"

"The part about you."

"About me?"

"Yes, about you. You would be in my book."

"Me? Me?" he asked, his eyes getting bigger and bigger.

"Yes, you. Of course I would write about you."

"About me? The things I do, the things I say?"

"Yes. I write about what I experience. I've spent a lot of time with you, so you will be in the book, just the way you sit before me now."

He grabbed his rifle, threw down the piece of meat that he had been holding over the fire during our conversation, jumped up, pointed his rifle at me threateningly, and cried:

"I'm asking you in total seriousness and in front of all these witnesses whether you really mean to do that."

"Naturally!"

"So! Then I order you to drop that plan this instant, and to swear to me that you will never undertake it!"

"Why?"

"Because otherwise I'll kill you on the spot with this old Liddy here. All right then, do you agree?"

"No."

"OK, here goes!" he cried, pulling out his Liddy.

"Go right ahead!" I answered calmly.

The barrel swept over my head for a few moments, then he lowered it, threw the gun on the grass, pounded his fist into his hand in despair and wailed:

"This guy is drunk, he's gone crazy, completely crazy! I suspected it when he first talked about writing those books and teaching those readers, and now it has really taken hold. Only a crazy person could sit there calmly with my Liddy pointed at his head. What am I going to do with this guy? I doubt if he can be cured."

"No cure is required, Sam," I answered. "My mind is completely clear."

"But why won't you take my advice? Why would you rather be struck dead than take an oath?"

"Pshaw! Sam Hawkens would never strike me dead, that's for sure."

"You think so? OK, so it's true. I have to admit it. I'd rather kill myself than harm a single hair on your head."

"And I'm not going to swear to anything. When I say I'll do something, my word is as good as an oath. And anyway, I'm not about to let a threat force me to promise something, even if your Liddy is backing it up. The business with the books is not as dumb as you think. There are good reasons for it, and I'll explain it to you when we have more time."

"Thanks anyway," he said, sitting back down and picking up his chunk of meat again. "I don't need explanations for things that can't be explained. Instructing your readers! Earning money from making books! The whole thing is crazy."

"And think of the honor, Sam!"

"What honor?" he asked, turning quickly back to me. He waved the meat high in the air. "Sir, now stop right this instant, or I'll throw this twelve-pound piece of steak right at your head! It belongs there anyway: you're at least as dumb as the dumbest grizzly. Fame from writing books! That's about the most pathetic idea I've ever heard. What do you even know about fame? I'll tell you how to become famous. See that bear skin lying there? Cut off the ears and put them on your hat. Take the claws and the teeth and put them on a chain around your neck. That's what every smart frontiersman and Indian would do if they had the great good fortune to kill a grizzly. Then, no matter where you go, people say, 'Look at that man! He battled the grizzly and won!' Everyone would gladly clear a place for you, and your name would be passed from tent to tent and from town to town. Understand? But suppose you put a book on your hat, and some more books on a chain around your neck. What do you think they would say then? They'd think you were crazy, totally crazy. That's the only fame that writing books will bring you!"

"But Sam, why is this making you so upset? What difference does it make to you what I do?"

"So? It shouldn't make any difference to me? My Lord, this fellow is unbelievable, if I'm not mistaken! I've treated him like a son and really started to cotton to him, and I'm not supposed to care what he does? That's a good one. The fellow has the strength of a buffalo, the muscles of a mustang, the sinews of a deer, the eye of a falcon, the hearing of a mouse, and a good five or six pounds of brains in his head. He shoots like a veteran, rides like the spirit of the prairies, and takes on a grizzly like it was a guinea pig. And this person, this prairie hunter, this fellow who was born to be a frontiersman and can already do more than most hunters that have been running around the prairies for twenty years—he's supposed to go home and write books? That's ridiculous. Is it any wonder that an honest frontiersman who is trying to help him out gets angry?"

He looked at me, waiting for an answer, but I didn't give him one—I had caught him. I pulled my saddle over and lay down, using it as a pillow, stretched out, and closed my eyes.

"Well, what kind of behavior is that?" he asked, still waving his piece of meat. "I'm not worth answering?"

"Sure," was my only answer. "Good night, Sam, my friend. Sleep well!"

"You're going to sleep?"

"Yes. You told me to a few minutes ago."

"That was then. Right now, we are not quite finished talking."

"We are too!"

"No. There's still something I want to discuss."

"Not me. I now know what I wanted to know."

"What you wanted to know? What was that?"

"What you've been trying so hard to avoid saying up to now."

"Trying to avoid? I'd sure like to know what that is. Out with it!"

"Not much, really, except that I was born to be a frontiersman, that I can already do more than some hunters who have been at it for twenty years."

He lowered the chunk of meat, gave an embarrassed cough, and said:

"Tarnation! This kid, this greenhorn, I can't believe he . . ."

"Good night, Sam Hawkens, and sleep well!" I repeated and turned on my side.

He came after me: "Sure, go ahead and sleep, you varmint! We're all better off that way. When you have your eyes open, no honest man is safe. My word, the way you lead people around by the nose! Well, it's over between us. You've ruined it with me. Now I see through you. You're a devil, and a man's got to keep an eye on you!"

He was as angry as I had ever heard him. Given his words and his angry tone, I had to assume that our friendship really was over. But after a minute, he added in a softer, friendlier voice:

"Good night, Sir. Get some sleep. You'll need your strength tomorrow."

He really was a warm, good, honest man, that Sam Hawkens!

And so I did sleep soundly until Sam woke me. Parker and Stone were already up. The others were fast asleep, even Rattler. We ate some meat, washed it down with water, watered our horses as well, and, as soon as Sam had given the other two instructions for every conceivable eventuality, we rode off. The sun hadn't risen yet as we set off on a ride which I knew could easily become dangerous. My very first experience with tracking! I was very curious about how it would turn out.

Naturally, we started off in the direction in which the two Apaches had disappeared, down the valley and along the edge of the woods. The tracks were still easy to see in the grass. Even I, the greenhorn, saw them; they lead northwards, whereas we expected to find the Apaches to our south. Once we had passed the curve of the valley, the forest that lined the valley sides began to look a bit barren, perhaps from some kind of insect infestation. The tracks led up into the forest. The barren appearance continued a long way until we eventually came to a prairie which formed a smooth, green surface rising gently to the south. Here, too, it was very easy to follow the tracks. We could now see that the Apaches had detoured around our camp. Once we crossed the ridge, a wide, flat, grassy expanse stretched out before us southwards, with no apparent end. Even though 18 hours had passed since the Apaches had left, the tracks led in a straight line across the flat landscape. Sam, who had not said a word until that moment, shook his head and grumbled in his beard:

"I don't like the look of these tracks, not a bit."

"And I like them better and better," I said.

"That's because you're a greenhorn, even if you did dispute it yesterday, Sir. Where did you get the idea that I thought you could measure up to a real frontiersman? Impossible! Forget it! Anyone who listened to what you just said would be onto you. You like these tracks? I can believe it: they're so clear a blind man could follow them by touch. But my experience makes me suspicious of them."

"Not me."

"Shut up, honorable Sir! I didn't bring you along to be bombarded by your youthful opinions. When two Indians leave such obvious tracks, you have to consider the reason, and particularly when they just left under hostile circumstances. It's likely they are trying to lead us into an ambush. Of course they know that we'll be following them."

"What kind of ambush would it be?"

"Can't tell yet."

"And where would it take place?"

"Somewhere to the south, of course. They've made it very easy for us to follow them there. If they weren't planning something like that, they would have taken more trouble to hide their tracks."

"Hmm," I grunted.

"What?" he asked.

"Nothing."

"Nothing? It sounded like you had something to say."

"I'll keep it to myself."

"Why?"

"Why should I talk? You'll just think I'm 'bombarding' you with opinions, but I assure you I have neither the talent nor the inclination to do that."

"Don't talk nonsense. Friends don't take words like those so seriously. You want to learn; how are you going to learn if you won't talk? Now, what did you mean by that 'Hmm' a moment ago?"

"I don't share your opinion. I don't believe they're planning an ambush."

"No? Why not?"

"The two Apaches want to get back to their tribe. They want to quickly assemble a war party against us, and they're traveling with a dead body in this heat. Those are two good reasons to ride as fast as possible: the body could start to decompose, and we might leave before they came back to attack us. They didn't want to take the time to cover their tracks. In my opinion, that's the only reason the tracks are so obvious."

"Hmm." It was Sam's turn to grumble.

"And if I'm wrong," I continued, "we can still follow the tracks without too much worry. As long as we're on this flat plain, we have nothing to fear. We can spot any enemy at a distance and retreat if we need to."

"Hmm," Sam repeated, giving me a sidelong glance. "You mentioned the body. Do you think they will continue traveling with it in this heat?"

"Yes."

"They won't bury it along the way?"

"No. The dead man was highly respected. Their ways require them to bury him with the highest of Indian ceremony. The ideal would be to have his murderer die alongside the corpse as part of the ritual. So they will be quick to leave the body with their people and return to capture Rattler and the rest of us. From what I know of them, that's what we can expect."

"From what you know of them? So you were born around here?"

"Nonsense."

"Well, what makes you think you know anything about Apaches?"

"I've read books about them. The books you don't want to hear about."

"Fair enough," he nodded. "Let's keep riding."

He didn't say whether he agreed with my opinion, but when he glanced over at me from time to time, a slight twitch emerged from his tangle of beard. I knew that twitch. It was always a sign that his mind was preoccupied with something that was difficult to swallow.

Chapter 11

Now we were riding at a gallop across the plain. It was one of those short-grass savannahs that can be found up in the regions between the headwaters of the Red River and those of the Rio Pecos. There were three sets of tracks, as parallel as the trace of a three-tined fork. So the horses were still being ridden side by side, as they had been when the Apaches departed from our camp. It must have been very strenuous, trying to keep the corpse upright on a horse on such a long ride. But we hadn't found any sign that they had found an opportunity to unload it.

Sam Hawkens now decided the time had come to exercise his role as teacher. He explained to me the features of the tracks from which you could tell whether the horses were walking or galloping. This was easy to see and note.

After half an hour, we came to a place were the plain began to be forested. But not really: there was a bend in the savannah, which we followed, and the forest remained to our left. The trees were so far apart that it would be easy for a troop of riders to pass through in single file. But the Apaches were riding three abreast and would have had trouble riding through. It was clear that this had forced them to detour around the forest, and we gladly followed their path, since it kept us in the open. In later years, once I really knew what I was doing, it would never have occurred to me to slavishly follow the tracks in this way. I would have ridden straight through the woods and found the tracks again on the other side, saving myself extra riding and extra time.

Later, the prairie got narrower and became a strip of meadow dotted with occasional clumps of bushes. We came to a place where the Apaches had stopped. It was at a thicket from which tall, thin oaks and boxwood trees grew. We circled it cautiously, approaching only when we were convinced that the Indians were long gone. On one side of the thicket the grass had been completely trampled. When we examined it, we found that the Apaches had dismounted and had laid the body in the grass. Then they had gone into the thicket to cut oak branches. They had stripped these of their twigs—we found the twigs on the ground.

"What do you think they did with these branches?" asked Sam, looking at me like a schoolmaster looks at a pupil.

"A drag or a stretcher for the corpse," I answered confidently.

"Who says?"

"I do."

"Why?"

"I've been expecting something like this. Keeping the corpse upright for such a long time must not have been easy. So I expected they would stop at the first opportunity to ease their burden."

"Not a bad piece of thinking. Did you read that in a book, Sir?"

"Not literally, and not relating to this specific set of circumstances. Everything depends on who reads the book and how they read it. You really can learn a lot that can be used in other, similar cases."

"Hmm, remarkable. Perhaps these book writers really have been in the West, if they know about something like this. Anyway, we agree on what the Indians probably did. Now let's see if our guess is right."

"I'm betting they made a drag, not a stretcher."

"Why?"

"To carry a body, or anything else, with a stretcher requires two horses either side by side or one behind the other. The Apaches only have three horses, and one horse is enough for a drag."

"Right. But a drag makes a devil of a track, which could be disastrous for them. And we can figure that they were here just before evening yesterday, so we'll soon find out whether they camped for the night or kept going."

"I imagine they kept on going through the night. They have good reasons for hurrying."

"Right you are. Now let's see what the tracks show."

We stayed on foot, leading our horses and slowly following the tracks. Now they looked quite different from the earlier ones. There were still three tracks. In the middle was the broad track made by the hooves of the three horses, and on either side was a narrow furrow created by the branches of the drag. It had evidently been constructed from two long branches tied to several cross-branches, with the corpse tied on top of that.

"They're riding single-file now," Sam said. "There must be a reason, since there's plenty of room to ride side by side here. Let's follow!"

We mounted again and rode off at a trot. I began thinking of possible reasons why the Apaches had switched to riding single-file. I pondered and pondered and suddenly came up with what I thought was the answer. So I said:

"Sam, keep a sharp eye on these tracks. There will soon be a change that we're not supposed to notice."

"How so? A change?" he asked.

"Yes indeed. They didn't just make the drag to make riding easier. They did it so they could split up without being noticed."

"You're crazy! Split up? They wouldn't dream of that, heeheehee!" he laughed.

"They might not dream of it, but they'd do it while they're awake."

"So tell me, how did you hit on this idea? Your books have really misled you this time."

"It isn't from a book. I thought of it myself. But it does come from having read those books very carefully and thinking hard about their contents."

"And?"

"You've been the teacher so far. Now I'd like to pose a few questions to you."

"Must be something pretty smart. I'm very curious!"

"Why do Indians generally prefer to ride in single file? Surely not for comfort or sociability."

"No, they do it so that someone looking at their tracks can't tell how many riders there are."

"Right! I think the same reasoning applies to the tracks we're following."

"Fat chance."

"But why are these two riding single file when there's plenty of room for more than three horses?"

"Just chance. Or, more likely, because of the corpse. One of them is riding ahead as pathfinder, then comes the horse with the body, and finally the other one, who has to make sure that the drag doesn't come apart and the body doesn't fall off."

"Could be. But I have to consider that they're in a hurry to return and capture us. Transporting the dead body is slowing them down. One of them will want to ride ahead to alert the Apache warriors."

"Your straying off into fantasy. I'm telling you, it would never occur to them to split up."

I didn't bother to argue. I could easily have been wrong. In fact, it was highly likely: he was an experienced scout and I was just a greenhorn. So I remained silent, but I kept a sharp eye on the ground and the tracks.

Not long after that we came to a flat, shallow stream bed, wide but completely dry. This was a hollow that filled with melt-water from the mountains in the spring, but was dry the rest of the year. Between the low banks, the streambed consisted mostly of gravel which the water had rounded, but with a few areas of fine, light sand as well. The tracks went right across.

As we slowly crossed, I examined the gravel and sand closely on both sides. If my previous guess was right, this would be an excellent place for one of the Apaches to part company. If he rode into the dry streambed, taking care to ride only on the gravel (where tracks could not be seen) and not on the sand, he could turn up or downstream and disappear without leaving a trace. If the other continued on with the drag horse behind him, this track could easily be mistaken for the tracks of all three.

I stayed behind Sam Hawkens. I was almost across when I noticed, on the edge of a sandy area where it met the gravel, a round depression whose sides had collapsed. It was about the width of a coffee cup. Back then, I didn't have the sharp eye, the quick judgment, and the experience that I would later possess, but at least I sensed what I would later have instantly known: that this little depression was created by a horse's hoof slipping from the gravel into the slightly lower sand. Once we had reached the other bank, Sam wanted to continue following the trail. But I summoned him:

"Come over here to the left for a minute, Sam!"

"Why?" he asked.

"I want to show you something."

"What?"

"You'll soon see. Come on!"

I rode along the bank of the dry stream. It was covered with grass. We had not gone more than two hundred paces when the tracks of a single rider appeared, emerging from the sand and heading southwards across the grass.

"What's this, Sam?" I asked, quite proud of myself for having been right.

His tiny eyes seemed to want to crawl back into their sockets, and his little face drooped.

"Horse tracks," he answered, astonished.

"Where are they from?"

He glanced across the streambed, and, seeing no sign of tracks on the far side, he said:

"From the dry bed here, that's for sure."

"Certainly. And who might the rider be?"

"How should I know?"

"Well, I know: one of the Apaches."

His face drooped even more, a capability which I wouldn't have known he had, and he cried out:

"One of these two? That's not possible!"

"Oh yes it is! They split up, like I thought they would. Let's go back to the other track. If we look at it closely, I bet we'll see the hooves of only two horses."

"That would be astonishing! We'll see. Now I'm really curious."

We rode back and investigated the tracks carefully. We were able to determine that only two horses had continued from this point. Sam coughed a few times, looked at me suspiciously from head to toe, and asked:

"Where did you get the idea that the second track would come up out of the dry bed over there?"

"I noticed a hoof-mark down there in the sand and I figured it out from there."

"You're kidding! Show me the hoof-mark."

I led him to the mark. He looked at me even more suspiciously than before, then asked:

"Sir, will you tell me the truth?"

"Yes. Do you really think I have ever lied to you?"

"Hmm. You seem to be a truth-loving and honest person, but in this case I don't believe you. You've never been on the prairie?"

"No."

"Never anywhere in the Wild West?"

"No."

"Not anywhere in the United States?"

"Never."

"Are there other countries with prairies and savannahs like these where you've been?"

"No. I never left my own country until I came here."

"Well, the devil take you, you're a completely incomprehensible son of a gun!"

"Oh, Sam Hawkens, you claim to be my friend, but that's not the way a friend pays a compliment!"

"Well, don't hold it against me if a thing like this bugs me! A greenhorn like you shows up in the West—never saw the grass grow, never heard a cricket sing—and on his very first attempt at tracking he makes old Sam Hawkens blush with shame. Why, I'd have to be an Eskimo in winter to keep my face from turning red, if I'm not mistaken. When I was your age, I was ten times smarter than you, but now, in my old age, I seem to be ten times dumber. It's sad for an old frontiersman who has a certain degree of pride."

"Don't take it so hard, Sam."

"Oh, it's painful! I have to admit you were right about them splitting up. But where did that notion come from?"

"I just tried to think logically and draw the right conclusion. The conclusion is the key."

"What do you mean? You're talking over my head."

"Well, here's my conclusion: When Indians ride single file, they want to hide their tracks; the two Apaches rode single file; therefore, they wanted to hide their tracks. You understand that much, right?"

"Of course."

"That line of thinking led me to my discovery of the hoof print. A true frontiersman must be able to think logically above all. Let me illustrate with another logical sequence. Do you want to hear it?"

"Why not."

"Your name is Hawkens. That comes from 'hawk', right?"

"Yes."

"OK. Hawks eat field-mice, correct?"

130

"Yes, when they catch field-mice, they eat them."

"Well, then, here's the conclusion: hawks eat field-mice, your name is Hawkens, so therefore you eat field-mice."

Sam opened his mouth, both to catch his breath and his thoughts, looked at me absently for a while, and then let loose:

"Sir, I don't permit people to make fun of me! I'm no clown that you can jump around on the back of. You have injured me, injured me deeply with this devilish story about eating mice—and pathetic field-mice at that. I want satisfaction. Shall we duel?"

"Great!"

"Terrific. You've been to the university, right?"

"Yes."

"So you know what satisfaction requires. I will send you my second. Agreed?"

"Yes. But have you been to the university?"

"No."

"So you may not know what satisfaction requires, and I will therefore send you my third and my fourth. Agreed?"

"Wait, I don't understand that part," he said, embarrassed.

"Well, if you don't know the rules of a duel, you can't challenge me to one. I will make it up to you another way."

"What way?"

"I'll give you my grizzly hide."

Immediately, his eyes were blazing again. "You need that yourself!"

"No. I'm giving it to you."

"Really?"

"Yes."

"Well I declare! I accept. Thank you, sir, thank you extremely! Think how annoyed the others will be! Do you know what I'll make out of it?"

"Well?"

"A new hunting jacket, a jacket of grizzly leather! What a triumph! I'll make it myself. I'm an expert at making jackets. Just look at this one, the way I've improved it!"

He pointed to the prehistoric sack that he wore. It had one piece of leather patched on top of the other until the whole thing was as thick as a board.

"But," he added in his great enthusiasm, "the ears, the claws, and the teeth are yours. I don't need them for the jacket, and they are trophies of the dangerous fight. I'll make you a necklace out of them—I know how such things are done. Would you like that?"

"Yes."

"Excellent, excellent. This way, each gets what he wants. You're a clever fellow, a really clever fellow. You give Sam Hawkens a grizzly pelt, and then he doesn't care if you claim he eats field-mice. Even rats would be all right; it wouldn't upset me in the least. And all that stuff with the books—I can see now that it isn't quite as crazy as I thought at first. You really can learn something from them. Will you really write one?"

"Maybe several."

"About your experiences?"

"Yes."

"And I'll be in them?"

"Only my best friends will make it in. It will be a kind of written monument to them."

"Hmm. A monument. That sounds a lot different from yesterday. I must have misunderstood what you meant. So will you include me?"

"Only if you want me to."

"Listen, Sir, I do want you to. I'd like that very much."

"Good. Consider it done."

"Wonderful! But will you do me a favor?"

"What?"

"You're going to write about everything that we did together?"

"Yes."

"Well, how about leaving out the part where I didn't notice that the Apaches had split up. Me, Sam Hawkens, and I missed that hoof-print! I'd be embarrassed in front of all those readers, that will be learning from your book. If you would do me the favor of leaving that out, then you can include all that stuff about mice and rats. I don't care what people think about what I eat, but if they take me for a frontiersman that lets an Indian ride away without noticing the tracks, that would rankle me, rankle me something fierce!"

"Sorry, Sam. I can't do that."

"No? Why not."

"Because I have to describe each person that I include exactly as he is. I guess I'd better leave you out."

"No, no, I want to be in the book, warts and all. It's better to be truthful. When you describe my blunders, it can be a caution to those readers that are just as dumb as me, hee-hee-hee! But now that I know I'm going to be published, I'll be extra careful not to make that kind of mistake again. So, we are agreed?"

"Yes."

"Let's go, then."

"Which track shall we follow? The rider that split off?"

"No, this one here."

"Yes, that will be Winnetou."

"What makes you think so?"

"This one will be traveling more slowly with the corpse. The other one will be riding ahead to assemble the warriors, so that one has to be the chief."

"Yes, you're right. I came to the same conclusion. The chief doesn't matter to us. We'll follow the son."

"Why him?"

"Because I want to know if he camped for the night. That's the key. Forwards, Sir!"

We continued following the track without finding anything worth mentioning. Nor would a description of the area we traveled through be particularly interesting. Finally, an hour before noon, Sam halted and said:

"OK, that's enough. We'll turn back. Winnetou must have ridden throughout the night, and that means they're in a big hurry and we can expect an attack soon—maybe within the five days of surveying we have left."

"That would be bad."

"Indeed. You should quit the surveying, and we should get out of here. The work won't be completed, but if we stay there we'll be attacked and the work won't get done that way either. We need to have a serious talk with Bancroft."

"Perhaps there's an alternative."

"I don't know what that would be."

"We could retreat to a safe spot and then, when the Apaches have left, finish the work."

"Yes, that might work. We'll have to see what the others say. We'll have to hurry to get back to camp before dark."

Chapter 12

We struck back along the same path as we had come. We hadn't spared our horses, but my chestnut stallion was still fresh, and the new "Mary" behaved as if she'd hardly left the stall. We quickly covered a large stretch, then stopped by a stream to let the animals drink and rest a bit. We dismounted and stretched out between some bushes on the soft grass.

We had already said what needed to be said, so we lay there without talking. I thought about Winnetou and the battle with him and his Apaches that apparently lay ahead. Sam Hawkens closed his eyes and slept, as I could tell from the regular movements of his chest. He hadn't slept much the night before, and he could risk a quick nap here with me awake. We hadn't noticed anything ominous in the area during our homeward ride.

I was about to experience an example of how sharp the senses of men and animals become in the Wild West. The mule was in the middle of the bushes, so it couldn't see out, and it was nibbling leaves from the twigs. It was not a social animal. It avoided the horses and preferred to be alone. My stallion stood near me and chewed clumps of grass with its sharp teeth. Sam was asleep, as I mentioned.

Then the mule gave a short, strange snort, almost like a warning, and instantly Sam was awake and on his feet.

"I was asleep. Mary snorted and it woke me up. Someone or something is coming. Where's the mule?"

"There in the bushes. Come on!"

We crept through the bushes and saw Mary, hiding behind the branches. Here long ears were moving, and her tail was going up and down. When she saw that we had come, she relaxed. Her ears and tail were still. The animal had really been in good hands, and Sam could congratulate himself on catching her instead of one of the horses.

As we looked out through the branches, we saw six Indians,

riding one after the other. They were coming from the north, where our camp was, following our tracks from the morning. The leader, a muscular figure though not tall, kept his head down and kept his eyes fixed on the tracks. They all wore leather leggings and dark wool tunics. For weapons, they carried rifles, knifes and tomahawks. Their faces had been smeared with fat, and across this there was a blue stripe and a red stripe.

I was beginning to get worried about this encounter, but Sam said, without lowering his voice:

"What an encounter! This will save us, Sir!"

"Save us? How so? Shouldn't we talk more softly? These guys are so close, they'll surely hear us."

"And so they should. These are Kiowas. The one in front is Bao, which means 'fox' in their language. He's a capable and sly warrior, as his name suggests. The chief of this tribe is Tangua, an ambitious Indian but a good friend of mine. They're wearing war paint, so they're probably spies—I don't think that any of the tribes are actually fighting each other."

The Kiowas are thought to be a mixed tribe, descended from the Shoshonees and the Pueblos. They have been given specific reservations in the Indian Territory, but there are still many groups wandering the Texas prairies, particularly in the so-called "panhandle," and over into New Mexico. These groups are excellent riders and have lots of horses. Their thievery makes them dangerous to whites, and the settlers of border regions hate them bitterly. They aren't on good terms with the various Apache tribes either—the Kiowas are just as happy to steal from the Apaches. In a word, they are marauding bands of thieves. How they got that way is not a question that needs to be asked.

The six spies had now approached us. How they were supposed to "save" us, I had no idea. Six Indians would be little or no help to us. But I would soon learn what Sam had meant. For the moment, I was just happy that they knew Sam and that therefore we probably had nothing to fear from them.

They had been following our outward track, and now they came to our return track, which led into the bushes. From this, they concluded that people would be in the bushes. They immediately turned their powerful and graceful horses and retreated, to be out of shooting range of our guns. Then Sam emerged from the bushes, cupped his hands around his mouth, and made a shrill call that echoed in the distance. They seemed to recognize it, for they stopped their horses and looked back. Sam called again and waved his arm. They understood the call and wave. They saw Sam, whose unique appearance was not to be confused with anyone else, and they returned at a gallop. I had joined Sam. They came riding up as if to trample us, but we stood our ground. Just a few feet from us, they reined in their horses, and jumped from their saddles, leaving the horses to their own devices.

"Our white brother Sam is here?," asked the leader. "What causes his path to cross that of his red friend and brother?"

"Bao, the sly fox, has found me by following my tracks," Sam responded.

"We thought they were the tracks of the red dogs that we are searching for," said the Fox, in broken but understandable English.

"What dogs does my red brother mean?"

"The Apaches of the Mescalero tribe."

"Why do you call them dogs? Is there war between them and my brothers, the brave Kiowas?"

"The war-hachet has been dug up between us and these mangy coyotes."

"Ugh! I'm glad to hear that! Let my brothers sit with us, for I have something important to tell them."

The Fox looked suspiciously at me and asked:

"I have never seen this paleface before. He is young. Is he already a warrior among the white men? Has he earned a name?"

If Sam had simply said my German name, it would have had no effect. He recalled the word that Wheeler had used, and answered:

"This is my good friend and brother. He recently came from over the great water, where he was a great warrior among his people. He had never seen a buffalo or a bear in his life, but still he saved my life by killing two old buffalo bulls the day before yesterday, and yesterday he killed the gray grizzly of the Rocky Mountains with his knife, without getting a scratch on his skin."

"Ugh, ugh!" cried the Indians, looking at me in astonishment, and Sam continued, in a somewhat exuberant manner:

"His rifle shots never miss, and his fist is so powerful that he knocks every enemy to the ground with a single blow. That's why the white men of the West have given him the name 'Old Shatterhand'."

Thus it was, quite without my consent, that I got the nickname by which I have always been known from that day to this. Such nicknames are the custom in the West: frequently, even best friends don't know each other's real names.

The Fox held out his hand and said, in a friendly voice:

"If Old Shatterhand allows it, we will be his friends and brothers. We love such men, that can knock down enemies with one blow. You will be most welcome in our tents."

What he really meant was: we need young scamps with that kind of strength, so come join us. If you pilfer, steal, and rob with us, you'll probably do well among us. Nevertheless, I answered with as much dignity as I could muster:

"I love the red men, for they are the sons of the great spirit, as the white men are. We are brothers and will support each other against all enemies that don't honor you and us."

A satisfied smile spread across his painted face, and he assured me:

"Old Shatterhand speaks well. We want to smoke the peace pipe with him."

They sat down with us by the side of the stream. The Fox pulled out a pipe whose charmingly vile odor could be smelled from a distance. He stuffed it with a mixture that appeared to consist of crushed red beets, hemp leaves, chopped acorns, and sorrel, lit it, stood up, took a puff, blew the smoke to the sky and the earth, and said:

"The Great Spirit lives above, and here on the earth grow the plants and animals that he has created for the warriors of the Kiowa."

He took two more puffs and, after blowing the smoke toward the north, south, east, and west, he continued:

"In these directions, there are red men and white men that have taken the plants and animals for themselves. But we will find them and take back what is ours. I have spoken. How!"

What a speech! So unlike all the others that I had read before or that I would so often hear later. This Kiowa was saying, in the plainest of words, that he viewed all of the plant and animal kingdom as belonging rightfully to his tribe, and that stealing it back was therefore not only a right, but a duty! And I was supposed to be a friend of these people? But if you fall among musicians, you'd better play along.

The Fox handed the not-so-peaceful peace pipe to Sam. He gamely took his six puffs and said:

"The Great Spirit doesn't pay attention to the color of men's skin, for they can smear it with other colors to deceive him, but he looks directly at their hearts. The hearts of the warriors of the famous Kiowa tribe are brave, fearless, and true. My heart is attached to theirs as my mule is to the tree I tied it to. And so it will remain, if I'm not mistaken. I have spoken. How!"

Now that's the real Sam Hawkens, the sly, cheerful little man who knows how to find a tolerable side to everything and every situation. His speech was applauded with a universal "Ugh, ugh, ugh!" Unfortunately, he committed the crime of shoving the stinking clay pipe into my hand. I would have to grin and bear it, and I undertook to preserve my dignity. I assumed the most earnest expression I could muster. I am very fond of smoking, and I have never had a cigar that was too strong for me. I have even smoked the famous "three-man tobacco" which got its name from its awful taste; whoever smokes it must be held up by three men to keep from collapsing. So I did not expect that this Indian peace pipe would be too much for me.

I stood up, made a prayerful gesture with my left hand, and took the first puff. Yes, the ingredients I expected were all there—beet, hemp, acorn, sorrel—but also a fifth which I hadn't detected but which I now tasted. There seemed to have been a bit of shoe felt mixed in. I blew the smoke to the sky and the earth and said:

"From the heavens come the sun and the rain; all good things and all blessings come from there. The earth receives the warmth and the moisture, and it nourishes the buffalo and the mustang, the bear and the deer, the pumpkin, the corn, and above all the noble plants from which the clever red men prepare kinnikinnick for the peace pipe of love and brotherhood."

I had read that the Indians call their tobacco mixture "kinnikinnick" and this seemed the right place to use that knowledge. Now, I took another mouthful of smoke and blew it toward the four points of the compass. The smoke seemed fuller and more complicated this time. I thought I detected two more ingredients, namely sap and fingernail clippings. After this splendid discovery, I continued:

"In the west, the rocky mountains rise, and in the east lie the prairies. The lakes are to the north, and the vast ocean is in the south. If all the land between these borders were mine, I would give it to the Kiowa warriors, for they are my brothers. Let them each catch ten buffalo and fifty grizzly bears this year. Let the kernels of their corn be like pumpkins, and let their pumpkins be so large that you can carve twenty canoes from a single shell. I have spoken. How!"

It didn't require much effort on my part to offer them these marvels, but they were as pleased as if they had actually received them. My speech was the cleverest that I had given in my life, and it was received with such a celebration as I would not have expected from the Indians, who were normally calm and cool. No one, and especially not a white man, had ever wished them so much. Hence the repeated "Ugh, ugh!" went on seemingly without end. The Fox shook my hand repeatedly, assured me of his friendship forever, and opened his mouth so wide with his

"How, how" that I was able to get rid of the peace pipe by shoving it between his yellow teeth. He immediately turned silent in order to enjoy its contents further.

This was my first "sacred ceremony" among the Indians, for they really view the smoking of the peace pipe as a celebration which has a serious purpose and equally serious consequences. Many a time I have since had to smoke the calumet and have been made fully aware of the seriousness and dignity placed on the event. On this particular occasion, however, it nauseated me from start to finish; and then, hearing about Sam's heart "tied like a mule to a tree," the whole procedure seemed a bit comical to me. My hand stank from the pipe, and my whole soul rejoiced that it was now in the Fox's mouth, not mine. To clear the memory of the taste of the pipe from my mouth, I pulled out a cigar and lit it. Suddenly, the greedy eyes of all the Indians were focused on me! The Fox opened his mouth, dropping the pipe, but as a trained warrior he had the presence of mind to retrieve it and stick it back between his lips. But it was easy to see that, at this moment, a single cigar was more appealing to him than a thousand peace and kinnikinnick pipes.

Since we were in constant communication with Santa Fe, and could have whatever we required sent up from there by wagon, it hadn't been hard for me to get cigars. They didn't cost much, and I liked to enjoy them when the others were drinking brandy. I had brought enough along for two days, since I didn't know exactly when we would get back to camp. So I was able to satisfy the obviously keen appetites of the Indians by giving them each a cigar. The Fox immediately put away the pipe and lit his, but his men behaved differently. They didn't just put the end of the cigars in their mouths, but rather shoved the whole thing in and started chewing. People have differing tastes, I guess. I silently swore never again to given them anything that was intended for smoking, not eating.

Now we had finished all the formalities and Indians were in a good mood. Sam began to speak, starting with a question:

"My brothers say that the war-hatchet has been dug up between them and the Mescalero Apaches. I haven't heard about that. How long has it been since it is no longer buried?"

"It is since the time that the palefaces call two weeks. My brother Sam must have been in a distant place if he did not hear of it."

"That is true. But your peoples have lived in peace. Why has my brother taken up his weapons?"

"The Apache dogs have killed four of our warriors."

"Where?"

"On the Rio Pecos."

"But you have no village there."

"The Mescaleros have a village."

"Why were your warriors there?"

The Kiowa reflected a moment about how truthful to be.

"Our warriors went in the night to take the horses of the Mescalero Apaches. But the stinking dogs watched well. They defended themselves and killed our brave men. That is why the war hatchet has been dug up."

So the Kiowas tried to steal horses, but were caught in the act and driven off. It was their own fault that several of them had lost their lives in the process. And now the Apaches, who were in the right in defending their property, were to suffer. I wanted to tell the Fox what I really thought, straight to his face, and in fact I had started to open my mouth, but Sam gave me a warning signal and continued his questions:

"Do the Apaches know that your warriors are riding against them?"

"Does my brother think that we will tell them this? We will attack them in secret and kill as many as we can. We will take what we can use of their animals and possessions."

This was terrible! I could not keep myself from injecting the question:

"Why did my brave brothers want the Apaches horses? I have heard that the Kiowa tribe has many more horses than its warriors need."

The Fox smiled at me and answered:

"My young brother Old Shatterhand has come over the water and so does not know how the people on this side of the water think and live. Yes, we have many horses. But white men came to us to buy horses, so many horses that we did not have enough. They told us of the horse herds of the Apaches and said that they would give us the same amount of goods and brandy for an Apache horse as for a Kiowa horse. So our warriors went to get Apache horses."

So I had guessed right. Whose fault was the death of the warriors and the bloodshed to come? White horse traders who paid with brandy and who practically sent the Kiowas off to steal horses. I would have given voice to my thoughts, but Sam gestured at me energetically and said:

"My brother the Fox has been sent as a spy?"

"Yes."

"When will your warriors follow?"

"They are a day's ride behind us."

"Who is leading them?"

"Tangua, the Chief, himself."

"How many warriors does he have?"

"Two times a hundred."

"And you think you will surprise the Apaches?"

"We will come down on them like the eagle comes down on the crows that have not seen him."

"My brother is mistaken. The Apaches know that the Kiowas will attack them."

The Fox shook he head in disbelief and answered:

"How can they know? Do their ears reach the tents of the Kiowas?"

"Yes."

"I do not understand my brother Sam. He must say what he means by these words."

"The Apaches have ears that can walk and ride. We saw two of these ears yesterday. They had been to the Kiowas, to spy."

"Ugh! Two ears? That means two spies?"

"Yes."

"Then I must go back to the chief immediately. We have brought only two hundred warriors because we do not need more if the Apaches do not know we are coming. But if they know, we need many more."

"My brothers have not thought over everything completely. Inchu-chuna, the Chief of the Apaches, is a very wise warrior. When he saw that his people had killed four Kiowas, he said to himself that the Kiowas would want revenge for these deaths. He went to spy on the Kiowas."

"Ugh! Ugh! He himself?"

"Yes, and his son Winnetou."

"Ugh! Him too! If we had known, we would have captured these two dogs. Now they will gather a great number of warriors to meet us. I must tell my chief, so that he stays where he is and sends for more warriors. Will Sam and Old Shatterhand ride with me?"

"Yes."

"Then let us go quickly!"

"Not so fast! First, I have something very important to talk with you about."

"Let us talk as we ride."

"No. I will ride with you, but not to Tangua, chief of the Kiowas. I want you to ride with me to our camp."

"My brother Sam is mistaken."

"No. Listen to what I am telling you. Do you want to capture Inchu-chuna, chief of the Apaches, alive?"

"Ugh!" cried the Kiowa as if electrified, and his people perked up their ears.

"And his son Winnetou as well?"

"Ugh, ugh! Is that possible?"

"It is very easy."

"I know my brother Sam. If I did not, I would think a joke was upon his tongue, and I would not permit it."

"Pshaw! I'm serious. You can capture the chief and his son alive."

"When?"

"I thought in five, six, or seven days. But now I know it can be much sooner."

"Where?"

"At our camp."

"I do not know where it is."

"You will see. We will gladly take you there, after you have heard what I want to tell you now."

He told about the section we were surveying, about the reason for our work (to which they voiced no objection at all), and about the encounter with the two Apaches. At this point Sam added this comment:

"I was surprised to see the two chiefs alone, and I assumed that they were on a buffalo hunt and had left their warriors briefly. But now I know the real reason. The two Apaches were at your village, spying. And they must believe that the situation is very important, for otherwise the two leaders would not have made the ride themselves. Now, they have gone home. Winnetou's trip was slowed by the body. But Inchu-chuna hurried ahead. He would have ridden his horse to death, if necessary, to gather his warriors together quickly."

"That's why I must tell my chief just as quickly!"

"Let my brother wait a minute and let me finish speaking! The Apache thirst for two kinds of revenge: revenge on you and revenge on us for the death of Kleki-petra. They will send a large war party against you and a smaller one against us. The chief and his son will ride with the smaller one, and they will plan to join the larger one after they have attacked us. You will ride to your chief after I have showed you our camp, so that you can find it later. You will tell him everything I have told you. Then he must come to us, with his two hundred warriors, to wait for Inchu-chuna and his smaller war party. You will have two hundred warriors, and he will not bring more than fifty. We have twenty white men who will help you, and it will be easy to overpower the Apaches. When you have the two chiefs in your hands, that is just as good as capturing the whole tribe, and you can demand whatever you want. Does my brother agree with all this?"

"Yes. The plan of my brother Sam is good. When my chief hears of it, he will be pleased and he will quickly follow it."

"Then let us ride quickly, so that we reach our camp before night."

We mounted our horses, which were now fully rested, and rode off at a gallop. We didn't bother following the trail, but took the most direct route back.

Chapter 13

I must say that I was not exactly delighted by Sam's behavior. On the contrary, it made me angry. Winnetou, the noble Winnetou, and his father were to be ambushed, along with fifty of their warriors! If it succeeded, they and the other Apaches were lost. How could Hawkens suggest such a thing! He knew well how highly I thought of Winnetou, for I had told him; and I knew that he too was favorably inclined toward the young Apache.

All of my efforts to pull Sam aside on the trail and get him away from the Kiowas for a moment were futile. I wanted to persuade him to drop his plan and adopt another one, without the Kiowas hearing it, but he seemed to suspect this and he stayed close to the side of the leader of the Kiowas. This made me even angrier at him. If there ever was a time when I (who have not the slightest inclination toward moodiness) was in a bad frame of mind, it was on that day, as we returned to camp at dusk. I dismounted, removed my saddle, and lay disconsolate on the grass. I could not bring myself to a frank discussion with Sam. He had ignored all my signals and was now telling the rest of the camp how we had encountered the Kiowas and what was to happen next. At first, they were shocked to see the Kiowas, but they were delighted to learn that these were our friends and that we no longer needed to worry about the Apaches. We would be able to complete our work, protected by two hundred Kiowas. Everyone was now convinced that the expected attack could not hurt us.

The Kiowas were treated as guests, got plenty of bear meat to eat, and then rode off. They planned to ride all night, to get word back to their people as quickly as possible. Only then, once they had left, did Sam come over to me. He lay down beside me and said, in his usual superior tone of voice:

"You're making an awful face this evening, Sir. Must be some problem behind it, either something you ate or your spiritual intestines, hee-hee-hee! Which is it, then? I think the second. Right?"

"You've got it," I responded, and my tone may not have been particularly friendly.

"Well, pour out your heart and tell me what's bothering you. I'll cure it for you."

"It would be great if you could, Sam, but I doubt it."

"Oh, but I can. You can depend on it."

"So tell me, Sam, what do you think of Winnetou?"

"He's marvelous. I think you share my opinion."

"And you plan to lure him to certain death! I don't get it."

"To certain death? Why, such a thing wouldn't occur to me in a million years."

"But he'll be captured."

"True enough."

"And that will be his death!"

"There's not the slightest question of that, Sir! I have so much regard for Winnetou that I'd risk my life to rescue him if he were in danger."

"Then why draw him into a trap?"

"To save us from him and his Apaches."

"And then?"

"And then? You really want to help out this young Apache, Sir?"

"Not only do I want do it, I will! If he is captured, I'll set him free. And let me be clear: if weapons are to be used against him, I'll fight on his side."

"So? You'll really do that?"

"Yes. I promised that to a dying man. And since I never break my word, a promise like that is as sacred as an oath."

"That's excellent! Then we're in total agreement, the two of us."

"Wait a minute. I don't see how your fine words can be reconciled with the hostile arrangements you've been making."

"Ah, so that's what you want to know? Yes, old Sam couldn't help noticing how badly you wanted to talk while we were riding. It couldn't be done, though. It would have ruined my whole beautiful plan. I'm not the man I appear to be, and my intentions are not what they seem. I just don't want to let everyone see my cards, hee-hee-hee! But I'll share it with you; you'll help me out. So will Dick Stone and Will Parker, if I'm not mistaken. All right then: the way I judge Inchu-chuna, he wasn't just out spying with Winnetou; he had already armed his warriors and gotten them on the move. So they've probably covered a good bit of territory already. And since Inchu-chuna probably rode all night, like Winnetou did, he probably figures on meeting up with the warriors tomorrow morning early, or at least before noon. Otherwise, he wouldn't be pushing his horse so hard. So he could make it back here the day after tomorrow, in the evening. So you see what kind of danger we're in, and how close it is. Thank goodness we followed them. I would never have expected them back so soon. And how lucky we encountered the Kiowas and learned everything from them! They'll be back with their two hundred riders and . . ."

"I'm going to go and warn Winnetou about the Kiowas," I interrupted.

"For God's sake, no!" he cried. "That would only hurt us. The Apaches would escape, and then we'd have them on our necks in spite of the Kiowas. No, they must really be captured and look death in the face. Then, when we secretly set them free, they will have to be grateful to us and give up their thoughts of revenge. At most, they would insist on getting Rattler from us, and I wouldn't prevent them from that. Now what do you say, my angry young gentleman?"

After a moment's reflection, I shook his hand and answered:

"I'm completely reassured, Sam. Your plan is well thought out!"

"Don't you think so? It may be, as some say, that Sam Hawkens eats field mice, but he does have his good side too, hee-hee-hee! So, I'm back in your good graces?"

"I guess you are, Sam."

"Well then, you better hit the hay and get some sleep. There's plenty to do in the morning. I'll go tell Stone and Parker what's happening, so they know the plan."

Good old Sam Hawkens. Wasn't he a wonderful, warm-hearted fellow? And when I say "old," that's exactly how he looked. He may not have been much over forty, but the jungle of beard that covered his face almost totally, the awful nose that poked out above it like a watch tower, and the jacket cobbled together out of board-like strips of leather—they all made him look much older than he really was.

Maybe this is the moment to make a comment about the word "old." In German, the word "alt" (old) is used not only to indicate age, but also as a term of endearment. You can talk about "a good old pal" or "a good old sport" and they needn't be especially old. In fact, you often hear very young people described this way. And there's another meaning to this word as well. You commonly encounter expressions such as: an old fuddy-duddy, an old grouch, and old miser, an old driveller. Here, "old" gives extra emphasis or intensity. The characteristic expressed by the noun gets raised to a higher level or degree by the word "old."

That's exactly how the word "old" is used in the Wild West. One of the most famous frontiersmen is named Old Firehand. Once he takes his gun in his hands, his fire is always deadly. That is how he got the name "Firehand." And the "Old" attached to it emphasizes this skill in shooting. Similarly, the nickname I received, "Shatterhand," was always accompanied by "Old" as well.

When Sam left me, I tried to sleep but couldn't. The rest of the party was very excited about the expected protection of the Kiowas and discussed it so loudly that it was hard to fall asleep, and my own thoughts kept me awake as well. Hawkens spoke so confidently about his plans that he seemed to see no chance of failure, but I was not so sure I shared his opinion. We planned to free Winnetou and his father. But what of the other captured Apaches? Nothing had been said about them. Were we to leave them in the Kiowas' hands while the chiefs went free? That seemed unjust to me. But it would be difficult or impossible for just four men to free all the Apaches, especially since it would have to be done secretly, so that no suspicion would fall on us. And, I asked myself, exactly how would the Apaches fall into the Kiowas hands? Surely not without a fight, and that meant that the two we planned to rescue, who were the bravest of fighters, were also in the greatest danger of being killed. How could we prevent that? If they didn't allow themselves to be overpowered and captured, then surely the Kiowas would kill them. That had to be prevented at all costs.

I thought over these questions, tossing and turning, and I couldn't come up with a solution. The only thought that finally gave me some reassurance was that little, cheerful old Sam would think of something to save the day. But in any case, I was resolved to step in to rescue the two chiefs, protecting them if necessary with my own body. In the end, I fell asleep.

The next morning, I worked doubly hard on my surveying, since I had not done any the previous day. Since the others were working with urgency too, we made much better progress than ever before. Rattler stayed away from us. He wandered around aimlessly, but his "scouts" were as friendly to him as if nothing had happened. This confirmed for me that we would not be able to count on their help if it came to a conflict with Rattler. By evening, we had surveyed almost twice the usual distance, even though the terrain was difficult. But we were worn out and we went to sleep soon after supper. As usual, we had moved the camp to the new location of our surveying work.

The next day, we worked just as hard. Around noon, the Kiowas arrived. Their scouts had easily found us by following our trail from our previous camp.

These Indians were powerful, war-like figures. They had excellent horses, and each man had a gun, a knife, and a tomahawk. I counted two hundred men. Their leader was of really imposing stature, had a powerful, dark expression and eyes like a beast of prey from which no trace of good could be expected. They seemed to express nothing but lust for war and plunder. His name was Tangua, which meant "chief" in his language. From this one could conclude that he did not have to worry about competitors for his position. When I looked into his eyes, I feared for Inchu-chuna and Winnetou, if they should really fall into his hands.

Tangua came as our friend and collaborator, but he was anything but friendly in his manner with us. He behaved like a tiger that has teamed up with a leopard for purposes of hunting, but that plans to eat the leopard afterwards, along with the rest of the kill. He was at the head of the Kiowa party, along with the Fox, his scout. Instead of dismounting to greet us, he made a gesture with his arm, upon which his people surrounded us. Then he rode to our wagon and raised the canvas to look inside. The contents seemed to attract him, for he dismounted from his horse and climbed into the wagon to examine what was inside.

"Oh ho!" said Sam Hawkens, who was standing next to me. "He seems to see us and our goods as spoils, before he even speaks a word with us, if I'm not mistaken. If he thinks Sam Hawkens is dumb enough to let the fox guard the hen-house, he's mistaken. In a moment he'll see."

"Don't do anything rash, Sam!" I urged him. "They have a two-hundred-man advantage on us."

"They've got us beat on numbers, but not on tricks, hee-hee-hee!" he answered.

"But we're surrounded!"

"Well, I can see that, same as you. Or do you think I'm blind? It looks like we may not have invited especially good rescuers to help us out. Since he's surrounded us, it looks like he has in mind to capture us along with the Apaches. But he's biting off more than he'll want to chew, and that's a fact. Come on over to the wagon and listen to Sam Hawken's method for dealing with rascals like him! Tangua and I know each other well, and even if he hasn't seen me yet, he certainly knows that I'm here. So it's not just that his behavior annoys me, but it's got me worried and I figure it should worry us all. Just look at the hostile faces on all those warriors! I better let them know that Sam Hawkens is around. Come on!"

Carrying our guns, we went to the wagon where Tangua was poking around. I wasn't feeling to good about the direction the proceedings were heading. When we arrived, Sam asked in a warning tone:

"Is the famous Chief of the Kiowas almost ready to go to the eternal hunting ground?"

Tangua, who had his back to us, straightened up, turned around, and answered roughly:

"Why are the palefaces bothering me with this foolish question? One day, Tangua will rule as a great chief in the eternal hunting ground, but a long time must pass before he goes there."

"This time may be just one minute."

"Why?"

"Get out of the wagon and I will tell you, but be quick!"

"I will stay here!"

"OK, then you will fly through the air."

Saying this, Sam turned and started to leave. But the chief jumped quickly from the wagon, grabbed his arm, and cried:

"Fly through the air? Why does Sam Hawkens speak such words?"

"To warn you."

"About what?"

"About death. You would have been killed if you had stayed in the wagon a few moments more."

"Ugh! Is there death in the wagon?"

"Yes."

"Where? Show me!"

"Perhaps later. Have your scouts not told you why we are here?"

"They told me. You wish to build a road for the fire-horse of the palefaces."

"Right! Such a road goes over rivers and valleys and through cliffs that we must blow apart. I think you know about that."

"I know it. But what does that have to do with the death that threatens me?"

"A lot, and much more than you know. Have you heard about what we use to blow up cliffs that are in the path of our fire-horse? Like the powder you use to shoot your guns?"

"No, I have not heard of it. The palefaces have another invention to blow up whole mountains?"

"Right! And this invention is on that wagon. It is well secured in packages, but someone who does not know how to handle it will be killed as soon as he touches one of the packages, for it will blow up in his hand and smash him into a thousand pieces."

"Ugh, ugh!" he cried, now visibly shocked. "Was I near these packages?"

"So near that you would be in the eternal hunting ground right now, if you hadn't jumped out of the wagon. But what would have been left of you then? Your medicine pouch, your scalps, it would all be gone. Nothing would be left but little bits of flesh and bone. How could you rule as a great chief in the eternal hunting ground in that form? Your remains would be crushed and trampled by the spirit-horses there."

An Indian that goes to the eternal hunting grounds without scalps or medicine pouch is received with contempt by the dead heroes there and must hide from their eyes while they feast on everything that Indians enjoy. This is what the Indians believe. What a misfortune to arrive there in small, scattered pieces! One could see in spite of his dark skin that the blood had gone out of the chief's face, and he cried:

"Ugh! It is good that you told me in time! But why do you keep this invention on the wagon, where so many other useful things are found?"

"Should we leave these packages on the ground where they will be spoiled and the least movement might cause a disaster? They are dangerous enough on the wagon. When one of them blows up, everything in the area flies through the air."

"People too?"

"Of course. All the people and all the animals that are within ten times a hundred lengths of a horse."

"Then I must tell my warriors that none of them must get near this dangerous wagon."

"Please do that. Otherwise, someone's carelessness might kill us all! You see how concerned I am for you, for I think that the warriors of the Kiowas are our friends. But it looks like I may be mistaken. When friends meet, they greet each other and smoke the peace pipe. Do you not want to do that today?"

"You have already smoked the pipe with my scout, the Fox."

"Only me and the white warrior next to me here. The others have not. If you do not want to greet them too, I have to think that your friendship is not real."

Tangua stood thinking for a moment and then answered:

"We are on the warpath and have not brought the kinnikinnick of peace with us."

"The mouth of the Chief of the Kiowas speaks one thing, his heart thinks something else. I see the bag of kinnikinnick there on your belt and it looks full. We don't need it, because we have enough tobacco here. Everyone does not have to smoke—you can smoke for your warriors and I can smoke for myself and the white men that are here. Then there will be a bond of friendship for everyone that is here."

"Why should we smoke? We are already brothers! Let Sam Hawkens assume that we smoked the calumet for everyone."

"Just as you like. But then we will do what we want and you will not capture the Apaches."

"Will you warn them?" asked Tangua, his eyes flashing.

"No, that wouldn't occur to me. They are our enemies and want to kill us. But I won't tell you the way that you can catch them."

"I don't need that. I know it myself."

"Oh ho! Do you know when and from what direction they will come, and where we will meet them?"

"I will find out. I will send scouts to spy on them."

"You won't do that, because you are smart enough to know that the Apaches will find the tracks of the scouts and will be prepared for the battle. They would take each step very cautiously and it is not certain whether you could capture them. But if you follow the plan that I want to use, you will surround them completely and capture them before they know you are there, if I'm not mistaken."

I saw that this explanation had made an impression. After a short period of consideration, Tangua said:

"I will speak with my warriors."

Then he left us. He went to the Fox, summoned several other Indians, and then we watched the way they discussed the matter.

"By saying he wants to talk to the others, he's confirming that he's plotting something against us," Sam said.

"That doesn't speak well for him, seeing that you are his friend and you haven't done anything to him," I answered.

"Friend? What does "friend" mean among these Kiowas? They are scoundrels and live from plunder. You're only their friend if they can't take something from you. But we have a wagon full of victuals and other items that are of great value to the Indians. The scouts told their chief about that, and from that moment on they decided to take everything we have."

"And now?"

"Now? For now, we are safe."

"I'd be happier if I thought that was true."

"I believe it is true. I know these people. That was a brilliant idea of mine, making them think we had blasting powder here in the wagon, hee-hee-hee! He already thought everything in there was his for the taking. The first thing he did was climb right in.

Now I doubt any of the Indians will risk touching anything in the wagon. Yes, I think we may even be able to make further use of their fear later on. I'll get me a can of sardines to carry around and I'll persuade them it's full of blasting powder. You already have one, with the papers in it. Bear it in mind in case it comes in handy later!'

"Good! I hope it will have the desired effect. But what was all that about smoking the peace pipe?"

"They obviously didn't plan on smoking it, but now I think they may decide to after all. My argument persuaded the chief, and he'll convince the others. Even so, though, we won't be able to trust them."

"See, Sam, I was at least partly right the day before yesterday. You wanted to go through with your plan with the Kiowas, but now they've got us outnumbered. I'm curious what the outcome will be!"

"Exactly what I expected, nothing else! You can depend on it. Certainly, the chief wanted to steal our goods and then capture the Apaches himself. But now he must be aware that they're too clever to be caught and butchered the way he had in mind. Like I told him, he would have to send scouts, and the Apaches would be sure to find their tracks. He couldn't just wait for them to walk into his hands like blind prairie hens. Look, they're finished and he's coming back. Now we'll find out what's going to happen."

We found out even before he got to us, for the Fox cried out a command and the circle of Indians around us dissolved. The warriors got back on their horses. We were no longer surrounded. Tangua looked a little less hostile than before:

"I have met with my warriors," he said. "They agreed with me that I will smoke the calumet with my brother Sam, and that will be as if all had smoked it."

"That is what I expected, for you are not only a brave man, but a clever man as well. Let the warriors of the Kiowas make a half-circle and let them be witnesses that we have exchanged the smoke of peace and friendship."

And so it was. Tangua and Sam Hawkens smoked the calumet in a ceremony like the one I described earlier, and then all of us whites went from one Indian to the next, shaking hands with each one. This allowed us to assume that, at least for the next day or two, they bore us no hostile intentions. How they might behave after that, we had no way of knowing.

When I speak of "smoking" the peace pipe or the calumet, I'm using the language we used among ourselves. But the Indians didn't speak of "smoking" tobacco, they spoke of "drinking" it. And "drinking" is a good description of what Indians do when they smoke: they breathe in the smoke, collect it in their stomach, and blow it back out in individual slow puffs.

It's similar to the way the Turks smoke, and, in the same way, the word for smoking in Turkish is the same as the word for drinking.

The high regard in which the pipe is held among the Indians is revealed by the fact that the same word is used for both "chief" and "pipe" in the Jemes language and in all the Apache dialects. In Jemes, "chief" is "fui" and the pipe is "fuitshash." In Apache, "chief" is "natan" and pipe is "natan-se." The "se" ending means "stone" and it is used equally for pottery pipes and for those whose bowl is literally made of stone. The bowl of a pipe that is used as a calumet is supposed to be cut from sacred stone that is found in Dakota.

Once this degree of harmony had been established, at least for the time being, Tangua requested that a big meeting be held, in which the whites were to participate. I was against it, since it would take us away from our work, which we urgently needed to complete. So I asked Sam to see if it could be postponed until the evening. I had read and heard that these palavers, once started, can go on practically forever. Hawkens spoke with the chief and reported back to me:

"In true Indian fashion, he's not willing to budge. The Apaches aren't expected anytime soon, so he wants to sit down and have a council to listen to my plan, and no doubt there will be a big meal afterwards. We've got provisions, and the Indians have brought plenty of dried meat on their pack horses. Fortunately, I managed to persuade them that only Dick Stone, Will Parker, and I need to participate. The rest of you will be allowed to go about your work."

"Allowed? Since when do we need permission from the Indians? I plan to behave so that they see that I'm a completely independent person."

"Don't go stirring up a hornet's nest, Sir! Better to behave as if you noticed nothing. We can't afford to get on their bad side if we want our plan to succeed."

"But I want to participate in the council!"

"That's completely unnecessary."

"No! I disagree. I need to know what gets decided."

"You'll be told immediately."

"But what if you settle on something that I don't approve of?"

"Don't approve of? Will you take a look at this greenhorn? He seems to think that Sam Hawkens can't make a decision without asking him for approval! I reckon I ought to ask you for permission before I cut my nails or patch my shoes!"

"That's not at all what I meant. I only want to be sure that nothing is agreed to that could endanger the lives of our two Apaches."

"Rely on old Sam Hawkens where that's concerned. I give you my word that they will escape completely unharmed. Is that enough for you?"

"Yes. I respect your word. Once you've given it, I think you'll see to it that it is fulfilled."

"Well! Get to work, then, and rest assured that the matter will be handled to your satisfaction, even without you there to stick your nose into it."

Chapter 14

I had to hurry. It would be mostly up to me if we were actually going to finish our surveying before the arrival of the Apaches. We worked with redoubled zeal on our task and made extraordinary progress, since Bancroft and his three men were working as fast as they could. This was because of something I had told them.

If we did not work quickly, the Apaches would come before we were finished, and we might be in trouble with them or with the Kiowas. But if we finished, it was possible that we could hustle ourselves and our survey work out of there safely. That's what I told them, and they worked with a level of speed and endurance that I had never seen in them before. For myself, though, I would never have considered hightailing it like that. I was worried about Winnetou. The others could do as they liked, but I was resolved not to leave until I was convinced that Winnetou was out of danger.

I actually had two jobs. I had to do the surveying, but I also recorded the results and made the drawings, the latter in duplicate. One copy went to the engineer, who was the man in charge. I created the second copy in secret, to have a spare in case of need. Our situation was so dangerous that this seemed a prudent step to take.

The council did indeed last until evening, just as I had feared. It was just ending when we returned, forced by the gathering darkness to stop working. The Kiowas were in high spirits, for Sam Hawkens had made the mistake of sharing (or maybe had been clever enough to share) the rest of our brandy with them. It had evidently not occurred to him to seek Rattler's agreement first. Several fires were burning, around which the feasting Indians now sat. The horses grazed nearby, and farther out in the dark, sentries had been posted by the chief.

I sat down by Sam and his inseparable companions Parker and Stone, ate my dinner, and let my eyes roam the camp. For me, newly arrived in the West, it had an appearance like nothing I had ever seen. It certainly had a warlike look. As I searched one Indian face after another, I found none that I would judge capable of any feeling of sympathy for an enemy. We only had enough brandy to provide five or six swallows per man, so no one appeared drunk. But they had had so little exposure to the fire-water that it had a rousing effect on them. The Indians were much livelier in their movements and they spoke much louder than they normally would.

Naturally, I asked Sam about the results of the council.

"You can rest easy," he replied. "Your favorite Indians won't be harmed."

"But what if they try to fight?"

"It will be futile. They'll be overpowered and tied up before they even realize anything is happening."

"Really? How do you plan to do that, Sam?"

"Very easy. We know the direction the Apaches will be coming from. Do you know why, Sir?"

"Yes. They'll naturally go where they found us last, then follow our tracks."

"Right! You're really not as dumb as a fellow would think, just judging by your face. OK, then, the first piece of information we need is already known, namely where they'll be coming from. The second is the time they will arrive."

"We can't predict that exactly, but we can estimate it."

"Yes, anyone with a few brains in his head could estimate it, but an estimate is not good enough. Anyone in a situation like ours who relies on estimates is in danger of losing his hide. Certainty is what we need, absolute certainty."

"The only way we'll get it is to send out scouts, and you've already rejected that approach, Sam. You were of the opinion that the tracks of the scouts would betray us."

"The tracks of Indian scouts, mind you, I said Indian scouts, Sir! The Apaches know that we're here, and when they encounter the tracks of a white man, they won't get worried. But Indian hoof prints would be something entirely different. They would take that as a warning and would be exceedingly careful. Since you are such an exceptionally clever young man, you can imagine what they would conclude."

"That Kiowas are in the area?"

"Yes, you figured it out! If I didn't have to take such good care of my old wig, I would take my hat off to you in salute. I won't, but let's just pretend I did."

"Thanks, Sam! I sure hope your new-found confidence doesn't fizzle out. But back to the subject. You're saying that we'll send white scouts out to check on the Apaches?"

"Yes, but not scouts. Just one scout."

"Is that enough?"

"Yes, if you've got one guy who you can really depend on. We do, and his name is Sam Hawkens, if I'm not mistaken. He eats field-mice, I believe, hee-hee-hee! Perhaps you know him, Sir?"

"Yes," I nodded. "If he takes it on, we have nothing to worry about. The Apaches will never spot him."

"They won't spot him, but they'll see him."

"What? They'll see you?"

"Yes."

"They'll capture or kill you!"

"Not likely. They're far too clever for that. I'm going to make it so they can't miss seeing me. Then, it won't occur to them that others have joined us. If I parade around as if I had no cares, they'll think that we're feeling as safe as if we were in Abraham's palace. They won't do anything to me, because they want to avoid the suspicions that would be created back in camp if I didn't return. The way they figure, they'll have me soon enough."

"But Sam, isn't it possible that they'll see you but you won't see them?"

"Sir," he roared, "if you continue to insult me in this way, I will have nothing further to do with you! Me, not see them? Sam Hawkens' eyes are small, it's true, but they're sharp. The Apaches won't arrive in a bunch; they'll send scouts ahead. But they won't be able to evade me. I'll position myself where I'm bound to see them. There are areas where even the best scout can't find cover and has to come out in the open. That's the kind of spot you need, if you want to spy on scouts. As soon as I see them, I'll alert you. That way, you can just act natural when they spy on the camp."

"But they'll see the Kiowas and report back to their chief!"

"They'll see who? The Kiowas? My dear greenhorn and esteemed young man, do you think that Sam Hawkens' brain is made out of wadding or blotting paper? I will have arranged things so that the Kiowas will not be seen, and there will be no trace of their presence, not the slightest trace, understand? Our very dear friends the Kiowas will hide themselves very well, only to appear again at the appropriate moment. Of course the Apache scouts can only be permitted to see the people who were in the camp when Winnetou and his father were in it."

"Oh, that makes sense!"

"You bet. So the Apache scouts can sneak around as much as they like and convince themselves that we're not expecting an attack. Then, when they leave, I'll follow them to find out when the attack is planned. They'll come at night, of course, and get as close to our camp as they can. Then the noble Apaches will be all over us."

"And they'll capture or even kill us, at least some of us!"

"Stop, Sir, it's painful to listen to you! You claim a certain amount of intelligence, but you don't even know that you have to take to your heels if you don't want to get caught! Every rabbit knows that. Why, even the little black biting bugs that can jump 600 times their body length know that. But you, you have no idea! Hmm. I guess they left that out of all the books you've been reading."

"No, but I'm not sure even an expert frontiersman could jump as far as that insect you mentioned, 600 times his height. So you're saying we'll retreat to a safe place?"

"Yes. Of course we'll have a campfire, so they get a good look at us. As long as it burns, they'll stay hidden. We'll let it burn down, and as soon as it is dark, we'll slip out quietly and quickly, and join the Kiowas. Then the Apaches will attack our camp and there'll be nobody home, hee-hee-hee! They will be baffled. They'll re-light the fire so they can look for us. Then we'll be able to see them as clearly as they saw us before, and the tables will be turned: it'll be us capturing them. What a shock they're in for! They'll be talking about this one for years to come. And they'll say, 'It was Sam Hawkens that cooked this up,' if I'm not mistaken."

"Yes, it would great if it worked out just that way."

"And it will. I'll make sure of it."

"What happens then? We secretly rescue the Apaches?"

"At least Inchu-chuna and Winnetou."

"Not the others?"

"As many as we can. But we can't afford to get caught."

"Then what will happen to the rest?"

"Nothing really terrible, Sir, I can assure you of that. The Kiowas will initially be more interested in recapturing the escapees than in the rest of the Apaches. And if they do get bloodthirsty, Sam Hawkens will still be there. Anyway, whatever happens afterwards, there's no point taxing your brain worrying about it now. We'll just have to wait and see what transpires. Right now, we have to find the right spot to execute our little plan. Not just any place will do. I'll work on that first thing in the morning. We've done enough talking for today. Starting tomorrow, it'll be time to act."

He was right. Talking or making more plans was superfluous now. Now we could only wait for events to play themselves out.

That was an uncomfortable night. A wind came up, and gradually it turned into a storm. Toward morning it got very cool, a rare thing in these parts. We were roughly at the same latitude as Damascus but were still wakened by the cold. Sam Hawkens checked the sky and observed:

"Something is going to happen here today that is very uncommon: it's going to rain, if I'm not mistaken. And that's perfect for our plan."

"What makes you say that?" I asked.

"Just think about it. Look around. See how all the grass has been trampled? When the Apaches arrive, they would probably easily see that more men and horses were here than just the ones we have. But if it rains, the grass will perk up again. Otherwise, the signs of our camp here would last three or four days. I'll get the Indians to move out of here as quickly as possible."

"You'll go looking for a place for the ambush?"

"Yes. I could leave the Kiowas here and then fetch them later, but the sooner they leave, the sooner their tracks will disappear. The rest of you can continue with your work."

He went to the chief to discuss his plan, and he agreed to it. Within a short period, the Indians rode off with Sam and his two partners. It was self-evident that the place Sam wanted to select must lie in the same direction as our surveying took us. Otherwise, we would have wasted time and the Apaches would have noticed our changed direction.

After the Indians had left, we followed along slowly, moving forward as the requirements of our work permitted. Around noon, Sam's prediction came true. It rained, and did so in a way that occurs only in these latitudes, on those few occasions when it does rain. It was as if an ocean fell from the sky.

In the middle of this downpour, Sam, Dick, and Will returned. We didn't see them until they were perhaps twelve or fifteen paces away, so thick was the rain. They had found a suitable spot. Parker and Stone were to show us the way there; Hawkens stopped only long enough to pick up a few provisions, then he was off on his spying mission, in spite of the storm. He went on foot—that way, he could hide better than if he had his mule with him. As he disappeared behind the thick curtain of rain, I had the sense that a catastrophe was rapidly heading our way.

As unusual as the downpour was—it was like a cloudburst—it

ceased just as quickly. The floodgates of the heavens suddenly closed, and then the sun appeared, shining just as hot as the day before. We had stopped work during the rain, and now we resumed it.

We found ourselves on a flat savannah, not too large and bounded on three sides by forest. A clump of bushes interrupted the grass here and there. It was very favorable terrain for surveying, and we made good progress. As we moved along, I noticed that Sam Hawkens had been right about the effect of the rain. The Kiowas must have ridden right through the area where we were working, but no trace of their horses' hoof prints was visible. If the Apaches followed us, they would never be able to tell that we had two hundred reinforcements in the area.

As it began to get dark and we had to stop working, Stone and Parker told us that we were close to the spot that had been picked out for the battle. I would have liked to go and take a look, but it was too dark.

The next morning, we resumed our work and it didn't take us long to reach a stream which formed a large bowl-shaped pool. This basin looked as if it would normally have standing water, whereas the bed of the stream would be half dry much of the time. At that moment, both basin and stream were full to their banks as a result of the previous day's rain. The pool was fringed on the right and left by trees and bushes. A tongue of the savannah led up to it, and at that spot there was a large peninsula. It was narrow where it connected to the shore, but got wider farther out, becoming almost circular. It looked a bit like a frying pan, connected to the land by its handle. On the other side of the pool lay thickly wooded rising ground.

"This is the spot Sam picked out for us," said Stone, looking around with a practiced eye. "For our purposes, you couldn't find a better one."

This, of course, caused me to take a harder look around.

"Where are the Kiowas, Mr. Stone?" I asked.

"Hidden, well hidden," he answered. "As hard as you might try, you'll find no sign of them, although they can see us very well and can observe everything we do."

"So where are they?"

"Wait a moment, Sir! First, I have to explain why Sam, the clever one, chose this place. There are clumps of bushes scattered over the savannah where we've just come. That will make it easy for the Apache scouts to follow us unnoticed, because they can use the bushes for cover. See the open area of grass near the peninsula? We can have our campfire there and it will be visible well out into the savannah, and that will draw the Apaches to us. They'll be able to approach us because they'll have the protection of the bushes and trees that surround the open area. I tell you, Sir, we couldn't find a better place to be attacked by Indians!"

His long, haggard, weather-beaten face gleamed with absolute satisfaction as he said this. The engineer, who was listening, had a different opinion. He said, shaking his head:

"What kind of man are you, Mr. Stone? How can you get excited about being in a prime spot to be attacked? Not me. I'm planning to hightail it out of here."

"So that you can be all the more certain of capture by the Apaches? Forget that idea, Mr. Bancroft. Of course I'm enthusiastic about this spot. If it makes it easier for the Apaches to catch us, then it will be still easier for us to catch them later. Take a look at that hillside on the far side of the water. That's where the Kiowas are hiding. They've got scouts among the top branches of those trees and have certainly seen us coming. They'll see the Apaches coming too. You get a great view of the savannah from up there."

"But what good will it do us to have the Kiowas up there, on the other side of the stream, when we're attacked?" asked the engineer.

"They are only waiting there for the time being, so they can't be spotted by the Apache scouts. As soon as the scouts leave, the Kiowas will come down and join us. They'll hide on the peninsula, where they won't be seen."

"Couldn't the Apache scouts investigate the peninsula?"

"They could, but we won't let them."

"Then we'd have to chase them away. But we're not supposed to even know they are around. How is that supposed to work, Mr. Stone?"

"Very easy. Of course we can't actually look for them, and therefore can't prevent them directly from exploring the peninsula. But it's only thirty paces across where it connects to the land, and we can block that area with our horses."

"How do we do that?"

"We'll tie our horses there. The Indians know that, if they come too close, the horses would alert us by their snorting and whinnying. So we can let the spies come and look around. They won't come onto the peninsula. When they leave, to bring their warriors, the Kiowas will come down and hide on the peninsula. Then the Apaches will sneak up and wait for us to go to sleep."

"What if they don't wait that long?" I asked. "Then we won't have a chance to pull back."

"That isn't much of a danger," he replied. "The Kiowas would be right there to help us."

"But blood would surely be shed, and that's exactly what we're trying to avoid."

"Sir, in the West nobody gets too upset about a few drops of blood. But don't worry. For exactly that reason, the Apaches will not attack while we're still awake. They know we'll defend ourselves, and even if there are only twenty of us, they know they'd lose a few of their own before they could overpower us. No, they value their lives just as highly as we do ours. That's why they'll wait until they think we're asleep. We'll let the fire go out and then we'll retreat to the peninsula."

"And what do we do in the meantime? Can we continue working?"

"Yes, as long as you're here when the time comes."

"OK, let's not lose any time. Come on, fellows, let's see what we can get done!"

Chapter 15

They followed my request, although they clearly didn't feel like working. I'm convinced that they would all have just left, but then the work would never have gotten finished and, according to the contract, they wouldn't get paid. They weren't ready to give that up. And if they had taken off, the Apaches would have immediately been on their trail. No, they recognized that they were actually safer if they stayed, and so they did.

For my part, I honestly must confess that I was certainly not indifferent to the events that lay ahead. I was experiencing a condition that is sometimes called "canon fever." It wasn't really fear—if I was going to be afraid, I had had plenty of opportunities for that when I killed the buffalo and the bear. But now it was people we were dealing with, and that unsettled me. I wasn't so worried about my own life. I knew I could defend myself. But Inchu-chuna and Winnetou! I had thought so much about Winnetou during the preceding days that he seemed closer than ever to me. He had become precious to me, although we hadn't had a chance to become friends or even to observe each other. It was certainly an odd turn of the mind; perhaps you could even call it a psychological puzzle. And what is even stranger: I later learned from Winnetou that he had been thinking just as often of me during this period!

Working didn't calm my inner unrest, but I was certain that it would disappear at the moment of decision. Since that moment was now unavoidable, I longed for it to arrive quickly. That wish came true soon enough. Around noon, we saw Sam Hawkens approaching. The little man was obviously tired, but his eyes were gleaming even brighter than usual from behind his dark beard.

"Everything went OK?" I asked. "The way you look, Sam, I'd guess it did."

"Really?" he laughed. "It's that obvious? Is it written on my forehead, or are you just imagining it?"

"Imagining? Pshaw! No one who saw your eyes could have any

doubt."

"Oh, so my eyes betray me. I'll make a note of that for future reference. But you're right. I succeeded—much better than I could even have hoped."

"Did you see the scouts?"

"The scouts? More, much more. Not just the scouts, but the whole war party. And I didn't just see them, I heard them. Snuck right up on them."

"You heard them? Quick, what did you learn?"

"Not just yet. Gather your instruments and bring them back to camp. I'll be right there. First, I have to make a quick visit to the Kiowas to tell them what I learned and what they need to do."

He strode to the stream above the pool, jumped over it, and disappeared into the woods on the other side. We packed up our various bits and pieces and made our way back to camp, where we waited for Sam's arrival. We didn't see or hear him coming, but suddenly there he was in our midst. He said, in a theatrical high-spirited voice:

"Well, here I am, my lords! Have you no eyes or ears? You could get trampled by an elephant that a normal person would hear a quarter mile away!"

"Well, you didn't exactly arrive like an elephant," I answered.

"Could be. I just wanted to demonstrate how to go about sneaking up on someone without them noticing. You were just sitting there and not talking. But you still didn't hear me when I sneaked up. That's exactly how it was yesterday when I crept up on the Apaches."

"Come on, tell us about it!"

"OK, I'll tell you in a moment. First, I need to sit down. I'm pretty tired. My legs are used to riding, and they're no good for walking anymore. And it's nobler to serve in the cavalry than the infantry, if I'm not mistaken."

He sat down near me, blinked at us, one after the other, and then said, nodding his head for emphasis:

"Well, tonight's the night!"

"Tonight? That soon?" I asked, half surprised and half excited, since I was anxious to be done with the waiting. "That's good, that's very good!"

"Hmm. You seem to be pretty keen on falling into the Apaches' hands! But you're right. It is good, and I'm also glad that we don't need to wait any longer. It's no fun, waiting for something to happen that could have an unexpected outcome."

"Unexpected? Has something come up that has you worried?"

"Absolutely not. Quite the opposite! Only now am I beginning to be convinced that everything will work out well. But a wise man knows that sometimes the most promising child grows up to be the worst kind of rascal. That's the way it is with incidents too. Some chance event can send the best of plans off down the wrong path."

"So what did you learn? Tell!"

"Easy now, my young Sir! Everything in sequence. I can't tell you what I heard until you hear what happened before that. I left in the middle of the downpour. I didn't have to wait for it to end, since even the heaviest rain can't make it through this jacket of mine, hee-hee-hee! I had almost reached our old campsite, where the two Apaches visited us, but then I had to hide because I saw three Indians nosing around. Those will be the Apache scouts, I thought to myself, and they're hanging around here because they've been told not to go any farther. And that's how it was. They looked around the area, without noticing my tracks, and then they sat down under the trees since it was too wet to sit out in the open. They sat waiting close to two hours. I waited the same two hours under another tree, watching. I wanted to know what would happen next. Then a group of riders in war paint arrived. I recognized them right away: Inchu-chuna and Winnetou with their Apaches."

"How many were there?"

"It was just like I thought. I counted about fifty of them. The scouts came out from the trees and made a report to the chiefs. Then they scouts headed out again and the rest followed slowly behind. As you might imagine, gentlemen, Sam Hawkens followed right along behind them. The rain had washed away all the normal tracks, but your surveying stakes were still there and they served as unmistakable guideposts. I wish someday I would get a chance to follow tracks that were marked as well as that! But they had to be very cautious, the Apaches, because they knew they could come upon us around any bend in the woods or behind any clump of bushes. So they moved slowly. They did it very cleverly and cautiously. It was a joy to watch. It reinforced the opinion I've long held, that the Apaches are a notch above all the other red nations. Inchu-chuna is a clever fellow, and Winnetou is just as smart. Every move they made, even the smallest, was for a reason. No one said a word. They communicated with signs. Two miles from the place where I first saw them, it began to get dark. They dismounted, hobbled their horses, and disappeared into the woods, where they spent the night."

"And that's where you overheard them?" I asked.

"Yes. They were smart enough not to light a fire, and since Sam Hawkens is just as smart, I figured they'd have a tough time seeing me. So I followed them into the woods and crawled along on my belly until I was close enough to hear everything they said."

"Could you understand everything they said?"

"Stupid question! If they said it, I heard it."

"I mean, did they use broken English?"

"They used the dialect of the Mescaleros, which I happen to know pretty well. I crawled further and further until I was near the two chiefs. They talked briefly from time to time. You know how Indians are: they don't say much, but every word is important. I learned enough to know what they're up to."

"So what did you hear? Spit it out, then!" I urged him, since he had fallen silent.

"Spit it out? Better step to one side, Sir, if you don't want to be in my line of fire! They've got their eye on us. They really want to take us alive."

"They don't want to kill us?"

"Oh, yes. They want to kill us, a bit at a time, but not right away. First they want to capture us without hurting us, then take us to their villages on the Rio Pecos where they plan to tie us to stakes and stew us alive. Just like a fish you might catch and take home in a pail, then serve boiled with a plate full of vegetables. I wonder what sort of a dish old Sam would make, especially if they throw me whole into the frying pan, leather jacket and all, hee-hee-hee!"

He laughed to himself in his quiet, secretive way and then continued:

"Really, it's Mr. Rattler that they've got their eye on; him that's sitting so quiet and cheerful over there, watching me as if heaven with all its blessings were just waiting for him to arrive. Yes, Mr. Rattler, you've landed in a pretty pot of soup, and I wouldn't want to be the one that had to ladle it out. You'll be speared, staked, poisoned, stabbed, shot, strung on the wheel, and hanged, one right after the next, and only a little of each. They'll keep you alive as long as possible so you get a proper taste of every form of suffering and death. And if you're still alive at the end of it, they'll put you in the grave of Kleki-petra, the man you shot, and bury you alive with him."

"Oh, Lord! Did they say that?" asked Rattler, whose face had gone pale.

"Certainly they said that. And you earned it, too. There's no helping that. I only hope that after you have all that torture behind you, you never think of doing such a dastardly act again. Come to think of it, I imagine you'll probably pass up the chance. The body of Kleki-petra has been given to a medicine man who is taking it back to his home. You know these southern Indians—they understand how to preserve the bodies of their dead. I myself have seen Indian mummies that look so fresh after a hundred years, you'd think they were alive yesterday. If we all get caught, they'll entertain us by showing us how they can turn Mr. Rattler into a mummy like that before he's even dead."

"I'm getting out of here!" cried Rattler. "I'm leaving right now! They're not going to get hold of me!"

He tried to jump to his feet, but Sam pulled him back down and warned him:

"Don't budge from this camp, if you value your life! I'm telling you, the Apaches have probably staked out the whole area around here already. You'd be walking right into their hands."

"Do you really think so, Sam?" I asked.

"Yes. It's not an empty threat. I have every reason to believe it. I was also right about another thing. The Apaches really have sent warriors on the warpath against the Kiowas, a whole army that the two chiefs plan to join as soon as they are finished here. That's the only reason they got back here so quickly. They didn't have to ride all the way back to their villages to recruit warriors. They met up with the war party heading for the Kiowas, gave Kleki-petra's body to the medicine man and a few others to take home, and came back here with fifty good riders to find us."

"Where are the troops that are supposed to attack the Kiowas?"

"I don't know. They didn't say a word about it. And it makes no difference to us anyway."

But Sam was wrong about that. It did make a difference where the other warriors were, as we would discover a few days later. Sam continued:

"Once I had heard enough, I could have just left. But it's hard to cover your tracks in the dark, and they would have noticed them in the morning. And besides, I wanted to observe them in the morning. So I stayed hidden in the woods all night, and I only came out after they had left. I followed them to a spot about six miles from here, and then I made a detour to get here without being noticed. Well, there you have it. That's all I have to say."

"So they never saw you?"

"No."

"And you made sure they won't find your tracks?"

"Yes."

"But you said before you wanted them to see you."

"I know, I know. I would have, too, but it wasn't necessary, because. . . . Wait! Did you hear that?"

He had been interrupted by three cries of an eagle.

"That's the Kiowa scouts," he said. "They're sitting up there in the trees. I told them to give this sign when they spotted the Apaches out there in the savannah. Come, Sir. Let's find out how good their eyes really are."

This invitation was directed at me. He stood up to go, and I picked up my gun to follow him.

"Hold on!" he said. "Leave that gun here. A frontiersman should never part company with his weapon, it's true, but this is the exception to that rule. We have to pretend that we don't suspect any danger at all. We'll make it look like we're just gathering firewood. That will convince the Apaches that we're camping here this evening."

We strolled together, looking as innocent as we could, among the trees and bushes and out onto the open savannah. We collected branches from the edges of clumps of bushes while secretly keeping an eye out for Apaches. If they were in the neighborhood, they would have to be hiding behind the bushes that were scattered across the savannah, some close to us and some farther away.

"See any?" I asked Sam after a while.

"No," he answered.

"Me neither."

We looked as hard as we could, but discovered nothing. And yet I later learned from Winnetou himself that he had observed us from behind a bush no more than fifty paces away. It's not enough to have sharp eyes. They also have to be experienced eyes, and mine, at least, were not yet experienced. Today, I would find Winnetou instantly, even if only by the fact that the mosquitoes would be thicker where he was hiding, drawn there by his body.

We thus returned to the others, not having accomplished anything, and all of us now busied ourselves gathering wood for the campfire. We gathered more than we actually needed.

"We'll need the extra," said Sam. "We have to leave a pile for the Apaches. When they try to capture us and find that we've disappeared, they'll need to be able to get a fire going quickly."

In the meantime, it was getting dark. Sam, the most experienced among us, positioned himself at the front, out where the strip of grass we were camped on joined up with the savannah. We were sure that Apache spies would be sent out to investigate our camp, and Sam wanted to spot them when they came. The fire was lit, and it illuminated our strip of grass and far out into the savannah. What careless and inexperienced people the Apaches must have thought us! The fire was a perfect beacon for leading enemies to us.

We ate supper and lay down as if we had were completely unsuspecting. We left our guns at a distance from us, but in the direction of the peninsula, so that we could collect them later. The peninsula itself was, as Sam had suggested, blocked by our horses.

Three hours after darkness had set in, Sam appeared silently. He reported, in a quiet voice:

"The spies have come, two of them, one on this side and one on the other side. I heard them and even saw them."

So they were observing us from the bushes on either side of the grassy strip. Sam sat down with us and began conversing in a loud voice about anything that occurred to him. We answered, and thus a lively conversation ensued, designed to reassure the spies. We knew they were there and were watching us closely, but we avoided even a single suspicious glance into the bushes.

Now the critical thing was to find out when they left. We wouldn't be able to hear or see them, and yet we couldn't waste a moment once they'd left, for it was likely that the rest of the warriors would soon sneak up, and we had to get all the Kiowas onto the peninsula in the meantime. So it seemed best not to wait for them to leave, but to force them to. With that in mind, Sam stood up and pretended to go and gather firewood in the bushes on one side, and I did the same thing on the other side. Now, we could be sure that the spies had left. Sam put his hands to his mouth and made three bull-frog calls, to let the Kiowas know they should come. Since we were next to the water, the bull-frog sounds would not be out of the ordinary. Then Sam sneaked back to his lookout post near the savannah, so that he could alert us to the approach of the enemy warriors.

No more than two minutes after the frog-call, the Kiowas slid up silently, one right behind the next, a long string of two hundred warriors. They hadn't waited in the woods, but had come down near the stream so that they could respond more quickly to Sam's signal.

They slipped like snakes in the shadows along the ground and out to the peninsula. It all happened so skillfully and quickly that the last one had passed by us in three minutes at the most.

We now waited for Sam. He soon came and whispered quietly to us:

"I heard them coming, on both sides. Don't put any more wood on the fire! And after the fire dies out, we'll have to make sure that enough coals remain for the Apaches to relight it quickly."

We piled up some of the extra wood around the fire so that the last coals would not throw off any light and disclose our departure prematurely. After that, each of us had to become an actor. We knew there were fifty Apaches close by, but we couldn't pay any attention to that. Everything, even our very lives, depended on what happened next. We assumed that they would wait until we seemed to be asleep, but what would happen if they didn't, if they attacked right away? We did have two hundred Kiowas to help us out, but it would be a bloody battle, and that could cost some of us our lives. Catastrophe hung in the balance. And what I knew would occur did in fact occur: I was calm, as calm as if we were playing a game of chess or dominos. It was very interesting to observe the others. Rattler was stretched out on the ground. He was lying on his stomach and pretending to sleep. The fear of death had him in its icy grip. His "famous frontiersmen" looked at each other with pale faces. They could only manage an occasional word, although they were supposed to participate in our conversation. Will Parker and Dick Stone sat there as cheerfully as if there were no Apaches in the whole world. Sam Hawkens made one joke after another, and I laughed as heartily as possible at his stories.

After half an hour of this, we were convinced that the attack wasn't supposed to occur until we were asleep—otherwise, it would have long since begun. The fire was burning low, and it seemed prudent to me not to put things off any longer. So I yawned a couple of times, stretched and said:

"I'm tired. I'm ready to hit the sack. How about you, Sam Hawkens?"

"Sounds good to me. I'll do the same," he answered. "The fire's going out. Good night!"

"Good night," said Stone and Parker as well. Then we positioned ourselves well away from the fire—but not so far as to be obvious—and stretched out on the ground.

Chapter 16

The flame got lower and lower, until they finally went out. Only the ashes were still glowing, but their light was blocked by the stacked wood and didn't reach us. We lay in total darkness. Now we had to retreat to safety, but quietly, very quietly. I reached for my gun and slowly crept forward. Sam came alongside, and the others followed. Once I got to the horses, I pulled one of them back and forth, making it stamp its hooves. That would mask any noise that one of our group might happen to make. Soon, we had all joined the Kiowas, who were like panthers lying in wait, ready for a fight.

"Sam," I whispered to him, "if the two chiefs are really to be spared, we can't let the Kiowas take them on. Do you agree?"

"Yes."

"I'll take Winnetou myself. You, Stone, and Parker take Inchuchuna."

"You take one by yourself, and we three only get one? There's something wrong with your arithmetic, if I'm not mistaken."

"No, it makes sense. I'll deal with Winnetou quickly, but it will take the three of you to make sure his father doesn't get a chance to fight. If he gets enough time and enough room to defend himself, he could get injured or even killed."

"OK, you're right. But if we want to make sure no Kiowas get there ahead of us, we'd better get out front a bit. That way we can get there first. Come on!"

We inched a few paces toward the fire and waited anxiously for the war cry of the Apaches. They never attack without it. The leader gives a cry as the signal to attack, and the others echo the cry in as ferocious a manner as possible. This howling serves to unnerve the victims so that they lose the courage to fight back. You can get a sense of how the cry of most tribes sounds if you give a long "Hiiiii!" at a high pitch while clapping your hand rapidly against your mouth, giving the cry a kind of trilling sound.

The Kiowas were just as tense as we were. Each of them wanted to be first, and so they inched their way forward, pushing us in front of them. This could become dangerous if we got too close to the Apaches, so I hoped that the attack would come quickly.

Finally, I got my wish. We heard the expected "Hiiii!" in such a shrill, penetrating tone that it went through us to the marrow. It was followed by a terrible howling like the cry of a thousand devils. In spite of the softness of the ground, we could hear quick steps and leaps. Then, suddenly, everything was still. For a few seconds, nothing happened. You could have heard, as they say, a pin drop. Then, we heard Inch-chuna cry out the word "Ko!"

This word means "fire." The coals of our fire were still glowing, and the dry wood and twigs that lay nearby burned easily. The Apaches obeyed the command and quickly threw wood on the glowing coals. In just a few seconds, the flames sprang up again, illuminating the area around the fire.

Inchu-chuna and Winnetou stood next to each other, and soon a circle of warriors formed around them as the Apaches saw, to their astonishment, that we were gone.

"Ugh, ugh, ugh!" they cried, bewildered.

Then Winnetou showed, despite his youth, the prudence that would so often impress me in later years. He realized that we must still be nearby, and that the Apaches were at a disadvantage by remaining in the firelight, where they were easy targets for us. He cried out:

"Tatisha, tatisha!"

This word means "get away." He was on the verge of springing into the bushes, but I got to him first. Four or five quick steps had gotten me as far as the circle of warriors around him. I threw aside Apaches to the left and right, fighting my way through with Hawkens Stone and Parker right behind. Just after his cry of "tatisha," as he turned for cover, he stood before me and we looked each other in the face for a moment. Then, he made a lightning grab for the knife in his belt, but I was even faster with a blow to his chin. He swayed and fell to the ground. At the same moment, I saw Sam, Will, and Dick taking on his father.

The Apaches howled with rage, but their howl could not be heard over the awful bellowing of the Kiowas, who were now throwing themselves on the Apaches.

Since I had broken through the circle of the Apaches, I was in the middle of the fighting and tangle of men struggling with each other. Two hundred Kiowas against perhaps fifty Apaches—four to one! But Winnetou's brave warriors put up a terrific fight. I now had to call on all my skill to keep several of them off of me. And because I was right in the middle of them, I had to spin like a top in a circle. I used only my fists, because I didn't want to kill or even seriously wound anyone. Once I had knocked out four or five more, I began to get a little more room, and at the same time, the overall level of resistance began to fall off. Within five minutes after it had started, our battle was at an end. Just five minutes! But in that situation, it felt like a very long time.

Chief Inchu-chuna lay bound on the ground. Next to him was Winnetou, out cold. We tied him up too. Not a single Apache got away, probably because it wouldn't occur to these brave people to abandon their two chiefs and flee. Many of them were wounded, as were many of the Kiowas. Unfortunately, three of the Kiowas and five of the Apaches had been killed. That certainly hadn't been our intention, but the ferocious resistance of the Apaches had given the Kiowas reason to use their weapons more aggressively than we would have liked.

All the captured Apaches were tied up. That wasn't much of a feat, given that we had about four men (or if you include the whites, almost five) for every one of them. It only took three Kiowas to hold an Apache while a fourth quickly tied him up.

The bodies were carried off to the side. The wounded Kiowas were tended to by their own people, so we whites checked and bandaged the wounded Apaches. As we did so, we not only got defiant looks, but actual resistance. They were too proud to let themselves be tended by an enemy, and would rather let their wounds bleed. But I didn't worry too much about that, since their wounds were generally superficial.

Once this work was finished, we began to think about how the prisoners should spend the night. I wanted to make it as easy as possible for them, but Tangua, the Chief of the Kiowas, intervened:

"These dogs don't belong to you, but to us, and I alone decide what will happen to them."

"What is your decision?" I asked.

"We will keep them until we have them back in our villages. But we want to attack their people, and their villages are far, so we will not keep them long. They will die at the stake."

"All of them?"

"All!"

"I don't believe that."

"Why not?"

"Because you have already made an error."

"When?"

"When you said that the Apaches belong to you. That is not true."

"It is true!"

"No. According to the law of the West, a prisoner belongs to the person who has captured him. You can keep the Apaches that you captured and I will say nothing against it. But those that we captured are ours."

"Ugh, ugh! You speak with such cleverness. You want to keep Inchu-chuna and Winnetou?"

"Of course."

"And if I do not let you have them?"

"You will let us have them."

He spoke with a menacing tone. I answered him calmly and with certainty. Then he drew his knife, thrust it into the ground as far as the hilt, and said, eyeing me threateningly:

"If you touch even a single Apache with one hand, your flesh will be like this spot my knife is sticking in. I have spoken. How!"

He was clearly in earnest. But I still would have shown him my distaste for being intimidated if Sam hadn't been wise enough to give me a warning glance, which persuaded me to choose caution and silence. I decided not to say anything.

The tied-up Apaches lay all around the fire, and it would have been easiest to just leave them there, where they could be guarded without difficulty. But Tangua wanted to show me that he regarded them as his property and could deal with them as he liked. So he gave the order to tie them upright to nearby trees.

This was done, and done in a very rough manner, as you can imagine. The Kiowas were merciless and tried to make the process as painful as possible. None of the Apaches changed their expression in the slightest. They had been brought up and trained to endure all kinds of suffering. The Kiowas were roughest with the two chiefs, whose limbs were tied so tightly that blood oozed from the swollen flesh.

It was completely impossible that any of the prisoners could have escaped by his own efforts, but even so Tangua posted guards all around the camp.

As I have mentioned, our campfire (now burning once again) was situated at one end of a strip of grass leading down to the water. We lay down around it. We planned not to let any of the Kiowas near us, since that would make it difficult or impossible to set Winnetou and his father free. But they had no intention of staying close to us in any case. From the time they arrived, they had not been friendly to us, and my latest exchange with their chief had not improved our relations. The cold, almost contemptuous glances that they gave us were not reassuring. We began to think we could count ourselves lucky if we were able to part company with the Kiowas without coming to blows.

They lit several other fires farther out toward the savannah, and camped around them. There, they spoke among themselves in their own language, not the broken English used between white men and Indians. We were obviously not supposed to hear what they were saying, which had to be viewed as an unhealthy sign. They considered themselves to be in charge, and their behavior was like that of a lion that tolerates a puppy in the vicinity.

Only four people—Hawkens, Parker, Stone, and I—could be permitted to know of our plan, which made it harder to carry out. We couldn't let the others in on the secret, since they would probably oppose the plan and try to prevent it. They might even tell the Kiowas what we were up to. They had settled down with us, and we had to hope that eventually they would all go to sleep. Because of this, and because carrying out our plan might well eliminate any later sleeping opportunity, Sam suggested it would be wise for us to try to get in a bit of sleep right away. So we lay down, and I was fortunate enough to go to sleep promptly, in spite of my state of agitation. Sam woke me later on. At that time, I had not yet mastered the art of telling time by the position of the stars, but it was probably soon after midnight. Our comrades were asleep and our fire had burned out. The Kiowas had maintained one fire, but had let the others go out. We were able to talk, although only softly. Parker and Stone were awake too. Sam whispered to me:

"First and foremost, we have to decide who's going. Two are enough."

"I'll be one of them, of course!" I answered confidently.

"Oh ho! Not so fast, my good Sir. This involves risking your life."

"I know."

"You're willing to risk your life?"

"Yes."

"Well, I'll be! You're a brave fellow, if I'm not mistaken. But we have to take another danger into account, not just the danger of losing our own lives."

"What danger do you mean?"

"The success of our plan depends on the people who carry it

out."

"That's right."

"I'm glad you agree. So I imagine you'll also agree to let others carry it out."

"Not a chance!"

"Be sensible, Sir! Let Dick Stone and me go."

"No!"

"You're still too new at this. You know next to nothing about sneaking up on people."

"Possibly. But tonight I'll prove to you that you can sometimes do something you don't completely understand, as long as you really want to do it."

"You also need skill, Sir, skill! You just don't have it. You have to be born with a knack for it, and then develop it through practice. And you haven't had any practice."

"A test would show whether that's true or not."

"You want to be tested?"

"Yes."

"What kind of test did you have in mind?"

"How about this: Do you know whether Chief Tangua is asleep?"

"No."

"But that would be important for us to know. Right, Sam?"

"Right. In a bit, I'll slip over there and find out."

"No. I'll do it."

"You? Why?"

"That will be my test."

"I see! And what if you're caught?"

"No harm done—I've thought of a good excuse. I'll say I just wanted to make sure the guards were doing their job."

"Well, that should work. But what's the point of this test?"

"I want to show you what I can do. If I can manage this, I think you'll be willing to take me along when you go to set Winnetou free."

"Hmm. We'll discuss that afterwards."

"That's fine with me. So, can I go spy on the chief?"

"Yes. But take care! If they find you sneaking around, they'll get suspicious. Maybe not right now, but later, after Winnetou disappears. They'll think you set him free."

"And they won't be far off the mark."

"Use every tree and bush for cover, and avoid any spots where there's light from the fire. Never leave the dark!"

"I'll stay in the dark, Sam."

"I sure hope so. There are still at least thirty Kiowas awake, if I'm not mistaken, plus the guards. If you can get through without being spotted, I'll be impressed. Why, I might even consider it possible that someday—maybe in ten years or so—I'll actually be able to make a decent frontiersman out of you, even though you're still as green a greenhorn as you could ever find, in spite of all my good teaching, hee-hee-hee!"

I stuck my knife and my revolver in my belt as far as possible, so as not to lose them along the way, and crept away from the fire. Now, looking back, I recognize how much responsibility I took on so blithely. It was the audacity of the plan that I had hatched. For I actually wasn't planning to spy on the chief at all!

I was very taken with Winnetou, and I wanted to prove to him how much I admired him, if possible by risking my life for him. Here was the perfect opportunity for that: I could set him free. But I wanted to do it by myself! And then along came Sam with his second thoughts. He wanted to take Dick Stone along and do exactly what I longed to do. Even if I succeeded in spying on Chief Tangua, I was pretty sure Sam would still have his misgivings. So I decided not to pester him or trouble myself by trying to convince him. No, I wasn't going to spy on Tangua, I was going find Winnetou!

But I wasn't just risking my own life, but also those of my companions. If I were caught while carrying out my plan, it would be over for them as well as for me. I knew this even then, but in my youthful enthusiasm, I paid little heed to it.

I had often read about sneaking up on people, and had often heard about it since arriving in the West. Sam in particular had often talked to me about it and shown me how to do it. I had imitated his examples. But nothing I had done had given me anything like the level of skill that I would need for this task. But that didn't stop me from being perfectly confident that I would achieve my objective.

I lay down in the grass and worked my way forward into the bushes. It was roughly fifty paces from our camp to the area where Inchu-chuna and Winnetou were each tied to a tree. I ought to have slid forward with only my fingertips and the toes of my boots touching the ground, but for that I would have needed more strength and endurance in the fingers and toes than I then possessed. Developing that kind of strength requires years of practice. So instead, I crawled along on my knees and forearms like a four-legged animal. Before I put my hand down in a new spot, I felt to see if there was a dry twig there that might break under my weight and make a noise. If I had to pass under or between branches, I carefully wove them together to create an opening that I could pass through. It was slow work, very slow, but I gradually moved forwards.

The Apaches had been tied to trees on either side of the strip of grass. The two chiefs were on the left-hand side (coming from our camp). Their trees were on the edge of the strip and four or five paces in front of them, an Indian sat facing them. Because of their importance, he had been given the task of guarding just the two of them. This was certain to make my task harder, maybe even impossible, but I had thought of a way to divert his attention, at least briefly. I needed a few stones, but there didn't seem to be any around.

I had covered perhaps half the distance to Winnetou, taking perhaps half an hour in the process. Think of it—twenty-five paces in half an hour! I noticed something bright a few feet off to one side. I crept over and found, to my delight, a small depression filled with sand, perhaps three yards in diameter. At some point, the rain must have caused the stream and the basin to overflow, depositing sand at this spot. I quickly filled a pocket with it and continued to creep forward.

After another half hour, I finally found myself behind Winnetou and his father, perhaps four paces away. The trees they were tied to weren't quite big enough to hide a person. I wouldn't have been able to get closer to them if it hadn't been for some low, leafy bushes that fortunately stood at the foot of the trees. These appeared to be sufficient to hide me from the guard. I should mention that I had noticed a clump of briars several paces behind and to one side of the guard.

First, I slipped up behind Winnetou and lay still for a few minutes, observing the guard. He seemed tired. He mostly kept his eyes closed, opening them from time to time with an apparent effort. I took that as a good sign.

Next, I had to determine how Winnetou was tied. I cautiously reached around the trunk and touched his foot and calf. Of course he must have felt this, and I was concerned that he might make a movement that would give me away. But that didn't happen. He was too clever and had too much presence of mind to do that. I found that his feet were bound at the ankles, and that an additional cord passed around them and the tree. So two cuts would be necessary.

Then I looked upwards. By the flickering firelight, I could tell that his arms had been put around either side of the tree and his wrists had been tied together behind it. That would require only one cut.

Now something occurred to me that I hadn't thought of before. When I cut Winnetou loose, I could probably expect that he would instantly flee. That would put me in great danger. I tried to think of ways of avoiding this, but couldn't come up with any. I just had to risk it. If the Apache took off, I'd have to do the same.

How mistaken I was about Winnetou! I really didn't know him. When we spoke about his escape later, he shared the thoughts he'd had at the time. When he felt my hand on his foot, he thought it was an Apache. He knew that all the men that had come with him were captured, but it was possible that a scout or a messenger had been sent out from the larger war party, perhaps bringing news. He was immediately confident that he would escape, and he was waiting for his bonds to be cut. But he would most certainly not have changed his position. He would not leave without his father, and he didn't want to put the man that freed him in danger by immediately taking flight.

I cut through the two lower cords. I couldn't reach the upper one from my lying position. And even if I could have reached it, I still had to be careful not to cut Winnetou's hands. I would have to stand up, but if I did, the guard would surely see me. I had brought the sand to distract him. Small stones would have been better. I reached into my pocket, got a small amount of sand, and threw it past Winnetou and the guard into the briars. This caused a rustling noise. The Indian turned and looked at the bush, but soon settled down again. A second handful roused his curiosity. Perhaps a poisonous snake was hidden in the bush. He stood up, went over, and looked closely at the bush. Immediately, I was up and cutting through the leather thong. As I cut it, Winnetou's long hair, which was gathered at the back of his head, fell in my face. Grabbing a few strands in my left hand, I cut them with my right and dropped silently back down to the ground.

Why did I do that? To have proof, if I ever needed it, that it was I who had freed him.

To my delight, Winnetou did not make the slightest movement. He stood there exactly as before. I wrapped the hair around my finger and stuck the circle of hair in my pocket. Then I crept over to Inchu-chuna and checked his bonds in the same way. He had been tied just as Winnetou had, and he stayed just as still when he felt the touch of my hand. I cut his feet loose first. Once again, I was able to distract the guard in the same way, and that allowed me to free his hands as well. He was just as careful as his son and didn't move a muscle.

Then it occurred to me that it would be better not to leave the leather thongs lying on the ground where they had fallen. The Kiowas didn't need to know how their prisoners had been freed. If they found the thongs, they would see that they had been cut and suspicion would fall on us. So first I collected the cut bits near Inchu-chuna, then snuck back over to Winnetou and did the same. I put them in my pocket and then made my way back to our camp.

If the chiefs disappeared, the guard would immediately sound the alarm, and then it would be unfortunate if I were still in the area. I had to move quickly. So I crept farther back into the bushes until I was far enough away that I couldn't be seen if I stood up. Then I slipped back to our camp, still very carefully, but much more quickly than before. Only as I approached camp did I once again drop down to the ground to finish the trip on my hands and knees.

Chapter 17

My three companions had been very concerned about me.

Once I was back and lying down with them, Sam whispered:

"We were really getting worried, Sir! Do you know how long you've been gone?"

"How long?"

"Almost two hours."

"Right: half an hour to get there, an hour there, and half an hour back."

"Why did you have to stay there so long?"

"I wanted to know for sure that the chief was asleep."

"And just how did you do that?"

"I watched him for a long time, and he didn't move, so I gradually became convinced that he was asleep."

"Oh, very good! Did you hear that, Dick and Will? He stares at the chief for an hour to tell if he's awake or asleep, hee-hee-hee! What a greenhorn, an incurable greenhorn! You couldn't think of anything better than that? Don't you have a single brain cell in that head of yours? You probably could have picked up a little stick or piece of bark along the way, right?"

"Sure," I answered, realizing that he was once again speaking to me.

"Well, all you had to do was get close enough to toss a little stick or dirt in his direction. If he were awake, he'd have moved instantly. But all tossed were glances, if I'm not mistaken, one glance after another for a whole hour, hee-hee-hee!"

"Could be. But I did pass my test!"

As I spoke, I looked over at the two Apaches, who were just visible from our camp. I couldn't believe they were still standing there as if they were still tied. They could have been long gone. I later learned the reason. Winnetou had assumed that I had freed him first and had then gone to free his father, and he waited for a sign from me that both were free. Inchu-chuna thought I was still occupied with freeing Winnetou. When no sign from me was forthcoming, Winnetou waited for the guard to close his tired eyes, then moved his arm to signal his father that he was no longer tied. His father responded with the same sign. Then they knew what the situation was and slipped silently away.

"Yes, you passed your test," Sam Hawkens admitted. "You watched the chief for a whole hour without being caught."

"That means you can trust me to get close to Winnetou without doing anything dumb."

"Hmm. What do you think, that you can free the two chiefs by staring at them for an hour?"

"No. We'll cut them free."

"You say that as if it was as easy as cutting a twig off a bush. You see that guard sitting in front of them?"

"I certainly do."

"He's doing what you were doing: he's staring at them. To cut them free while he's guarding them, that's something you're not ready for yet. Why, I don't even know if I could manage it. Just look over there, Sir. Just managing to sneak over there undetected would take a real master. And if you did manage to get close to them, then good luck setting them free. Wait, what's that?"

He had looked over toward the two Apaches, and, not seeing them there, he stopped in the middle of what he was saying. I pretended not to have noticed, and asked:

"What's the matter?"

"Well, am I seeing things? I'll be durned!"

He rubbed his eyes and then continued:

"Yes, by God, it's true! Dick, Will, look over there and see if you still see Winnetou and Inchu-chuna."

They looked, and before they could express their astonishment, the guard, who now noticed that his prisoners were missing, sprang up, stared at the two trees for an instant, and let out a loud, piercing cry. At this, all the sleeping Indians awoke. The guard shouted rapidly in the Kiowa tongue, which I didn't understand, evidently explaining what had happened, and an indescribable chaos broke out.

Everyone, including all the whites, ran to the two trees. I followed them, since I had to behave as if I knew nothing about the escape. On the way, I emptied the rest of the dirt from my pocket.

Too bad that I was only able to free Winnetou and Inch-chuna! How gladly I would have freed more of them—maybe even all of them—but it would have been madness to try it.

Two hundred men, and more, swarmed around the spot where, a few moments earlier, the escapees had stood. The howl that filled the air served to remind me what awaited me if anyone should find out the truth. Finally, Tangua called for quiet and gave a series of commands. At least half of his people immediately left to spread out on the savannah and search for the Apaches in spite of the darkness. The chief was really foaming with rage. He hit the inattentive guard in the face with his fist, then tore the medicine pouch from his neck and trampled it under his foot. This meant the poor devil had lost his honor and standing in the tribe.

Don't be confused by the word "medicine." The word was introduced to the Indians by the white man, and they don't use it to mean herbs for healing wounds or treatment of sickness. To them it means a kind of magic, one of the secrets beyond knowing, which is what the medicines of the white men initially seemed to be. The Indians came to use the word for everything that seemed to be magic, for which they had no explanation, or which seemed to be the results of higher powers or a higher inspiration. Each tribe had a word in its own language for this concept, that got translated as "medicine." Thus, for example, the Mandans have "hopenesh," the Tuscaroras have "yunnju quet," the Blackfoot have "netowa," the Sioux have "wehkon," and the Riccares have "werooti." But when any of them talk about it in English, it's "medicine."

Every adult male, every warrior, has his own medicine. The youth who wants to be accepted as a warrior must abandon the tribe and seek out loneliness. He must fast and even avoid drinking any water. He thinks about his hopes, his wishes, his plans. The striving of his spirit, along with the physical deprivation, puts him into a feverish state in which he can no longer separate appearance from reality. He believes he is receiving higher guidance. His hallucinations become, for him, an opening to another world. Once he reaches this state, he waits for the first object that is presented to him, in his dream or in any other way. If this is a bat, for example, he does not rest until he has caught a bat. Once he has done so, he returns to his tribe and gives the bat to the medicine man, the shaman, who uses it to prepare new medicine. The medicine then takes its place in the medicine pouch. These pouches, always uniquely decorated, must be worn at all times, and they are considered the most valuable possession of any Indian. To keep your honor, you must keep your medicine. If you are unlucky enough to lose your medicine, there is only one cure: you must kill a notorious enemy and take his medicine, which now becomes yours.

Now you can see what a severe punishment it was for the guard to have his medicine taken away and trod upon. He didn't try to make an excuse or show any sign of anger. He simply shouldered his gun and disappeared into the bushes. From that day on, he was dead as far as his tribe was concerned and, with the exception noted above, would never be allowed to return.

The anger of the chief not only directed at the guard. It was directed at me as well. He came up to me and yelled:

"You wanted these two dogs for yourself. Now follow them, catch them and bring them back!"

I tried to turn away from him without answering, but he grabbed my arm and cried:

"Did you hear my command? You must follow them!"

I shook myself loose and responded:

"Command? You give me commands?"

"Yes. I am the chief of this camp, and you must obey me!"

I pulled the sardine tin out of my pocket and said:

"Shall I answer you by blowing you and all your men into the air? Say one more word that I don't like, and I'll demolish you all with this medicine!"

I was curious whether this bluff would have the desired effect. It did, and how! He jumped backward, and cried:

"Ugh, ugh! Keep that medicine to yourself. You're a dog just like all the Apaches!"

This was an insult I wouldn't generally have accepted so readily, but it seemed prudent to take into account Tangua's state of agitation and the fact that we were greatly outnumbered. We whites went back to our campfire, where every aspect of the disappearance was discussed, without a reasonable explanation being hit upon. I kept my role secret from everyone, including Sam, Dick, and Will. I enjoyed being the only one who knew the secret of the escape, while the rest so eagerly sought it, but in vain. I kept the lock of Winnetou's hair with me throughout my wanderings in the West, and I have it still today.

Chapter 18

The behavior of the Kiowas made us concerned about our well-being, although we couldn't really view them as enemies. So when we lay down again to sleep, we set up a rotating watch, each man for an hour, until morning. Of course the Indians noticed that we had taken this precaution, and of course they took it as a slight and showed us even less friendliness than before.

At dawn, we were awakened by our watchman. We saw that the Indians were engaged in a search for the tracks of the vanished Apache chiefs. They found them, and followed them back to a spot where the Apaches had left their horses, in the care of a few guards, prior to the attack. Inchu-chuna and Winnetou had ridden off with the guards. Instead of taking the rest of their horses along, they had left them where they were. When we learned this, Sam Hawkens made one of his sly faces and asked me:

"Can you tell, Sir, why they went and did that?"

"Yes. It's not hard to figure out."

"Well, Sir! A greenhorn like you can't expect to hit on the right explanation by pure chance. You need experience to answer that question correctly."

"But I have enough experience!"

"You? Experience? You think I believe that? I'd like to know where you got it from."

"The experience I'm talking about is something I gleaned from my books."

"Those books again! I'll grant you that now and then something you read might come in handy here, but don't you assume that frontier smarts gets dished out with a spoon like that! You'll soon learn that you know nothing, not a thing. All right then, tell me why the two chiefs took only their own horses and left the others behind."

"For the sake of the other captives."

"Ah. And why would that be?"

"Because the captives will soon need them."

"You think so? What can captives do with horses?"

I didn't feel that he was attacking my honor with his questions. It was just his way. I answered:

"There are two possibilities. The first is that the two chiefs are planning to return immediately with enough warriors to free the captives. If so, why take the horses away only to bring them back? The second possibility is that the Kiowas won't wait for the Apaches to return, but will leave as quickly as possible with the captives. In that case, it's much easier for them if the captives can ride. The Apache chiefs might then hope to free them on their way to the Kiowa villages. If they had no horses, the Kiowas would be faced with taking the captives on a long and slow march, and they might be tempted to kill all the Apaches right here to avoid that problem."

"Hmm. That's really not as dumb an answer as I would have thought you'd give, just looking at you. But you left out a third possibility: the Kiowas might just kill their captives in spite of the horses."

"No. That's not possible."

"No? Sir, what makes you so sure that something is impossible when Sam Hawkens thinks it could easily happen?"

"Because Sam Hawkens seems to have forgotten that I'm here."

"Ah. You're here? Really? You consider your exalted presence an extraordinary and earth-shaking event?"

"No. I simply mean that the captives will not be killed, so long as I am here and I can raise an arm in their defense."

"Really? What a noble fellow you really are, hee-hee-hee! The Kiowas have two hundred men and you, the greenhorn, plan to stop them from doing what they want to do!"

"Hopefully I won't have to do it by myself."

"No? Who's going to help you?"

"You, Sam. And Dick Stone and Will Parker! I happen to trust you enough to have confidence that you also would seriously resist such a massacre."

"So! You trust us! Well, I'm most grateful, for it's really a compliment to have the trust of such a man as you. I feel extraordinarily flattered by that, if I'm not mistaken!"

"Listen, Sam, I'm serious about this. I have no intention of making jokes about a situation like this. When you're dealing with the lives of this many people, it's no joking matter!"

He glared at me with a particularly ironic and crafty expression in his tiny eyes and said:

"I'll be a monkey's uncle! You're actually serious! All right, then let's talk seriously about this. How do you see the situation, Sir? We can't count on the others, so there's only four of us to take on two hundred Kiowas. Are you trying to say that this is as good a place as any for us to make our final stand?"

"I'm not interested in discussing final stands. I just refuse to tolerate such killing in my presence."

"Then it will happen anyway, and the only difference will be that you'll be killed along with the rest. Or do you plan to depend on your new name 'Old Shatterhand'? Do you think you can take on two hundred Indians with your bare fists?"

"Nonsense! I didn't give myself that name, and I know full well that four of us can't survive against two hundred of them. But is the use of force necessary? Trickery is often better."

"Oh yeah? Is that something you read?"

"Yes."

"I see. You know, reading made you a fearfully smart fellow. But I'd really like to see you be crafty sometime. Would you be looking at me with that smug expression then? I'm telling you, you can be as smart as you want but you'll accomplish nothing. The Indians will do what they want to do, and they won't even notice what kind of faces we're making at them. "

"Good. I see I can't count on you, so I'll act on my own if I have to."

"For God's sake, don't do anything stupid, Sir! You don't need to do anything on your own. Just look to us for direction. I don't mean to say I won't help the Apaches if they are threatened, but it has never been my style to ram my head into stone walls. I'm telling you, walls are always harder than heads."

"And I had no intention of saying that I wanted to do the impossible. We don't know what the Kiowas have decided to do about the captives, so we don't need to burden ourselves with that concern now. If the time comes when we need to do something, the right approach will become evident."

"Possibly. But a careful man shouldn't depend on it. I don't worry about what might become evident. The question we have to answer is clear enough: what do we do if they decide to kill the Apaches?"

"We won't let them."

"What does that mean? Won't let them? Tell me what you mean."

"We'll object to it."

"That won't accomplish anything."

"I'll force the chief to comply against his will."

"And how will you do that?"

"If I have to, I'll grab him and hold my knife to his chest."

"And stab him?"

"If he won't obey, yes."

"The devil you will! Aren't you the brutal one!" he cried. "You'd really do that?"

"I assure you, I would indeed do it."

"There you have it." He was quiet for a moment. His face, first shocked, then concerned, gradually took on another expression. Finally he said: "Listen, that thought is really not so crazy. Putting a knife to the chief's throat might be the only way to force him to do what we want. It really is true: now and then a greenhorn can come up an idea, however modest. Let's think about that one for a moment."

He was about to continue speaking, but Bancroft came up to me and called on me to resume work. He was right. We didn't have an hour to lose if we hoped to finish our assignment before Winnetou and Inchu-chuna showed up with their warriors.

We worked at top speed, without a break, until noon. Then Sam Hawkens came to me and said:

"Sorry to interrupt, Sir, but the Kiowas seem to be about to do something with the captives."

"Something? That's pretty vague. Do you have any idea what?"

"I can guess, if I'm not mistaken. They're planning to kill them at the stake."

"When? Right away or later?"

"Right away, of course. Otherwise I wouldn't have bothered you. They've made preparations from which I conclude they're going to be killed. And they appear to be planning to begin right away."

"We can't let that happen! Where's the chief?"

"In the middle of his warriors."

"So we'll have to draw him away from them. Will you do that, Sam?"

"Sure. Any ideas about how it might be done?"

I looked back at the camp. The Kiowas weren't where they had camped the previous night. They had followed along behind as we did our surveying and had sat down at the edge of a patch of woods. Rattler and his people were with them. And Sam had been hanging around in their vicinity, to see what was going on. Parker and Stone, meanwhile, had sat down near me. Between the Indians and the place where I now stood, there was a clump of bushes that was perfectly suited for what I had in mind, since it prevented the Kiowas from seeing what we were doing. I answered Sam's question:

"Just tell him I have something I want to say to him, but I can't leave my work. He'll come."

"I hope so. But what if he brings some of his men along?"

"I'll leave them to you and Stone and Parker; I'll take on the chief. Have ropes ready to tie them up. We'll have to do this as quickly and quietly as possible."

"Well, I don't know if your plan is the right one, but nothing better occurs to me, so we'll go with yours. We'll be risking our lives, but I'm not ready to die just yet so I think we'll come out of this more or less intact, hee-hee-hee!"

He went off, laughing to himself in his unique way. My colleagues were not far away, but they hadn't heard our conversation. It would never have occurred to me to fill them in on our plans, since I was sure they would only try to keep us from carrying them out. They considered their lives more valuable than those of the Apache prisoners.

I knew exactly what I was risking. Could I draw Dick Stone and Will Parker into such a dangerous situation without briefing them in advance? No. I therefore asked them if they would rather not be involved. Stone answered:

"What in the world are you thinking of, Sir! Do you think we're a couple of rascals that leave their friends in the lurch in an emergency? What you're planning to do is the right thing, a real frontiersman's deed, and we're delighted to take part. Right, Will?"

"Yes," Parker nodded. "I wouldn't mind a test of my theory that the right four men to take on two hundred Indians! I'd be pleased if they came after us with a roar and still couldn't do anything to us."

I worked quietly a while longer without looking back. After a while, Stone called out:

"Get ready, Sir. They're coming!"

Now I turned around. Sam was approaching with Tangua. Unfortunately, three other Indians were with them.

"Each of us gets one of them," I said. "I'll take the chief. But grab them by the throat so they can't cry out. Don't do anything until I make the first move."

I went slowly up to Tangua. Stone and Parker followed me. When we met, we were standing where the Kiowas could not see us because of the bushes I mentioned earlier. The chief's expression was not very friendly, and he spoke in an equally unfriendly tone:

"The paleface who is called Old Shatterhand has asked me to come. Have you forgotten that I am the chief of the Kiowas?"

"No. I know that you are," I answered.

"Then you should have come to me, instead of me to you. But I know that you have not been long in this land and you must still learn how to be polite, so I will excuse this mistake. What do you want to say to me? Speak quickly, for I have little time."

"What do you have to do that is so important?"

"We will make the Apache dogs howl."

"When?"

"Now."

"Why so soon? I thought you would take the prisoners back to your wigwams, to make them die at the stake there, in the presence of your squaws and children."

"We wanted to do that. But that would prevent us from continuing on our war party. So they must die here."

"I ask you not to do this!"

"You are not allowed to ask!" he shouted.

"Will you not be as polite to me as I am with you? I have only made a request. If I had given a command, you would perhaps have reason to be rude."

"I want to hear nothing from you, no command and no request. When I decide something, I will not change it because of any paleface."

"Maybe so. Do you have the right to kill the prisoners? I don't want to hear your answer, because I know what it is and I don't want to fight about it. But there is a difference between killing a man quickly and painlessly, and torturing him slowly. We will not permit torture in our presence."

He drew himself to his full height and answered in a contemptuous tone:

"Not permit? Who do you think you are? Against me, you are like a toad that wants to rebel against a mountain bear. The prisoners are mine, and I will do with them what I want."

"They fell into your hands only because of our help, so we have the same right to them as you. We want them kept alive."

"You can want what you want, you white dog. I laugh at your words!"

He spit on the ground in front of me and started to turn away. My fist caught him and he fell. But he had a hard skull. He wasn't completely knocked out and tried to get to his feet. I had to bend over him to give him another punch, so for a moment I couldn't pay attention to the others. By the time I had hit him again and had stood up, I saw Sam Hawkens kneeling on one Indian, who he had by the throat. Stone and Parker held the second, but the third was running off, yelling.

I came to Sam's aid. Once we had his Kiowa tied up, Dick and Will were finished with theirs.

"That wasn't too smart," I said to them. "How come you let the third one get away?"

"Because Stone and I had both picked the same one," answered Parker. "We only lost a moment, but it was long enough for the other scoundrel to take off."

"No damage done," Sam Hawkens reassured them. "It just means the dance gets started a little sooner. No need to beat ourselves over the head. In two or three minutes the Indians will be here. Let's make sure there's plenty of open ground between us and them."

We tied up the chief. The surveyors were horrified to see what we had done. The engineer came running over and cried indignantly:

"What's the matter with you people? What did the Indians do to you? Now they'll kill us all!"

"Indeed they will, Sir, if you don't join us pronto," answered Sam. "Call your people over and come with us! We'll protect you."

"Protect us? That's . . . "

"Quiet!" Sam interrupted him. "We know exactly what we want to do. If you don't stick with us, you're as good as dead. So make it quick!"

As quickly as we could, we carried the three bound Indians some distance out into the open prairie. There, we stopped and laid them on the ground. Bancroft followed with the three surveyors. We had picked our spot because we were safer in open terrain than in an area where we couldn't see everything around us.

"Who will speak with the Indians when they come? Shall I?" I asked.

"No, Sir," answered Sam. "I'll do it. You haven't mastered the half-Indian, half-English mishmash they speak. But back me up at the right moment by looking as if you're about to stab the chief."

Chapter 19

He had hardly finished speaking when were heard a howl of rage from the Kiowas, and a few moments later they had already reached they bushes that had curtained us from their view. They were running toward us, but since some were faster than others, they didn't appear like an organized crowd, but rather a long row of individual runners. That was better for us, for it would have been harder to bring a closed rank of men to a stop.

Sam boldly strode out a short distance toward them and held out both arms in a signal to stop. I heard him call out something, but couldn't understand it. It didn't immediately have the desired effect, but after a few repetitions, I saw the nearest Kiowas come to a halt, and those behind them did the same. He spoke to them, pointing repeatedly at us. I asked Stone and Parker to pull the chief to his feet, and swung my knife threateningly toward him. The Indians let out a howl of terror.

Sam continued speaking to them, and then we saw one of them, the second in command, leave the group and come toward us in slow, dignified strides. Sam came with him. As they reached us, Sam pointed to our three captives and said to him:

"You see that I have told you the truth. They are completely at our mercy."

It was easy to see the fury that came over the Kiowa. He answered:

"The two warriors are still alive, but our chief looks dead."

"He is not dead. Old Shatterhand's fist knocked him to the ground and took away his consciousness, but it will soon return. Sit with us and wait until it does. When the chief is awake and can speak again, we will talk things over with you. But if any Kiowa raises a weapon against us, Old Shatterhand's knife will go into Tangua's heart. You can be sure of that."

"Why did you raise you hand against us? We are your friends!"

"Friends? You yourself do not believe the words you speak."

"I believe it. Did we not smoke the pipe of peace with you?"

"Yes, but this peace cannot be trusted."

"Why not?"

"It is the custom of the Kiowas to offend their friends and brothers?"

"No."

"Well, your chief insulted Old Shatterhand. Therefore, we no longer consider you brothers. Look, he's starting to move!"

Tangua, who Stone and Parker had laid back down on the ground, was indeed stirring. In a moment, his eyes opened and he looked at each of us, one after the other, trying to understand what had happened. Then, as his full consciousness returned, he cried out:

"Ugh, ugh! Old Shatterhand knocked me down. Who tied me?"

"I did," I answered.

"Take away the ropes. I command it!"

"Earlier, you ignored my request. Now, I ignore your order. You have no right to give orders."

He gave me an enraged look and he ground his teeth: "Quiet, boy, or I will crush you!"

"It is you who should be quiet. You insulted me earlier, and I knocked you down for that. Old Shatterhand does not let anyone call him a toad and a white dog without punishment. If you are not polite, something worse may happen to you."

"I demand to be set free! If you do not obey, my warriors will exterminate you from the earth!"

"Then you would be the first to die. Listen to me: your people are right over there. If even one of them lifts a foot to come nearer without permission, the blade of my knife goes straight into your heart. How!"

I placed the tip of the knife against his chest. It was obvious to him that he was completely in our hands. Nor did he seem to doubt that I would follow through on my threat if I had to. For an interval, he rolled his eyes wildly, as if to devour us. Then, with an effort, he controlled his anger and asked in a more moderate voice:

"What do you want from me?"

"Nothing more than what I asked you to do before. The Apaches must not die at the stake."

"You want us not to kill them at all?"

"Later, you can do what you wish. But as long as they are here and we are here, they are not to be harmed."

Another few moments passed in silence. In spite of the war paint that covered his face, you could see the impression of various emotions crossing it—anger, hate, malicious pleasure. I had expected that our negotiations would go on for quite a while, so I was quite surprised when he said:

"It will be as you wish. Yes, I will do even more than you ask, if you agree to my next proposal."

"What proposal is that?"

"First, you must know that I do not fear your knife. You wouldn't stab me, because then my warriors would tear you to pieces in a few minutes. You may be brave, but you cannot overcome two hundred warriors. So I laugh at your threat, that you would stab me. Even if I said I would not agree to your wish, you would not do anything to me. But still, the Apache dogs will not die at the stake, I promise you that, if you agree to a fight to the death."

"With whom?"

"With one of my warriors, who I will choose."

"What weapons?"

"Only knives. If he stabs you, the Apaches must die. If you stab him, they can live."

"And you will set them free?"

"Yes."

I figured he had some ulterior motive behind this proposal.

Perhaps he thought I was the most dangerous of the white people there and he wanted to eliminate me as a threat. Of course he would choose only a master knife-fighter to oppose me. So I answered, without much hesitation:

"I agree. We will work out the rules and smoke the peace pipe over it. Then the fight can start immediately."

"What are you talking about?" cried Sam Hawkens. "I can't stand by and permit you to agree to this dumb idea, Sir!"

"It's not dumb, Sam."

"It's as dumb as they come! In a fair and honorable fight, each fighter has an equal chance. This one isn't fair."

"Oh yes it is!"

"No, absolutely not. Have you ever fought a man to the death with a knife?"

"No."

"Well, there you have it! You'll be up against an opponent who is a knife virtuoso. And think about the unequal results! If you get stabbed, then all the Apaches die. If your opponent gets stabbed, who dies then? Nobody!"

"But the Apaches will be set free."

"Do you really believe that?"

"Yes. If we smoke the calumet, that's as good as an oath."

"The devil take your oaths! He could make an oath and have second thoughts! And even if he really means what he says, you're a greenhorn and. . ."

"Forget that 'greenhorn' business, Sam!" I interrupted. "You've already seen that this particular greenhorn always knows what he's doing."

But he continued trying to dissuade me, and Dick Stone and Will Parker advised me against it as well. But I stuck with my decision. Finally, Sam yelled angrily:

"OK, fine. Bang your thick skull against ten or twenty walls, for all I care! But I plan to make absolutely sure that it's a fair fight. Anyone who tries any funny business, toward you or toward the rest of us, had better look out! I'll blast him to a thousand little bits with my Liddy, if I'm not mistaken!"

Now, the terms of the fight were agreed to. On a grass-free area not far away, two touching circles making a figure eight were to be drawn in the sand. Each fighter was to stand in one of the circles, and he could not leave his circle during the fight. No mercy was to be shown: one of the two must die. But no revenge on the victor was to be taken by the supporters of the dead man. The rest of the conditions and the reward for the winner had already been agreed upon.

Once we had settled all this, the chief was untied and I smoked the calumet with him. Then we released the other two Indians as well, and all four of the Indians rejoined the other warriors, to tell them about the spectacle they were soon to witness.

The engineer and the other surveyors gave me various suggestions, but I didn't pay attention to them. Sam, Dick, and Will still didn't agree with my decision, but at least they didn't squabble with me. Hawkens said, with a note of concern in his voice:

"You might have chosen something better to get involved with than this devlishness, Sir! But I've always said—and I'll say it again—you're a thick-headed fellow, extraordinarily thick-headed! What's the result of getting stabbed to death? Tell me that!"

"The result? Death, nothing more."

"Nothing more? Come on, don't try to make this humorous. Death is the last thing you can experience. Once you're dead, that's the end of the road."

"Not really."

"No? How do you figure?"

"You might get buried."

"Shut up, Sir! If all you're going to do is irritate me even more, you'll make me wish I had expended my fondness on a worthier subject."

"Are your feelings really hurt, then, Sam?"

"Of course my feelings are hurt. Don't ask such stupid questions! It almost a certainty that you'll be killed, dead as a doorknob. Then what will I do in my old age? Well, what will I do? I've got to have a greenhorn that I can bicker with. But what will happen, who will I bicker with, if you get stabbed to death?"

"You'll just have to find another greenhorn to bicker with."

"That's easier said than done. I may never find such a complete and utter, unredeemable greenhorn as you for the rest of my life. But I'm telling you, Sir, if anything happens to you these Indians better look out for me! I'll fall upon them like a band of raging Gothics and . . ."

"Goths, not Gothics. The word is Goths, Sam," I interrupted.

"I couldn't care less if I'm a raging Goth or a raging Gothic. I'm not going to just let someone stab you. And what about your respect for humanity, Sir? You have a good heart and you don't like killing people. You're not thinking of sparing the man you have to fight, are you?"

"Hmm."

"Hmm? I don't like the sound of that 'Hmm'! This is a fight to the death, Sir!"

"What if I just wound him?"

"That doesn't count. You heard that."

"I mean, what if I wound him so that he's unable to fight?"

"It still doesn't count. You aren't considered the winner and you have to fight somebody else. You heard it, the loser must die! No ifs, ands, or buts! If you injure you opponent so he can't fight, then you have to finish him off. Put him out of his misery. Otherwise, it doesn't count. You can't let it bother you. If you want to become a real frontiersman, you'll have to carve a bit of human flesh now and then. Look, these Kiowas are all a bunch of thieving swine, and they're to blame for everything that's happened, because they wanted to steal horses from the Apaches. If you kill a rogue like that, you save all those good Apaches. If you spare him, they're dead. That's something to consider, if I'm not mistaken. Now tell me straight: are you going to fight like a worthy frontiersman, who doesn't go all weak with fear when he sees a drop of blood? Tell me you'll really fight!"

"If it's any comfort to you, you can be sure that I won't be lenient. I know he won't be thinking about sparing me either. I'm in a position to save many lives. It's like a duel. Back in the old country, the most respected gentlemen went at each other over trivialities. But here, there's more at stake, and I'm not facing a gentleman, I'm facing an Indian rascal and murderer. I promise you, I won't be harboring any sympathetic thoughts or misgivings."

"Good. I'm glad to have your word on that. I can look at things a little more calmly now. But still, I feel like my own son is being sent to the slaughterhouse. I wish I could fight in your place. Would you let me do that, Sir?"

"No, Sam. First of all, to put it honestly, it's better that a greenhorn dies than an accomplished frontiersman like you, and second. . ."

"Be quiet! It's no big deal, when an old man dies. But one so young, I hope . . ."

"No, you be quiet!" I interrupted him, as he had interrupted me. "And second, it would be pretty dishonorable and cowardly if I backed out and let somebody else fight in my place. Anyway, the chief wouldn't accept it — he specifically has it in for me."

"That's just what I can't fathom! He has it in for you, you in particular. I sure hope his canoe doesn't go where he thinks he's paddling it. Look, here they come!"

The Indians marched up slowly. Not all two hundred came, since some stayed back to guard the Apaches. Tangua led them past us to the spot where the fight would take place. When they got there, they gathered around it in a three-quarter circle, leaving a space for the whites. We joined them. The chief lifted his arm, and a warrior with a Herculean body stepped forward. He laid down all his weapons except his knife. Then, he stripped to the waist. Anyone seeing the muscles he revealed would have feared for my life. The chief took him to the center of the circle and informed us, in a voice that rang with the certainty of victory:

"This is Metan-akva, 'Lightning-knife', the strongest warrior of the Kiowas. No warrior has ever withstood his knife. Enemies fall under its blade as if lightning had hit them. He will fight Old Shatterhand, the paleface."

"Lord have mercy!" Sam whispered to me. "This fellow's a real Goliath. Listen, Sir, it's all over for you!"

"Pshaw!"

"Don't get any crazy ideas! There's only one way to beat this fellow."

"What's that?"

"Don't let the fight drag out. Press for a quick end; otherwise, he'll wear you down and you're a goner. How's your pulse?"

He grasped my wrist for a moment, then continued:

"Not more than sixty beats, thank God, completely normal. You're not excited? Aren't you frightened?"

"Do I really need that? Excitement and fear in a situation where a cool head and a keen eye are essential? The name of this giant says as much as his bulk. It's because he's the strongest and most invincible with a knife that the chief proposed a knife fight. Well, we'll see just how unbeatable he is."

As I softly spoke these words to Sam, I too stripped to the waist. This was perhaps not required by the rules of the fight, but I didn't want to give the impression that I sought even the slightest protection from my opponent's knife. I gave my bear-killer and revolvers to Sam, then stepped into the middle of the circle. Good old Sam's heart was pounding overly loud, but I felt calm. Believe me, that's the first requirement in any kind of danger.

Now, a fairly large figure eight was drawn in the sand with the handle of a tomahawk, and the chief gave the order for us to take our places. "Lightning-knife" looked me over with a most contemptuous glance and said in a loud voice:

"The body of this paleface is shaking with fear. Will he dare to step forward and take his place?"

He had hardly said these words before I had stepped into the more southern of the two circles in the sand. I had two reasons for this. I got the sun at my back, which meant he would have to look into it, and wouldn't see me as well. You could say this was taking unfair advantage of him, but he had made fun of me, and he lied when he said I was trembling. This was my way of getting even. This was the wrong situation to give him a break by letting him take my circle. I repeat: it was awful, but one of us had to die. It is horrible to have to kill a man, but if I now yielded in the slightest it would cost me my life. I was totally resolved to stab this Samson to death. I was calm in spite of his stature and his impressive name. I had no reason to think I would be a poor knife fighter, in spite of the fact that I was facing a man with a knife for the first time in my life.

"He will really try it!" he sneered. "My knife will eat him. The Great Spirit has delivered him into my hands by taking away his understanding."

Such talk is typical of the Indians. I would have been considered a coward if I had remained silent, so I answered:

"You fight with your mouth, but I am standing here with a knife. Take your place, unless you're afraid."

In a single bound, he jumped into the other circle and cried angrily:

"Afraid? Metan-akva is never afraid! Did you hear it, warriors of the Kiowas? I will take this white dog's life with the first stroke of my knife!"

"My first stroke will take yours! Now stop talking! You should really be called Avat-ya, not Metan-akva."

"Avat-ya, Avat-ya! This stinking coyote thinks he can make fun of me! Wolan the vulture will eat his entrails!"

This last threat revealed carelessness—almost foolishness—on his part, for it made me aware of the way he planned to use his weapon. My entrails! So he apparently was not planning on going for the heart, but rather a low stab, followed by an upward pull, to slit my body open!

We were close enough together that it would only be necessary to bend forward to reach the other man with a knife. His gaze bored into my eyes. His right arm hung straight down. He held his knife with the end of the handle near his little finger and the blade sticking out in front, between his thumb and forefinger. The sharp side of the blade was facing upwards. So he really was planning an attack from below, as I suspected. If he had planned a stroke from above, he would have held the knife in the opposite orientation, with the blade emerging from his fist near the little finger.

So I knew the direction of his attack. Now the question became the timing of it. I would have to learn that from his eyes. I was familiar with the characteristic, lightning twitch that can always be seen an instant ahead of time in all such situations. I lowered my eyelids, to make him think I wasn't attentive, but watched him all the more closely through my eyelashes.

"Go ahead and stab, you dog!" he demanded.

"Don't talk, just fight, red boy!" I responded.

That was a great insult, which would have to be followed by a angry answer or an attack. In this case, it was the latter. A lightning-quick widening of his pupils warned me of it, and in that instant he thrust his knife powerfully ahead and upwards, in order to split me open. If I had expected a stroke from above, it would have been the end of me. But I parried his thrust by thrusting my knife downwards into his forearm, cutting it open.

"Mangy dog!" he growled, pulling his arm back in terror and pain, and letting his knife fall to the ground.

"Don't talk, fight!" I repeated, raising my arm and thrusting my knife down into his heart. I instantly withdrew it. The wound was so well placed that a warm, red stream of blood the width of a finger spurted out on me. The giant wobbled back and forth for a moment, and tried to cry out. But he only managed a groaning sigh, and collapsed dead on the ground.

Chapter 20

An angry howl rose up from the Indians. Only one of them, Tangua, the chief, did not join in. He came forward, bent down to my opponent, felt the edges of his wound, stood up again and looked at me with an expression that I will never forget. It was a mixture of rage, horror, fear, wonder, and recognition. He turned to go without a word. I said:

"You see, I'm still in my circle. But Metan-akva left his and is lying outside it. Who is the winner?"

"You!" he answered angrily, and stalked away. But he had only gone five or six paces before he turned and hissed at me: "You are a white son of the evil black spirit. Our medicine man will take your magic, and then you will have to give us your life!"

"Let your medicine man do what he likes, but keep the word that you gave us!"

"What word?" he asked scornfully.

"That the Apaches will not be killed."

"We will not kill them. I have said it."

"And they will be freed?"

"Yes, the will get their freedom back. What Tangua, Chief of the Kiowas, says, that is what will be done."

"Then my friends and I will go and untied their ropes."

"I will do that myself, when the time comes."

"The time has come. I won, and that means the time is now."

"Quiet! Did we speak before of the time?"

"It wasn't specifically mentioned. But it was understood that. . ."

"Quiet!" he thundered at me again. "I will say when it is time. We will not kill the Apache dogs, but what can we do if they die because they have nothing to eat and no water? How can I help it if they starve or die of thirst before I can free them?"

"Swine!" I shouted in his face.

"Dog! If you say one more word like that. . ."

He wanted to complete his threat, but stopped and stared in shock at my face, whose expression probably didn't please him. But I finished his interrupted threat:

". . .then I will smash you to the ground with my fist, you who are the worst of all liars!"

He quickly stepped back a few steps, pulled out his knife, and threatened:

"You won't get so close with your fist again. If you get close enough to touch me, I'll stab you."

"That's what 'Lightning-knife' said too. And now he's lying there dead. That's how you would end up. I will speak with my white brothers about what will happen to the Apaches. If you so much as touch a hair of one of them, that's the end for you and all your people. You know that we can blow you all into the air."

Only after saying this did I finally leave the figure-eight in the sand and go over to Sam. He had not been able to hear my exchange with Tangua because of the howls of the Indians. He ran up to me, grabbed me with both hands, and cried in delight:

"Welcome, welcome, Sir! Welcome back from the realm of death—I reckon you've been there and back. Friend, buddy, boy, man, greenhorn, whatever sort of creature you are! Never saw a buffalo in his life and shoots down the strongest in the herd! Never saw a grizzly before, but stabs one to death, the way you'd core an apple! Never saw a mustang, but pulls my new Mary right out of the pack! And now he takes on the strongest and most famous Indian knife-fighter and stabs him through the heart, first try, without losing a drop of his own blood! Dick and Will, come over here and take a look at this German surveyor. Can you figure him out?"

A journeyman," Stone grinned.

"A journeyman? What do you mean?"

"He's shown many times over that he's no greenhorn, no

apprentice. Let's promote him to journeyman. Later, he'll become a master."

"Not a greenhorn? Make him a journeyman? If you really have to say something, can't you do better than that? The kid is a greenhorn through and through, otherwise he'd have known better than to lock horns with this huge, powerful Indian. But that's the way he is: a dumb, half-wit greenhorn! Fools have all the luck—the stupidest farmers grow the biggest potatoes. He can chalk his survival up to his pure stupidity, if I'm not mistaken. When he got in that ring, my heart stopped beating and I could hardly breathe. I kept thinking about whether his will was in order. Then, he raises the knife, plunges it in, and the Indian falls to the ground! Well, we've got what we wanted: freedom for the Apaches."

"You're wrong about that," I answered, without getting angry about he way he'd been speaking of me.

"Wrong? Why?"

"When the chief gave us his promise, he was keeping his real plan secret. He has his own ideas about what happens next."

"I suspected he might be hiding something. So what is his real plan?"

I repeated what Tongua had said. He was so incensed by it that he immediately went to find him. I took the opportunity to put my shirt and jacket back on and collect my weapons.

The Kiowas had been completely convinced that "Lightning-knife" would kill me. The unexpected outcome had saddened and angered them. Certainly, they would have preferred to simply capture us, but they couldn't do that because we had agreed (and had even smoked the peace pipe to confirm) that the losing side would not take revenge. That much was settled and there was nothing they could do about it. But it wouldn't take them long to find some other pretext for declaring us enemies. They were in no hurry, since we were in their hands. So they held back their fury for the time being and occupied themselves with the body of their fallen comrade. The chief was involved in this as well. Under the circumstances, Sam Hawkens could not expect to get much of a hearing. He came back very morose and reported:

"This guy won't keep his word. It appears he plans to let the prisoners die of exposure. And he calls this 'not killing' them! But we'll keep our eyes open, if I'm not mistaken, and we'll put one over on him yet, hee-hee-hee!"

"As long as we don't get one put over on us!" I remarked. "It's hard to protect others when you're in need of protection yourself."

"Why, I think you're afraid of these Indians, Sir!"

"Pshaw! You know as well as I do how little I fear them."

"With one difference: where I would tread carefully, you go charging in like a bull after a red cloth. And where real bravery is required, you get all doubtful. But that's how greenhorns are. So what's your opinion?"

"About what?"

"About the knife fight you just won."

"I think perhaps you might be satisfied with my performance."

"I don't mean that. I'm talking about possible accusations."

"Accusations? Did someone make accusations? You perhaps?"

"My heavens, you sure are slow to catch on. Tell me straight, Sir, did you maybe face hanging for a murder of somebody or other over in the old country?"

"I don't think so. I can't remember doing anything like that," was my answer to his remarkable question.

"So you didn't kill anybody?"

"No."

"Then today was your first chance to try your hand at killing. How do you feel about it now? That's what I want to know."

"Hmm! It's certainly not a pleasant thing to think about. I doubt it will ever be as easy for me to take a man's life again. It provokes something akin to a guilty conscience inside of me."

"Now don't get conceited, and don't start getting any dumb ideas!

Around here, you never know from one day to the next when you'll have to kill a man to save your own skin. In a case like that . . . my heavens, here comes a case like that!" he interrupted himself. "The other Apaches have returned already! Now there'll be some bloodshed! Get ready for a fight, gentlemen."

From the area around the prisoners and their guards range out the high and schrill "Hiiiiii" of the Apache war cry. Contrary to all expectations, Inchu-chuna and Winnetou had already returned, and they attacked the Kiowa camp. The Kiowas that were near us jumped to their feet in shock. The chief cried:

"Enemies are attacking our brothers down there! Quick, to the rescue!"

He started to dash off, but Sam blocked his path and cried:

"Don't go there! Stay here! We're already surrounded. Or do you think the two chiefs of the Apaches are stupid enough to attack your guards without knowing where you are? In a moment they'll. . ."

He was speaking very quickly, but still didn't finish before a terrible war cry arose all around us, piercing us to the marrow. We were in the open, but there were bushes here and there, and Apaches had hidden behind them while we were occupied with the knife fight. Now we were totally surrounded. The colorful crowd came running at us from all sides. The Kiowas shot at them, and hit a few, but not enough to make a difference. Then they were upon us.

"Don't kill any Apaches, not one!" I called to Sam, Dick, and Will. We were immersed in hand-to-hand combat. We four did not fight. But the engineer and the three surveyors pulled out their guns. They were shot down. That was grim. As I watched this, we were attacked by a substantial group and pulled apart from each other. We tried to yell to the Apaches that we were their friends, but without success. They came at us with knives and tomahawks so that we had to defend ourselves, even though we didn't want to. We knocked down several of them with our rifle butts, so they backed off a little.

I used that moment for a quick glance around. There were no Kiowas without several Apaches attacking them. Sam saw this also. He called:

"Quick! Into the bushes over there!"

He ran for the clump of bushes that lay between us and the camp. Dick and Will followed him. I hesitated a moment, looking at the spot where the surveyors had been. They were white men, and I would have liked to help them, but it was too late. I turned toward the bushes. I had barely reached them when I saw Inchu-chuna appear.

He and Winnetou had been with the group of Apaches who had the task of taking on the guards and freeing the prisoners. Once they had done this, the two chiefs had run to join the larger group that we were fighting with. Inchu-chuna arrived ahead of his son. As he rounded the clump of bushes, he spotted me.

"The land-thief!" he cried, and swung at me with the butt of his sliver rifle, trying to knock me down. I yelled to him, trying to explain that I was not his enemy. He paid no attention, but redoubled his blows and punches. I saw that if I wished to avoid being injured or killed, I'd have to fight back. Just as he raised his arm to strike, I threw aside my bear-killer, with which I had parried his blows, and in an instant I had my left hand on his throat and I hit him several times with the right. He let his rifle drop, choked briefly, and fell to the ground. A jubilant voice called out behind me:

"That is Inchu-chuna, the leader of the Apache dogs! I must have his scalp!"

I turned and found Tangua, the Kiowa chief, who had (for whatever reason) ended up near me. He tossed his gun aside, pulled out his knife, and dropped beside the unconscious Apache, ready to scalp him. I grabbed his arm and said:

"Don't touch him! I brought him down, so he belongs to me, not you!"

"Be quiet, you white vermin!" he answered. "You can't tell me what to do. The chief is mine! Let me go, or I'll . . ."

He swung the knife toward me, catching me in the left wrist. I didn't want to stab him, so I left my knife in my belt. Instead, I threw myself at him and tried to drag him away. Failing at this, choked him until he no longer moved. Then I bent over Inchu-chuna, whose face was bloodied from my blows. At that moment, I heard a noise behind me and I turned to look. That movement saved my life. A the powerful blow from a rifle butt caught me in the shoulder. It was meant for my head. If it had hit its mark, it would have split my skull. It was Winnetou that had hit me.

As I said, he had followed at a distance behind his father. As he came around the clump of bushes, he saw me kneeling by his father, who looked lifeless and bloodied. Winnetou immediately tried to deliver a deadly blow, but fortunately hit only my shoulder. Then he dropped his gun, pulled out his knife, and came after me.

My situation couldn't have been worse. The blow had shaken my entire body and had paralyzed my arm. I longed to explain the situation to Winnetou, but things were happening so fast that there wasn't time for a single word. His arm was raised, ready to stab, to drive his knife-blade into my heart. I only managed a small movement, but the knife hit my left shirt pocket and struck the sardine tin containing my papers. It glanced off the metal and struck me under the chin, piercing through my mouth and tongue. He pulled the knife back out and, grabbing me by the throat with his left hand, got ready to stab again. The fear of death doubled my strength. I could only use one hand and one arm, and he was to one side of me. I turned a bit more and was able to grasp his right hand, pressing it so hard that he had to let the knife fall. Instantly, I grabbed his left arm by the elbow and pressed it upward so hard that he had to let go of my neck or risk having his arm broken. Now I drew in my knees and raised myself with all my strength. He slid off of me, so that his chest touched the ground. In the next moment, I was on his back, just as he had previously been on mine.

Now I had to keep him down, for if he got to his feet, I was lost. I got one knee onto his thighs and the other on one of his arms. With my good hand, I grabbed the scruff of his neck. Meanwhile, he was trying to reach his knife with his free hand. Fortunately, it was out of reach. Now began a satanic wrestling match between us. Think of it! Winnetou, who had never been conquered (and who never would be conquered), with his suppleness, his iron muscles and steel sinews. Now I had time to speak, and a few words of explanation would have been enough, but the blood was pouring from my mouth, and as I attempted to speak with my wounded tongue, only unintelligible babbling came out. He used all of his strength to try to throw me off, and I lay on him like a nightmare that could not be shaken off. He began to pant more and more severely. I pressed my fingertips into his larynx so hard that he lost his breath. Should I choke him to death? No, absolutely not! I released the pressure on his neck for an instant. He immediately raised his head, and I immediately delivered two or three well-placed punches, one after the other. Winnetou was out cold. I had conquered the unconquerable. (I had previously knocked him out, true, but that couldn't be called a victory—there hadn't been a fight.)

I took a deep, deep breath, taking care not to breathe in the blood that filled my mouth. I had to hold it wide open, giving the blood a chance to run out. Blood was spurting from the wound under my jaw, too. As I started to get up from the ground, I heard an angry Indian voice behind me and was struck a blow to the head that left me unconscious.

Chapter 21

When I came to, it was evening. I had been out cold the whole time. At first, I thought I was dreaming. I had fallen into the deep walled enclosure of a mill-wheel. The wheel couldn't turn because I was stuck between the wheel and the wall. The water rushed over me, and the force with which it pushed the wheel pressed me tighter and tighter against the wall until I thought I would be crushed. All my limbs ached, especially my head and shoulder. Gradually, I realized it was not a dream. The rushing and roaring sounds were not water—they were inside my head, a result of the blow that had knocked me out. And the pain in my shoulder was not from a mill wheel that was crushing me, but from Winnetou's blow. Blood still ran from my mouth. It ran down my throat, too, threatening to choke me. I heard a terrible rattling and gurgling that brought me fully awake. I was I who had gurgled that way.

"He's moving! Thank God, he's moving!" I heard Sam's voice cry.

"Yes, I saw it too," answered Dick Stone.

"He's opening his eyes! He's alive!" added Will Parker.

I had indeed opened my eyes. And the scene that immediately greeted me was not reassuring. We were still on the scene of the battle. More than twenty campfires were burning, and more than five hundred Apaches moved among them. Many of them were wounded. I could also see quite a few dead bodies, in two separate groups. The first was Apaches and the second, Kiowas. The Apaches had lost eleven of their warriors, and the Kiowas had lost thirty. All around us lay captured Kiowas, thoroughly tied up. Not one of them had gotten away. Tangua, the chief, was also among them. I couldn't see the engineer and the three surveyors. They had made the unwise choice of reaching for their weapons and had died instantly.

Not far away lay a man whose body had been bound in a circle, wrists and ankles behind him, in the manner that they used to call the "Spanish goat torture" back in the Middle Ages. It was Rattler. The Apaches had tied him that way, to prepare him for future pain. He moaned so painfully that I felt sorry for him in spite of his lack of morals. He had been spared because, as the murderer of Kleki-petra, he had been kept alive for a slower and more painful death.

My hands and my feet were tied, as were those of Parker and Stone, who lay to my left. Sam Hawkens was on my right. His right hand was tied behind his back, but his left had been left free, as I later learned, so that he could help me.

"Thank heavens you've come back to your senses, Sir!" he said, stroking my forehead with his free hand. "How did you get knocked out?"

I tried to answer, but couldn't because my mouth was full of blood.

"Spit it out!" he said.

I did so, but I still could only utter a few incomprehensible syllables before my mouth filled with blood once more. I had suffered a massive loss of blood and was deathly pale. I could only answer in short, widely-spaced phrases, and my voice was so soft that Sam could hardly understand me:

"Fought Inchu-chuna. So Winnetou stabbed mouth. Hit over head, don't know."

"I'll be jiggered! Who would have thought it! We'd have gladly surrendered, but these Apaches wouldn't listen to us. So we headed into the bushes to wait until their fury settled down a bit, if I'm not mistaken. We thought you did the same, and we looked for you. When we didn't find you right away, I snuck up to the edge of the clump of bushes to see if I could see you. A bunch of howling Apaches were standing around Inchu-chuna and Winnetou, who looked to be dead. But they came to soon enough. You were lying next to them, and I thought sure you were dead as well. I was so upset, I fetched Will and Dick, here, and we ran over to you to see if there might still be life in you. Of course they captured us right away. I told Inchu-chuna that we were friends of the Apaches and had planned to set the two chiefs free the night before. But he laughed at me grimmly, and it's only because of Winnetou's goodwill that I have this one hand free. He's the one that bandaged your neck wound, too. Otherwise, you never would have come to. You would have bled to death, if I'm not mistaken. Is it a deep cut?"

"Through the tongue," I mumbled.

"What the devil? That's dangerous. I'd rather not have the fever you're going to suffer before that heals. But I'd gladly take it on if I could, since an old raccoon like me survives a thing like that easier than a greenhorn like you, that hasn't seen blood except maybe in a sausage. But you are feeling a little better?"

"Bashed head and shoulder," I answered.

"Oh, so they knocked you down? I thought the stab wound was what got you. Well, your head will be buzzing a bit, I don't doubt. But that will pass. The main thing is, the few brains you had before, you seem to have back. The danger now is from that tongue wound. It can't be bandaged. I'll . . ."

I heard no more, but sank back into unconsciousness.

When I woke up again, I felt that I was moving. I could hear the horses' hooves. I opened my eyes. I lay, to my astonishment, on the hide of the grizzly that I had killed. It had been stitched together roughly in the shape of a hammock, and it was hung between two horses which carried it along. I was stuck so deeply in the hide that I could see only the sky and the heads of the two horses, nothing more. The sun beat down on me and it flowed through my veins like melted lead. My mouth was swollen and full of blood. I tried to dislodge it with my tongue, but my tongue wouldn't move.

"Water, water!" I wanted to cry, for I felt an almost intolerable thirst. But I couldn't utter a word, not even an audible breath. I told myself that this was the end, and tried, as every dying man should, to think of God and that which awaited me on the other side of this earthly life. But I was overcome with weakness.

Later, I would go on to fight with Indians, buffalo, and bear; to make death-marches through parched deserts; to drift for months on boundless oceans. But it was the fever from that wound with which I wrestled for a long, long time on the verge of death. From time to time, I heard Sam Hawken's voice, as if from far, far away. From time to time, I saw two soft dark eyes before me, the eyes of Winnetou. Then I died, was laid in a coffin, and buried. I heard the clumps of earth being shovelled into the grave, and I laid there for an eternity without being able to move, in the earth, until finally the cover of my coffin silently lifted and disappeared. I saw the sky above me. The four sides of the grave dropped away. Was this happening? Could this happen? I moved my hand toward my face and...

"Halleluja, Halleluja! He's waking from the dead!" Sam cried in excitement.

I turned my head.

"Did you see that? He reached up to his head with his hand, and now he's turning his head!" the little man cried.

He bent over me. His face was truly glowing with delight—as I could tell, even in spite of the thicket of beard that almost totally covered it.

"Can you see me, Sir?" he asked. "You opened your eyes and moved, so you're alive. But can you see me?"

I tried to answer, but I couldn't—firstly because of overwhelming weakness and secondly because my tongue felt as heavy as lead in my mouth. So I just nodded.

"And you can hear me?"

I nodded again.

"Look here! Take a look at him!"

His face disappeared and was replaced by the two heads of Stone and Parker. Both those good men had tears of joy in their eyes. They wanted to speak to me, but Sam shoved them aside and said:

"Let me in there! Let me do the talking. Me, me!"

He took both my hands, pressed them to the spot on his beard under which his mouth apparently lay, and asked:

"Are you hungry, Sir? Are you thirsty? Could you eat or drink something?"

I shook my head. I felt no need to eat or drink anything. I was so weak, I couldn't even contemplate drinking a single drop of water.

"No? Really? Lord, is that possible? Do you know how long you've been lying here?"

I answered again with a slight shake of my head.

"Three weeks, three full weeks! Think of it! You have no idea what happened after you were wounded or where you are now. You had a terrible fever, and then you went rigid with tetanus. The Apaches were ready to bury you, but I couldn't believe you were dead, and I pleaded and pleaded until Winnetou spoke to his father and got his permission to wait until your body started to go bad before burying you. We have Winnetou to thank for that. I've got to go find him and bring him over here!"

I closed my eyes and lay still again. But I lay in blessed weariness, in blessed peace, and not in a grave. I wished I could lie like that forever. Then I heard steps. A hand felt me and moved my arm. Then I recognized Winnetou's voice:

"Is Sam Hawkens mistaken? Was Old Shatterhand really awake?"

"Yes, yes. We three all saw it. He even answered my questions by nodding and shaking his head."

"Then a great wonder has happened. But it would have been better if it had not happened, if he had remained dead. He has survived, only to die. He will be killed along with you."

"But he is the Apache's best friend!"

"Twice he knocked me out!"

"Because he had to!"

"He did not have to!"

"Oh, yes. The first time, it was to save your life. You would have found the Kiowas and been killed. And the second time, he had to protect himself from you. We wanted to surrender, but we couldn't because your warriors would not pay attention to our reassurances."

"Hawkens says this only to save himself."

"No, it's the truth!"

"Your tongue lies. Everything you have said to avoid death at the stake has only convinced us that you were even greater enemies to us than the Kiowa dogs. You spied on us. If you were our friends, you would have warned us about the Kiowa. Then we would not have been captured by the water and tied to the trees."

"But you would have avenged Kleki-petra's death on us, or if you didn't do that, you would at least have prevented us from finishing our work."

"You couldn't have done it anyway. You make arguments that any child can see through. Do you think Inchu-chuna and Winnetou are as dumb as childern?"

"I would never think of such a thing. Old Shatterhand is unconscious again. If he were awake and could talk, he'd tell you that I'm telling the truth."

"Yes, he would lie just like you. Palefaces are all liars and betrayers. I have only known one white person who had truth living in his heart. That was Kleki-petra, who you have killed. I almost made a mistake with Old Shatterhand. I saw his cleverness and his strength and was amazed. I thought I saw that sincerity lived in his eyes, and I thought he could be my friend. But he was a land thief like the rest. He didn't keep you from drawing us into the ambush, and twice he struck me down with his fist. Why did the Great Spirit create such a man and give him such a false heart?"

I tried to look at him when he touched me, but my muscles wouldn't obey my will. My body seemed to be made of ether, to be constructed of something that couldn't be detected by human senses, and therefore incapable of doing anything perceptible by others. But now, as I heard Winnetou's judgment of me, my eyelids finally obeyed me. They opened, and I saw him standing near me. He was wearing a light linen garment, carried no weapons, and held a book in his hand with the word "Hiawatha" in large gold letters on the cover. So this Indian, this son of a race that people call "wild," could not only read, he even appreciated and enjoyed higher things. Longfellow's famous poem in the hand of an Indian! I would never have imagined it possible!

"He opened his eyes again!" cried Sam, and Winnetou turned to me. He came up to me, gazed long into my eyes, and then asked:

"Can you speak?"

I shook my head.

"Are you in pain?"

The same answer.

"Be honest with me! When you awake from the dead, you cannot lie. Did the four of you really plan to rescue us?"

I nodded twice.

He made a scornful, disparaging gesture with his hand. "Lies, lies, lies! Lies even on the edge of the grave! If you had told me the truth, perhaps I would have thought that you were different, that you could become better, and I would have pleaded with Inchu-chuna, my father, for your life. But you are not worth such a request, and you must die. We will take special care of you, and quickly make you healthy and strong again, so that you will be able to hold out for a long time against the suffering that awaits you. To die quickly, as a sick, weak man—that is no punishment."

I closed my eyes—I couldn't hold then open any longer. If only I could talk! Sam, the otherwise so cunning Sam Hawkens, defended us in what could only be called an astute way. I would not have spoken very differently. Now, as if reading my mind, he confronted the young Apache chief:

"But we have proven, clearly and irrefutably proven, that we were on your side. Your warriors were supposed to be martyred. To prevent it, Old Shatterhand fought with "Lightning-knife," and beat him. He risked his life for you and now you want to repay him by torturing him to death!"

"You have proved nothing. This story is a lie as well."

"Then ask Tangua, the Chief of the Kiowas, who you still have as your prisoner."

"I have asked him."

"What did he say?"

"That you lie. Old Shatterhand did not fight with Lightning-Knife. Lightning-Knife was killed by our warriors."

"That's absolute wickedness on Tangua's part. He knows we were secretly on your side, and now he's trying to take revenge by sending us to our death."

"He swore by the Great Spirit, so I believe him and not you. I say again what I just said to Old Shatterhand: if you had openly confessed, then I would have intervened for you. Kleki-petra, who was friend and teacher to my father, put belief in peace and mildness in my heart. I do not lust after blood, and my father, the chief, always does what I request of him. That is why we have not killed any of the Kiowas that we still hold as prisoners here. They will pay with horses, weapons, tents, and blankets, but not with their lives. We have not yet settled on a price with them, but that will come soon. Rattler is Kleki-petra's murderer. He must die. You are his companions, but we would have perhaps had leniency if you were honest. But since you are not, you will share Rattler's fate."

In later years, I rarely heard Winnetou speak this much, and then only in the most important circumstances. He was quiet by nature. It was clear that our fate lay heavier on his heart than he wanted to admit.

"How can we admit to being your enemy when we're your friends?" Sam responded.

"Quiet! I can see that you will die with this great lie still on your lips. Until now we have given you more freedom than the other prisoners, so that you could help Old Shatterhand. You are not worthy of this consideration and will be confined from now on. The sick man does not need you any more. Follow me! I will show you the place where you will be kept and not permitted to leave."

"Not that, Winnetou, please not that!" Sam cried in shock. "I can't leave Old Shatterhand!"

"You can, because I command it! What I say, that is what will happen!"

"But I ask you at least. . ."

"Still!" the Apache interrupted him in the strongest tone of voice. "I will hear no word of opposition! Will you go, or will my warriors tie you up and carry you?"

"You're in charge, and we have to obey. When can we see Old Shatterhand again?"

"On the day of your death, and his."

"No sooner?"

"No."

"Then let us say goodbye before we follow you."

He gripped my hands, and I felt his tangle of beard on my face as he gave me a kiss on the forehead. Parker and Stone did the same. Then they left with Winnetou, and I lay alone for a while, until several Apaches came and carried me away. I couldn't tell where, since I was too weak to open my eyes again. I fell asleep even as they were carrying me.

Chapter 22

I don't know how long I slept. It was a sleep of recovery, which always tends to be very long and very deep. When I awoke, it wasn't hard at all for me to open my eyes, and I was not nearly as weak as before. I could move my tongue a bit, and could reach my finger into my mouth, to clean it of some of the coagulated blood and puss.

To my astonishment, I found myself in a four-sided room with walls of stone. It received light from its doorway, which had no door. My bed was in the back corner. I lay on grizzly pelts that had been laid on top of each other, and a very beautiful Indian blanket had been spread over me. In the corner near the door sat two Indian women, one old and one young, to tend and guard me. The older one was ugly, like many old Indian squaws. This is a result of overwork: the women have to do all the hardest tasks by themselves, while the men only fight and hunt, and are idle the rest of the time. The younger woman was very beautiful. If she had been dressed in European clothes, she would have attracted notice in any salon. She wore a long, bright blue dress-like garment which fit tightly around her neck. A rattlesnake skin at the waist served as a belt. She wore not a single piece of jewelry, such as the glass beads or the cheap coins that Indian women like to decorate themselves with. Her only decoration was her marvelous long hair that fell in two great blue-black braids to below her hips. Her hair reminded me of Winnetou's. The shape of her face was also similar to his. She had the same velvet-black eyes, which lay hidden beneath long, heavy lashes, like secrets that must not be fathomed. There was no trace of the prominent Indian cheekbones. The soft and warmly pigmented full cheeks joined beneath in a chin, whose dimple might well have led to trouble in a European woman. She spoke softly with the older woman, to avoid waking me, and when she opened her beautifully chiseled mouth to smile, her teeth gleamed like the purest ivory between her red lips. The finely fluted nose might have suggested Greek, rather than Indian, ancestry. The color of her skin was a bright copper-bronze with a touch of silver. This girl might have been perhaps eighteen years old. I would have bet anything that she was Winnetou's sister.

These two squaws were decorating a white-tanned leather belt with red stitches and patterns.

I sat up—yes, sat up—and it was surprisingly easy, although I had been so weak when I was previously awake that I could hardly keep my eyes open. The older woman heard my movement, looked over at me, and cried, pointing:

"Ugh! Aguan inta-hinta!"

"Ugh" is the exclamation of astonishment, and "Aguan inta-hinta" means "he is awake." The girl looked up from her work and, seeing that I was sitting up, got up and came over to me.

"You are awake," she said (to my astonishment, in reasonably fluent English). "Do you need anything?"

I opened my mouth to answer, but closed it again. It suddenly occurred to me that I couldn't talk. But I had been able to sit up, so perhaps it would be possible to speak also. So I made the attempt:

"Yes, I need several things."

How glad I was to hear my own voice. It did sound strange to me. The words came out cramped and wheezing and it hurt the back of my mouth to talk. But I was able to speak, and for three weeks I hadn't been able to utter a syllable.

"Speak softly, or just make signs," she said. "Nsho-chi hears that it is painful for you to speak."

"Nsho-chi is your name?" I said.

"Yes."

"Well, the person who named you that deserves thanks. You could not have gotten a more fitting name. You are like a beautiful spring day on which the first flowers of spring start to bloom."

Nsho-chi means "beautiful day". She blushed slightly and reminded me:

"You wanted to tell me your wishes."

"First tell me if you are here because of me."

"Yes. I have been commanded to tend to you."

"By whom?"

"By Winnetou, who is my brother."

"I thought so. You look very much like him."

"You tried to kill him!"

This sounded half like an accusation and half like a question, and as she said it, she looked searchingly into my eyes as if to fathom the mystery of my whole inner being.

"No," I replied.

"He doesn't believe that and he considers you his enemy. Twice, you have knocked him, who no one can conquer, to the ground."

"Once to rescue him, and the other time because he was trying to kill me. I have always liked him, from the moment I first saw him."

Her dark eyes rested again for a time on my face. Then she said:

"He doesn't believe you, and I am his sister. Does your mouth hurt?"

"Not now."

"Will you be able to swallow?"

"I would like to try. Can you give me water to drink?"

"Yes, and for washing too. I will get you some."

She left with the old woman. What was going on? How could I make sense of it? Winnetou considered us his enemies, did not believe our affirmations to the contrary, and yet had put me in the care of his sister! Perhaps the reason for this would become clearer later.

After a while the two squaws returned. The younger one had a vessel of brown clay, similar to the cups that the Pueblo Indians make, in her hand. It was filled with cool water. Assuming I would not be strong enough to drink without help, she held it to my mouth. Swallowing was hard, very hard and very painful. But I could do it, I had to do it. I drank in small sips, with long pauses in between, until finally the cup was empty.

How the water rejuvenated me! Nsho-chi must have observed this, for she said:

"You have done that well. I will bring other things for you later. You must be very hungry and thirsty. Do you want to wash?"

"I don't know if I will be able to."

"Try!"

The old woman had brought a carved-out gourd full of water. Nsho-chi put it by my bed and gave me a piece of netting, something like a handkerchief, made of a fine, soft material. I tried, but I couldn't manage it. I was still too weak. So she dipped a corner of the netting in the water and began to wash my face and hands—the face and hands of one whom she believed to be the mortal enemy of her brother and father. When she was done, she asked with a slight, but clearly sympathetic smile:

"Are you always as thin as you are now?"

Me thin? I hadn't given it any thought. But of course the three long weeks of fever and then the tetanus, which almost always led to death, must have taken their toll. And not a speck of food or drink the whole time! I felt my cheeks, and then said:

"I have never been thin."

"Look at yourself in the water here!"

I looked in the gourd and drew back in shock. Looking back at me was the head of a ghost, a skeleton.

"It's a wonder I'm still alive," I cried.

"Yes, Winnetou said that too. You even survived the long ride back here. The Great, Good Spirit has given you an body that is stronger than most. Others would not even have lasted five days on the trail."

"Five days? Where are we?"

"In the pueblo on the Rio Pecos."

"Did all the warriors that captured us come back here?"

"Yes, all. They live near the pueblo."

"And the captured Kiowas are here too?"

"They too. They ought to be killed. Any other tribe would kill them at the stake, but the good Kleki-petra was our teacher and taught us of the goodness of the Great Spirit. Once the Kiowas have atoned for what they did, they can go home."

"And my three friends? Do you know where they are?"

"They are in a room like this one, but dark. They are tied up."

"How are they?"

"They have all they need. One who will die at the stake must be strong enough to survive much, otherwise it is no punishment."

"So they must really die?"

"Yes."

"Me too?"

"You too!"

There was not a trace of regret in her voice as she said this. Was this beautiful girl so unfeeling that the agonizing death of a man did not move her?

"Can I speak with them?"

"That is forbidden."

"Perhaps just see them, from a distance?"

"Also forbidden."

"May I send them a message through you?"

"I am not allowed to do that."

"Can you just tell them how I am doing?"

She thought for a moment, and then said:

"I will ask my brother, Winnetou, to let them know how you are."

"Will Winnetou come to see me?"

"No."

"But I need to speak with him!"

"He has no need to speak with you."

"What I have to tell him is very important."

"For him?"

"For me and my companions."

"He will not come. Perhaps I can say it to him, if it is something you can say to me."

"No. Thank you, though. I could easily say it to you. I know I can trust you with anything. But if he is too proud to speak with me, then I will have enough pride not to speak to him through a messenger."

"You will not see him again before the day of your death. Now we will go. If you need anything, make a sound with this. We will hear it and someone will come right away."

She took a small, clay whistle from her pouch and gave it to me. Then she and the old woman left.

It was a perilous spot in which I found myself. Here I was, sick unto death, and I was to be nursed back to health so that I would be strong enough to die slowly! And the man who insisted on my death assigned his sister to take care of me, rather than some dirty old squaw!

It hardly needs to be mentioned that my conversation with Nsho-chi was not as easy as the impression you get by reading it. Speaking was hard and quite painful for me. I spoke very slowly and often had to pause to recover. This exhausted me, and so I fell asleep as soon as Beautiful Day had left.

When I awoke several hours later, I was very thirsty and as hungry as a bear. I decided to see if the magic whistle would work. Sure enough, a moment after I blew it, the old woman, who must have been sitting outside the door, stuck her head in and asked a question. I caught the words "ichha" and "ishtla" but I didn't know what they meant. She had asked me if I wanted to eat or drink. I made gestures to indicate eating and drinking, and she disappeared. A few minutes later Nsho-chi came with a clay bowl and a spoon. She kneeled next to me and spoon-fed me, like a child who isn't old enough to feed himself. In the wild, the Indians don't use vessels and utensils like this. This was one more thing the dead Kleki-petra had taught them.

Eating was, of course, more difficult for me than drinking. I could hardly stand the pain, and I felt like crying out after each spoonful. But we need food to live, and if I was not to starve, I had to eat something. So I made a point of ignoring the pain, but I couldn't prevent the tears from coming to my eyes. This did not escape Nsho-chi's notice and she said, after I had finally managed to get down the last spoonful:

"You are weak enough to fall over, but you are still a strong man, a hero. If only you were born as an Apache and not a lying paleface!"

"I don't lie. I never lie! You will see in the end."

"I would like to believe you, but there was only one paleface who told the truth—Kleki-petra, who we loved. His body was crooked but he had a pure spirit and a good and beautiful heart. You killed him when he had done nothing to you. Therefore you must all die and be buried with him."

"What? Is he not yet buried?"

"No."

"But how can his body have lasted so long?"

"He lies in a tight coffin, through which no air can pass. But you will get to see his coffin shortly before you die."

After this bit of reassurance, she left. I was left to imagine how heartening it would be for one who is about to be tortured to death to see someone else's coffin beforehand! I didn't really think seriously about my death at that point. On the contrary, I was convinced that I would survive. I had an infallible means of proving my innocence, namely the lock of Winnetou's hair that I had cut off when I set him free.

But did I really still have it? Had they taken it away? A moment of panic swept over me. In the few moments that I had been awake, I hadn't recalled the fact that Indians generally take all the valuables of their prisoners. I checked my pockets.

I still had the same clothes on—no one had removed a stitch. I will leave to your imagination what the result of three weeks of fever in an outfit like that were. There are circumstances that one can go through and survive, but which one should definitely omit from a book. The reader of a book such as this may envy my travels and experiences, but probably wouldn't mind missing dealing with some of the things I am omitting here. I often receive letters from enthusiastic readers of my works, telling me that they plan to undertake similar travels. They ask about costs, about equipment and the associated know-how, and about the languages one should learn beforehand. I can always dissuade these adventuresome readers by my forthright answers, in which I reveal some of the things I am silent about in my books.

In any case, I checked my pockets and found to my astonishment and relief that I still had everything—every single thing. Only my weapons had been taken away. I pulled out the sardine tin. My surveying notes were still there, and among them was the lock of Winnetou's hair. I closed it up again, put it in my pocket, and lay down, relieved, to sleep once more.

Chapter 23

It was nearly evening when I awoke, and Nsho-chi appeared right away. I didn't have to use the whistle. She brought me food and fresh water. This time, I was able to eat without help. As I ate, I asked her many questions. She answered some, but not others, depending on their content. Naturally, she had been given rules of conduct which she had to follow strictly. There was much that I was not allowed to know. I asked her, among other things, why my things had not been taken.

"Winnetou, my brother, commanded it," she answered.

"Do you know why?"

"No. I did not ask. But there is something else, something better, that I can tell you."

"What?"

"I have visited the three palefaces that were caught along with you."

"You did?"

"Yes. I wanted to say to them that you were much better and would soon be healthy. The one that is called Sam Hawkens asked me to give you something that he made during the three weeks that he cared for you."

"What is it?"

"I asked Winnetou if I could bring it to you, and he permitted it. Here it is. You must be a strong and clever man to kill the gray bear with only a knife. Sam Hawkens told me about it."

She gave me a necklace that Sam had made from the teeth and claws of the grizzly. The tips of the two ears were also attached.

"How did he make this?" I asked, astonished. "And with just his hands. Did he get to keep his knife and his other possessions?"

"No, you are the only one that kept everything. But he said to my brother that he wanted to make this necklace, and asked to get back the teeth and claws of the bear. Winnetou granted this request, and also gave him the tools he needed to make the necklace. Put it on today. You will not have long to enjoy it."

"Because I must die soon?"

"Yes."

She took the necklace from me and put it around my neck. From that day on, I always wore it whenever I was in the Wild West. I now answered the beautiful Indian:

"You could have brought me this souvenir later. There's no hurry. I hope to wear it for many more years."

"No, the time is short, very short."

"You must not believe it! Your warriors won't kill me!"

"Yes they will. The council of the elders has decided it."

"They will change their minds, when they hear that I am innocent."

"They will not believe it."

"They will believe it. I can prove it."

"Then prove it, prove it! I would be very, very happy if I heard that you were not a liar and traitor! Tell me how you can prove it, so that I can tell my brother Winnetou!"

"Let him come to me to find out."

"He will not do that."

"Then he will not find out. I am not used to begging for friendship, or talking to someone who could come to me, through messengers."

"You warriors are such hard people! I would have loved to bring you the forgiveness of Winnetou, but you would not accept it."

"I do not need forgiveness, for I have done nothing that needs to be forgiven. But I would like to ask you to do another favor."

"What?"

"If you see Sam Hawkens again, tell him not to worry. As soon as I am well again, we will be free."

"I don't believe that! This hope will never be fulfilled."

"It is not a hope, but a total certainty. Later, you will tell me that I was right."

I said this with such a tone of certainty that she gave up trying to argue and left.

I knew the place I was being kept was on the Rio Pecos, or rather, on a tributary—when I looked out the door, I could see the cliffs on the opposite side of the canyon, not far away. The valley of the Rio Pecos itself would have to be much wider. I would have enjoyed seeing the pueblo in which I was being held, but I wasn't yet strong enough to get off my bed, and in any case, I didn't know if the Indians would let me leave my room.

At dusk, the old woman came and sat in the corner. She brought along a lamp made of a small, hollowed-out gourd, which burned all night long. This old woman had to do all the coarse tasks, whereas Nsho-chi served as my host, if I may use that expression.

Once again, I spent the night in a deep, restorative sleep, and when I woke I felt much stronger than the previous morning. On this day, I received no less than six meals, always consisting of a thick bullion with cornmeal. This was as nourishing as it was easy to chew. I continued getting it on the following days until I was able to swallow better and could eat more solid food, particularly meat.

My condition improved from day to day. I gradually got some flesh on my bones, and the swelling in my mouth steadily grew less. Nsho-chi never changed, always showing a friendly concern, totally convinced that I would soon have to die. Later, I noticed that, when she thought I wasn't watching, her eyes would occasionally rest on me with a sad, silently questioning look. It seemed that she was beginning to sorry for me. I had clearly judged her unjustly in thinking she had no heart. I asked her if I was permitted to leave my room, whose door was always open. She said I was not, and she explained that two guards were constantly stationed outside my door, day and night. It was only because of my weakness that I had not been tied up, and she thought it wouldn't be long until they would come with ropes to tie me.

This prompted me to think about precautions. I was depending on my lock of Winnetou's hair, but it was possible that it might not work as I hoped. Then I would be on my own and would have to depend on the strength of my body. I needed to build up my muscles. But how?

By this time, I lay down only to sleep. At other times, I sat or paced up and down the room. I told Nsho-chi that I was not accustomed to sitting on the floor, and asked her if I could not have a stone to use as a seat. This request was relayed to Winnetou, and he sent several of various sizes. The heaviest probably weighed a bit over a hundred pounds. I exercised with this stone whenever I was alone. To the women who tended me, I still feigned weakness. But in reality, in two weeks I was strong enough to easily lift the big stone into the air many times in a row. This improvement continued, and by the end of the third week, I knew I had recovered my full strength.

I had been there six weeks and had not heard that the captured Kiowas had been released. That must have been quite an undertaking, to feed two hundred men for so long! But of course the Kiowas had to pay for it all. The longer they stayed without accepting the Apache's terms, the more they would have to pay to be released.

Then, one beautiful, sunny late fall day, Nsho-chi brought me my morning meal and sat down near me while I ate. Previously, she had kept at a distance. She watched me with a moist gleam in her soft eyes, and finally a teardrop rolled down her cheek.

"You are crying?" I asked. "What has happened that troubles you so?"

"It will finally happen, today."

"What?"

"The Kiowas are being released and they will leave. Their people came last night to the river down below, with all the things that they must pay us."

"And that upsets you? You should be happy about it!"

"You don't know what you are saying. You don't understand what will happen to you. The departure of the Kiowas will be celebrated by tying you and your three white brothers to the stake."

I had known this was coming, but still I was startled when I heard it. So this was to be the decisive day, maybe even my last day! What would my situation be when dusk approached this evening? I pretended indifference and continued eating, outwardly calm. When I finished, I gave her the dish. She took it, stood up, and left. In the entrance, she turned around, came back to me, gave me her hand and said, unable to hold back her tears:

"This is the last time I will be able to speak to you. Farewell! You are called Old Shatterhand, and you are a strong warrior. Be strong when they torture you! Nsho-chi is very troubled about your death, but she will be pleased if you make no sound of pain and no wailing in spite of all the suffering. Do this for me and die as a hero!"

After making this appeal, she hurried out. I walked to the door to watch her go. Instantly, I faced the barrels of two rifles. The guards were doing their duty. Had I gone one step further, I would have been shot to death, or at least sufficiently wounded to prevent me from proceeding. There was no chance of escape, and an escape wouldn't have been successful anyway, since I didn't know the area. So I quickly retreated into my jail.

What should I do? The only thing to do was to wait calmly for the command and, when the right time arrived, to see if the lock of hair would have the effect I hoped for. My brief glimpse of the world outside had served to convince me that any thought of flight was foolhardy. I had read about Indian pueblos, but I hadn't seen one until then. They are built to be easy to defend, and their construction is uniquely suited to this purpose.

They usually fill deep gaps in the cliff, are built of nothing but solid stonework, and are composed of several individual stories, in accordance with the available space. Each successive story is set slightly back from the one below, so that the roof of one level creates a platform at the front of the next-higher level. The whole construction has the appearance of a stepped pyramid which sits deeper into the cliff the higher you go. Thus the ground floor sticks out farther than any other, and it is also the widest. The upper levels decrease in size. These buildings are not like ours, with internal stairs that connect the levels. Rather, you reach the upper levels via ladders which are placed against the outside walls, and which can be removed if need be. If an enemy approaches, the ladders are pulled up. The enemy can't get to the upper levels unless he brings ladders of his own. But even then, he would have to attack the levels one by one, and survive the bullets of the defenders standing on the levels above, who would still be completely safe from his weapons.

It was in such a pyramidal pueblo that I found myself. From what I had seen, I was probably on the eight or ninth level. How could you escape from a place like that, with Indians on every level below? No, I had to remain. So I lay down and waited.

These were terrible, almost unbearable hours. Time passed at a snail's pace, and by noon nothing had happened to confirm what Nsho-chi had told me. Finally, I heard outside the approaching steps of several people. Winnetou came in, followed by five Apaches. I remained lying down, trying to behave naturally. He gave me a long, searching glance and then said:

"Old Shatterhand must say if he is healthy again!"

"Not completely," I answered.

"But I can hear that you can speak."

"Yes."

"And you can walk?"

"I think so."

"Do you know how to swim?"

"A little."

"That is good, because you will have to swim. Do you know on which day you are supposed to see me again?"

"On the day of my death."

"You remembered. That day has arrived. Stand up. You will be tied."

It would have been crazy not to follow this order. There were six of them, and they could easily have overpowered me. Perhaps I might have knocked out a few of them, but that wouldn't have accomplished anything except to make the rest more hostile. So I stood up and held out my hands. They were tied together in front of me. Two thongs were tied to my feet so that I could walk or climb slowly, but I couldn't run. Then they took me out to the platform.

From there, a ladder led to the next level down. It was not the kind of ladder we are used to, but rather a big wooden pole into which notches had been carved that served as steps. Three of the Indians went down first. I had to follow them, which was not really hard in spite of my ropes. Then the other two followed me. In this way we went down from one story to the next. Women and children quietly watched our progress on each level, and then came down after us. By the time we reached the bottom, there must have been several hundred of them. They were to be our audience, our public, who were to enjoy the spectacle of our death.

It was as I had deduced. The pueblo was in a small side canyon that opened into the wide valley of the Rio Pecos, down to which I was led. The flow of water in the Rio Pecos is limited, and it is considerably less in the summer and fall than in the winter and spring. But there are deep areas where, even in the dry months, the flow of water is not noticeably less. These are surrounded by rich grasslands and thickets of trees. Indians tend to settle in these areas, which provide year-round grazing for their horses. I saw that I was being led toward such a spot. The width of the river valley at this point was a good half-hour's walk, and both banks of the river were covered with bushes and woods, surrounded by strips of green grass. Directly in front of us, there was a break in the woods on both banks, the cause of which I didn't have time to contemplate at that moment. Right where the side canyon opened into the main valley, there was a stretch of sand, at least five hundred paces wide, that led straight to the river and continued on the far side of it. It was like a yellow stripe crossing the green valley of the Rio Pecos. Along this wide, sandy line there wasn't a blade of grass, not a bush, not a tree to be seen, with the exception of a single huge cedar that stood on the far side, right in the middle of the otherwise barren strip of sand. Thanks to its strength, it had withstood whatever the natural event was that had deposited the strip of sand across the valley. It was not on the riverbank, but stood a distance back. It had been chosen by Inchu-chuna to play a role in the day's events.

The near bank was full of life. I noticed our wagon, which the Apaches had seized and brought back with them. On the other side of the sandy strip, the horses that the Kiowas had brought as ransom were grazing. There, too, were the tents and the weapons that the Kiowas had brought. Inchu-chuna was moving among them with some of his people whose task it was to count up the booty. Tangua was with him, for the Apaches had already released him and his warriors. A glance at the milling crowd of fantastically clothed red figures told me that easily six hundred Apaches were present.

When they saw us coming, they quickly gathered around the wagon, forming a half-circle. The Kiowas joined the crowd.

When we reached the wagon, I saw Hawkens, Stone, and Parker. They were each tied to a pole that had been set firmly and deeply into the ground. A fourth pole was empty, and I was tied to it. These were the stakes where we were to end our lives in slow, painful suffering! They were set up in a line, with only a little space between them. Sam was next to me, then came Stone, and then Parker. Not far from us lay many bundles of dry wood that would be piled around us when the time came to burn us like the many martyrs before us.

My three friends seemed not to have suffered during their captivity. They looked well fed, but they didn't look very happy.

"Ah, Sir, you're here too!" said Sam. "It's a miserable, sad operation they have in mind for us, and I don't believe we'll live through it.

Getting killed and being beaten to death are hard enough on the body that you're not likely to survive them. And after that, they plan to burn us, if I'm not mistaken. What do you think, Sir?"

"Do you have any hope of rescue?" I asked him.

"I can't think who might turn up to save us. I've been straining my wits for weeks, but I haven't come up with a single suitable idea. We were stuck in a dark hole in the cliff, we were tied up, and we had guards to boot. How can you escape from that? How was it for you?"

"Very good!"

"I believe it. You look healthy. They fattened you up like a gander that is to be grilled for the feast of St Martin! How are your wounds?"

"Passable. I can speak again, as you hear, and the swelling I still have will be gone soon."

"I don't doubt that! That swelling will be cured so dramatically today that not a trace of it will be left. Same with the rest of you—nothing left but a pile of ashes. I can't see how we get out of this one, and yet I'm not really in a dying frame of mind. Believe it or not, I'm not fearful or worried. It's as if these Indians somehow can't do anything to us, as if someone will suddenly turn up and set us free."

"Possible! I haven't lost hope either. I'm even willing to bet that tonight, at the end of this perilous day, that we will be completely fine."

"Sure, you can say that—you're nothing but an egregious greenhorn. We'll be completely fine? That's dumb. Forget about 'completely fine.' I'll thank God if I even live to see the evening."

"I've given you plenty of examples to prove that German greenhorns are different from the local ones."

"So? What do you mean by that? That's quite a tone of voice. Did you think up a good plan?"

"Yes."

"What is it? When did you think it up?"

"That evening when Winnetou and his father managed to escape the Kiowas."

"You thought of the plan then? That's weird. It's not likely to help us now, because back then you didn't know we'd be lodging with the Apaches this way. So what's the nature of this plan?"

"A lock of hair."

"A lock of hair?" he repeated, astonished. "Tell me, Sir, what in the world do you have in that head of yours? A rat's nest, maybe?"

"I don't think so."

"But what is this blathering about a lock of hair? Did some old girlfriend of yours send it to you, so you could make a present of it to the Apaches?"

"No. It comes from a man."

He looked at me as if he doubted my sanity, shook his head, and said:

"Listen, Sir, there's something not right in your head. You must have ended up with something stuck in there from your wound that doesn't belong there. Maybe you have a lock of hair in your head instead of your pocket. I just don't see how a lock of hair is going to get us untied from these stakes."

"Hmm. Yes, I guess it's a greenhorn idea, and we'll just have to see if it works or not. And as far as getting untied from the stake goes, I'm certainly not planning to hang around."

"Right you are. Once they've burned you, you won't be hanging around."

"Pshaw! I'll be free before they even start to torture us."

"Is that so? What gives you that idea?"

"I'm supposed to swim."

"Swim?" he asked, giving me a look akin to that of a psychiatrist dealing with a difficult patient.

"Yes, swim. And I can't do that tied to a pole. So they'll have to untie me."

"I'll be jiggered! Who told you you would have to swim?"

"Winnetou."

"And when are you supposed to swim?"

"Sometime today."

"I declare! If he said that, why, it's like a gleam of sunlight breaking through the clouds. Sounds like you'll get a chance to fight for your life."

"That's what I think too."

"Then they'll do the same with us. I don't think they'll treat you any different than us. This means our situation isn't quite as doubtful as I figured."

"I agree. We'll probably be able to save ourselves."

"Oh ho! Don't get too confident! If they're going to let us fight for our lives, they'll make it as difficult as possible. But there have been some cases where white captives have survived. Do you know how to swim, Sir?"

"Yes."

"How well?"

"Well enough that I don't think I need to fear any Indian."

"Listen, don't get cocky. These fellows swim like fish."

"Then I'll swim like an otter that catches fish and eats them."

"You're bragging."

"No. Swimming was always one of my favorite activities. Have you ever heard of treading water?"

"Yes."

"Can you do it?"

"No, and I've never seen it done."

"Well, maybe you'll see it done today. If they actually give me a chance to save my life by swimming, I'm pretty sure I'll survive this day."

"I sure hope so, Sir! And I hope they give us the same chance. At least that's better than being tied to this pole here. I'd rather die fighting than be tortured to death."

Chapter 24

We were not prevented from talking to each other. Winnetou stood talking with his father and Tangua, without paying any attention to us. The other Apaches that had been my guards were busy bringing order to the half-circle of Indians around us.

The children sat in the front row, and behind them were the girls and women, Nsho-chi among them. I noticed that she rarely took her eyes off me. Next were the young men, with the warriors behind them. Things had settled down by the time Sam uttered the words just mentioned. Then Inchu-chuna, who stood between Winnetou and Tangua, said in a voice loud enough for all to hear:

"My red brothers, sisters, and children, and also the men of the Kiowa tribe: listen to what I have to say!"

He paused. Once he saw that he had everyone's attention, he continued:

"The palefaces are the enemies of the red man. There are very few of them that look at us with a friendly eye. The most noble of these few white men came to the Apache people, to be our friend and father. That is why we gave him the name 'Kleki-petra,' white father. My brothers and sisters all knew him and loved him. Let them confirm it!"

A "How!" of affirmation rose from the circle. Then the chief continued:

Kleki-petra was our teacher in all things that we did not know, but that were good and useful. He also spoke of the religion of the white people and of the Great Spirit who created all people and cares for all people. This Great Spirit commanded that the red man and the white man should be brothers and should love each other. Have the white people fulfilled his command? Have they shown us love? No! Let my brothers and sisters confirm it!"

There was another chorus of "How!"

"Instead they came to take our possessions and to wipe us out.

They succeeded because they were stronger than we were. Where the buffalo and the mustangs grazed, they built their cities, from which come all the evils that overwhelm us. Where the red hunter went through the woods or over the plains, the steaming fire-horse runs with its great wagons, bringing enemies to us. And when the red man flees to the place that they have left for us, and where he just wants to starve and die, soon the palefaces follow to make new paths for the fire-horse on the ground that belongs to the Indians. We met such palefaces and spoke with them peacefully. We told them that this land was ours and did not belong to them. They could not say anything against this, and they agreed that it was true. But when we called on them to go and not to bring the fire-horse to our grazing lands, they did not follow our demand and they shot Kleki-petra, who we loved and honored. Let my brothers and sisters confirm that I speak the truth!"

A loud and unanimous "How!" confirmed this.

"We brought the body of the dead man back here and awaited the day of revenge. That day has dawned today. Kleki-petra will be buried today along with the man that killed him. Along with him, we captured four palefaces who were with him when he shot Kleki-petra. They are his friends and they delivered us into the hands of the Kiowas, but they deny it. What they have done would earn them death at the stake from any other tribe. But we want to follow the teachings of our white father Kleki-petra and act justly. Since they do not admit that they are our enemies, we will question them. Their fate will be determined by what we learn. Let my brothers and sisters show that they agree!"

"How!" echoed all around.

"Listen, Sir, that sounds promising for us," Sam said to me. "If they want to question us, then we aren't in as much trouble as I thought. I hope we can prove our innocence. I'll make everything so clear to these people that they'll be persuaded and they'll let us go."

"Sam, it'll never work," I answered him.

"No? Why not? You think I don't know how to talk to people?"

"Oh, I'm sure you learned how to talk to people as a child. But we've been prisoners here for six weeks, and in all that time you weren't able to convince the Apaches."

"You didn't either, Sir!"

"True enough, Sam. First of all I couldn't talk, and then, once I was able to move my tongue again, none of the Indians came to see me. You'll have to admit that I haven't really had a chance to defend us to the chiefs."

"And you shouldn't try it now!"

"Why not?"

"Because you wouldn't succeed. You're a greenhorn and inexperienced in such things. You would only make things worse. Sure, you're exceptionally strong, but that doesn't help us here— what's needed is the right kind of experience, a sharp mind, a bit of slyness, that you don't have. You can't help it. Nobody's born with these things, but that's exactly why you need to leave our defense to me."

"Well, I wish you better success than you've had so far, Sam!"

"I'm an old hand at this stuff. You'll see."

We were able to have this exchange undisturbed, for our questioning did not begin immediately. Inchu-chuna and Winnetou talked quietly with Tangua, often looking in our direction as they did so. They were clearly talking about us. The faces of the two Apaches grew steadily darker and sterner. The movements and expressions of the Kiowa were those of a man who speaks eagerly to someone in order to make them suspicious of someone else. Who knows what lies he was telling about us in order to see us dead! Then they came over to us. The two Apaches stood to our right, while Tangua positioned himself at the left, near me. Now Inchu-chuna said to us, but in a loud voice so that all could hear:

"You heard what I said before. You must tell us the truth and you may defend yourselves. Answer the questions that I ask you! Do you belong to the white men who have measured the new path for the fire-horse?"

"Yes. But I must tell you that the three of us here did not do any measuring but were brought along only for protection," Sam answered. "And as for the fourth, called Old Shatterhand, he. . ."

"Quiet!" the chief interrupted him. "Answer my questions and speak no more. If you say more, I will have you whipped so that your skin jumps! So, you belong to these palefaces? Answer yes or no!"

"Yes," answered Sam, to avoid being hit.

"Old Shatterhand helped to measure?"

"Yes."

"And you three protected these people?"

"Yes."

"Then you are even worse than them. Someone who protects robbers and thieves has earned twice the punishment. Rattler, the murderer, was your companion?"

"Yes, but we were not his friends, but rather. . ."

"Quiet, dog!" Inchu-chuna interrupted. "You are to tell me what I want to know, nothing more! Do you know the laws of the West?"

"Yes."

"What is the punishment for stealing a horse?"

"Death."

"What is more valuable, a horse or the great, wide land that belongs to the Apaches?"

Sam did not answer. He would have been condemning himself to death.

"Speak, or I will have you whipped until you bleed!"

Little, brave Sam grumbled:

"Well then, whip away! Sam Hawkens is not a man who can be forced to talk when he doesn't want to!"

I turned to him and pleaded:

"Speak, Sam. It's better for us!"

"Well," he answered. "If you want me to, I'll give it a try, though I really shouldn't be saying anything."

"So, what is more valuable, a horse or the land?"

"The land."

"So a land-thief has earned death even more than a horse-thief, and you were trying to steal our land. Also, you are the companions of the man that murdered Kleki-petra. That makes the punishment greater. As land-thieves, you would be shot without having to suffer, but since you are murderers, you will have to suffer death at the stake. But we have not finished listing your deeds. Did you not deliver us into the hands of the Kiowas, who were our enemies?"

"No."

"That is a lie!"

"It is the truth."

"Did you not ride after us with Old Shatterhand, when we left you?"

"Yes."

"That is certainly a sign of being an enemy!"

"No. You threatened us, and so we needed to know if you had really left. That's a rule you follow if you live in the Wild West. You could have been hiding, waiting to shoot at us. That's why we followed you."

"Why not just you? Why did Old Shatterhand come along?"

"To teach him how to follow a trail, since he's new around here."

"If your intentions were peaceful and you followed us only out of caution, why did you call upon the Kiowas to help you?"

"Because we saw that you had hurried away. You wanted to gather your warriors quickly, to attack us."

"Was it really necessary to turn to the Kiowas?"

"Yes."

"Was there no other alternative?"

"No."

"You are lying again. You could have avoided us simply by doing what I had told you to do. You could have left our lands. Why didn't you do that?"

"Because we could not leave until our work was done."

"So you wanted to complete the theft that I had forbidden, and that's why you asked the Kiowas for help. Whoever sets our enemies against us, is also our enemy and must be killed. This is yet another reason for us to take your lives. But you didn't just let the Kiowas attack and capture us, you helped them. Do you admit it?"

"What we did, we did only to avoid bloodshed."

"Do you want to make me laugh? Did you not attack us when we came?"

"Yes."

"Did you not spy on us?"

"Yes."

"And spend a whole night near us? Is it so or not?"

"It is so."

"Did you not lead the palefaces to the water, to draw us there, and then hide the Kiowas in the woods, so that they could attack us?"

"That is true, but I must . . . "

"Quiet! I want a short answer, not a speech. We were led into an ambush. Whose idea was that?"

"Mine."

"This time, you are telling the truth. Several of us were wounded, a few died, and the rest were captured. You are to blame. This blood that was spilled will come back over you and is another reason you must die."

"My plan was that . . ."

"Quiet! I didn't ask you a question. The Great, Good Spirit sent us an unknown, invisible rescuer. My son Winnetou and I were freed. We went quietly to our horses, but took only those we needed so that the prisoners would have their horses when we freed them. We rode off to get our warriors, and brought them to face the Kiowas. They were on the Kiowas' trail and had been following them, so we met them quickly, on the next day. Much blood flowed again, and we had sixteen dead, without speaking of the blood and pain of the wounded. This is still another reason why you must die. You can expect no pity or mercy, and . . ."

"We don't want pity, just justice," Sam interrupted. "I can . . ."

"Will you not be quiet, dog?" Inchu-chuna interrupted him angrily. "You are to speak only when I ask you a question. And now I am completely finished with you. But since you speak of justice, I will not only judge you by what you say, but I will also put a witness before you. Tangua, the Chief of the Kiowas, may deign to raise his voice in this situation. Are these palefaces our friends?"

"No," answered the Kiowa, who was plainly pleased that matters were taking a turn that was so worrisome to us.

"Did they want to spare us?"

"No. They tried to stir me up against you, and they asked me to have no pity, but rather to kill you, to kill you all."

This untruth angered me so much that I ended my silence and said to his face:

"That is such a huge, barefaced lie, that I would knock you to the ground in an instant if I had just one hand free!"

"Dog, stinking dog!" he thundered. "Shall I be the one that hits you?"

He raised his fist. I answered:

"Hit me, if you are not ashamed to hit someone who cannot defend himself! You speak of a hearing and of justice? Is it a hearing, and is it justice, if a man can't say what he has to say? Are we supposed to defend ourselves? How can we do that, if we'll be beaten when we say one more word than what you want to hear? Inchu-chuna is behaving like an unjust judge. He gives us questions that can only be answered so that we condemn ourselves. We are not allowed to give any other answers, and when we want to speak the truth to save ourselves, he interrupts us, will not let us speak, and threatens us with punishment. We do not need such a hearing and such justice. We prefer that you begin the torture that you have planned for us! You will not hear a single sound of pain from us."

"Ugh, Ugh!" I heard a female voice cry in wonder. It was Winnetou's sister.

"Ugh, Ugh!" many of the Apaches answered.

Courage is what the Indian always respects and recognizes even in his enemy. Hence the cries of wonder which I now heard. I continued:

"When I saw Inchu-chuna and Winnetou for the first time, my heart told me that they were brave and honest men who I could love and honor. I was wrong. They are no better than all the others, for they listen to the voice of a liar and will not let the truth be spoken. Sam Hawkens let himself be intimidated, but I will not listen to your threats and I despise anyone who oppresses a prisoner just because he cannot defend himself. If I were free, I would speak very differently with you!"

"Dog, you call me a liar?" cried Tangua. "I will break apart your bones!"

He lifted his gun, turned, and would have hit me with the butt, but Winnetou sprang forward, held him back, and said:

"Let the Chief of the Kiowas remain calm! This Old Shatterhand has spoken very boldly, but I agree with some of his words. Let Inchu-chuna, my father, the Chief of all the Apaches, give him permission to say what he wants to say!"

Tangua had to restrain himself, and Inchu-chuna decided to grant his son's request. He walked up to me and said:

"Old Shatterhand is like a bird of prey, that still bites when it is captured. Did you not knock out Winnetou twice? Did you not knock me out with your own fist?"

"Did I do that freely? Did you not force me to do it?"

"Force you?" he asked, astonished.

"Yes. We wanted to surrender without fighting, but your warriors would not listen to us. They attacked us so fiercely that we had to defend ourselves. But ask them. Didn't we only wound them, when we might have killed them? We tried to flee, rather than kill them. Then you came and attacked me, without listening to what I was trying to say. I had to defend myself, and I could have stabbed you or shot you, but I only knocked you out because I was your friend and wanted to spare you. Then Tangua, the chief of the Kiowas, came and wanted to take your scalp. I wouldn't let him, and so he fought with me, but I beat him. So I not only spared your life, but saved your scalp. Then, when. . . "

"This accursed coyote lies as if he had a hundred tongues!" cried Tangua angrily.

"Is it really a lie?" Winnetou asked him.

"Yes. I hope my red brother Winnetou does not doubt the truth of my words."

"When I arrived, you were lying still and so was my father. That is true. Old Shatterhand may continue!"

"Well, I had subdued Tangua in order to rescue Inchu-chuna, then Winnetou arrived. I didn't see him, and he hit me with the butt of his gun, but it missed my head. Winnetou stabbed me in the mouth and through my tongue, so I could not speak. Otherwise, I would have said that I liked him and wanted to be his friend and brother. I was wounded and one arm was lame, but still I beat him. He lay unconscious before me, just as Inchu-chuna did. I could have killed them both. Did I?"

"You would have done it, but an Apache warrior came and knocked you out."

"No. I would not have done it. Didn't these three palefaces, tied up here next to me, didn't they come freely to you and turn themselves over to you? Would they have done that if they viewed you as enemies?"

"They did it because they saw that they could not escape. They decided it was smarter to give up. I admit that there is something in your words that is almost worth believing, but the first time you knocked out my son Winnetou, you were not forced to."

"Oh, yes."

"Who forced you?"

"It was as a precaution. We wanted to save you and Winnetou. You are brave warriors. You would certainly have defended yourselves and would have been wounded or even killed. We wanted to prevent that. That's why I knocked out Winnetou, and you were captured by my three friends. I hope you will believe my words."

"They are lies, nothing but lies!" cried Tangua. "I came just as he had knocked you out. It is he who wanted your scalp, not me. I tried to stop him, but his hand, in which the great, evil spirit lives, struck me. No one can withstand it, not the strongest man."

I turned back to him and said, in a threatening voice:

"Yes, no one can withstand it. I only use it because I don't want to shed the blood of a man. But if I fight you again it will be with a rifle, not my hand, and you will not escape with just a headache. Mark my words!"

"You? Fight with me?" he laughed scornfully. "We will burn you and spread your ashes to the wind!"

"I don't think so. I will be free sooner than you think, and then you will have to answer to me!"

"I wish your words could be fulfilled. I would be glad to fight with you, for I know that I would crush you."

Inchu-chuna intervened to end this exchange. He said to me:

"Old Shatterhand is very bold, if he thinks he will be set free. He should consider how many cases there are against him. If one of them were given up, it would not change his fate. He has only made claims, and has given no evidence."

"Did I not strike down Rattler when he shot at Winnetou and hit Kleki-petra? Is that not evidence?"

"No. You could have done this for another reason. Do you have anything else to say?"

"Not now, but perhaps later."

"Say it now. You will not be able to say it later!"

"No, not now. If I say it later, you will hear that Old Shatterhand is not a man whose word can be doubted. I will keep quiet now, for I want to hear what judgment you will pass on us."

Inchu-chuna turned from me and made a gesture with his hand. Several old warriors emerged from the half-circle and sat down together with the three chiefs. During their council, Tangua did everything he could to make the judgment as harsh as possible. While this was going on, we had a chance to exchange a few words.

"I'm curious what they'll brew up," Dick Stone observed. "I don't think it'll be very pleasant."

"I bet we're really in for it," said Will Parker.

"Right," agreed Sam Hawkens. "These fellows don't believe a word, no matter what we say! By the way, you didn't do half bad, Sir! I was surprised at Inchu-chuna."

"Why?" I asked.

"The way he let you run on. He practically jumped down my throat whenever I opened my mouth."

"Run on? Do you really mean that, Sam?"

"Yes."

"Well, thanks for the compliment."

"Running on is what I call any talking that doesn't accomplish something, if I'm not mistaken. I you accomplished just as little as I did."

"I disagree."

"On what grounds?"

"I have very good grounds. Winnetou spoke of swimming. That was already decided. So I think they only made the hearing so tough in order to frighten us. The sentence will be much lighter."

"Don't count on it, Sir! Perhaps you're thinking they'll let you swim for your life?"

"Yes."

"Nonsense, complete nonsense! Yes, they may decide to let you swim, but do you know where?"

"Well?"

"Straight to your own death, that's where. Then, when you're dead, you'll be thinking 'Hey, old Sam was right', hee-hee-hee!"

This remarkable little man managed, even in this awful situation, to find enough humor in his dubious jokes that he actually laughed to himself. His amusement lasted only a moment, however, for the Indians had finished their council. The warriors that had taken part went back to their places in the half-circle, and Inchu-chuna announced in a loud voice:

"Hear, you warriors of the Apaches and Kiowas, what we have decided about these four paleface prisoners. In the council of elders, it was previously decided that we would drive them into the water, then make them fight each other, and then burn them. But Old Shatterhand, the youngest of them, has spoken words that contain much wisdom. They have earned death, but it seems that their intent was not as bad as we believed. So our original decision has been changed, and we will let the Great Spirit decide between us and them."

He paused for a moment, perhaps to increase the suspense among his listeners. Sam used the opportunity to remark:

"How about that! This is getting interesting, very interesting! Do you know what he means, Sir?"

"I have an idea," I answered.

"Well, what?"

"A duel, a so-called decision of the gods. Am I right?"

"Yes, a two-man fight, for sure. But who will the fighters be? I can't wait to hear."

The chief continued:

"The paleface that is called Old Shatterhand seems to be the most noble of them, so the decision will be laid in his hands. And it will depend on the highest-ranking one among us. That is me, Inchu-chuna, Chief of the Apaches."

"Well bless my soul!" whispered Sam, very excited.

"Ugh, ugh, ugh!" came the cries of surprise from the ranks of Indians.

They were astonished that he wanted to fight me himself. He could have avoided the danger that he might find himself in by assigning the task to someone else. He continued, explaining his choice:

"The reputation of Inchu-chuna and Winnetou has been damaged because they were knocked out by the fist of a paleface. One of them must fight the paleface to wash away this stain. Winnetou must let me fight, for I am the older and the highest chief of the Apaches. He agrees that I will clean both my honor and his by killing Old Shatterhand."

Again he paused.

"You can be happy about that, Sir!" said Sam. "At least you'll have a quicker death than us. You wanted to spare this guy, and now he's going to wipe you out!"

"We'll see about that!"

"Forget it, it's a forgone conclusion. Or do you think you'll get an even chance against him?"

"I don't see any chance of that."

"No, indeed! They always set these things up so that the white man doesn't stand a chance. If somebody escapes with their life every once in a while, well, that's the exception that proves the rule. Listen!"

Inchu-chuna continued:

"We will untie Old Shatterhand and let him jump into the water. He must swim across the river, but he will have no weapon. I will follow him with only my tomahawk. If Old Shatterhand makes it across the river and reaches the cedar tree in the clearing over there, he is saved, and the other palefaces will be set free also. They can go wherever they wish. But if I kill him before he reaches the cedar, then they must also die. But they will not be tortured and burned, they will just be shot. Let all the warriors confirm that they hear my words and take heed of them!"

"How!" was the unanimous answer.

Chapter 25

As you can imagine, we were very excited, though I was less so than Sam, Dick, and Will. Sam said:

"Those fellows were very sly about this. You get to swim because you're the 'most noble' of us. That's nonsense! It's because you're a greenhorn, that's why. It's me, me that they should let in the water! I'd show them how Sam Hawkens can swim like a trout through the waves! But you? Listen, Sir, think how our lives depend on you! If you lose and we have to die, I'll refuse to ever speak to you again. You can depend on it, if I'm not mistaken!"

"Don't worry, Sam!" I answered. "What I can do, I will do. I disagree with you: the Indians haven't made a bad choice. I think I can save you a lot easier than you could save us."

"I sure hope so! Our lives are in the balance. Don't even think about sparing Inchu-chuna. Get that idea out of your head!"

"We'll see!"

"Forget it! There's nothing to see! If you don't kill him, you're lost, and then we die too. You're planning to depend on your fists?"

"Yes."

"It won't work! It will never come to hand-to-hand combat."

"I think it will."

"No it won't!"

"How's he going to kill me, then?"

"With his tomahawk, of course. You know they don't use that up close. They're deadly at a distance. These Indians practice until they can cut off the tip of your finger at a hundred paces if you hold it in the air. Inchu-chuna won't try to hack you up with his hatchet, he'll throw it at you as you try to flee and kill you with the first throw. Believe me, you could be the best swimmer in the world and still not make it to the far bank. He'll fling that tomahawk right into your skull, or more likely your neck, while you're swimming. I don't care how clever or strong you are, it won't help."

"I know that, Sam. And I also know that in some situations a thimbleful of cunning does more than a huge pot of strength."

"Cunning? And where would you get that kind of cunning from? I'm telling you, old Sam Hawkens is known as a smart guy, but I sure don't see how this cunning of yours is going to outstrip the chief. What defense is all the cunning in the world against a well-aimed tomahawk?"

"It helps, Sam, it helps!"

"How so?"

"You'll soon see, or rather, you soon won't see. But I will tell you I'm almost certain I will succeed."

"You're not just doing all this bragging to give us encouragement?"

"No."

"Yes, you are. To buck us up! But what's the point of that, if it ends in disgrace the next minute?"

"Relax. I have an excellent plan."

"Plan? What now? There's no plan here, except to swim to the other side, and a tomahawk will get you before you make it."

"No. Now pay attention! If I drown, we are saved."

"Drowning saves us? Sir, you're half-dead already, or you wouldn't be talking so crazy."

"I know what I'm doing. Mark my words: if I drown, we have nothing more to fear."

I spoke these words quickly, since the three chiefs were approaching. Inchu-chuna said:

"Now we'll untie Old Shatterhand. But he must not think he can run away! Several hundred warriors would be after him immediately."

"I wouldn't think of it," I answered. "Even if I could escape, it would not be right for me to abandon my friends."

They untied my ropes and I moved my arms around, to see how well I could move. Then I said:

"It is a great honor for me to compete with the most famous chief of the Apaches, or rather, to swim for my life. But for him it is no honor."

"Why not?"

"Because I am not a good opponent for him. I have washed myself in streams and avoided going under water. But to cross such a wide, deep river—I'm not sure I can do it."

"Ugh, ugh! I am not pleased. Winnetou and I are the best swimmers of our tribe. It would mean nothing to conquer such a bad swimmer!"

"And you have a weapon, but I don't! So I'm going to my death, and my friends are resigned to death as well. So tell me again how to think about this fight. Who goes into the water first?"

"You!"

"And you follow me?"

"Yes."

"And when do you attack me with your tomahawk?"

"When it pleases me," he answered, with the proud, even contemptuous smile of a virtuoso speaking with a bungler.

"So that could happen while I'm still in the water?"

"Yes."

I behaved as if I were getting increasingly uneasy, worried, and hopeless. I asked:

"So you can kill me. Can I kill you?"

He made a face that made his answer clear without actually saying it: "You poor worm, don't bother thinking about it! This question can only have come from your fear of death." He said aloud:

"It is a fight to the death. Kill me if you can. That's the only way you're going to reach the cedar."

"And if you die I won't be harmed?"

"No. If I kill you, you won't reach the cedar and your friends must die. But if you kill me, you will reach the cedar, and from that moment you will be free. Come!"

He turned, and I took off my jacket and boots. The things I had in my pockets and belt, I laid on the ground. Sam wailed:

"It's all going wrong, Sir, completely wrong. If you could only see your face! And the pathetic tone of your last questions! I'm deathly scared, for you and for us!"

I couldn't answer him, since the three chiefs would have heard me. But I knew exactly why I was feigning fear. I wanted to make Inchu-chuna overconfident and, as they say, lead him down the garden path.

"One more question!" I pleaded, before I followed him to the river. "If we are freed, will we get our possessions back?"

He gave a short, impatient laugh. He thought this question was practically insane. He answered:

"Yes, you will get it back."

"Everything?"

"Everything."

"Our horses? Our guns?"

He sanpped at me angrily:

"Everything! I said it already! Do you have no ears? A turtle wanted to have a flying contest with an eagle and asked the eagle what he would give the turtle if he won! If your swimming is as bad as your questions, I'll be ashamed that I didn't choose an old squaw to be your opponent!"

We went out through the half-circle, which opened to let us through to the river bank. I passed close by Nsho-chi and she gave me a glance with which she said goodbye forever. The Indians followed behind us, and then selected spots to sit down and enjoy the interesting drama that was about to take place.

It was obvious that I was in grave danger. I could swim straight across or zig-zag, it didn't matter—I would be lost. The chief's tomahawk would find me. There was only one way to save myself: by diving. And fortunately, in diving I wasn't the bungler that Inchu-chuna had taken me for.

But I couldn't depend on diving by itself. I'd have to surface sometime, to breathe, and that's when I'd get a tomahawk in the head. No, I would not be able to come back up to the surface, at least not where the Indians could see me. But how could I do that? I looked up and down the river and saw, to my relief, that the situation was favorable for me.

We were, as I mentioned, on a clear, sandy area—a bit upstream from the middle of it. The upstream edge of it, where the forest began, was only a bit more than a hundred paces from me, and farther up there was a bend in the river that my eye was drawn to. Downstream, the sandy area continued for about four hundred paces.

If I jumped in the water and never surfaced, they would think I had drowned, and they would look for my body—downstream, of course. So upstream would be my salvation. Then I noticed a spot where the bank of the river had been undercut. The overhang there was well suited to provide a brief refuge. Farther upstream, all kinds of driftwood had washed up along the bank, and it was solid enough that I could use it the same way. But first, I needed to make a show of fear.

Inchu-chuna stripped down to his light Indian-style pants and stuck the tomahawk in his belt, having gotten rid of everything else he carried there. Then he said:

"We can begin. Jump in!"

"Can I check first, to see how deep it is?" I asked half-heartedly.

A smile of complete contempt went across his face. He called for a spear. It was brought to me, and I stuck it in the water. It didn't reach the bottom. That was ideal, but I tried to act even more defeated than before. I knelt by the water and washed my forehead, like one who fears he will get a heart attack if he doesn't cool off before going in the water. I heard a murmur of general disdain behind me, a sure sign that I was having the desired effect, and Sam's voice cried out:

"For God's sake, just come back here, Sir! I can't stand this. Let them torture us to death. That would be better than having to watch such a miserable sight!"

In spite of myself, I found myself wondering what Nsho-chi must be thinking of me. I turned around. Tangua's face was scorn made flesh; Winnetou's upper lip was curled, so that you could see his teeth; he was regretting having intervened on my behalf. And his sister had lowered her eyes. She could no longer watch me.

"I'm ready," commanded Inchu-chuna to me, "so jump in! Why are you hesitating?"

"Do I really have to?" I asked. "Is there no other way?"

A roar of laughter erupted from the onlookers, and Tangua cried out:

"Set the frog free! Give him his life! No warrior should touch such a coward!"

With the grim growl of a enraged tiger, Inchu-chuna yelled:

"In! Or in a moment I will cut your neck with my tomahawk!"

I looked shocked, turned to the bank of the river, put my foot in the water, then my other foot up to the shin, and behaved as if I wanted to get in nice and slowly.

"In with you!" cried Inchu-chuna again, and pushed me over with a kick in the back. That's what I wanted. I waved my arms helplessly, gave a cry of fear, and plopped into the water. In the next instant, though, the masquerade was over. I felt the bottom, turned upstream and swan, underwater, along the bank. Immediately I heard a noise behind and above me.

Inchu-chuna had jumped into the water after me. As I later learned, he had first thought of giving me a head start, pursuing me to the far side, where he planned to kill me. Because of my cowardly behavior, he gave up this plan and jumped in right away, to kill me as soon as I came to the surface. One must make short work of such a coward.

I reached the overhanging area of the bank and came up, but only high enough to let my mouth clear the surface. No one could see me there except the chief, who was the only one in the water. Fortunately, he was facing downstream. I took a quick, deep breath, went back down to the bottom, and continued swimming. Then I reached the driftwood and I surfaced again behind it and caught my breath. I was so well hidden that I could stay above water a bit longer. I saw the chief lying in wait like a bird of prey that is ready to pounce on its victim. Now I had the last, but also the longest, stretch of water before me—the stretch between me and the beginning of the woods, where bushes hung over into the water from the bank. I managed to get there safely, and I climbed onto the bank, completely hidden by the bushes.

Now I had to reach the bend in the river mentioned earlier, where I could cross over to the other side. Before hurrying off, I took one more look back through the bushes at those I had deceived. They were standing on the bank, calling and gesticulating, while the chief swam back and forth, still waiting for me, even though I could never have stayed under water that long. I wondered if Sam had remembered my words: if I drown, we are saved.

I ran as quickly as I could through the woods, until I reached the river-bend. There, I ran into the water and happily swam across, thinking about my deception—that they thought I was a bad swimmer and afraid of the water. Furthermore, it had been a rather crude bit of cunning to fool them this way. From what they knew of me previously, they should never have taken me for a coward.

On the other side, I proceeded downstream until I reached the end of the woods. Watching from the bushes, I could see that several of the Indians had jumped into the water and were poking around for the drowned Old Shatterhand. I could have gone to the cedar at my leisure and won, but I didn't want my victory to depend on cunning alone. I wanted to teach Inchu-chuna a lesson and make him obligated to me at the same time.

He was still swimming back and forth, searching. He didn't think to look across to the other bank. I slipped back into the water, floated on my back so that only my nose and mouth were out of the water, and slowly, by slight movements of my hands, moved downstream. No one noticed me. When I was opposite them, I ducked under water again, swam a bit toward them, surfaced, and, treading water, cried out:

"Sam Hawkens, Sam Hawkens, we have won, won!"

It appeared as if I were standing on a shallow spot. The Indians heard me and looked across. What a howl went up! It sounded like a thousand devils had been let loose and were competing at howling. Anyone who heard that sound would never forget it their whole life long. As soon as Inchu-chuna saw me, he struck out with long, powerful strokes and came rushing toward me. I could not let him get too close. I went back to the bank, climbed up, and waited there. "Go farther, Sir!" Sam cried out. "Get over to the cedar!"

Yes, no one could stop me from doing that. Inchu-chuna himself couldn't. But I wanted to teach him a lesson, and so I went no further until he was about forty paces away. Then I ran toward the tree. If I had still been in the water, he would have gotten me with his tomahawk, but I was convinced that he would not really be able to use his weapon until he reached the bank.

The tree was about three hundred paces from the bank. I covered about half the distance at a fast pace, and then I stopped and looked back. The chief was just emerging from the water. He was caught in the trap I had set for him: it was too late to catch up with me, so his only chance was the tomahawk. He pulled it from his belt and ran forwards. I held my ground, but once he got close enough to be dangerous, I turned to run—or at least I pretended to. I told myself that he would not throw the tomahawk while I was standing still, for I would see it coming and could avoid it. He, on the other hand, could attack me with it once he reached me. He would only throw it if I started to run; then my back would be turned and I would not see the tomahawk coming. So I decided to pretend to flee, but after no more than two steps, I stopped and turned quickly.

Right! He had stopped running to take good aim, and had swung the tomahawk around his head. Just as I turned to face him, he let it go. I took two or three quick steps to the side and it flew by me and buried itself in the sand.

That was what I wanted. I ran over to it, picked it up, and instead of running to the tree, I slowly walked back to the chief. He cried with fury and came running at me like one enraged. I swung the tomahawk over my head and cried threateningly:

"Halt, Inchu-chuna! You were mistaken about Old Shatterhand once again. Do you want your own hatchet in your head?"

He came to a stop and cried out:

"Dog, how did you escape me in the water? The evil spirit helped you again!"

"That's not true! If there is a spirit at work here, then it is the good Manitou that has stood by me."

As I spoke, I could see that his eyes, which were fixed on me, had the flicker of a secret decision in them. I continued:

"You plan to surprise me, to attack me, I can tell. Don't do it! It will mean your death. No harm will come to you. I am really fond of you and Winnetou. But if you attack, I will defend myself. You know I'm stronger than you, even without a weapon, and now I have the tomahawk. So do the wise thing and. . .

I couldn't finish. The fury that consumed him robbed him of the ability to think calmly. He threw himself at me, his hands outstretched like open claws. He thought he had me, but I ducked and slipped to one side, and he fell to the ground from the very power of the his lunge. I was on him instantly, one knee on each arm. I grabbed him by the neck with my left hand, and, raising the tomahawk in my right, cried:

"Inchu-chuna, do you plead for mercy?"

"No."

"Then I'll split your skull."

"Kill me, dog!" he panted, struggling vainly to get loose.

"No, you are Winnetou's father and you must live. But I'll have to knock you out. You're forcing me to do it."

I hit him in the head with the flat side of the tomahawk. It was a rattling blow. His limbs jerked and then went limp. It looked to the Indians on the other bank as if I had struck him dead. An even more terrible howl went up than the one I had heard earlier. I tied his arms with his belt, carried him to the cedar, and laid him there. I had to make this detour, because I was obliged by the wording of our agreement to reach the cedar. But I left him lying there and ran back to the riverbank. I saw that many of the Indians had jumped into the water and were swimming over, with Winnetou in the lead. If they weren't forced to keep their word, it could get dangerous for me and for my friends. So when I reached the water, I called out to them:

"Go back! The chief is alive, I have done nothing to him. But if you come, I will kill him. Only Winnetou may come. I want to speak with him!"

They did not heed this warning. Then Winnetou raised himself in the water so they all could see him, and called out several words that I didn't understand. They obeyed him, and turned back. He alone came across. I waited for him at the edge of the water and said, as he climbed out:

"I'm glad you sent your warriors back. They might have put your father in danger."

"You cut him with the tomahawk?"

"No. He forced me to knock him out, since he wouldn't submit to me."

"You could have killed him. He was in your hands!"

"I don't kill enemies gladly, and I certainly wouldn't kill a man who is the father of Winnetou, whom I like so much. Here, take his weapon! You decide whether I have won and whether the promises made to me and my friends will be kept."

He took the tomahawk, and he looked me over for a long, long time. His face got milder, its expression changed to one of astonishment, and then he cried out:

"What kind of a man is Old Shatterhand? Who can understand him?"

"You will learn to understand me."

"You give me this hatchet without knowing whether I will keep my word! You could have used it to defend yourself. Do you know that you have given yourself into my hands?"

"Pshaw! I'm not worried. I still have my arms and my fists, and Winnetou is not a liar but a noble warrior who will never break his word."

He reached out his hand to me and answered, with his eyes gleaming:

"You are right. You are free, and the other palefaces are too, except for the man called Rattler. You trust me. I wish I could trust you!"

"You will soon trust me as I trust you. Just wait a bit. Now, let's go to your father!"

"Yes, come! I must see him, for when Old Shatterhand hits someone they can easily die, even if it was not intended."

We went to the cedar and untied the chief's hands. Winnetou checked him over and then said:

"He is alive, but it will take time for him to wake up and his head will hurt for a long time. I cannot remain here, so I will send several men over to him. Would my brother Old Shatterhand like to come with me?"

This was the first time he ever called me "my brother." How often I would later hear this phrase from his lips, and how earnestly, truly, and loyally it was always meant!

We went down to the river and swam across. The Indians were anxiously waiting and watching on the other side. Seeing us swimming in such a relaxed way next to each other, they recognized not only that we had settled our differences, but also that they had misjudged me badly in making me the butt of their jokes and scornful laughter. As we climbed up the bank, Winnetou announced in a loud voice, taking me by the hand:

"Old Shatterhand won. He and his three friends are free!"

"Ugh, ugh, ugh!" cried the Apaches.

But Tangua stood there and looked at me darkly. I would still have to reckon with him. His lies and his efforts to have us killed needed to be punished, not just for our sake, but for the sake of the future and of the whites who might encounter him in later.

Chapter 26

Winnetou walked right past him without a glance. He led me to the poles where my three friends were bound.

"Hallelujah!" cried Sam. "We are saved! We won't die after all! My good man, friend, boy, greenhorn, how in the world did you do that?"

Winnetou gave me his knife and said:

"Cut them loose! You earned the right to do this yourself."

I did so. As soon as they were free, they flung themselves on me and took me in their six arms, pressing and squeezing me so hard that it almost frightened me. Sam even kissed my hand and affirmed, with tears flowing from his tiny eyes and down his tangled beard:

"Sir, if I ever forget what you did for me here, then let the first bear that I meet swallow me, beard and all! How in heaven's name did you do it? You disappeared. You were so scared of the water, we all thought you had drowned."

"Didn't I tell you: 'if I drown, we're saved'?"

"Old Shatterhand said that?" asked Winnetou. "So that was all acting?"

"Yes," I nodded.

"My brother knew what he was doing. He swam upstream under water, then came back on the other side, I think. My brother is not only as strong as a bear but also as clever as a prairie fox. His enemies must beware of him."

"And Winnetou was my enemy?"

"I was, but I am no longer."

"So you believe me, not the liar Tangua?"

He looked at me searchingly as he had earlier on the other bank, then held out his hand to me and answered:

"Your eyes are good eyes, and your face is honest. I believe you."

By this time, I had put on the clothing that I had earlier removed. I took the sardine tin out of my jacket pocket and said:

"My brother Winnetou is right, and I will prove it to him. Perhaps he will recognize what I will show him now."

I removed the rolled-up lock of hair, straightened it out, and held it out to him. He reached for it, but didn't take it. Instead, he jumped back a step, completely astonished, and cried:

"That is hair from my head! Who gave you that?"

"Earlier, Inchu-chuna told of the unseen rescuer sent by the Great, Good Spirit when you were tied to the trees. Yes, you did not see him, for he had to keep hidden from the Kiowas. But he does not need to keep hidden any longer. Now you will surely believe that I was not your enemy, but always your friend."

"You . . you untied us! We have you to thank for our freedom and our lives!" he managed to blurt, still stunned—he, who usually was not fazed by anything. Then he took me by the hand and led me to the place where his sister stood, who had been following our every move and word with her eyes. He put me in front of him and said:

"Nsho-chi sees here the brave warrior who secretly freed me and our father when the Kiowas had tied us to trees. Perhaps you may want to thank him."

With these words, he gave me a hug and kissed me on both cheeks.

She held out her hand to me and said only: "Forgive me!"

She was supposed to thank me and instead asked my forgiveness! Why? I understood her perfectly. She had silently doubted me. As my caretaker, she should have known me better than the others, and yet, when I had pretended to be afraid, she had believed it was true. She had believed me to be a cowardly fool, and rectifying this was more important to her than the thanks that Winnetou asked her to give. I pressed her hand and answered:

"Nsho-chi will remember all the things I said to her. Now they have come true. Will my sister believe me now?"

"I believe my white brother!"

Tangua was standing nearby. I could see how enraged he was. I walked up to him and said, looking him directly in the eye:

"Is Tangua, Chief of the Kiowas, a liar, or does he love the truth?"

"Do you mean to insult me?"

"No. I only want to know where I stand with you. So give me an answer!"

"Old Shatterhand knows that I love the truth."

"We will see! Do you keep your word when you make a promise?"

"Yes."

"That is important. Beware of those who do not do what they say. Do you remember what you said to me?"

"When?"

"A while ago, when I was still tied up."

"I said many things."

"Indeed. But you know the words I mean."

"No."

"Then I will help you remember. You wanted to settle matters with me."

"Did I say that?" he asked, raising his eyebrows.

"Yes. You also said that you would be glad to fight with me, because you knew that you would crush me."

He must have been unsettled by the tone in my voice, for he answered carefully:

"I don't remember these words. Old Shatterhand must have misunderstood me."

"No. Winnetou was there. He will be my witness."

"Yes," Winnetou willingly confirmed, "Tangua wanted to settle things with Old Shatterhand and boasted that he would be happy to fight with him and crush him."

"So you see, you did say these words. Will you keep them?"

"Is that what you demand?"

"Yes. You called me a frog with no courage, you slandered me and tried to get me killed. One who is audacious enough to do this must also be willing to risk defending himself against me."

"Pshaw! I only fight with chiefs."

"I am a chief!"

"Prove it!"

"Fine! I will prove it by hanging you on that tree there with a rope, if you refuse to settle with me."

Threatening an Indian with hanging is a greater insult than almost any other. He ripped his knife from his belt and cried:

"Dog, shall I stab you to death?"

"Certainly, but not that way. It has to be an honest fight, man against man and knife against knife."

"I will not do that. I want nothing to do with Old Shatterhand!"

"But earlier, when I was tied up and couldn't defend myself, you were interested in me, you coward."

He wanted to stab me, but Winnetou stepped between him and me and said:

"My brother Old Shatterhand is right. Tangua slandered him and wanted to settle accounts with him. If he now does not keep his word, he is a coward and should be thrown out of his tribe. This matter must be settled right now, for it must not be said that the Apache welcome cowards as guests. What does the Chief of the Kiowas want to do?"

Before he answered, Tangua glanced around. There were almost four times as many Apaches as Kiowas present, and the latter were deep in the former's territory. It would be imprudent to let it come to a quarrel between the tribes, now that he had had to pay such a huge ransom and was still, practically speaking, to some extent a prisoner.

"I will think about it," he answered, edging away.

"For a brave warrior, there is nothing to think about. Either you fight or you will be seen as a coward"

At this, he gathered himself together and cried:

"Tangua a coward? Anyone who says that, I will stab in the chest with my knifet!"

"I will say it," answered Winnetou, proudly and calmly, "if you do not stand by the words that you said to Old Shatterhand."

"I do stand by them!"

"Then you are ready to fight him?"

"Yes."

"Right now?"

"Right now! What I want most is to see his blood as soon as possible."

"Very good. Now it must be decided what kind of weapons will be used for this fight."

"Who chooses?"

"Old Shatterhand."

"Why?"

"Because you insulted him."

"No. I will choose."

"You?"

"Yes, me. He insulted me, and I am a chief while he is an ordinary white man. So I am much more than he is."

"Old Shatterhand is more than an Indian chief."

"That is what he claims, but he cannot prove it. A threat is no proof."

I settled the question:

"Tangua can choose. It makes no difference to me what weapon I beat him with."

"You will not beat me," he growled. "Do you think I would choose to fight with fists? You knock out everyone with your fists. Or do you think I would choose knives, when I saw you fight 'Lightning-Knife'? Or even a tomahawk, with which you overcame Inchu-chuna?"

"Well then, what?"

"Rifles. We will shoot at each other, and my bullet will find your heart!"

"Fine! I agree. But did my brother Winnetou hear what Tangua just admitted?"

"What?"

"That I fought 'Lightning-Knife' and stabbed him to death. I did that to save the captured Apaches from death at the stake, but Tangua has denied it until this moment. You can see how right I was when I called him a liar."

"A liar? Me?" the Kiowa thundered at me. "You will pay for this with your life! Let the fight begin immediately, so that I can quiet this yapping dog!"

He had his rifle in his hand. Winnetou sent one of his Apaches to the pueblo to fetch my rifle and the ammunition that I had had with me when I was captured. It had been carefully taken care of, because Winnetou, although he had thought I was his enemy, took such an interest in me. Then he asked me:

"Let my white brother say how many shots and from what distance apart."

"It makes no difference to me," I answered. "He chose the weapons. He can decide this too."

"Yes, I will decide," said Tangua. "Two hundred paces, and we will keep shooting until one of us falls and cannot stand up again."

"Good," said Winnetou. "I will be in charge. First one of you will shoot and then the other. I will have my rifle, and if anyone shoots when it is not his turn, I will put a bullet through his head. But who will shoot first?"

"I will, of course," cried the Kiowa.

Winnetou shook his head disapprovingly and said:

"Tangua wants to have all the advantages for himself. Old Shatterhand may shoot first."

"No," I answered, "let him have his wish. He'll shoot once, I'll shoot once, and then it will be done."

"No," replied Tangua. "We will keep shooting until one of us falls!"

"Indeed. You will fall with my first shot."

"Braggart!"

"Pshaw! I really should kill you, but I won't. But the minimum punishment for what you have done is to be lamed. I will shatter your right knee. Mark my words!"

"Do you hear?" he laughed. "This paleface, who is called a greenhorn by his friends, says he can hit me in the knee from two hundred paces! Laugh at him, you warriors, laugh at him!"

He looked around with a gesture of invitation, but nobody laughed. He continued:

"You're afraid of him! But I will show you how I laugh at him. Come, let us measure the two hundred paces!"

While this was happening, my bear-killer was brought to me. I checked it over and found it in good condition. Both barrels were loaded. To be on the safe side, I shot both barrels and reloaded them, as carefully as the current situation warranted. Sam came up to me as I did this and said:

"Sir, I have a hundred questions for you, and no opportunity to ask them. For now, I'll just ask one: are you really going to try to hit this fellow in the knee?"

"Yes."

"Nothing more?"

"That's enough of a punishment."

"No, it certainly is not. Such a vermin must be wiped out, if I'm not mistaken. Think of everything he is guilty of, and all the trouble he caused just because he wanted to steal the Apaches' horses!"

"The white men that put him up to it are at least as guilty."

"He shouldn't have let himself be tempted! If I were in your shoes, I'd give him a bullet through the head. You know he'll be aiming at yours!"

"That or the chest; no doubt about it."

"But he'll miss. His rifle is a piece of junk."

The distance was measured and we positioned ourselves at either end. I was as calm as ever, but Tangua indulged in unrepeatable curses against me. Finally Winnetou, who was standing halfway between us and slightly to the side, said:

"Let the Chief of the Kiowas be silent and listen! I will count to three, and then you can shoot. Anyone who shoots sooner will get my bullet in his head!"

As you might expect, all the on-lookers were gripped by the suspense. They had formed two rows to the right and left of us, so that a broad corridor was formed with us at its ends. A deep quiet set in.

"Let the Chief of the Kiowas begin," said Winnetou. "One, two, three!"

I stood still and showed my opponent the full width of my body. At the first word from Winnetou, he lifted his rifle into position and aimed carefully. He shot. The bullet flew right by me. The shot evoked no cries from anyone.

"Now let Old Shatterhand shoot," Winnetou cried out. "One, two, ..."

"Wait!" I interrupted him. "I faced the chief of the Kiowas directly and honestly. But he has turned so that I see only his side, not his face."

"I can do that," he answered. "Who says I cannot? We did not agree on how we should stand."

"That is true, and Tangua can stand as he pleases. He turns his narrow side to me because he thinks I cannot hit him as easily. But he is wrong. I will certainly hit him. I could shoot without saying anything, but I want to be honest with him. I wanted to hit his right knee, but that can only happen if he faces me. If he turns his side to me, then the bullet will shatter both his knees. That is the difference. He can stand however he wants to. I have warned him."

"Do not shoot words, shoot bullets!" he jeered, ignoring my warning and continuing to face sideways.

"Old Shatterhand will shoot," repeated Winnetou: "One, two, three!"

My shot cracked. Tangua gave a sudden loud cry, dropped his gun, waved his arms, tottered, and fell.

"Ugh, ugh, ugh!" came cries from all around. Everyone crowded toward him, to see where I had hit him.

I followed, and they made way for me.

"Both knees, he was hit in both knees!" I heard them saying right and left.

When I reached him, he was lying on the ground, whimpering. Winnetou knelt by him and checked his wounds. He saw me coming and said:

"The bullet went exactly where my white brother said it would go. It shattered both his knees. Tangua will never again be able to ride out after the horses of other tribes."

When the wounded man saw me, he heaped a flood of insults on me. I barked at him so that he paused for a moment, and I said:

"I warned you, and you didn't pay attention. It is your own

fault."

He didn't dare to cry out. An Indian must not do this even when in the most intense pain. He bit his lip, looked darkly at the ground in front of him, and then, through his clenched teeth, said:

"I am wounded and cannot go home. I must stay with the Apaches."

Winnetou shook his head and answered very forcefully:

"You will have to go home. We have no place for those who steal our horses and murder our warriors. We have not taken revenge in blood, but satisfied ourselves with horses and goods. You cannot ask for more than that. A Kiowa does not belong in our pueblo."

"But I cannot ride!"

"Old Shatterhand was more seriously wounded than you and he could not travel, but still he had to. Think of him often! It will do you good! Let the Kiowas leave us today. They must do this, because any who are still around in the morning will be treated as they wanted to treat Old Shatterhand. I have spoken. How!"

He took my hand and led me away. As we left the crowd, we saw his father come swimming across the river with the two men that Winnetou had sent to him. Winnetou went to meet him at the riverbank, while I sought out Sam Hawkens, Dick Stone, and Will Parker.

"Finally, finally we get our turn with you!" said Sam. "First of all, tell us what that hair was that you showed Winnetou."

"I had cut it from his head."

"When?"

"When I cut him and his father loose."

"So you . . . What the devil? You cut. . . You, the greenhorn, cut. . . you cut them loose?"

"Absolutely."

"Without saying a word to us?"

"It wasn't necessary!"

"But how in the world did you do it?"

"Just the way any greenhorn would do it."

"Please talk sense, Sir! That was an extraordinarily difficult feat!"

"Yes, you even doubted whether you would be able to do it."

"And yet you did it! Either I've lost my wits, or they aren't working at the moment!"

"I think it's the former, Sam."

"Don't make stupid jokes! Such maliciousness! He frees the chiefs and carries the lock of hair that works wonders around with him, without saying a word about it! Such an honest face he has, too. You just can't trust anybody any more! And how about what happened today! A couple of things are still unclear to me. He was drowned and then he suddenly reappeared!"

I told him the whole story. When I was done, he cried out:

"My good man, friend, and greenhorn, you are an awful varmint, if I'm not mistaken! I must ask you once again: have you never been in the Wild West before?"

"No."

"Not anywhere in the United States?"

"No."

"I just can't make you out. You're a beginner at everything, but you learn everything instantly. I really have never met a type like you. I have nothing but praise for you. That was really clever, the way you worked things out, hee-hee-hee! Our lives hung by a hair. But don't you let this praise go to your head. You'll just go out and do something dumber than ever. I'll be astonished if you ever turn into a serviceable frontiersman!"

He would have continued with these words of wisdom, but just then Winnetou and Inchu-chuna came up to us. Inchu-chuna looked at me long and searchingly, just as his son had done earlier, and then said:

"I have heard everything from Winnetou. You are free and you must forgive us. You are a very brave and very clever warrior, and you will defeat many enemies. He who makes himself your friend, he is wise. Will you smoke the calumet of peace with us?"

"Yes. I want to be your friend and brother."

"Then come with me and Nsho-chi, my daughter, into the pueblo! I want to provide a worthy place for the one that conquered me. Winnetou will stay here, to make sure everything is in order."

As free men, we climbed with him and Nsho-chi up into the pueblo from which, earlier in the day, we had been herded off to face our deaths.

Chapter 27

As we approached the pueblo, I saw for the first time what a powerful and imposing piece of stone construction it was. Some think the American natives are incapable of culture, but only people with a sophisticated culture could move such masses of stone and build a fortress, level upon level, that is completely impervious to the weapons of the day. There are those who say that the builders were of a past generation, and that today's Indians are not their descendants. I can't confirm or disprove that, but even if it is true, it is not grounds for saying that Indians aren't capable of mental sophistication. Naturally, if they are allowed no opportunity and no place in which to develop, these capabilities will wither and die.

By means of the ladders, we climbed up to the third-level platform, where the best rooms in the pueblo were located. Inchu-chuna lived there with his two children, and there we were shown our rooms.

Mine was large. While it had no window openings and received light only from the doorway, it was such a wide and high doorway that there was plenty of light. The room was empty, but Nsho-chi immediately fixed it up with furs, blankets, and other furnishings, so that I felt far more comfortable than would be expected for the circumstances. Hawkens, Stone, and Parker were given a similar room to share.

As soon as my "guest room" was ready for me to occupy, "Beautiful Day" brought me a magnificently-carved peace pipe, as well as tobacco. She filled the pipe herself and lit the tobacco. As I drew the first puffs, she said:

"Inchu-chuna, my father, sends you this calumet. He himself brought the stone from the sacred quarry, and from it I carved the bowl. It has not been in the mouth of any man, and we ask you to accept it from us as your possession, and to accept our thanks to you as you smoke it."

"You are very generous," I answered. "I am almost ashamed, because I have no gift to give in return."

"You have already given us so much—the lives of Inchu-chuna and Winnetou, my brothers—that we have no way to thank you enough. Both of them were in your hands, and you did not kill them. Again today, you could have taken Inchu-chuna's life without being punished for it, but you did not do it. Therefore our hearts are turned towards you, and you shall be our brother, if will you permit our warriors to look upon you as a brother."

"If that happens, my greatest wish will be fulfilled. Inchu-chuna is a famous chief and warrior, and I have liked Winnetou from the first moment that I saw him. It is not just a great honor, but also a great joy to be the brother of such men. I only wish that my three friends could join in this honor."

"If you wish, they will be treated as if they had been born as Apaches."

"We thank you for that! So, you carved this pipe from the sacred stone yourself? How gifted your hands are!"

She blushed at this praise and answered:

"I know that the women and daughters of the palefaces are much more skillful and clever than we are. Now I will get something for you."

She left, and returned with my revolver, my knife, all my ammunition, and the rest of the objects that had not been in my pockets. (The contents of my pockets had been left untouched.) I thanked her and, realizing that not the least item was missing, asked:

"Will my comrades also get back what was taken from them?"

"Yes, everything. They already have it, for while I was helping you here, Inchu-chuna was taking care of them."

"And what about our horses?"

"They are here too. You will ride yours again, and Hawkens will have his Mary."

"Oh, you know the name of his mule?"

"Yes, also the name of his old gun, that he calls Liddy. I often spoke with him, without telling you about it. He's a man that likes to joke, but also a real hunter."

"Yes, he certainly is, and much else besides: a true companion, ready to sacrifice himself. It's impossible not to like him. But I would like to ask you something. Will you give me an accurate answer? Will you tell me the truth?"

"Nsho-chi does not lie," she answered proudly and simply. "She would certainly never tell you something that was not true."

"Your warriors took everything from the captured warriors that they had with them?"

"Yes."

"And they did the same with my three comrades?"

"Yes."

"Then why not me? No one touched the contents of my pockets."

"Because Winnetou, my brother, ordered it so."

"And do you know why he made this command?"

"Because he loved you."

"Even though he thought I was his enemy?"

"Yes. You said before that you liked him from the first moment that you saw him. That was true for him as well. It was very painful for him to have to treat you as an enemy, and not as a friend."

She was quiet, for she had something more to say that she thought would offend me.

"Go on," I urged her.

"No."

"Then I will speak for you. Just to treat me as an enemy could not cause him pain, because you can respect an enemy. But he thought I was a liar, a false and deceitful man. Right?"

"You have said it."

"I hope he can now see that he was mistaken. And now, one more question: what has happened to Rattler, the murderer of Klecki-petra?"

"He is being tied to the stake right now."

"What? Now? Right this moment?"

"Yes."

"And no one told me? Why was it kept from me?"

"Winnetou wished it so."

"Yes, but why?"

"He thought your eyes could not bear to see it and your ears could not bear to hear it."

"He is probably right, and yet it is possible for me to see and hear it, if my wish is taken into consideration."

"What wish?"

"First, tell me where the stake is."

"Down by the river, where you were before. Inchu-chuna took you away from there, because you were not supposed to observe."

"But I want to observe! What tortures is he to endure?"

"All that can be done to a captive. He is the most evil paleface that the Apaches have ever had in their hands. He killed our white father, who we loved and honored, the teacher of Winnetou— killed him for no reason. Therefore he will not die from just a few sufferings, he will experience all the tortures that we know of, one after another."

"That can't be permitted. That's inhumane!"

"He has earned it!"

"Are you allowed to watch?"

"Yes."

"You, a girl?"

She lowered her long lashes. For a moment, she looked down at the ground, then raised her head again, looked me in the eye in an earnest, almost reproachful way, and answered:

"Are you surprised?"

"Yes. A woman should not be permitted to see such a thing."

"Is that the way it is among white people?"

"Yes."

"Really?"

"Yes."

"You say an untruth, but you are not a liar. You say it unintentionally, without knowing it. You are mistaken."

"You think the opposite is true?"

"Yes."

"Then you must know our women and girls better than I do!"

"Perhaps you do not know them. When your criminals stand before the judge, other people can listen. Is that true?"

"Yes."

"I have heard that men and women can listen. Does a squaw belong there? Is it good for her to let her curiosity take her to such a place?"

"No."

"And when a murderer is sentenced, if he is hung or his head is cut off, are no white women present?"

"That was long ago."

"They are forbidden to see it now?"

"Yes."

"And the men are forbidden too?"

"Yes."

"So no one can watch! If it were permitted, the squaws as well as the men would watch. Oh, the women of the palefaces are not as delicate as you think. They are good at enduring pain, but only the pain of others — men or animals. I have not been among white people, but Klecki-petra told us about it. Then Winnetou went to the great cities in the East, and when he came back he told me everything he had seen and observed. Do you know what your squaws do with animals that they are going to cook, broil, and then eat?"

"Well?"

"They take off their skin while they are still alive. They also pull our their intestines and throw them in boiling water. And do you know what the medicine men of the white people do?"

"What do you mean?"

"They throw living dogs in boiling water to see how long they can live, and they take the scalded hide from their bodies. They cut out their eyes and tongues, they cut openings in their bodies, they torture them in many other ways, and then make books about it."

"That is called vivisection, and is only done for the good of science."

"Science! Kleki-petra was my teacher as well, and so I know what you mean by this word. What must your Great Good Spirit say about this science, that can teach nothing without torturing his creatures to death! And your medicine men do this torture in houses, where there are also squaws who must see it! Or do they not hear the cries of pain of the poor animals? Do your squaws not have birds in cages in their rooms? Do you know what a torture that is for a bird? Do your squaws not sit and watch as horses are ridden to death in contests? Are not thousands of squaws there when your boxers tear each other apart? I am a young, inexperienced girl and you probably think I am only a "wild" person, but I can tell of many more things your delicate squaws do without feeling the shudder that I would feel. Count how many thousands of delicate, beautiful white women tormented their slaves to death, or stood by smiling while a black servant was whipped to death! And here, we have a criminal, a murderer.

He should die the death he has earned. I will be there, you will see! Am I really wicked because I can calmly watch a man like that die? And if it is wicked, who is to blame that the eye of the red man has become used to seeing such things? Is it not the white man, who has forced us to repay their cruelty with hardship?"

"I don't think a white judge would sentence a captured Indian to death at the stake."

"Judge! Don't be angry with me if I call you the name that I have so often heard from Hawkens: Greenhorn! You don't know the West. Where are there any judges, the kind that you mean when you say this word? The stronger is always the judge, and the weaker is sentenced. Let them tell you what has happened around the campfires of the whites! More Indians than can be counted lost their lives, and did they die of a swift bullet or knife wound? How many were tortured to death? And they had done nothing but try to defend their rights! And now, a murderer is to die, who has earned his punishment, and I am supposed to turn my eyes away because I am a squaw, a girl? Yes, once we were different, but you have taught us to watch blood flow without blinking. I will go now, to be there when the murderer of Klecki-petra suffers his punishment!"

I had come to know the beautiful young Indian as a soft, quiet being. Now, she stood before me, eyes blazing and cheeks glowing, the very image of a goddess of revenge who knew no mercy. She looked almost more beautiful than before. Was I to condemn her? Was she wrong?

"Then go," I said, "but I will come too."

"It is better if you stay here," she pleaded, speaking once more in her old tone of voice. "Inchu-chuna and Winnetou will not be pleased if you come."

"Will they be angry with me?"

"No. They do not wish it, but they will not forbid it. You are our brother."

"Then I will come, and they will forgive me for it."

As I walked out onto the platform with her, Sam Hawkens was

standing there. He was smoking his old, short prairie pipe, for he too had been given tobacco.

"Everything's different, Sir," he said, smiling to himself. "Been a prisoner until a little while ago, and now I get to play the nobleman. What a difference. How are you doing in the new circumstances?"

"Good, thanks," I answered.

"Me too, outstanding. The chief himself was taking care of us. Now that's a treat, if I'm not mistaken!"

"Where is Inchu-chuna now?"

"Gone. He was heading for the river."

"Do you know what's happening there?"

"I've got a hunch."

"Well, what?"

"A fond farewell for the beloved Kiowas."

"That's the least of it."

"What else, then?"

"Rattler is being tortured."

"Rattler is being tortured? And they sent us here? I want to be there! Come, Sir! Let's get down there!"

"Hold on! Can you witness such a thing without turning away in horror?"

"Witness? Horror? You are an unbelievable greenhorn, dear Sir! Once you've been here in the West for a while, you won't think about horror either. That guy has earned his punishment and he'll be executed the Indian way, that's all."

"But it's gruesome."

"Pshaw! Don't you start talking about things being gruesome! He has to die. Or are you still not convinced of that?"

"Oh yes. But they could make it quick. He is human!"

"The kind of man who would shoot down someone who hadn't done the least thing to him is not really a human. He was as drunk as a skunk."

"Well, that's a mitigating circumstance. He didn't know what he was doing."

"Don't be a fool! Yes, over in the old country, the lawyers sit around and figure that whisky is a mitigating circumstance for anyone who likes to get drunk and commit mayhem. What they should do is make the punishment harsher, Sir, harsher! Anybody who drinks himself into a state where he attacks his neighbors like a wild animal should get twice the punishment. I don't have the smallest bit of sympathy for this Rattler. Think how he treated you!"

"I remember it well, but I'm a Christian and not an Indian. I will do everything I can to make his death a quick one."

"Let it lie, Sir! First, he doesn't deserve it, and second, your efforts will be for naught. Kleki-petra was the teacher and spiritual father of the tribe. His death was an irreplaceable loss for the Apaches, and he was killed without provocation. You'll never get the Indians to be lenient."

"But I'll try!"

"It'll never work!"

"In that case I'll shoot Rattler through the heart."

"To end his suffering? For God's sake, let it lie! You'll make yourself the enemy of the whole tribe. They have every right to determine his punishment, and if you kill him like that, the new friendship we've just begun will vanish, like a late snow in the sun. So you're coming?"

"Yes."

"OK, but no foolishness! I'll get Dick and Will."

He disappeared through the door of his room and returned with the other two. We climbed back down. Nsho-chi had gone ahead of us and was nowhere to be seen. As we emerged from the side canyon, into the main valley of the Rio Pecos, we saw that the

Kiowas had left. They had taken their wounded chief and ridden off. Inchu-chuna was wise and prudent enough to send spies after them secretly. They might have decided to double back to take revenge.

Chapter 28

I mentioned earlier that our ox wagon was standing near the stakes. When we arrived, the Apaches had formed a large circle around the wagon. In the middle stood the two chiefs and a few warriors. Nsho-chi was with them, speaking to Winnetou. Although she was the daughter of the chief, she was not permitted to participate in men's affairs, so the fact that she was not with the women meant that she must have something important to say to Winnetou. When she saw us coming, I noticed that she alerted him to our presence and then slipped away to join the squaws. So she must have been talking to him about us. Winnetou broke through the circle of warriors and came up to us. He said, in a serious voice:

"Why do my white brothers not stay up in the pueblo? Are they not pleased with the rooms which they have been given?"

"They please us," I answered, "and we thank our red brother for the good care he has taken of us. We have come back because we heard that Rattler was to die. Is this true?"

"Yes."

"I don't see him!"

"He lies in the wagon with the body of the one he murdered."

"What sort of death must he suffer?"

"He will be tortured to death."

"This decision cannot be changed?"

"No."

"My eyes cannot bear to see such a death!"

"That is why Inchu-chuna, my father, took you to the pueblo. Why did you come back? Why do you want to witness something that you cannot bear to see?"

"I hope I can be present at his death without having to turn away in horror. My religion makes me plead for Rattler."

"Your religion? Was that not his religion too?"

"Yes."

"Did he follow the commands given by that religion?"

"Unfortunately, no."

"Then you do not need to plead for him. Your religion forbids killing, but he killed anyway. So the teachings of your religion do not apply to him."

"I cannot consider what he did. I must do my duty without asking about the thoughts, beliefs, and deeds of other people. I ask you to moderate your severe rules and let this man die a quick death!"

"What has been decided must be carried out!"

"There is no possibility of changing it?"

"No."

"So there is no way to grant my wish?"

"There is only one."

"What is it?"

"Before I tell my white brother what it is, I must ask him not to use it. It would be very, very damaging to you in the eyes of our warriors."

"What do you mean?"

"They would not be able to respect you, even though that is what I wish."

"So is this a dishonorable way, a despicable way?"

"As the Indian understands it, yes."

"Tell me what it is!"

"You would have to call upon our gratitude."

"Ah! But no good man would do that!"

"No. We have our lives, thanks to you. If you were to call upon that, you would force me and Inchu-chuna, my father, to do what you wish."

"In what way?"

"We would hold a new council and would speak for you, so that our warriors would know the thanks that we owe you. But after that, everything you have done would be worthless. Is this Rattler worth such a sacrifice?"

"Indeed not!"

"My brother hears that I speak forthrightly to him. I know what thoughts and feelings lie in his heart, but my warriors will not understand such emotions. A man who calls upon gratitude will not have their respect. Should Old Shatterhand, who could be the greatest and most famous warrior of the Apaches, leave us tomorrow because my warriors spit before him?"

It was hard for me to answer this. My heart told me to persevere in my plea, but my reason (or rather, my pride) was against it. Winnetou sympathized with the dilemma I was grappling with and said:

"I will speak with Inchu-chuna, my father. Let my brother wait here."

He left.

"Don't do anything stupid, Sir!" pleaded Sam. "You have no idea what could be at stake—maybe even your life."

"Certainly not that!"

"Oh yes! It's true: the Indian does not respect anyone who trades on his gratitude, who makes demands based on his indebtedness. He'll do what he's asked, sure enough, but after that he doesn't know that person anymore. We would have to leave immediately, and the Kiowas would be just ahead of us. I don't have to tell you what that means."

Inchu-chuna and Winnetou spoke earnestly with each other for a while, then returned to us. Inchu-chuna said:

"If Kleki-petra had not told us so much about your faith, I would consider you a man who is too low to speak with. But I am able to understand your wish. My warriors would not understand it and would despise you."

"This does not involve just me, but also Kleki-petra, who you just mentioned."

"Why does it involve him?"

"He had the same faith that causes me to make my request, and he died with this faith. His faith required him to forgive his enemies. Believe me, if he was still alive he would not permit his murderer to die this way."

"Do you really think so?"

"Yes, I am certain of it."

He shook his head slowly and said:

"What kind of men are these Christians? Either they are bad, and then their badness is so great that no one can understand it. Or they are good, and then their goodness is just as hard to understand!"

At this, he looked over at his son, who returned the look. They understood each other. It was as if they could converse through these glances. Inchu-chuna turned back to me, and asked:

"This murderer was your enemy, wasn't he?"

"Yes."

"Have you forgiven him?"

"Yes."

"Then hear what I say! We will find out if there is even a tiny, tiny trace of good left in him. If there is, I will try to fulfill your wish, without hurting you. Sit down here and wait to see what happens. When I wave my hand toward you, come over to the murderer and get him to ask you to forgive him. If he does that, he can die quickly."

"Can I tell him this?"

"Yes."

Inchu-chuna and Winnetou went back to the circle, and we sat down where we had been standing.

"I wouldn't have believed it," Sam said. "The chief is willing to consider your wish. He must think the world of you."

"He doesn't. He has another reason."

"What?"

"It's the influence of Kleki-petra, that is felt even in his death. These Indians picked up more true, inner Christianity from him than they realize. I'm very curious to see what happens now."

"You'll soon see. Watch!"

The canvas was removed from the wagon. We saw a long, box-like object being removed, on top of which a man was tied.

"That's the coffin," Sam Hawkens said. "It's made of hollowed-out logs and covered with hides that have been kept wet. When the leather dries out, it pulls together, and that will make the coffin air-tight."

Not far from the spot where the side canyon joined the main valley, there was a cliff. A square arrangement of stones, open at the front, and been constructed there. Many other stones lay nearby. To this stone square, the coffin, with the man still tied to it, was carried. The man was Rattler.

"Do you know why they put all those stones over there?" asked Sam.

"I can imagine."

"Well, why?"

"They will use them to build a grave."

"Right! A double grave."

"For Rattler too?"

"Yes. A murderer is buried with his victim. It's supposed to happen after every murder if possible."

"That's awful! To be bound to the coffin of a dead man, and to know that it will be your final resting place!"

"I do believe you really sympathize with the man! I can grasp why you tried to plead for him, but sympathizing with him? I just can't understand that."

Now the coffin was set on end, so that Rattler was standing up. The casket and the man were tied securely to the wall of stone. The Indians—men, women, and children—approached the spot and formed a half-circle around it. A deep, expectant silence set in. Winnetou and Inchu-chuna stood near the coffin, one to the right of it and the other to the left. Then the chief raised his voice:

"The warriors of the Apache have come together here to hold court, for the Apache people have had a great and heavy loss for which the guilty one must pay with his life."

Inchu-chuna continued in the picturesque Indian way, describing Kleki-petra, his character, and his works. He described in full detail the way in which the murder had occurred. He recounted how Rattler had been captured, and finally announced that Rattler was to be tortured to death, and that he was to be buried with his victim, tied to the coffin as he now was. Then he looked over at me and gave me the expected gesture.

We stood up and walked to the half-circle, which opened to let us in. Earlier, we were far enough from the condemned man that I had not been able to see him clearly. Now I stood before him and, as evil and godless as he might be, I felt a deep sympathy for this man.

The coffin, which was standing on end, was more than twice as wide as a man and over 15 feet long. It looked as though a log had been sawed from a thick tree trunk and covered with leather. Rattler was tied to the coffin with his arms behind him and his feet spread apart. You could see that he had not had to suffer either hunger or thirst. A gag closed his mouth so that he could not speak, and his head was tied so that he could not move it. As I approached, Inchu-chuna removed the gag from his mouth and said to me:

"My white brother wishes to speak with this murderer. Let him speak!"

Rattler saw that I was free. I must have befriended the Indians, that much he could conclude. So I assumed he would ask me to put in a good word for him with them. Instead, as soon as the gag was removed, he shouted angrily at me:

"What do you want of me? Get out of here. I don't want nothing to do with you!"

"You have heard that you are sentenced to death, Mr. Rattler," I answered calmly. "That can't be changed. You will certainly be killed. But I would like. . ."

"Get away, you dog!" he interrupted me. He tried to spit at me, but missed because he couldn't move his head.

"You will certainly be killed," I continued without wavering, "but you can determine the manner of your death. You're supposed to be tortured to death. They're planning on making you suffer for a long, long time. Maybe the rest of today, maybe all day tomorrow. That is outrageous, and I want to prevent it. I have spoken with Inchu-chuna, and he has agreed to let you die quickly if you fulfill the conditions he has set."

I waited a moment, assuming that he would ask what these conditions were. But instead, he cursed at me in such a foul manner that I can't repeat it here.

"The condition is that you must ask my forgiveness," I explained.

"Your forgiveness? I'm supposed to apologize to you?" he cried. "I'd rather bite out my own tongue and endure whatever torture these red swine can come up with!"

"These aren't my conditions, Mr. Rattler. I don't need you to ask me for anything. Inchu-chuna wants it this way, and he wanted me to tell you. Well, I've done my part. But I think you should consider you situation and what you're about to face! It's grim, a terrible death, and you can avoid it by just saying two little words: I'm sorry."

"Not in a million years! Never! Get out of here! I don't want to see your villainous face. You can go to the devil—and farther, for all I care!"

"If I do as you say and leave you, it's all over for you. I won't come back. Be reasonable and say those words."

"No, no, no!" he bellowed.

"I implore you!"

"Get away from me! Damn it, why am I tied up? If my hands were free, I'd show you the way!"

"Well, you'll have you wish, but I'm telling you: you can call for me all you like later on and I won't be coming back."

"You think I'd call for you? You? Don't flatter yourself. Just get out, get out!"

"OK, I'm going. But one last thing. Do you have a last wish? I'll see that it is fulfilled. A greeting to anyone? Any relatives I can send word to?"

"Go to hell, and when you get there, tell them you're a damned rogue! You cut a deal with these Indians and delivered me into their hands. So you can . . ."

"You're mistaken," I interrupted him. "So, do you have a last wish?"

"Just that you follow me as soon as possible, nothing else!"

"Good. That's done, then, and the only thing I can do as a good Christian is to give you this advice: do not cross over in sin, but think about your deeds and about the compensation that awaits you on the other side!"

Once again, I will omit his response, which sent a shiver down my spine. Inchu-chuna took my hand and led me away, saying:

"My young white brother sees that this murderer has not earned the help of a peace-maker. He says is a Christian. He calls us heathens. But would a red warrior say such words?"

I didn't answer. What could I say? I had expected Rattler to behave differently. Earlier, he had been so cowardly, so fearful, and he had actually shuddered when we had talked about dying at the stake. But today he was behaving as if all the torture in the world meant nothing!

"Don't take that for courage," Sam told me. "It's rage, nothing but rage."

"About what?"

"About you, Sir. He thinks it's your fault that he fell into the hands of the Indians. He hasn't seen you since the day we were captured. Now he sees you and the rest of us, and we're free. The Indians are friendly to us. But he has to die. Naturally, that's grounds enough for him to conclude that we've dealt him a bad hand. But as soon as the suffering starts, he'll be singing a different tune, if I'm not mistaken!"

The Apaches didn't wait long to begin the tragic game. I had planned to leave, but since I had never seen anything like this before, I made up my mind to stay until I couldn't bear to watch anymore.

The onlookers sat down. Several young warriors walked forward with knives in their hands and took up positions about 15 paces from Rattler. They threw their knives toward him, being careful not to actually hit him. Instead, the blades lodged in the coffin to which he was tied. The first knife hit to the right and the second to the left of his foot, but so close that there was almost no intervening space. The next two knives struck a bit higher, and it continued in this manner until both legs were hemmed in on both sides by rows of knives.

Up to this point, he had kept himself reasonably under control. But now the knives came ever higher, for it was evident that the Indians planned to outline his whole body with them. He began to be afraid. As each knife flew toward him, he gave a cry of fear. And these cries got louder and shriller as the knives came higher and higher.

Once his upper body was surrounded by knives, the Indians started planting them around his head. The first knife lodged in the coffin just to the right of his throat, the next just to the left. The process continued on either side of his face, up around his head, until there was no more room for another knife. Then all of the knives were pulled out. This had just been by way of an introduction, conducted by the young warriors, which was supposed to demonstrate that they had learned how to take aim and throw accurately. They went back to their places and sat down.

Next, Inchu-chuna selected several seasoned warriors, who were to throw from thirty paces. When the first was ready, the chief walked up to Rattler, pointed at his right upper arm, and ordered:

"Hit him here."

The knife came flying, hit at exactly the designated spot, tore through the muscle, skewering it, and continued into the lid of the coffin. Now things were starting to get serious. Rattler felt the pain and gave a howl as if he were about to die. The second knife went through the same muscle of the other arm, and the howling was doubled. The third and fourth throws were directed at the thighs, and they hit at exactly the spots indicated by the chief. No blood was visible yet. Rattler was still fully clothed, and the Indians were aiming at spots where the wounds would not be life-threatening. This was done to avoid the possibility that the drama might be cut short.

Perhaps Rattler had believed that they weren't really serious about killing him. He now must have realized his error of judgment. An Indian at the stake behaves quite differently. Once the torture begins, he starts to sing his song of death, in which he praises his own deeds and mocks those who are torturing him. The greater the pain, the greater the insults he hurls at them; but he will never utter a word of complaint or a cry of pain. Once he is dead, his enemies proclaim his glory and bury him with full Indian honors. For it has also been an honor for them to play a part in such a glorious death.

It's different with a coward, who screams at the slightest wound and roars with pain, and even asks for mercy. To kill such a person is no honor. It's almost shameful. Eventually, no decent warrior is willing to deal with him any longer, and he is beaten to death or put to death in some other dishonorable way.

Rattler was that sort of coward. His wounds were small and not yet dangerous. They certainly caused him pain, but you couldn't really consider it serious suffering. But he howled and cried as if he were suffering the tortures of Hell, and he continued calling out my name, pleading for me to come to him. Inchu-chuna ordered for a temporary halt, and called me over:

"Let my young white brother go to him and ask him why he cries out. Up to now, the knives have not done him harm."

"Yes, come here, Sir! Come here!" cried Rattler. "I must speak with you!"

I went to him and asked:

"What do you want of me now?"

"Pull the knives out of my arms and legs!"

"I'm not permitted to."

"But I will die! Who could survive all these wounds?"

"Strange! Did you really think you would survive?"

"Well, you're alive!"

"I didn't murder anyone."

"It's not my fault, you know I was drunk when I did it!"

"That doesn't change the deed. I warned you about drinking brandy. You didn't heed me, and now you have to pay the price."

"You're a heartless and unfeeling man! Please intercede for me!"

"I already did that. Say you're sorry, and they won't torture you slowly. You'll die quickly."

"Die quickly? But I don't want to die! I want to live, live, live!"

"I'm sorry, that's impossible."

"Impossible? There is not hope of rescue?"

"No."

"No rescue!"

He bellowed this at the top of his lungs and then began such a sorrowful wailing and moaning that I couldn't bear to be near him and I turned to go.

"Stay here, Sir, stay with me!" he cried after me. "If you don't stay, they'll start again!"

The chief shouted at him:

"Stop howling, dog! You are a stinking coyote that no warrior wants to bother to shoot."

And turning to his people, he continued:

"Which of the sons of the brave Apaches would still like to deal with this coward?"

No one answered.

"Nobody?"

Still silence, as before.

"Ugh! This murderer is not worthy of being killed by us. He should not be buried with Kleki-petra. How could such a toad arrive at the eternal hunting ground with a swan? Cut him free!"

He gestured to two boys. They jumped up, ran over, pulled out the knives, and cut him free from the coffin.

"Tie his hands behind his back!" the chief commanded.

The boys, no older than ten, did so, and Rattler made not the slightest resistance. What a disgrace! I was almost ashamed of being white.

"Take him to the river and throw him in the water!" was the next command. "If he can get to the other bank, he can be free."

Rattler gave a cry of joy and let the boys lead him down to the river. They actually did have to push him in, for he did not even have enough self-respect to jump in himself. At first he went under, but then he started trying to swim on his back. It wasn't too hard, even though his hands were tied behind him. A person's body isn't dense enough to sink. He had his legs free, so he could use them to propel himself, which he managed to succeed in doing.

Would they let him reach the far side? Even I didn't really want that. He deserved to die. Anyone who let him escape now would be guilty for all the crimes he would be sure to commit in the future. The two boys were still standing by the water's edge. Inchu-chuna gave them the command:

"Get a rifle and shoot him in the head!"

They ran to the place where the warriors kept their rifles, and they each took one. These little boys knew very well how to use such weapons. They knelt on the bank and aimed at Rattler's head.

"Don't shoot, for God's sake, don't shoot!" he cried in horror.

The boys spoke a few words to each other. They handled the incident as little sportsmen, letting Rattler swim farther and farther. The chief said nothing. I concluded that he knew full well whether they could shoot or not. Then they gave a yell in their high boy's voices and shot. Rattler was struck in the head and quickly disappeared under the water.

No one cried out in joy, the way Indians usually do when an enemy is killed. Such a coward was not worth making any sound at all. The Indians' contempt was so great that they didn't even bother with his body. They let it be carried down-river without so much as a glance after it. I suppose it was possible that he had been wounded but not killed. He might even have pretended to be hit and might have, like me, swum underwater to some other spot where they couldn't see him surface. They just didn't think it was worth the effort to pay any more attention to him.

Inchu-chuna came to me and asked:

"Is my young white brother satisfied with me now?"

"Yes. Thank you!"

"You have no reason to thank me. Even if I hadn't known what you wished, I would have done the same thing. This dog was not worthy of a martyr's death. Today you have seen the difference between heathens and Christians, between brave Indian warriors and white cowards. The palefaces are capable of every evil deed, but when they have to show courage, then they howl with fear like dogs that know they will be hit."

"The Chief of the Apaches must not forget that there are brave and cowardly people, good and evil people everywhere!"

"You are right, and I do not want to offend you. But no people can think that they are better than some other people because their skin is a different color."

To steer him away from this prickly topic, I enquired:

"What will the Apache warriors do now? Bury Kleki-petra?"

"Yes."

"Can my friends and I watch?"

"Yes. If you had not asked, I would have asked you to come. I remember that you spoke with Kleki-petra while we went to get the horses. Was that just an ordinary conversation?"

"No, it was a very serious one, an important one, for him and for me. May I tell you what we talked about?"

I addressed this to Winnetou, who had just joined us, as well as to his father.

"Tell us!" Winnetou replied.

"When you left, we sat down together. We quickly found that his homeland was the same as mine, and we talked to each other in our native language. He had experienced much and endured much, and he told me about it. He told me how much he loved the two of you, and that his greatest wish was to be able to die for Winnetou. The Great Spirit gave him his wish just a few minutes later."

"Why did he want to die for me?"

"Because he loved you, and for another reason that I will tell you another time. He wanted his death to be an atonement."

"When he lay dying at my heart, he spoke to you in a language I did not understand. What was it?"

"Our native language."

"Did he speak of me?"

"Yes."

"What did he say?"

"He asked me to be loyal to you."

"To be loyal to me? You didn't know me!"

"I knew you. I had seen you, and anyone who sees Winnetou knows who he's looking at. And anyway, he told me all about you!"

"How did you answer him?"

"I promised to fulfill his wish."

"It was the last wish of his life. You are his legacy. You promised to be loyal to me, you protected me, watched over me, and spared me, while I treated hunted you as my enemy. The wound from my knife would have killed anyone else, but your strong body survived it. I am deeply, deeply in debt to you. Be my friend!"

"I already am."

"My brother!"

"Gladly, with all my heart."

"Then let us forge this bond on the grave of the one who gave my soul into your keeping! A noble paleface has departed from us and has given us, as he left, another just as noble. My blood shall be yours and yours shall be mine! I will drink yours and you will drink mine. Inchu-chuna, the greatest Chief of the Apaches, who is my father and creator, will permit me!"

Inchu-chuna gave each of us his hand and said in a voice that came from his heart:

"I will permit you. You will not just be brothers, you will be one single man and warrior with two bodies. How!"

Chapter 29

We went to the place where the burial building, a sort of mausoleum, was to be built. I learned what I could about its planned size and construction, then asked for several tomahawks. Sam, Dick, and Will went with me into the woods a bit upriver, where we selected and cut some branches using the tomahawks, and made them into a cross. By the time we had brought it back to the camp, the funeral proceedings had begun. The Indians had been working diligently on the mausoleum and had almost finished it. But most of them had stopped their work on it and were now singing their unique and deeply moving funeral chant. The muffled, monotonous sound was drowned out from time to time by a shrill, sharp cry of mourning which rose above it like a sudden lightning bolt from heavy, dark clouds.

A dozen Indians were still at work on the building, under the direction of the two chiefs. Between them and the chanting onlookers, a strangely-cloaked figure covered with all sorts of symbols danced with grotesque slow movements and sudden leaps.

"Who is that?" I asked. "The medicine man?"

"Yes," answered Sam.

"A Indian ceremony at the funeral of a Christian! What do you say to that, Sam?"

"You don't like it?"

"Not really."

"Just let it go, Sir! Please don't say a word against it! It would be a terrible insult to the Apaches."

"But I find this masquerade extraordinarily repulsive, more than you would guess."

"But their intentions are good. You think it's a bit on the heathen side?"

"It sure is."

"Nonsense! These brave, good people believe in a Great Spirit. That's where their dead friend and teacher has gone. They are performing their ritual of leave-taking and mourning in their own way, and everything the medicine man is doing is part of that. Just let them do as they like! They won't prevent us from adding our cross to the grave."

We laid the cross down next to the coffin. Winnetou asked:

"Should this sign of Christianity be added to the stones?"

"Yes."

"That is good. I would have asked my brother Old Shatterhand to make a cross, for Kleki-petra had one in his room and prayed before it. That is why I thought this sign of his faith should guard his grave also. Where shall it be placed?"

"It should rise above the top."

"Like the great, tall houses that the Christians pray in? I will make it as you wish. Sit down and watch, and tell me if it is right."

In a little while the construction was complete. It was crowned with our cross and had an opening at the front for the coffin, which had not yet been put inside.

Then Nsho-chi arrived. She had been back to the pueblo to fetch two pottery dishes, which she took to the river and filled with water. Then she brought them back and placed them on the coffin. I would shortly learn their purpose.

Now everything was ready for the burial. At a signal from Inchu-chuna, the chanting stopped. The medicine man squatted on the ground. The chief went up to the coffin and spoke slowly and formally:

"The sun rises in the east in the morning and sinks in the west in the evening. The year awakes in the spring and goes to sleep again in the fall. So it is with men. Is it so?"

"How!" came the low response from all around.

"Men rise like the sun and sink again in the grave. They come like spring to the earth and lie down like the winter to their rest.

316

But when the sun goes down, it comes up again the next day; and when the winter passes, the spring appears again. Is it so?"

"How!"

"Kleki-petra taught us this. A man is laid in the grave but he stands again on the other side of death, like a new day and like a new spring, to live again in the land of the Great Good Spirit. Kleki-petra told us this, and now he knows whether he told the truth, for he is gone like the day and like the year, and his soul has gone to live in the house of the dead, for which he always longed. Is it so?"

"How!"

"His faith was not ours, and ours was not his. We love our friends and hate our enemies; but he taught that we should love our enemies because they are also our brothers. We did not want to believe him, but when we followed his words, it led to useful things and happiness. Perhaps his faith really is ours, if we could understand it the way he wanted us to. We say that our souls go to the eternal hunting ground, and he believed that his soul would go to an eternal blessedness. I often think that our hunting ground is the same as this eternal blessedness. Is it so?"

"How!"

"He often told of the savior who had come to make all people holy. We believed the truth of his words, for a lie was never found in his mouth. This savior came for all people. Did he come to the red men as well? If he were to come, we would welcome him, for we are oppressed and stamped out by the palefaces and we long for him. Is it so?"

"How!"

"This was his teaching. Now I will speak of his end. It came upon us like a predator upon its prey. It was sudden and unexpected. He was healthy and sprightly and stood next to us. He was about to get on his horse and ride home with us, but he was hit by the bullet of a murderer. Let my brothers and sisters mourn him!"

A low cry of grief rang out, getting steadily stronger and higher until it ended in a piercing howl. Then the chief continued:

"We have avenged his death. But the soul of the murderer has left him. It cannot serve Kleki-petra on the other side of the grave, for it was cowardly and did not want to follow him in death. The mangy dog it belonged to has been shot by children, and his body has been carried away by the river. Is it so?"

"How!"

"Now Kleki-petra has left us, but his body remains with us, so that we can build a memorial by which we and those who come after us can remember the good white father. He was our teacher and we loved him. He was not born in this land, but came from a far kingdom on the other side of the great water where oak trees grow. So to honor him and to show our love, we have brought little oaks to be planted by his grave. As they sprout and grow from the earth, so will his soul awake from the grave and flourish on the other side. And as these oaks grow, so will the words that we heard from him, that have spread in our hearts, so that our souls can find shade under them. He always thought about us and cared for us. And he did not leave us without sending another paleface who will be our friend and brother in his place. Here you see Old Shatterhand, the white man who comes from the same land as Kleki-petra. He knows everything that Kleki-petra knew, and he is an even stronger warrior. He killed the grizzly bear with his knife, and with his fist he knocks every enemy to the ground. Inchu-chuna and Winnetou were delivered into his hands again and again, but he did not kill us. Instead, he let us live because he loves us and because he is a friend of the red man. Is it so?"

"How!"

"Kleki-petra's last word and last wish was that Old Shatterhand should follow in his path among the Apache warriors. Old Shatterhand promised him that he would fulfill this wish. So he will become part of the Apache tribe and will be treated as a chief. It will be as though he had red skin and was born among us. To confirm this, he would have to smoke the calumet with every grown Apache warrior, but that is not necessary. He will drink Winnetou's blood, and Winnetou will drink his. Then he will be blood of our blood and flesh of our flesh. Do the warriors of the Apache tribe agree to this?"

"How, how, how!" was the joyous three-fold response of all the onlookers.

"Then let Old Shatterhand and Winnetou go to the coffin and add their blood to the water of brotherhood!"

So Winnetou and I were to be joined as blood-brothers, something I had so often read about! Many primitive tribes have this ritual, in which the two people involved either mix their blood together, or each drinks the other's blood. The result is that these two are then held together more strongly, more deeply, and more selflessly than if they had been brothers from birth.

In this case, I was to drink Winnetou's blood and he was to drink mine. We went to opposite sides of the coffin, and Inchu-chuna bared the forearm of his son and slit it with his knife. A few drops of blood oozed from the small cut, and the chief let them fall into one of the dishes of water. Then he followed the same procedure with me, letting a bit of blood fall into the other dish. Winnetou received the dish with my blood in it, and I was given the one with his blood. Then Inchu-chuna said:

"The soul lives in the blood. Let the souls of these two young warriors be carried into each other, so that they become one soul. What Old Shatterhand thinks, let that also be Winnetou's thought, and what Winnetou wishes, let that be Old Shatterhand's wish as well. Drink!"

I drank the contents of my dish, and Winnetou did the same. It was just Rio Pecos water with a few drops of blood that you couldn't taste. The chief took my hand and said:

"Now you are just like Winnetou, the son of my body and a warrior of our people. The stories of your deeds will spread everywhere quickly, and there will be no greater warrior. You join us as a chief of the Apaches, and all our tribes will honor you as a chief!"

This was rapid career advancement! From a tutor in St. Louis to a surveyor, and now accepted as a chief among the Indians! But I confess that these "wild" Indians suited me far better than the whites I had recently associated with.

To avoid a possible misunderstanding, I should note something here. Even among Europeans, you sometimes encounter a similar form of blood-brotherhood among the more adventurous sorts of people. Sometimes this is celebrated with strange ceremonies based on superstition. Exceptional and secret powers are ascribed to such brotherhoods, such as the notion that both brothers will die at the same instant. If, for example, there is one who is weaker and more sickly, and that one travels to Italy and dies of cholera there, then the other (strong, healthy, and at home in Germany) will fall dead the same second. This is of course nonsense. There was no superstition of this kind involved in the ceremony involving Winnetou and me. No particular effect was ascribed, either by me or by the Apaches, to the drinking of the blood. It had a purely symbolic meaning.

And yet, strangely enough, from then on Inchu-chuna's words always rang true, that we were one soul in two bodies. We both understood, without having to tell each other, our feelings, thoughts, and decisions. We only had to look at each other in order for each to know what the other wanted. Actually, looking at each other wasn't required. Even when we were separated, we acted with remarkable like-mindedness, and not once has there ever been the slightest disagreement between us. But I don't think this was an effect of shared blood, but rather a natural result of our mutual inner attraction and the friendly way we each accommodated the other's perspective and peculiarities.

As Inchu-chuna spoke his final words, all the Apaches, including the children, rose to their feet and let out a loud and powerful "How!" Then the chief added:

"Now the new, living Kleki-petra is among us, and we can give the dead man over to his grave. Let my brothers do this now!"

He signaled to the warriors who had built the mausoleum. I asked if the work could wait for a moment and waved Hawkens, Stone, and Parker over. When they had joined me, I spoke a few words over the coffin and ended with a prayer. Then, the last remains of the one-time revolutionary and later penitent were shoved into the stone building, and the Indians began filling in the opening.

That was my first burial ceremony among the Indians. It touched me deeply. I will not criticize the opinion that Inchu-chuna expressed during the ceremony. It was a mixture of much truth and much that was incomprehensible. But out of it all had rung a cry of longing for redemption, for a redemption that he, like the people of Israel long ago, thought could come to them from the outside. Really, though, it had to be an inner, spiritual redemption.

While the mausoleum was being closed up, the laments of the Indians rose again. Only after the last stone had been put in place could the ceremony be considered complete, and everyone went off to attend to more cheerful activities. Foremost among these was eating, and Inchu-chuna invited me to eat with him.

His home was the largest residence of the level of the pueblo mentioned earlier. It was furnished very simply, but a rich collection of Indian weapons hung on the walls, which attracted my lively interest. Beautiful Day served us (meaning her father, Winnetou, and me) and I found that she was a master at cooking Indian dishes. Not much was said—actually, almost nothing. Indians generally preferred to keep quiet, and so much talking had already taken place that day that they prefer to postpone discussion of the topics that still had to be discussed. After the meal, twilight set in rapidly. Winnetou asked me:

"Would my white brother rather rest or go with me?"

"I'll go with you," I answered, without knowing where he was planning to go.

We climbed down from the pueblo and went toward the river. I had expected that. Such a deep-rooted nature as Winnetou's would surely be drawn toward the grave of the teacher who had been buried today. We soon reached it, and there we sat down next to each other. Winnetou took my hand and held it in his for a time without saying a word. I had no cause to break the silence.

I must note here that not all the Apaches I had encountered lived in the pueblo with their families. As big as it was, it was far too small to hold them all. Only Inchu-chuna and his most prominent warriors lived there, serving as a central point for the rest of the members of the Mescalero Apache tribe, who lived a nomadic life herding their horses and hunting. From this center, the chief ruled his tribe, and from here he undertook long rides to visit other tribes that acknowledged him as the highest chief. These were the Llaneros, Jicarillas, Tatcones, Chiriguais, Pinalenjos, Gilas, Mimbrenjos, Lipans, the copper-mine Apaches, and others. Even the Navajos, though not subject to his rule, followed his orders.

Most of the Mescaleros that didn't live in the pueblo left after the burial. Only enough of them remained to tend the horses that the Kiowas had turned over, which were grazing nearby. So Winnetou and I were unobserved as we sat by Kleki-petra's grave. I should mention that oaks were indeed planted around it on the following day. They grew into trees which are still there to this day.

Winnetou finally broke the silence. He asked me:

"Will my brother Old Shatterhand forget that we were his enemies?"

"It is forgotten already," I answered.

"But one thing you will not be able to forgive."

"What?"

"The insult that my father made to you."

"When?"

"When we met you for the first time."

"Ah, when he spit in my face?"

"Yes."

"Why shouldn't I be able to forgive that?"

"Because spit can only be washed away with the blood of the person who spits."

"Winnetou must not worry. That too has already been forgotten."

"My brother says a thing which I cannot believe."

"You can believe it. I have already proved that I have forgiven it."

"How did you prove it?"

"By not taking offense at Inchu-chuna, your father. Or do you think that Old Shatterhand lets himself be spit upon without answering it immediately with his fists, if he thinks he has been insulted?"

"Yes, we were very surprised that you did not do so."

"The father of Winnetou couldn't insult me. I wiped off the spit and then it was forgiven and forgotten. Let's not talk about it any more!"

"And yet I must speak of it. It is my duty to you, my brother."

"Why?"

"You must learn the ways of our people. No warrior likes to make a mistake, and it is even more important for a chief not to make one. Inchu-chuna knows that he was in error, but he is not allowed to ask your pardon. So he asked me to speak with you. Winnetou asks it in place of his father."

"That is completely unnecessary. We are even, for I have insulted you as well."

"No."

"Oh, yes! Is the blow of a fist not an insult? And I struck both of you with my fists."

"That was in battle, so it doesn't count as an insult. My brother is noble and good-hearted. We will not forget it."

"Let's talk about other things! Today I became an Apache. What about my comrades?"

"They cannot be taken into the tribe, but they are our brothers."

"Without a ceremony?"

"Tomorrow we will smoke the peace pipe. In the homeland of my white brother is there no calumet?"

"No. Christians are all brothers, without requiring any kind of ceremony."

"All brothers? Are there no wars between them?"

"Indeed there are."

"Then they are not different or better than us. They teach love but do not feel it. Why did my white brother leave his homeland?"

Customarily, such questions are not asked by Indians. But Winnetou, because he was now my brother and needed to get to know me, could ask. But he wasn't asking merely out of friendly curiosity. He had another reason.

"To seek my luck here," I answered.

"Luck? What is luck?"

"To be rich!"

As I said this, he let go of my hand, which he had held tightly up to now. Another pause ensued. I knew that he was feeling that perhaps he had misjudged me.

"To be rich," he whispered.

"Yes, to be rich," I repeated.

"So that's why. . ."

"What?"

"That's why we saw you. . ."

It was painful to him to speak the words. I completed the sentence for him:

"You saw me with the land thieves?"

"You have said it. You did this to get rich. Do you really think that being rich makes you happy?"

"Yes."

"You are mistaken. Gold has only made the red man unhappy. Because of gold, the white men still push us from one land to another, from one place to another, so that we will slowly but surely die away. Gold is the reason for our death. Let my brother not strive for such a thing."

"I will not."

"No? And yet you say that you seek happiness in being rich."

"That is true. But there are many ways to be rich. You can be rich with gold, with wisdom, with health, with honor and fame, with mercy from God and men."

"Ugh, ugh! So that is what you meant! What kind of riches do you strive for, then?"

"The last that I mentioned."

"Mercy from God! So you are a pious man, a very devote Christian?"

"I don't know if I am a good Christian. Only God knows that. But I would like to be."

"So you consider us heathen?"

"No. You believe in the Great Good Spirit and you don't pray to idols."

"Then grant me a request."

"Certainly! What is it?"

"Do not speak to me about faith! Do not strive to convert me! I like you very, very much and I don't want our bond to be torn. It is as Kleki-petra said. Your faith may be the right one, but we red men cannot yet understand it. If the Christians had not driven us from our land and tried to wipe us out, we would consider them good men, and would think their teachings were good. Then we would surely find time and space to learn what we need to know to understand their holy book and their priests. But he who is slowly but surely squeezed to death cannot believe that the religion of those who are killing him is a religion of love."

"You must see the difference between the religion and its members, who only outwardly claim it, but who do not behave according to it!"

"That is what the palefaces all say. They call themselves Christians, but do not behave that way. But we have our great Manitou who wants all men to be good. I try to be good, and so perhaps I am a Christian, maybe a better Christian than those who say they are Christians but who show no love and who strive only for what helps them. So you must never speak to me about faith, and do not try to make me a man who says he is a Christian, perhaps without being one! This is the request that you must fulfill for me!"

I honored his request and never spoke a word about conversion to him. But is speaking necessary? Aren't deeds a more powerful, a far more persuasive message than words? 'By their works shall ye know them,' says the Holy Scripture. Not by my words but by my life, my actions, I was Winnetou's teacher, until finally, years later on one unforgettable evening, he himself called upon me to speak. Then we sat together for hours, and in that consecrated night all the seeds sown in silence suddenly bore glorious fruit.

But for now, I was satisfied to simply press his hand, to indicate that I would honor his wish. Then he continued:

"How did it happen that my brother Old Shatterhand was associated with the land thieves? Did he not know that this was a crime against the red man?"

"I could have figured it out, but I simply did not think about it. I was glad to be allowed to be a surveyor, for I was very well paid."

"Paid? I think you did not finish the work. Did they pay you before the work was done?"

"No. I received a payment to start and the equipment I needed. What I earned by surveying was to be paid after the work was done."

"And now you will get this money?"

"Yes."

"Is it a lot?"

"For my situation, it is a great deal."

He was quiet for a while. Then he said:

"I'm very sorry that my brother suffered so much from us. You are not rich?"

"I am rich in many ways, but in money I am a poor devil."

"How much longer would you have to measure in order to be finished?"

"Only a few days."

"Ugh! If I had known you then as I know you now, we would have waited a few days to attack the Kiowas."

"So that I could have finished?" I asked, touched by this magnanimity.

"Yes."

"You mean, you would have allowed us to finish our theft?"

"Not the theft, but the measuring. The lines you draw on paper do not hurt us, for that is not how the theft is done. The theft begins when the paleface workers come to build the road for the fire-horse. I will take you. . ."

He stopped in the middle of his sentence, to make sure he was clear about the thought that had come to him. Then he continued:

"To get your money, must you have the paper that I just spoke of?"

"Yes."

"Ugh! Then you will never be paid. Everything that you drew was destroyed."

"And what happened to our instruments?"

"The warriors wanted to smash them, but I would not allow it. Although I have not been to the school of the palefaces, I know that such objects have great value, and so I ordered them to be carefully protected. We brought them here and we kept them well. I will give them back to my brother Old Shatterhand."

"Thank you. I accept your gift, even though I can't really use it. But I would really like to be able to return the instruments to their owner."

"You can't use them?"

"No. They would only be useful if I could complete the measuring."

"But you can't complete it, because the papers were destroyed!"

"No. I was careful to make the drawings twice."

"So you still have the second papers?"

"Yes. Here in my pocket. You were kind enough to command your people not to take anything from me."

"Ugh, ugh!"

This exclamation was partly one of astonishment and partly of relief. Then he was quiet once more. As I later learned, he was occupied with thoughts of such noble-mindedness that I, as a white, could hardly comprehend, let alone carry out. After a while, he stood up and said:

"Let us go home. My white brother has been damaged by us. Winnetou will find a way to replace this loss. Now, though, you must stay with us until your strength is fully back."

Chapter 30

We went back to the pueblo, in which we four whites slept as free men for the first time. The following day Hawkens, Stone, Parker, and the Apaches smoked the peace pipe amid great celebration. Of course, this was accompanied by long speeches. The best of them was Sam's, which, in typical fashion, he larded with such droll expressions that the Indians, ever serious, had to struggle to suppress the laughter that it evoked in them. In the course of that day, everything associated with the preceding events that had been unclear was explained. In the process, it was again mentioned that I had cut Inchu-chuna and Winnetou loose that night among the Kiowas, and Hawkens gave me the following harangue:

"You're a deceitful man, a totally and completely deceitful man, Sir! Don't you think you should be honest with your friends, especially when you have so much to be grateful for? What did you amount to when we first saw you in St. Louis? A tutor who drilled children on their ABCs and their times tables. And you would have remained a pathetic character if we hadn't been so generous and thoughtful as to take you on. We dragged you out of those unhappy ABCs and carried you across the prairie with astonishing gentleness, if I'm not mistaken. We watched over you, like a loving mother watches over her tiny baby or a hen watches over a duckling that she has hatched. We gradually brought you to consciousness, and we're the ones who cultivated your brain so that there started to be a little bit of dawn in the vast darkness inside it. The long and short of it is, we were father and mother, uncle and aunt to you. We lifted you up, fed your body with the sweetest morsels and your soul with our wisdom. And all we expected was a little respect, deference, and gratitude, and perhaps that the duckling wouldn't go running into the water that we hens would have to drink."

"But you did everything we told you not to," Sam continued. "It pains me to see so much love and sacrifice repaid with so much disobedience and ingratitude. If I was to list all your bad deeds one after the other, I don't think I'd ever reach the end. And the absolute worst of it was, you cut the two chiefs loose and didn't say a word about it to us. That ain't something I can forgive or forget, and I'll hold it against you for as long as I occupy this here skin. The results of this insidious silence weren't long in coming, either. Instead of getting nicely braised and roasted at the stake yesterday and waking up today in the lovely hunting grounds of the departed Indians, they didn't even find it worth their while to kill us. Now we have to sit around, alive and in good health, in this out-of-the-way pueblo, where everyone is trying to ruin our stomachs with delicacies, and to make you, a half-baked greenhorn, into a demi-god. And we have you to thank for this disaster, just because you're such a completely despicable swimmer. But love is always an incomprehensible being. The more it is abused, the more it is expressed. And so, even after all this, we are too kindhearted to cast you out of our company and our hearts. Instead, we want to pile glowing coals on your skin as we once more forgive you, in the fond hope that you will finally reflect and change your ways, if I'm not mistaken. Here is my hand. Will you promise me you'll do better, Sir?"

"Yes," I answered, shaking his hand. "I will strive to follow the noble example that you have always given me, so that someday soon people will mistake me for the true Sam Hawkens."

"My dear Sir, don't bother trying! You would be wasting your energy. A greenhorn, like you, being mistaken for Sam Hawkens? Not a chance! That would be the same as if a prairie toad wanted to be an opera singer. Why, I'll . . ."

Dick Stone interrupted him with a grin:

"Stop! Shut up, for once, you old curmudgeon! I can't stand it any more! You twist everything around, get everything backwards, and stick your left glove on your right hand! If I were Old Shatterhand, I wouldn't tolerate all this 'greenhorn' nonsense."

"What objection can he possibly have? It's the truth: that's what he is!"

"You're crazy! We have him to thank for our lives. You wouldn't find one experienced frontiersman in a hundred, us included, that could have done what he did yesterday. We were supposed to protect him, and he protected us—mark it well! If he hadn't been around, we wouldn't be here today, and you'd not be sitting there with your skin intact, under that silly old wig of yours!"

"What? Silly old wig? Don't you ever say that again! It is a superb wig. If you don't know that by now, you better look at it closely!"

He took it off and handed it to Stone.

"Get that pelt away from me!" Stone laughed.

Sam pulled it back on his head and said, in an accusatory tone:

"Dick, you ought to be ashamed, calling the ornament of my head a pelt! I wouldn't have expected it from a good comrade like you! None of you realizes the value of your old Sam. So I will punish you with contempt and go looking for my Mary. I need to find out is she's managed as well as I have."

He made a disdainful gesture with his arms and left. We laughed heartily, for it really was impossible to hold anything against him.

The next day, the scouts that had secretly followed the Kiowas returned. They reported that the Kiowas had travelled off without stopping and thus did not seem likely to engage in any more hostilities for the moment.

This was the beginning of a peaceful time, but one full of activities for me. Sam, Dick, and Will were delighted with the hospitality of the Apaches and they took the opportunity for a thorough rest. The only activity that Hawkens permitted himself was to go for a ride on his Mary every day so that, as he put it, she would "learn to appreciate his finesse" and become accustomed to his way of riding.

But I didn't lie around on my bearskins. Winnetou had made it his business to put me through "Indian school." We were often gone for whole days. We rode far and wide, and I had to master everything relating to hunting and fighting. We crept through the forests, and I got excellent training in techniques for spying. He took me through formal "field exercises." Often, he would separate from me and my job was to find him again. He tried hard to cover his tracks, and I tried just as hard to find them. He would often hide in a thicket or stand in the Rio Pecos, hidden behind overhanging bushes, watching me to see how well I could follow him. Then he would point out my mistakes and show me, through his own example, how I should behave and what I should do or not do. It was an excellent kind of training, for the enthusiasm he put into it was as great as the joy and wonder I experienced as his pupil. But not a word of praise ever crossed his lips, nor anything that you could really call criticism. A master in all the accomplishments of Indian life, he was also a master teacher.

I often came home dead tired, feeling like I had been put through a wringer. But even then I had no rest, since I was trying to learn the Apache language and I had lessons in the pueblo in the evening. I had three teachers: Nsho-Chi taught me the Mescalero dialect, Inchu-chuna that of the Llaneros, and Winnetou that of the Navajos. Since these languages are closely related to each other and have limited vocabularies, the work went quickly.

When Winnetou took me somewhere not too far from the pueblo, Nsho-chi would sometimes join us on our outings. She was always very pleased when I did my tasks well.

Once, the three of us were in the woods, and Winnetou told me to leave and return in a quarter of an hour. On my return, they would both be gone, and I was to search for Nsho-chi, who was very good at hiding. So I walked a fair distance away, waited for the allotted time, and then returned. It was easy to find both sets of tracks leaving the site. At first they were quite clear, but then Nsho-chi's footprints disappeared. To be sure, I knew that she was extraordinarily light on her feet, but the ground was soft, so there would have to be at least one print somewhere around, even if it were faint. But I found nothing, absolutely nothing, not a single tiny plant that was bent or broken, despite the fact that the area was covered with thick and receptive moss. Only Winnetou's prints were obvious, but I didn't pay much attention—it was his sister, not him, that I was supposed to find. He always hung around in the vicinity, watching secretly to see whether or not I made mistakes.

I searched again and again in a circle, but didn't find the slightest clue. This was strange. I thought it over. She would have had to leave a track, since no foot could have touched the ground here without leaving evidence in the soft moss. A foot touching the ground? Aha! What if she hadn't touched the ground at all?

I investigated Winnetou's footprints. They were deeply pressed into the ground, deeper than previously. Had he picked up his sister and carried her? He had set me a difficult problem, from his point of view, but as soon as I realized he had carried Nsho-chi, it was an easy one for me.

Because of the extra weight, his feet had pressed deeper into the moss. Now, what I needed to do was find some trace of Nsho-chi. I would have to find it, not on the ground, but higher up.

If Winnetou had been going through the woods alone, he would have had his hands free, and he would have been careful about how he went through the brush. But carrying his sister, he could not have avoided broken twigs. I followed his footprints, paying close attention to the bushes, not the tracks on the ground. Right! As he forced his way through the bushes, he had had his arms full and had not been able to carefully push the branches out of the way. Nsho-chi had apparently not thought to do it either, so I found many bent branches and damaged leaves — signs that I would not have found if Winnetou had come through by himself.

The path led straight to a clearing in the woods and continued straight across it. Probably the two of them were hiding on the far side of the clearing, taking quiet delight in their belief that I would find it impossible to complete my task. I could have gone directly across, but I wanted to do even better and really take them by surprise. So I snuck carefully around the clearing, staying concealed in the undergrowth.

Once I reached the other side, I first searched for Winnetou's tracks. I would be sure to see them if he had continued on. If I didn't find them, then he must be hidden with Nsho-chi. I stretched out on the ground and moved soundlessly in a half-circle, always keeping myself hidden behind trees and bushes. There was not a footprint to be found. So they had to be hiding at the edge of the clearing, just as I had suspected, and probably right where the tracks that I had been following reached the woods on this side of the clearing.

Quietly, very quietly, I slid toward the hiding spot. They were sitting still, and their practiced ears would not miss a sound. That meant I had to show an uncommon level of care. I succeeded better than I had thought possible. I saw the two of them. They were sitting next to each other in the middle of a wild plum bush, with their backs to me, facing the clearing. They expected me to come, if at all, from the far side. They were speaking to each other, but in a whisper, too softly for me to understand a word.

I was uncommonly pleased at the opportunity to surprise them, and I crept closer to them. Finally, I was so close that I could have touched both of them. I was about to reach out and grab Winnetou from behind, but before I could do this, I heard what he was saying and stopped.

"Should I go get him?" he asked in a whisper.

"No," answered Nsho-chi. "He'll come by himself."

"He won't come."

"He will come!"

"My sister is mistaken. He has learned everything very quickly, but your tracks went through the air. How will he find them?"

"He will find them. My brother Winnetou has told me that it is already impossible to trick Old Shatterhand. Why does he now say the opposite?"

"Because the task today is the hardest one that there is. His eyes can find any track, but yours can only be found by thinking, and he has not yet learned that."

"Still, he will come. He can do anything, anything that he wants to do."

These words were only whispered, but there was a confidence evident in her tone that I could take pride in.

"Yes, I have never known a man who picked up everything so easily. There is only one thing that he will never do, and it is painful to Winnetou."

"What is that?"

"The wish that we all share."

At this point, I ought to have revealed myself to them. But Winnetou spoke of a wish, and that made me decide to wait a bit longer. What wish would I not fulfill for these wonderful, warm people? They were harboring a wish and not telling me because they believed I wouldn't fulfill it. Maybe I would be able to learn what it was. I kept still and listened.

"Did my brother Winnetou already speak to him about it?"

"No," answered Winnetou.

"And Inchu-chuna, our father, did not speak either?"

"No. He wanted to say something, but I wouldn't let him."

"You wouldn't? Why not? Nsho-chi loves this paleface very much, and she is the daughter of the most powerful chief of the Apaches!"

"So she is, and more, much more. Every red warrior and every paleface would be happy to have my sister as his squaw, but Old Shatterhand would not."

"Did he say this?"

"No."

"Does his heart belong to some white woman?"

"Not that either."

"You are sure of that?"

"Yes. We have spoken of white women, and I learned from his words that he has not yet spoken his heart."

"Then he will speak it to me!"

"Let my sister not deceive herself! Old Shatterhand thinks and feels differently than you imagine. When he chooses a squaw, she must be among women as he is among men."

"Am I not that?"

"Among red women, yes. No squaw compares with my beautiful sister. But what have you seen and heard? What have you learned? You know the world of Indian women, but nothing of what a white squaw must learn and know. Old Shatterhand does not look at the shininess of the gold and the beauty of the face. He strives for other things, which he cannot find in a red woman."

She lowered her head and was silent. He stroked her cheek lovingly and said:

"It hurts me that I cause pain in the heart of my good sister, but Winnetou always tries to tell the truth, even when it is not a happy truth. Perhaps Winnetou knows a way for Nsho-chi to succeed in her goal."

She quickly raised her head again and asked:

"What way is that?"

"The way to the cities of the palefaces."

"Do you think I must go there?"

"Yes."

"Why?"

"To learn what you must know and what you must be able to do, if Old Shatterhand is to love you."

"Then I want to go, very soon! Will my brother Winnetou fulfill a wish for me?"

"What wish?"

"Speak to Inchu-chuna, our father, about this! Ask him to let me go to the great cities of the palefaces! He will not say 'no' to you, because. . . "

I did not hear more, but quietly crept away. It felt almost sinful to have overheard this conversation between brother and sister. As long as they didn't notice! What an embarrassment for them as well as me! Now I had to be even more careful in withdrawing than I had in approaching them. The least noise, the smallest accident could reveal that I had discovered the secret of the beautiful Indian. And if that happened, I would be obliged to leave my Indian friends that very day.

Fortunately, I was able to get away unnoticed. Once I was out of hearing range, I stood up and quickly circled the clearing back to where Winnetou's footprints were. I then followed them into the clearing two or three paces toward the other side, where I had just been and where Nsho-chi was expecting me. I called across:

"Let my brother Winnetou come over here!"

Nothing stirred on the other side. I continued:

"Let my brother come, for I see him there."

Still he didn't come.

"He is sitting there in the bush with the wild plums. Shall I come and get him?"

The twigs moved, and Winnetou walked out, but alone. He couldn't remain hidden, but he didn't want to give away his sister's hiding place. He asked me:

"Has my brother Old Shatterhand found Nsho-chi?"

"Yes."

"Where?"

"There, in the bush, where she is hiding."

"In which bush?"

"In the same one that your tracks lead to."

"Did you see her tracks?"

There was a note of wonder in his voice. He wasn't sure exactly what he was dealing with. He didn't believe that I would lie, but he knew of no tracks I could have found, and since he had left his sister only a moment earlier, he clung to the idea that I had not really found her. He assumed that I must be mistaken in some way, that I was confusing something.

"Yes," I answered, "I saw them."

"But my sister was so careful that her tracks cannot be seen!"

"You are mistaken. They can be seen."

"No."

"On the ground, no, but among the branches. Nsho-chi did not touch the ground with her feet, but when you carried her, you bent twigs and damaged leaves."

"Ugh! I carried her?"

"Yes."

"Who told you that?"

"Your footprints. They were suddenly deeper, because you were suddenly heavier. But you could not have changed your weight, so you must have been carrying something heavy. That was your sister, whose feet did not touch the moss."

"Ugh! You're mistaken. Go back and look some more!"

"That would be useless and completely unnecessary, for Nsho-chi is sitting where you were sitting. I will go and get her."

I went straight across the clearing, but she was already emerging from the bushes, and she said, with apparent satisfaction, to her brother:

"I told you he would find me, and I was right."

"Yes, my sister was right, and I was wrong. My brother Old Shatterhand can read a man's tracks, not just with his eyes, but with his thoughts. There is hardly anything more for him to learn."

"Oh, there's still a great deal more," I answered. "My brother Winnetou gives me praise which I have not yet earned. But what I can still learn from him, I will."

It really was the first praise I had ever heard from his mouth, and I can tell you I was at least as proud of it as of any praise I ever got from one of my professors.

That same evening he brought me a nicely-sewn hunting outfit of white tanned leather decorated with Indian designs in red thread.

"Nsho-chi, my sister, asks you to wear these clothes," he said. "Your clothing is not good enough for Old Shatterhand anymore."

He was certainly right about that. Any Indian would have easily seen how pathetic my clothes looked. And if I were caught wearing them in any European city, I would have been arrested immediately as a vagrant. But was it all right to accept such a present from Nsho-chi? Winnetou seemed to read my thoughts. He said:

"You may accept these clothes, because I requested them. They are a gift from Winnetou, who you rescued from death, and not from his sister. Is it forbidden among the palefaces for a man to take gifts from a squaw?"

"Yes, if it is not his own squaw, or a relative."

"You are my brother, so Nsho-chi is your relative. Anyway, the gift is from me and not from her. She only did the sewing."

Chapter 31

When I tried on the outfit the next morning, it fit like a glove. A New York tailor couldn't have done a better fitting job. Of course I modeled it for my pretty friend, who was delighted at the praise I gave her. A little later, Dick Stone and Will Parker came by to admire me. They had also been given new outfits (sewn by other squaws, not Nsho-chi). And not long after, I was down in the river valley practicing my tomahawk throwing when a small, odd figure approached me gravely. It was wearing a new Indian outfit of leather, which ended at the bottom in a pair of exceptionally large old Indian boots. On top, it wore an even older felt hat with a sadly drooping brim, under which a muddled forest of beard, a huge nose, and two tiny, crafty eyes appeared. I recognized Sam Hawkens. He planted himself, skinny legs spread far apart, before me and demanded:

"Sir, do you happen to know the man who now stands before you?"

"Hmm!" I anwered. "Let me take a look."

I took his arms and turned him around three times, observed him from every side, and then said:

"It does appear to be Sam Hawkens, if I'm not mistaken!"

"Yes, my good man, you're absolutely right. It's me, in person and life-size. Notice anything?"

"Spiffy new outfit!"

"You bet!"

"Where did you get it?"

"From the bearskin you gave me."

"I can see that, Sam. That's not what I meant. I'm interested in knowing who the person is that gave it to you."

"The person? Hmm! Right! The person, Sir. It's like this. Actually, it isn't really a person."

"What do you mean?"

"More like a young woman."

"How so?"

"Well, don't you know that pretty girl Kliuna-ai?"

"No. Kliuna-ai means moon. Is she a girl or a squaw?"

"Both, or really neither."

"A grandmother?"

"Nonsense! If she's a squaw or a girl or really neither, then naturally she must be a widow. She is the survivor of an Apache warrior who died in the battle with the Kiowas."

"And you want to offer her consolation?"

"Well, Sir," he nodded. "I don't see anything wrong with that. I've taken a glance at her—looked her over pretty carefully, really."

"But, Sam, an Indian woman?"

"What difference does it make? Why I'd marry the right woman no matter what color she was. Furthermore, Kliuna-ai is an excellent match."

"Why?"

"Because she tans the best leather in the whole tribe."

"Would you let her tan you?"

"Don't make jokes, Sir! This is serious. Home, sweet home. Don't you understand? She's got a lovely round face, just like the moon."

"Does it have a first and last quarter?"

"Please, no moon jokes! She's the full moon, and I mean to marry her, if I'm not mistaken."

"I hope that doesn't result in any new moons. How did you make her acquaintance?"

"Through the tannery, actually. I asked around for the best person to do tanning—because of the bearskin, you know—and she was recommended to me. I took the bearskin around to her, and I could tell right away she was attracted."

"To the skin?"

"Nonsense! To me, of course!"

"That shows taste, Sam!"

"Yes, she's got good taste. Oh, she's not ignorant at all! She proved that by not just tanning the skin, but also making me a new outfit from it. Well, how do I look?"

"A regular dandy!"

"A gentleman, right? Yes, a gentleman! She was astonished when she saw me in this outfit a moment ago. I'll marry her, Sir, you can depend on it!"

"Where's your old outfit?"

"I threw it out."

"Amazing! And I remember a day when you told me that you wouldn't part with your jacket for ten thousand dollars!"

"That was long ago. I didn't know Kliuna-ai. Times change. Well!"

The little suitor clothed in bearskin turned on his heel and stamped away indignantly. The empathy that I felt for that Indian widow did not stem from any moral compunctions or considerations. You only had to look at Sam to understand. The huge feet, the skinny, crooked legs, and then that face—good grief! It looked like some ancestor of his had been a vulture, and Sam had inherited the beak. It was too much for any woman. He hadn't gone far before he turned around again and called back to me:

"This new set of clothes changes everything, Sir! I feel like a newborn. I don't ever want to see the old ones. Sam's going courting, hee-hee-hee!"

The next day I encountered him near the base of the pueblo. He had a pensive expression.

"What kind of astronomical thoughts are going through your

head, Sam?" I asked him.

"Astronomical? Why astonomical?"

"Because you're making faces like someone puzzling about the discovery of a comet or a patch of cosmic fog."

"You've just about summed it up, Sir. I thought it was a comet, but it turns out to be fog."

"What?"

"Kliuna-ai."

"Aha! Yesterday's full moon is today's patch of fog! Why?"

"I asked her if she wanted to get married again. She answered 'No.'"

"That shouldn't stop you from looking confidently to the future. Rome wasn't built in a day."

"And my new outfit wasn't sewed together in an hour. You're right, Sir. I'm still going courting."

He climbed up the ladder, intent on visiting his Kliuna-ai. The next day, as I was saddling my chestnut stallion to go buffalo hunting with Winnetou, Sam Hawkens came up to me and asked:

"May I come along, Sir?"

"Hunting buffalo? Oh, no! You're hunting something much better."

"I'm afraid it doesn't really bear scrutiny."

"Really?"

"Yes. And it makes demands."

"How so?"

"I visited her again. She told me that Winnetou had ordered her to make my outfit."

"So it wasn't done for love?"

"Apparently not. Not only that, but she also said I had requested her to do the tanning, and what was I going to give her for it."

"So she wants payment!"

"Yes! Is that a sign of love?"

"I don't know. I don't have any experience in such things. Children love their parents, but the parents still have to pay for everything. Perhaps this is evidence that your 'full moon' shares your love."

"Full moon? Hmm! I'm afraid it may be the last quarter. So you won't take me along?"

"Winnetou wants to ride alone with me."

"Well, I can't object to that."

"You would ruin your new hunting jacket, Sam!"

"True enough. You wouldn't want splotches of blood on such fine duds."

He left, but then turned back again and asked:

"Don't you think my old outfit was much more practical?"

"It's possible."

"Not just possible. Pretty darn likely."

That was the end of the topic for that day. But in the course of the following days, Sam became more and more brooding and monosyllabic. His moon seemed to be on the wane. Then, one morning, he emerged from his quarters wearing his old clothes!

"What's this, Sam?" I asked. "I thought you had put these clothes away, or even 'thrown them out' as you put it."

"And I did."

"But you went and found them again."

"Yes."

"Because you're angry?"

"Of course! I'm really furious!"

"Down to the last quarter?"

"New moon. I can't, and won't, see Kluina-ai any more!"

"That's exactly what I predicted."

"Yes. It turned out just like you said. But it's the story behind it that drives me positively wild."

"May I ask what that is?"

"Yes, I'll tell you. I was with her yesterday. She treated me badly these last few days, very badly. She hardly looked at me, and answered me very curtly. I was sitting with her yesterday and I leaned back against a wooden pole. I guess it must have had a splinter that caught in my hair. When I got up to go, I felt a strong tug on my noble pate. I turned around, and what do you suppose I saw, Sir?"

"Your wig, I'm guessing?"

"Yes, my wig was caught on that splinter, and my hat had fallen off on the floor."

"And that's when the previously full moon became a new moon?"

"And how! First, she stood there and stared at me like . . . like I was a man with no hair on his head."

"And then?"

"Then she screamed and howled, as if it was she that had the bald head."

"And after that?"

"After that? Well, then she did turn into a new moon. She dashed out and disappeared."

"Maybe she'll appear as a first quarter again soon, and then as a full moon."

"Not her! She sent word to me."

"What word?"

"I'm not allowed to visit her any more. She stupidly insists on having a man who has hair. Isn't that the height of stupidity?"

"Hmm!"

"Don't give me that 'Hmm,' Sir! When a woman marries, she shouldn't care whether her husband has hair on his head or on his wig, if I'm not mistaken. It's actually more honorable to have a wig, because they cost money but real hair grows for free."

"Then I'd grow some, if I were in your shoes, Sam!"

"Let the devil take you, Sir! I look to you for comfort in my heartbreak and marriage troubles and all I get is teasing. I wish you had a wig and an Indian widow that threw you out the door. Farewell!"

He hurried away angrily.

"Sam," I called after him, "one more question!"

"Well, what is it?" he asked, stopping.

"Where did you leave it?"

"What?"

"Your new outfit."

"I sent it back. I don't want it. I thought it would be good for the honeymoon, maybe wear it for the wedding, but now that there's not going to be a honeymoon, I don't want any part of that outfit. How!"

Thus ended the friendship between Sam and Kliuna-ai, the ever-waning red moon. By the way, he was soon in good spirits again, and he assured me that he was pleased to remain a bachelor. He would never again part with his old hunting jacket, which was better, more practical, and more comfortable than all the hunting jackets made by all the Indian seamstresses in the world. So it worked out as I had thought. Sam as a husband—that was just unimaginable.

Chapter 32

That evening I ate, as usual, with Inchu-chuna and Winnetou. Winnetou disappeared after the meal, and I was about to go as well, but the chief started talking to me about Sam's adventure with Kliuna-ai and then about the general topic of relationships between whites and Indian women. I could tell he was sounding me out.

"Does my young brother Old Shatterhand think such a marriage would be right or wrong?" he asked.

"If it is conducted by a priest and the Indian woman had already become a Christian, I see nothing wrong with it."

"So my brother would never take an Indian girl as is squaw, just the way she is?"

"No."

"And is it difficult to become a Christian?"

"No, not at all."

"Can such a squaw still honor her father, even if he is not a Christian?"

"Yes. Our religion says that all children should honor and obey their parents."

"What kind of squaw would my young brother prefer, a red or a white one?"

Could I say a white one? No, I would have insulted him. So I answered:

"That is not so simple to answer. It depends on the voice in your heart. When it speaks, you listen, no matter what color the squaw is. Before the Great Spirit, all people are equal, and those who belong together and are intended for one another, they will find each other."

"How! If they belong together, they will find each other. What my brother says is very true. He always speaks truly and well."

I believed (and hoped) that this was the end of the discussion. I had intentionally emphasized that an Indian woman had to be Christian in order to marry a white man. I would not have begrudged Nsho-chi the best and noblest of all the red warriors and chiefs; but I had not come to the Wild West to take an Indian wife—nor a white one, for that matter. There was no room in my life's plans for marriage.

Two days later, I learned what success my discussion with Inchu-chuna had had. He took me into the first level of the pueblo, where I had not previously been. There, in a special little container, lay our surveying instruments.

"Look at these things and see if anything is missing," the chief requested.

I did so and found that nothing had been mislaid. The items had not even been damaged, with the exception of a few dents which could easily be repaired.

"These things have been medicine for us," he said. "That is why they have been so well guarded and preserved. Let my young white brother taken them. They are his again."

I tried to thank him for this most welcome gift. He dismissed my thanks, explaining to me:

"They were yours before, and we took them, because we thought you were our enemy. But now that we know that you are our brother, you must get back everything that is yours. There is nothing to thank us for. What will you do with these things?"

"When I leave here, I will take them along and give them back to the people who gave them to me."

"Where are these people?"

"In St. Louis."

"I know the name of this town and also where it lies. Winnetou, my son, has been there and told me about it. So, you would like to leave us?"

"Yes, but not right away."

"That's too bad. You have become a warrior of our tribe, and I have even given you the power and honor of a chief of the Apaches. We thought you would stay with us for ever, just as Kleki-petra stayed with us until he died."

"My situation is different than his was."

"You know what his situation was?"

"Yes. He told me everything."

"He must have had great confidence in you, even though he saw you for the first time."

"Perhaps because we came from the same land."

"That alone cannot explain it. He even spoke with you as he died. I could not understand a word, because I don't know the language he spoke in, but you told us what he said. Because of Kleki-petra's wish, you became Winnetou's brother, and yet you want to leave him. Is that not a contradiction?"

"No. Brothers do not need to always be together. They often separate when they have different tasks to do."

"But then they see each other again?"

"Yes. You will see me again, for my heart will send me back to you."

"My soul is glad to hear it. There will be great joy among us whenever you return. I am very sorry to hear you speak of other tasks. Can you not be happy here among us?"

"I don't know. I have been here for such a short time that I cannot answer that question. Perhaps it is like two birds who sit in the shade of a tree. One takes strength from the fruit of the tree and stays there. The other needs a different kind of food and cannot stay for long. He must leave."

"But you can be sure that we would give you everything you desired."

"I know that. But when I spoke of food, I didn't mean the kind of nourishment that your body needs."

"Yes, I know that you palefaces also speak of food for the spirit. I learned that from Kleki-petra. He did not find that food among us, and it sometimes made him very sad, although he tried to hide it from us. You are younger than he was, and so perhaps you will be drawn away sooner and more easily than he was. Therefore go, but we urge you to return. Perhaps you will change your mind and realize that you can feel at home among us. But I would like to know what you will do when you go back to the cities of a palefaces."

"I don't know that yet."

"Will you stay with the white men who want to build the road for the fire-horse?"

"No."

"That is a wise choice. You have become a brother of the red men and you must not help the palefaces when they want to cheat us of our land and our possessions again. But there you cannot live by hunting as you can here. You will need money, and Winnetou told me that you are poor. You would have gotten money if we hadn't attacked you. Therefore my son has asked me to offer to replace it. Do you want some gold?"

He looked at me so hard and searchingly as he asked this question that I hesitated to answer 'yes.' He was testing me.

"Gold?" I said. "You didn't take any from me, and so I desire none from you."

This was a diplomatic answer, neither a 'yes' nor a 'no'. I knew there were Indians that knew places where precious metals could be found, but they would never reveal them to white men. Inchu-chuna certainly knew of such places, and now he was asking me "do you want gold?" What white man would have answered that with a direct 'no'? I have never sought treasures, which can rust or be eaten by moths, but still the gold would have been useful to me as a means to good ends, I certainly can't deny that. The Apache chief might not have seen it that way, though.

"No, we didn't steal any gold from you," he answered, "but because of us, you did not get what you would have gotten, so

I want to repay you for that. I can tell you that great amounts of gold can be found in the mountains. The Indians know the places where it lies. They only need to go there and bring it back. Would you like me to get you some?"

Hundreds of men in my position would have accepted this offer, and gotten nothing. I could tell from the strange, expectant look in his eyes. So I said:

"I thank you! But receiving wealth as a gift, without earning it, brings no satisfaction. Only what you have worked for and earned has real value. Even if I am poor, there is no reason to believe that I will starve when I return to the palefaces."

The tension drained away from his face. He gave me his hand and said, in a hearty, supportive tone:

"Your words tell me that we have not been deceived about you. The gold dust that drives the whites to seek gold is the dust of death. Those who happen to find gold perish because of it. Never strive to obtain it, for it kills the soul as well as the body! I was testing you. I would not have given you gold, but you will get money — the money you had been expecting."

"That is not possible."

"If I want it to happen, then it is possible. We will ride back to the place where you were working. You will be able to complete the work and get the money that was promised to you."

I stared at him, astonished and at a loss for words. Was he joking? No, an Indian chief wouldn't joke about a thing like that. Or was this perhaps another test? That didn't seem likely either.

"My young white brother says nothing," he continued. "Does he not welcome what I offer?"

"I welcome it indeed! But I can't believe that you are speaking in earnest."

"Why not?"

"You are saying I can complete the work for which you killed the white men I worked with! You are saying I can do the thing that you objected to so strongly at our first meeting!"

"You worked without the permission of those that the land belonged to, but this time you will have permission. My offer comes not from me, but from my son Winnetou. He told me that it will not hurt us if you complete your work."

"That is not true. The tracks will be built, and the whites will certainly come!"

He stared darkly at the ground for a while, and then admitted:

"You are right. We cannot stop them from robbing us again and again. First they send small groups, like the one you were with. We can kill them, but it changes nothing, for later they come in great bands, from which we must retreat if we do not want to be crushed. But you cannot change this either. Or do you think that they will not come, if you refuse to finish your measurements?"

"No, I don't think so. We can do whatever we please, and the iron-horse is still sure to come to that area."

"Then accept my offer! You will benefit and we will not be hurt. I have spoken with Winnetou. We will ride with you, he and I, and thirty warriors will come with us. That is enough to protect you while you work, and also to help you with it. Then these thirty men will come with us to the East, far enough for us to find safe paths and to take the steam canoe to St. Louis."

"What is my red brother saying? Did I understand him correctly? He wants to come to the East?"

"Yes, with you, me, Winnetou, and Nsho-chi."

"Nsho-chi too?"

"My daughter too. She would like to see the great houses of the palefaces and stay there long enough to become like a white squaw."

Perhaps I looked at bit stunned at these words, for he added with a smile:

"My young white brother appears surprised. Does he not want us to go along with him? Let him say it honestly!"

"Not want you to come? How could I? On the contrary, I am

extremely happy about it! With you along, I will get back to the East without danger. That alone would make me pleased. And in addition, I will still have with me those whom I have learned to love."

"How!" he nodded, relieved. "You will finish your work and then we will travel east. Will Nsho-chi find people there with whom she can live and learn?"

"Yes. I will be glad to take care of that. But the chief of the Apaches must understand that the palefaces cannot offer the same hospitality as the Indians."

"I know it. Unless palefaces come to us as enemies, we give them everything they need without having to give us anything. But if we go to visit them, we must pay for everything, and we must pay twice as much as white travelers do. And even then, what we are given is not as good as what whites get. Yes, Nsho-chi will also have to pay."

"Unfortunately, that is true, but you don't need to worry about it. Because of your generous offer, I will get a lot of money, and then you will be my guests."

"Ugh, ugh! What is my young white brother thinking about Inchu-chuna and Winnetou, the chiefs of the Apaches? I told you before that the red men know the places where gold can be found. There are mountains with gold veins running through them, and valleys where the gold dust that has been washed down can be found under a thin blanket of earth. When we go to the cities of the whites, we will have no money, but we will have gold— enough gold that no one will have to make a gift of even a drink of water. And if Nsho-chi has to stay there for many suns, I will leave more gold with her than she will need for this long time. Only the inhospitality of the palefaces forces us to find the sources of this gold dust. Otherwise, we ignore them and never use them. When will my young brother be ready to leave?"

"Any time, as soon as you like."

"Then we will not delay, for it is near the end of the fall, and the winter will follow soon. A red warrior does not need to make preparations even for a long ride. We can leave tomorrow, if you are ready then."

"I am ready. Nothing needs to be done except to discuss what we need to bring, how many horses. . ."

"Winnetou will take care of that," he interrupted me. "He has already thought of everything, and my young white brother does not need to worry about anything."

We left the level where we were and went back up into the pueblo. As I was about to enter my room, I saw Sam Hawkens coming.

"I have news to tell you, Sir," he said, gleaming with excitement. "You'll be amazed, really amazed, if I'm not mistaken."

"About what?"

"About the news I'm going to tell you. Or do you already know?"

"Tell me what you mean, Sam!"

"We're leaving!"

"Aha! Yes, I do already know that."

"You already know? I wanted to bring you the happy news, but I guess I'm too late."

"I just learned it from Inchu-chuna. Who told you?"

"Winnetou. I ran into him down by the river, where he was picking out horses for the trip. Even Nsho-chi is coming along! Did you know that too?"

"Yes."

"It's a strange idea, but it's OK with me. Apparently, she's going to find a place to stay back East. Why she'd do that, I can't fathom, unless. . ."

He stopped in the middle of his sentence, gave me a brief but expressive look with his tiny eyes, and then continued:

". . . unless, unless, hmm. Nsho-chi might become your Kliuna-ai. Do you reckon, Sir?"

"My Kliuna-ai? You mean my moon? I leave such episodes to you,

Sam. What is the point of a moon that gets smaller and smaller until it completely disappears? Besides, I'd never lose an Indian woman on account of my wig."

"Your wig? Hey, cut it out. That was a pathetic joke. A smart guy like you should be able to do better than that. Besides, it's a good thing my love affair with that waning moon didn't work out."

"Why?"

"Because I wouldn't be able to leave it here. I'd have to take it with me. And who wants to carry a new moon across the prairie? Hee-hee-hee! There really is a silver lining to every storm cloud. Only one thing still bothers me about it."

"What?"

"That beautiful grizzly hide. If I had sewed it myself, I'd be wearing a splendid hunting jacket now. But the jacket and the hide are both gone."

"Too bad! Hopefully there will be another chance to kill a grizzly. Then I'll give you the hide."

"You'll give it to me? More likely I'll give it to you! Don't you go thinking that there's grizzlies just walking around waiting to be stabbed by the next greenhorn that comes along. That time was just an accident, and you have even less reason to take pride in that than the dumb joke you cracked a minute ago. Let's not go wishing for bears, especially with so much work to do right now. What an incredible idea, that you should continue surveying. Don't you think?"

"A noble thought, Sam, very noble."

"Yes! You'll get your pay, and we'll get ours too. Wait a second! Something just occurred to me that should make you very happy!

"What's that, Sam?"

"That you'll get all of the money—all of it!"

"I don't understand you."

"It's easy enough to understand. When the work is done, it must be paid for. The others are all dead, so you should get their share along with yours."

"Don't get your hopes up, Sam. They're not going to want to go along with your clever scheme."

"It's possible! If we just approach it right, we can demand it all. After all, you did just about all the work. Want to give it a try?"

"No. I wouldn't want to make a fool of myself by asking for more than I'm owed."

"Greenhorn, what a greenhorn! I'm telling you, German modesty is completely out of place in this country. I'm trying to help you, so pay attention. Just forget about becoming a frontiersman—you could work at it all your life and you'd never do it. You don't have the slightest talent for it. So you need to think about another line of work, and for that you need money, and lots of it. Now, if you're clever, you can land yourself a tidy sum, and that will keep you going for a while. But if you don't follow my advice, you'll miss the boat, and you'll be washed up like a fish out of water."

"We'll see about that. I didn't cross the Mississippi to become a frontiersman, so I won't lose any sleep if I never become one. You'd be the only unhappy one then."

"Me? Why would I be unhappy?"

"Because you tried so hard to make something out of me. I can just imagine how people will tell me, 'you must have been trained by someone who didn't know what he was doing.'"

"Didn't know what he was doing? Me? Sam Hawkens? Hee-hee-hee! I know what I'm doing, all right. And what I'm doing right now is leaving you standing here, Sir!"

He left, but turned back after a few paces and said:

"Mark my words: if you don't demand all that money, then I'll demand it and stuff it in your pockets! How!"

After these words, he strode off in a manner that was meant to be dignified but was actually the exact opposite. That wonderful little man only wanted the best for me—in this case, the entire sum, but I would never have considered it.

Chapter 33

What Inchu-chuna had said was true: a red warrior needed little preparation even for the longest ride. Even today, there was no change in the ordinary, even pace of life in the pueblo, and still everything possible was done to be ready for our imminent departure. Nsho-chi, too, served us our meal just as she always did. Among white women, there is such excitement and preparation for even a brief excursion! This Indian woman faced a long and dangerous trip to learn about the much-touted glories of civilization, and yet she showed not the slightest sign of change. She did not ask about anything, she did not solicit my advice, she did nothing at all to bother me. The only thing I had to do was to pack up the instruments in some soft wool blankets that Winnetou had given me for the purpose. We sat together, as usual, the whole evening, without a single word being spoken about the ride ahead. When I went to bed, it didn't seem as if I could possibly be on the verge of such a long trip. I had caught the calm and composure of the Indians. In the morning, Hawkens woke me up, saying that everything was ready for our departure. The dawn had hardly broken, a late fall morning whose coldness reminded us that the trip could no longer be postponed.

We had a bit of breakfast, and then the whole population of the pueblo, children and all, accompanied us down to the river, where a ceremony that I had not previously witnessed was to take place. The medicine man was to determine whether or not the trip would be a happy one.

The Apaches who were camping in the vicinity of the pueblo also joined the festivities. Our big wagon was still there. We would be leaving it behind, since it was much too heavy to move at the speed we had in mind. It had become the sanctuary of the medicine man, who had covered it with blankets which hid him from view.

A large circle formed around the wagon, and then the "sacred ceremony" (which seemed to me more like a "performance," though I didn't say so) began with a snarling and hissing sound

357

emanating from the wagon, like several cats and dogs getting ready for a fight.

I stood between Winnetou and his sister. The great similarity between the siblings was especially obvious that day, since Nsho-chi was wearing a man's hunting outfit, not women's clothing. Her outfit was just like her brother's, which I have described before. She, too, wore no head covering, but had her hair gathered in the back like his. Several pouches with various contents hung from her belt, as did a knife and a pistol, and she carried a rifle slung across her back. Her outfit was new, and was decorated with colorful fringing and needlework. She looked at once so fierce and so girlish and charming that all eyes were fastened on her. I was wearing the outfit I had been given, so the three of us were dressed almost identically.

I must have made a less than solemn face when the hissing began, for Winnetou said:

"My brother is not familiar with our ways. To himself, he will laugh at us."

"No sacred activity is to be laughed at, even one that I cannot understand or grasp."

"That is the right word: sacred. What you will see and hear is not a heathen performance. Every movement and sound of the medicine man has a meaning. What you are hearing now is the voices of good and evil battling each other."

Continuing in this way, he explained what the medicine man was doing throughout the medicine dance.

An ever-repeating howl, alternating with softer sounds, followed the hissing. The howl occurred whenever the medicine man, in investigating the future, perceived evil signs, while the softer sounds showed that he had foreseen something good. After this had gone on for awhile, he suddenly jumped out of the wagon and ran around in a circle, raging and bellowing. Gradually, he slowed down, the bellowing stopped. The well-acted "fear" that had driven him tapered off, and he began a slow, grotesque dance that looked all the more strange because he wore a ferocious mask and had all sorts of astonishing and monstrous objects hanging around his body. He accompanied the dance with a monotonous chanting. Both the dance and the chant were initially livelier, then got steadily calmer, until they finally stopped and the medicine man sat down, lowering his head between his knees. He remained for quite a long time without a sound or a movement, then suddenly jumped up and announced the results of his discernment in a loud voice:

"Hear, hear, you sons and daughters of the Apaches! This is what Manitou, the Great Good Spirit, has revealed to me. Inchu-chuna and Winnetou, the chiefs of the Apaches, and Old Shatterhand, who is our white chief, are riding out with their red and white warriors to take Nsho-chi, the young daughter of our tribe, to the place where palefaces live. The good Manitou is prepared to protect them. They will have some adventures, but will not be harmed, and will return to us safely. Nsho-chi will return safely too, after a long time with the palefaces. There is only one of the travelers that we will not see again."

He stopped speaking and lowered his head, to express his sadness at this fact.

"Ugh, ugh, ugh!" cried the Indians, in a mixture of curiosity and mournfulness. But none of them risked asking who it was that he meant.

The medicine man stood silent with his head bowed for a long time. Finally, little Sam Hawkens lost his patience and asked:

"Well, who is it that won't be coming back? Let the medicine man tell us!"

The medicine man made a gesture of reproval, waited quite a while longer, lifted his head, turned his eyes toward me and cried:

"It would have been better not to ask this question. I did not want to name him, but now Sam Hawkens, the curious paleface, has forced me to tell. It is Old Shatterhand who will not come back. Death will take him very soon. Those who I have said will return safely should stay away from him, if they do not wish to lose their lives along with his! They will be in danger when they are near him, but safe when they are away. These are the words of the Great Spirit. How!"

After these words, he went back into the wagon. The Indians were giving me sidelong glances and saying words of sympathy. For them, I was now an ostracized man, one to be avoided.

"What's that fellow talking about?" Sam said to me. "You're supposed to die? Can't the idiot come up with some other name? This infernal idea just popped into his addled brain. How else would he have come up with it?"

"Better to ask what his intent is! He doesn't wish me well. No Indian medicine man becomes a Christian's friend. This one never said a word to me, and naturally I repaid him in kind. I ignored him. It was as if he wasn't there. He fears my influence with the chiefs, and the possibility that it could spread to the whole tribe. Now he has seized the opportunity to head off that possibility."

"Should I go and give him a good punch in the jaw, Sir?"

"Don't do anything stupid, Sam! This isn't worth getting excited about."

Inchu-chuna, Winnetou, and Nsho-chi had looked at each other in dismay when they heard the medicine man's words. It didn't matter whether they believed the prophecy or not, they knew what its effect would be on their followers. Thirty men were to ride with us. If they believed that being near me would bring ruin, it would be impossible to avoid all kinds of unhealthy consequences. Since the medicine man's words could not be changed, the only way the leaders could head off these problems was to immediately show their people that their relationship with me was unchanged. Therefore, the chiefs took my two hands in theirs and Inchu-chuna said, loudly enough for all to hear:

"Let my red brothers and sisters hear my words! Our medicine brother has the vision to see the secrets of the future, and very often what his says comes true. But we have also seen that he can be mistaken. In the time of the great drought, he called for the rain but it did not come. Before our last expedition against the Comanches, he told us we would get great spoils, but though we gained the victory we only brought back a few old horses and three bad rifles. Two autumns ago, he told us we had to go to the waters of the Tugah if we wanted many buffalo. We followed his words, but got so little meat that we nearly starved during the winter. I could give you more examples to show that his eye is sometimes dark. So it is possible that he is wrong about our brother Old Shatterhand as well. I will treat his words as if they had not been spoken, and I call upon my brothers and sisters also to do this. We will wait and see if they are true."

Then little Sam Hawkens stepped forward and cried out:

"No, we will not wait! We don't need to wait. There is a way to learn right now whether the medicine man has pronounced the truth."

"What way does my white brother mean?" the chief inquired.

"I will tell you. It is not just Indians that have medicine men who understand how to find out the future. White people have them too, and I, Sam Hawkens, am the most famous of them."

"Ugh, ugh!" cried the Apaches, astonished.

"Yes, you're surprised, aren't you? I have been pretending to be an ordinary frontiersman, because I didn't know you, but there's more to me than meets the eye, and you'll soon get to know me, hee-hee-hee! Let several of the red warriors take tomahawks and dig a hole in the ground that is narrow but deep."

"Does my white brother want to look inside the earth?" asked Inchu-chuna.

"Yes, for the future is buried in the womb of the earth, and sometimes also in the stars. But since I can't see the stars when the day is bright, I must turn to the earth."

Several Indians followed his instruction, digging a trench with their tomahawks.

"Don't try to pull a fast one, Sam," I whispered to him. "If the Indians figure out that you're fooling around with them, you'll just make things worse."

"Pull a fast one? Fooling around? What do you think that medicine man does? Nothing but fooling around! What he can do, I can do too, if I'm not mistaken, Sir. I know what I'm doing. If nothing happens, the men we take with us will be stubborn. You can count on that."

"I agree completely, but I urge you: please, no funny business!"

"Oh, I'm completely serious. Don't you worry about that!"

In spite of his reassurance, I was still worried. I knew him only too well. He loved to have fun. I would have tried to warn him even more strongly, but he left me and went over to the Indians, to tell them how deep the hole needed to be.

Once it was finished, he dismissed the diggers and took off his old leather hunting jacket. Then, he buttoned it up again, and the old jacket was as stiff as if it had been made of tin or wood. He placed the jacket (which now formed a tall, hollow cylinder) over the hole. Then he turned to the crowd with a somber expression and cried:

"When the men, women, and children of the Apaches see what I do next, they will be astonished. After I speak my magic words, the earth will open her loins so that I can see all that will happen to us in the coming days."

He then stepped back from the hole, and then circled it in slowly and with much ceremony. During this process, to my annoyance, he recited the times-tables, from "one times one equals one" up to "nine times nine." Fortunately, he did it so fast that the Indians probably had no idea what he was saying. Once he was done with the "nines," his steps became faster and faster, until he was galloping around the hole. He uttered a loud cry and waved his arms like a windmill. Finally, out of breath, he approach the hole, made several deep bows, and stuck his head into the top of the jacket to look into the hole.

I was worried about the success of this childishness. But I looked around the circle and saw, to my relief, that the Indians were taking it all quite seriously. Nor did the faces of the two chiefs betray any sign of disapproval, though I was sure that Inchu-chuna was fully aware that Sam's performance was just trickery.

Sam's head remained in the collar opening of the jacket a good five minutes. During this time, his arms moved in a way that was meant to suggest that important and wonderful things were being revealed to him. Finally, he pulled out his head. His expression was deadly serious. He unbuttoned the jacket, put it on, and commanded:

"Let my red brothers close the hole. As long as it is open, I can say nothing!"

When this had been completed, he took a deep breath, as though he had suffered some sort of attack, and cried out:

"Your red medicine brother has not seen things correctly. It will be exactly the opposite from what he has said. I have learned everything that the next few weeks will bring to us, but I am forbidden from sharing it with you. There are only a few things I am permitted to say. I have seen guns in the hole, and have heard shots, so we will be involved in battles. The final shot came from Old Shatterhand's bear-killer. The person who shoots the last shot cannot have been killed, but must be the victor. Evil threatens my red brothers, and they can only escape it by staying close to Old Shatterhand. But if they follow the medicine man's advice, then they will perish. I have spoken. How!"

The effect of this prophecy was, at least for the moment, exactly what Sam had in mind. The Indians believed him, that much was clear. They looked over to the wagon with expectation. They obviously thought the medicine man would be emerging to defend himself. But he did not appear, so they assumed that he felt he had been bested. Sam Hawkens came over to me and, with a sly twinkle in his eye, asked:

"Well, Sir, how did I do?"

"You performed like a real, professional swindler."

"Well! So I did OK?"

"Yes. At least it appears you achieved what you set out to do."

"You bet I did. The medicine man is down for the count. He hasn't made a peep in response."

Winnetou gave us a quiet, but still very expressive, glance. His father was more vocal. He came over to us and said:

"My white brother is a clever man. He took the power out of the words of our medicine man, and he has a jacket that is full of important wisdom. That marvelous jacket will soon be known from one great water to the other. But Sam Hawkens went too far with his prophecy."

"To far? What do you mean?" Sam inquired.

"It would have been enough to say that Old Shatterhand brings us no danger. Why has Sam Hawkens added that we will face terrible times?"

"Because I saw it in the hole."

Inchu-chuna made a dismissive gesture and explained:

"The chief of the Apaches understands what is going on here. Let Sam Hawkens believe it. It was not necessary to speak of terrible things and to fill our people with worry."

"With worry? But the warriors of the Apaches are brave men who will not be fearful."

"They are not afraid. They will prove it if our trip, which ought to be peaceful, brings us together with enemies. Let us begin it now."

Our horses were brought to us. A considerable number of pack horses were to be taken along, a few carrying the surveying instruments and the rest carrying food and other necessities.

It was customary among the Indians for those being left behind to accompany the departing warriors for a while. But Inchu-chuna did not want that to be done in this case, and so it was not. If the thirty Indians that rode with us said goodbye to their wives and children, we did not observe it. Their warrior's dignity did not permit them to do so in public.

There was one person who did say a few words of farewell, and that was Sam Hawkens. He saw Kliuna-ai among the women, turned his mule toward her, and asked:

"Did Kliuna-ai hear what I saw in the hole in the earth?"

"You have said it, and I heard your words," she answered.

"I could have said much more, including something about you."

"About me? Was I in the hole also?"

"Yes. I saw your whole future before me. Shall I tell you?"

"Yes, do it!" she pleaded eagerly. "What will the future bring me?"

"It will not bring you something, but rather take something from you, something that is very precious to you."

"What is that?" she inquired anxiously.

"Your hair. You will lose it a few moons from now and you will get an awful bald head, just like the moon, which also has no hair. Then, I will send you my wig. Farewell, you sad moonbeam!"

He rode off laughing, and she turned away, much ashamed that she had let Sam lead her along because of her curiosity.

Chapter 34

The order we rode in evolved naturally. Inchu-chuna, Winnetou, his sister, and I were at the head. Next came Hawkens, Parker, and Stone, followed by the thirty Apaches, who took turns leading the pack animals.

Nsho-chi sat astride her horse, like a man. As I already knew, and as she was to show in the course of our journey, she was an excellent and tireless rider. She was equally expert with her weapons. Anyone encountering us who didn't know her would have taken her for Winnetou's younger brother at first, but a closer look would not have missed the womanly softness of face and figure. She was beautiful, truly beautiful, in spite of her man's clothing and her man's way of riding.

The first days of our trip went by without any incident worth mentioning. The previous trip from the location of the battle with the Kiowas to the pueblo on the Rio Pecos had taken the Apaches five days, but that had been slowed by the need to transport the prisoners and the wounded. It took us only three days to get back to the spot where Rattler had killed Kleki-petra. We camped there for the night. The Apaches gathered stones for a simple memorial. Here, Winnetou's mood was even more serious than usual. I told him, his father, and his sister everything that Kleki-petra had told me about his earlier life.

On the next morning, we continued until we reached the area where our surveying had been so suddenly interrupted by the attack. The stakes were still in place, and I could have resumed the work immediately. But I didn't: there was something more important to attend to first.

It had not occurred to the Apaches to bury the dead whites and Kiowas after the fight. They just left the bodies as they lay. What they neglected, the vultures and other scavangers took care of—admittedly in a different way. The bones lay scattered, some gnawed clean, some with rotting flesh still attached. It was a dreadful task for Sam, Dick, Will, and me to gather these remains and bury them in a common grave. The Apaches did not participate, of course.

Thus was spent the rest of the day, and I didn't get to start my work until the following morning. Apart from the warriors, who assisted me, it was Winnetou who was particularly helpful, and his sister rarely left my side.

The process was quite different from before, when I had to deal with so many disagreeable people. The Indians that weren't helping me wandered the surrounding area and often encountered game, which they hunted down and brought back in the evening.

It is easy to understand why we were able to make rapid progress. In spite of the difficulty of the terrain, I reached the boundary of the next section after only three days, and I needed only one additional day to complete the drawings and notes. Then I was finished—and a good thing, too. Winter was approaching fast, and the nights were already noticeably colder, so that we kept the fire burning throughout the night.

Though I have said that the Apaches helped me, I can't say they did so willingly. They obeyed the commands of their chiefs. Without this, they wouldn't have provided much help. You could see that each man that I called upon was happy once his assistance wasn't needed any more. And in the evening when we sat together, the thirty warriors always camped at a greater distance from us than was necessary or required as a sign of respect for their chiefs. The two chiefs certainly noticed this, but never mentioned it. Sam noticed it too, and said to me:

"Not too keen on working hard, these Indians. It's true and always will be: the red man is a marvelous hunter and brave warrior, but lazy in other respects. He has no taste for labor."

"What they're doing for me is not strenuous at all. You couldn't call it labor. There's a different explanation for their reluctance."

"So? What do you think the reason is?"

"They're thinking about the prophecy of their medicine man, and I'm afraid they believe it more than they believe yours, Sam."

"Could be. But they're dumb if they do."

"And what's more, my work is anathema to them. The local area belongs to them, and I'm surveying it for other people, for their enemies. They must be thinking about that too, Sam."

"But it's what their chiefs want!"

"True enough. But that doesn't mean they agree with it. They silently oppose it. And when I watch them, the way they sit together and speak quietly with each other, I can see in their faces that they're talking about me. And it isn't anything that I'd be happy about if I happened to hear it."

"That's about how I see it too. But it's no skin off our nose. Let them think what they like—it doesn't hurt us. We're just dealing with Inchu-chuna, Winnetou, and Nsho-chi, and we can't complain about them."

He was right. Winnetou and his father were always helpful and had a truly brotherly courteousness, and Nchu-chi even anticipated my every wish. It was as if she could read my thoughts. She always did what I had in mind without waiting to hear me say it, and this extended even to trivial things that no other person would have noticed. With each passing day, I was more grateful to her. She was a keen observer and an attentive listener, and I noticed with satisfaction that I was becoming her teacher, from whom she eagerly learned. When I spoke, she hung on my words, and when I did something, she did the same thing later, even when it contradicted the customs of her tribe. She seemed to be there for me alone, and she was much more concerned for my comfort and well-being than I myself was—I had never wanted preferential treatment.

Anyway, by the end of the fourth day, I was done. I packed up the surveying instruments in their protective blankets. We got everything ready for an early start, and broke camp first thing on the fifth morning. The two chiefs had selected exactly the same route that Sam had chosen in bringing us to this area initially.

Two days into the trip, we encountered riders. We were traveling through a flat, grassy region, dotted with clumps of bushes here and there. It provided a good view of our surroundings, which is always an advantage in the West. You never know what kind of people you may meet, so it's good to be able to see from a distance who is approaching you. We saw four riders approaching. They were whites. They observed us just as we did them, and they stopped, uncertain whether to continue towards us or to avoid us. Encountering thirty Indians can be pretty uncomfortable for just four whites, especially if they don't know what tribe they belong to. But they saw that there were whites with the Indians, and that seemed to reassure them. They continued to ride straight ahead.

They were dressed as cowboys and armed with rifles, knives, and revolvers. When they were within twenty paces of us, they brought their horses to a halt and held their rifles at the ready. One of them called out to us:

"Good day, Sirs! Do we need to keep a finger on the trigger?"

"Good day, Gents," answered Sam. "Have no qualms about putting away your shooting irons! We're not going to eat you. May I ask where you're coming from?"

"From across the old Mississippi."

"And where are you heading?"

"Up into New Mexico and from there over to California. We hear they need cow-hands there, and they pay better than where we come from."

"You could be right, Sir, but you've got a heck of a trip ahead of you before you get one of those fancy jobs. We're coming down from the mountains, heading for St. Louis. Is the trail clear?"

"Yes. At least we haven't heard anything to the contrary. But you don't need to worry. There's enough of you to take care of anything that might happen. Or are the red gentlemen not going the whole way?"

"Only the two warriors here, Inchu-chuna and Winnetou, the chiefs of the Apaches, with their daughter and sister."

"What's that you say? A red lady who wants to go to St. Louis? Do you mind if I ask your names?"

"Why not! They're honest names, we don't need to keep them secret. I'm called Sam Hawkens, if I'm not mistaken. These two are Dick Stone and Will Parker, and here next to me is Old Shatterhand, a kid who can kill a grizzly with just a knife and knock the strongest man to the ground with a blow from his fist. And will you do me the favor of mentioning your names?"

"Certainly. I've heard of Sam Hawkens, but not the other gentlemen. My name is Santer and I'm not a famous frontiersman like you, but just a poor, simple cowboy."

He named his three traveling companions, but I didn't catch the names. He asked a few more questions about the trail ahead, and then they rode on. Once they had left, Winnetou asked Sam:

"Why did my brother give these people such detailed information?"

"Should I have refused?"

"Yes."

"I don't see why. They asked politely enough, so I had to answer politely. That's what Sam Hawkens always does."

"I don't trust the politeness of the paleface. They were polite because we had many more people than they did. I am not pleased that you told them who we are."

"Why? Do you figure it can do us harm?"

"Yes."

"In what way?"

"In many ways. I didn't like these palefaces. The eyes of the one that spoke with you were not good eyes."

"Well, I didn't notice that. But even if it is true, they won't do anything to us. They're gone. They're headed that way, we're headed the opposite way. It won't occur to them to come back and bother us."

"Still, I want to know what they are doing. Let my brothers continue riding slowly ahead. Old Shatterhand and I will turn around and follow these palefaces for a while. I need to know whether they really continued to ride west, or whether they only pretended to do this."

While the others started off again, he rode with me back along our tracks, which the four strangers had followed as well. I have to say that I hadn't liked the looks of this Santer either, and his three companions looked no more trustworthy than he. But I couldn't see how or why they might harm us. Even if they were the sort of men who like to take the possessions of others for their own, I couldn't fathom what could possibly lead them to assume that they could get anything valuable from us. And even if this was their intent, it seemed highly unlikely that they would risk taking on 37 well-armed people with just four men. But when I asked Winnetou a question concerning these thoughts, he explained:

"If they are thieves, they will not care if we outnumber them. They won't plan to attack us openly. They are more likely to follow us secretly to discover the moment when the one they have their eye on separates from the group."

"Who could they have their eye on? They don't even know us."

"The one they think might have gold."

"Gold? How could they know if we have any, and which of so many people is carrying it? They'd have to be all-knowing."

"Oh, no. They only have to think a little in order to be almost sure of it. Sam Hawkens spoke carelessly in telling them that we are two chiefs on our way to St. Louis. They don't need to know more than that."

"Ah, now I see what my brother means. When Indians travel to the East, they need gold. Since they have no coins, they bring the raw gold that they know how to find in the mountains. And if they are chiefs, they are certain to know where to find it and to bring a lot of it along."

"My brother Old Shatterhand has guessed it. It is we two chiefs that the whites will be watching, if they plan to rob us. Even so, they wouldn't find us carrying any."

"No? But you were planning to take some gold along!"

"We'll get it tomorrow. Why carry it before we need it? Up to now, we haven't had to pay for anything. That won't start until we reach the first of the forts that lie along our path. That's why we waited until now to get some gold, and we will probably get it tomorrow."

"So there is a source of gold near our route?"

"Yes. There is a mountain that we call Nugget-tsil. Other people, who don't know that gold is there, give it other names. Tonight we will be near it, and we will go and get what we need."

I confess that I was overcome with admiration that was mixed with a little envy. These people knew where quantities of the valuable metal lay, and instead of using it, they led a life that knew almost none of the pretensions of civilized people! They had no stock exchanges and no money bags, but everywhere they went they had hidden treasure troves into which they only had to reach in order to fill their pockets with gold. Who would not covet at least this ability (if not their pretension-free life)?

We had to be careful so that Santer wouldn't know he was being followed. We used every rise, every bush to hide our presence. After a good quarter of an hour, we finally caught sight of the four men. They trotted on cheerfully and without pause. They seemed to be in a hurry to move on, and to have no thought of turning around. We stopped. Winnetou watched them until they disappeared, and then said:

"They have no evil intentions. We can relax."

Like me, he had no idea how wrong he was. They certainly did have bad intentions, but they were an extraordinarily sly bunch, as I was later to find out for myself.

They had assumed we would observe them for a while, and they made a pretense of being in a hurry. But later, they turned back and followed us.

We turned our horses, and by galloping we easily caught up with our companions. In the evening, we camped by a stream. The two chiefs, accustomed to being cautious, examined the surrounding area carefully before they gave the word to set up camp. The stream originated in a spring that bubbled up from the earth, clear and strong. There was plenty of grass for the horses, and since the place was surrounded by trees and bushes, we were able to make a substantial fire without it being visible from a distance. Inchu-chuna gave two men guard duty, and it seemed that everything necessary had been done to assure our security.

The thirty Apaches camped, as usual, farther from us than necessary, eating their shares of dried meat while the fire blazed. We seven sat at the edge of the bushes by our fire. We had picked the location because the bushes provided protection from the cool wind that blew that night.

After supper, as was our custom, we talked among ourselves for a while. In the course of the conversation, Inchu-chuna said that on the following day we would break camp later than usual—not until noon, in fact—and when Sam Hawkens asked him the reason for the delay, he explained with a directness that I sorely regretted later on:

"It is really supposed to be a secret, but I can trust my white brothers with it if they promise not to try to follow me."

When we had given our word, he continued:

"We need gold, so I will leave early tomorrow morning with my children to fetch nuggets. We won't be back until the middle of the day."

Stone and Parker cried out their astonishment, and Hawkens, no less surprised, enquired:

"So there's gold in this area?"

"Yes," answered Inchu-chuna. "No one has any idea about it. Even my warriors don't know it. I learned about it from my father, and he learned about it from his. Such secrets are passed on only from father to son and are kept as a sacred trust. No one would even tell his best friend. It is true that I am speaking of it now, but I would never mention or show the location, and I would shoot anyone who tried to follow us to learn where it is."

"Would you even kill us?"

"Even you! I have spoken to you in trust. If you betray my trust, you have earned death. But I know you won't leave this camp until we have returned from our errand."

He said this in a warning tone of voice, and then fell silent. The conversation moved on to other topics, until Sam Hawkens interrupted it a while later. Inchu-chuna, Nsho-chi, and I sat with our backs to the bushes; Sam, Dick, and Will occupied places on the other side of the fire, so they were facing the bushes. In the middle of the conversation, Hawkens cried out, raised his rifle, and sent a bullet into the bushes. Naturally, the shot sent the whole camp into a state of alarm. The Indians sprang up and ran over. We also jumped up and asked Sam why he had shot.

"I saw two eyes watching Inchu-chuna from the bushes," he explained.

The Indians immediately grabbed burning branches from the fire and charged into the bushes. Their search was futile. We gradually calmed down and resumed our seats again.

"Sam Hawkens must have been mistaken," said Inchu-chuna. "A flickering fire makes such mistakes very easy."

"That would surprise me. I believe I saw the two eyes quite clearly."

"The wind must have turned over two leaves. My white brother saw their lower side, which is lighter, and thought it was two eyes."

"Well, it could be. I probably killed a couple of leaves, hee-hee-hee!"

He laughed to himself in his typical fashion. Winnetou, however, did not find the matter amusing. He said, in a serious voice:

"In any case, my brother Sam has made an error which he must always avoid in the future!"

"An error? Me? What do you mean?"

"It was wrong to shoot."

"Wrong? That's crazy! If there's a spy hiding in a bush, I have the right to put a bullet through him, if I'm not mistaken."

"Do you know if the spy has bad intentions? He discovers us and sneaks up on us to see who we are. Maybe he comes out to greet us."

"Hmm. That's true enough," Sam admitted.

"The shot was dangerous for us," Winnetou continued. "Either Sam was mistaken and saw no eyes—then the shot was unnecessary and could only bring enemies to us if they happened to be nearby. Or there really was a man there, whose eyes Sam saw. In that case it was also wrong to shoot, since it could be assumed that the bullet would miss."

"Oh ho! Sam Hawkens doesn't miss! I'd like to meet the man that claims to have seen me miss!"

"I also know how to shoot, but I would probably miss. The spy can see that I am aiming at him. He knows that he has been seen and he will make a quick movement to avoid the mouth of my rifle. The bullet misses and the man disappears in the night."

"Yes, yes. But what would my red brother have done in my place?"

"I would either use a knee shot or else I would leave quietly, circle around, and try to come up behind the spy."

The knee shot is the most difficult shot there is. Many, many frontiersmen that are good shots otherwise cannot manage it. I had not known anything about it, but Winnetou had made me aware of it and I had been practicing it in recent days.

Suppose I am sitting by a campfire (alone or with others—it doesn't matter). My rifle is lying, as usual, where is it easily grasped by my right hand. Then I happen to notice two eyes observing me from a hiding place. I can't see the spy's face, which is in the darkness, but I can see the eyes unless he is careful to look only through his lowered eyelashes. Eyes have a soft, phosphorescent look that becomes more evident the harder the person stares. You must not think that it is easy to distinguish a pair of eyes from millions of leaves at night. You can't learn to do it. You have to be born with the necessary sharpness and sureness of vision.

If I am convinced that I am dealing with an enemy spy, the only way I can save myself is to render him harmless—to kill him—and I can only do that with a bullet between his eyes. That must be my target, since it is the only part of him that I can see. But if I raise the rifle to the normal shooting position, against my cheek, he will see that I am aiming at him and he will instantly disappear. So I must take my aim without him noticing. This is done with the knee shot. I bend my right leg so that the knee is raised and my thigh makes a line that, if extended, would end between the eyes I am observing. Then I reach absent-mindedly for my rifle, as if I am playing with it, lay the barrel on my thigh so it is aimed in precisely the same direction, and fire. It is hard, very hard, especially since it must be done with the right hand only. The necessary appearance of harmlessness would be lost if you used both hands. With one hand, you must aim the rifle, hold it tight against your leg, and then fire. Hundreds have tried to do this and could not. And that doesn't take into consideration how difficult it is to take good aim, in that position and without your eye to the sights. On top of that, the target consists of two barely visible points in the middle of a mass of leaves and foliage, illuminated by a flickering fire and perhaps moving in the wind! This is what Winnetou meant when he spoke about a knee shot, and he was a master of it. It was not an easy type of shot for me, since my bear-killer was so heavy and could barely be managed with just one hand. But with continued practice, I gradually achieved the desired level of success.

While the others were satisfied and reassured by the inconclusive search of the area, Winnetou was not. After a while, he stood up and left, in order to carry out and extend the search. More than an hour went by before he returned.

"No one is there," he said; "Sam Hawkens must have been mistaken."

Nevertheless, he posted four guards instead of the previous two, and instructed them to be as alert as possible and to make regular patrols around the camp. Then we lay down to sleep.

Chapter 35

My sleep was fitful. I awoke often, and when I did sleep, I had short, disquieting dreams in which Santer and his three companions played the leading roles. This was easily explained as the simple result of our encounter with him, but it gave him, when I got up the next morning, a significance that I tried in vain to talk myself out of. It has been my experience that when I dream about someone, they take on greater importance in my mind than they had previously.

After breakfast, which consisted of meat and a mixture of flour and water, Inchu-chuna prepared to depart with his son and daughter. Before they left, I asked for permission to accompany them, at least for a short distance. To reassure them that I wasn't doing this in order to find out where the gold was, I told them that I couldn't get Santer out of my mind. I was surprised myself, for early that morning I had harbored, without a shred of solid evidence, the conviction that he and his people had returned. This was probably a result of my dream.

"My brother does not need to worry about us," answered Winnetou. "To reassure him, I will look once more for tracks. We know our brother does not strive for gold, but if he came even a short way with us, he would surely get the fever for the deadly dust. The fever does not leave a paleface until it has it worked its way into his heart and soul. So it is not mistrust, but love and caution, that causes me to ask you not to come with us."

I had to be satisfied with that. He searched once more, without finding any tracks, and then they left. Since they went on foot, I concluded that the place they wanted to visit could not be very far away.

I lay down in the grass, lit my pipe, and talked with Sam, Dick, and Will—all in order to get rid of my groundless fears. But I got no rest, and soon I stood up again. Something inside me drove me on. So I threw my gun over my shoulder and left. Perhaps I would find some game to hunt, and that would distract me.

When I had been gone perhaps a quarter of a hour, to my astonishment I came upon some tracks made by three people. They had worn moccasins. I could distinguish two large, two middle-sized, and two small feet. The tracks were fresh. These must have been made by Inchu-chuna, Winnetou, and Nsho-chi. They had started out to the south, but had then turned north—to deceive us, of course. We were supposed to think the gold was to be found to the south.

Should I continue on? No. They might see me, and they would almost certainly see my footprints on their return. I didn't want them to get the idea that I had secretly followed them. But I also didn't want to return to camp, so I wandered off to the east.

I soon had to stop again, for I came upon a second set of tracks. I inspected them and saw that they had been made by four men wearing boots with spurs. I immediately thought of Santer. The tracks went in the direction where the two chiefs had gone, and they seemed to come from a thicket not far away, from which rose a few oaks whose leaves had not yet fallen. I now turned my attention there.

I was right: the tracks did come from this thicket, and as I penetrated it, I found tethered the four horses that Santer and his people had ridden. It was clear from the marks on the ground that the four had spent the night here. So they had doubled back after all! Why? Certainly because of us. Surely they had come up with exactly the idea that Winnetou had explained to me the day before. Sam Hawkens hadn't been mistaken the previous night. He really had seen those two eyes, but through his behavior had driven the spy away even before he fired a shot. So we had been observed. Santer had watched us, waiting for the moment when he could catch the person he had his eye on alone. But this spot was so far from our camp. How could he watch us from here?

I looked at the trees. They were very tall, but not terribly thick. They would be easy to climb. The bark of one of them had been torn, and that could only be the work of spurs. So they had climbed up, and even if they couldn't see the camp itself, they would certainly have seen anyone who left it. Heavens, what thoughts now swarmed in my head! What had we been talking about around the fire, before Sam noticed the eyes? About Inchu-chuna's plan to go and fetch gold with his children the next day! The spy would have heard that. He would have climbed the oak early this morning and from there he would have seen the three people he expected going by. Then he must have followed after them with his three partners in crime. Winnetou in danger! Nsho-chi and her father as well! I had to take off after the bandits, as quickly as possible. I couldn't take the time to go back to camp first, to raise the alarm. I quickly untied one of the four horses, led it out into the open, mounted, and galloped off along the trail of the scoundrels, which soon joined that of the chiefs.

Along the way, I looked for landmarks so that I could tell where to look for the source of the gold in case I lost the trail. Winnetou had spoken of a mountain that he called Nugget-tsil. Nuggets are bits of gold, which are found in various sizes; "tsil" is an Apache word that means "mountain." Nugget-tsil means Nugget Mountain. So I was looking for a mountain. North of me, in the direction I was travelling, were several substantial peaks covered with forest. One of them must be Nugget Mountain, that much was clear in an instant.

The old nag on which I sat was not fast enough for me. I tore a switch from a bush as I went by, and drove him on with it. He did as much as his strength permitted. The plain disappeared behind me and the mountains opened ahead. The tracks led between two of them, and soon I began to lose them, for here the rains had brought great boulders down from the heights. Still, I didn't dismount, because it was clear that the people I was following must have continued up the valley.

A bit later, though, a side canyon opened up on the right. Its floor was just as stoney. Now I had to determine whether they had turned right or continued straight ahead. I jumped from the saddle and examined the gravel. It wasn't easy to find the tracks, but I did find them. They went into the side canyon. I mounted again and followed them. But the canyon soon divided again and I dismounted once more. I anticipated that this would happen again, and the horse was becoming a hindrance to me. I tied it to a tree and, after checking to see where the tracks led, hurried ahead on foot.

I hurried into the narrow ravine, bordered with cliffs, in which no water was flowing at present. Fear drove me on a such a rapid pace that I gradually ran out of breath. As I came to the crest of a sharp-edged ridge, I had to stop for a moment to get my breathing under control. Then I was off again, down the other side, until suddenly the tracks turned left into the woods. More running than walking, I made my way through the woods. The trees stood close together at first, then farther apart, until I sensed from the light ahead that I was approaching a clearing. I had not quite reached it when I heard several shots ring out. An instant later, a cry went up that went through my body like a sword. It was the Apache death cry.

Now I was not just running, I was tearing down the path in huge strides, like a beast of prey chasing down its victim. Another shot, and then another—those were the two barrels of Winnetou's rifle, I could recognize the sound. Thank God! At least he was still alive. In a few more strides, I reached the clearing, then came to an abrupt halt under the last tree. What I saw stopped me in my tracks.

The clearing was not large. Almost in the middle lay Inchu-chuna and his daughter. Whether they were still alive, still moving, I couldn't immediately tell. Not far away was a small outcropping behind which Winnetou was crouched. He was occupied with the reloading of his rifle. To my left were two men standing behind trees, rifles raised and ready to shoot as soon as Winnetou showed any weakness. To my right, a third was creeping cautiously through the trees, trying to circle around and get in back of Winnetou. The fourth lay dead directly in front of me, shot through the head.

The pair at the left presented the most immediate threat to the young chief. I raised the bear-killer and shot them both down, then sprang toward the third without taking time to reload. He had heard my shots and turned around. He saw me coming, aimed his rifle at me, and fired. I jumped to the side and his shot missed. He gave up the fight and fled into the woods. I ran after him. It was Santer, and I wanted to catch him. But he had such a headstart on me that, while I could see him at the edge of the clearing, I quickly lost sight of him in the woods. So I had to follow his tracks, which meant I couldn't go as fast as I would have liked. It wasn't possible to catch up with him, so I soon turned back, thinking that Winnetou might need me.

When I reached the clearing again, he was kneeling by his father and his sister, anxiously looking for signs of life. As he saw me arrive, he stood up for a moment. I will never forget the look in his eyes. It spoke of an almost insane fury and pain.

"My brother Old Shatterhand can see what has happened. Nsho-chi, the most beautiful and best daughter of the Apache will never see the cities of the palefaces. There is still a little life in her, but she will never open her eyes again."

I wasn't capable of saying a word. There was nothing I could say and nothing I wanted to ask. What was there to ask about? The situation was painfully clear! They lay next to each other in a deep pool of blood. Inchu-chuna had been shot through the head, and Nsho-chi through the chest. He had died instantly, but she was still breathing, heavily and roughly, and her bronze face was getting paler and paler. Her full cheeks were sunken in and the expression of death was spreading over the features that I held so dear.

Then she stirred a little. She turned her head to the side where her father lay, and slowly opened her eyes. She saw Inchu-chuna lying in blood and was utterly stunned, except that she was so weak that her horror did not find the animated expression that it otherwise would have. She seemed puzzled for a moment, then she understood what had happened and raised her small hand to her chest. She felt the warm blood running out and gave a deep, gasping sigh.

"Nsho-chi, my dear, my only sister!" wailed Winnetou, and the expression in his breaking voice could never be described in words.

She turned her head to him.

"Winnetou, my brother!" she whispered. "Vengance! Avenge me!"

Then her eyes traveled over to me, and a happy smile flickered across her pale lips and then disappeared. "Old Shatterhand!" she breathed. "You are here! Now I can die. . ."

We heard no more, for death intervened and sealed her lips forever. I felt as if my heart would shatter. I needed air. I jumped up (we had been kneeling by her) and gave a loud, loud cry that echoed from the mountains all around.

Winnetou also stood up, slowly, as if he were weighed down by a huge burden. He threw his arms around me and said:

"Now they are dead! The greatest, noblest chief of the Apaches and Nsho-chi, my sister, who gave her soul to you. She died with your name on her lips. Never forget it. Never forget it, my brother!"

"I will never, never forget it!" I cried.

Then his expression changed, and his voice became threatening, like a far-off roll of thunder, as he asked:

"Did you hear what her last request was?"

"Yes."

"Revenge! I must avenge her death, and I will avenge her death as no death has ever been avenged before. Do you know who the killers were? You saw them. They were palefaces, to whom we had done nothing. That is the way it has always been, and that is the way it will be forever, until the last red man has been killed. And even if he should die a natural death, it is murder, a murder of my people. We wanted to visit the cities of these crazy palefaces. Nsho-chi wanted to be like a white squaw. She loved you and she thought she could win your heart by adopting the knowledge and customs of the whites. She paid for that with her life. It doesn't matter if we hate you or if we love you, wherever a paleface sets foot, for us ruin will follow. A lament will go through all the tribes of the Apaches, and a cry of fury and revenge will rise everywhere, in every place where the warriors of our Nation are found. Now the eyes of all Apaches will be on Winnetou, to see how he will avenge the death of his father and sister. Let my brother Old Shatterhand hear what I vow here, by these two dead bodies. I swear by the Great Spirit and by all my brave forefathers who are assembled in the great hunting ground, that from now on every white man, every single white man that I encounter, I will shoot with the gun that fell from my father's hand, or. . ."

"Stop!" I interrupted, shivering, for I knew that he would fulfill his oath inexorably and without mercy. "Stop! Let my brother Winnetou not swear an oath right now!"

"Why not now?" he asked, almost angrily.

"An oath must be spoken when the soul is calm."

"Ugh! Right now my soul is as calm as the grave in which I will bury my dead. Just as the grave will never give them back, so I will never take back a word of that which I. . ."

"Say no more!" I interrupted again.

There was almost a threat in his eyes as he glared at me, and he cried out:

"Will Old Shatterhand hinder me from doing my duty? Shall the old women spit at me? Shall I be cast out from my people because I don't have the courage to avenge what has happened here today?"

"Far be it from me to demand that of you. I too want the murderers punished. Three have already met a quick punishment. The fourth has fled, but he will not escape us."

"How could he escape!" he exclaimed. "But this is not only about him. He acted as the son of that white race that brings us destruction, the race that is responsible for all the lessons he learned from it. I will make that race pay, I, Winnetou, who am now the head and highest chief of all the tribes of the Apache!"

He stood proud and erect before me, a man who, despite his youth, felt himself king of all his people! Yes, he was a man who would see that his will was carried out. He, and he alone, would be capable of assembling the warriors of all the red nations under him and leading them into war against the whites. A desperate battle it would be, but still there could be no doubt about its end, though it might mean hundreds of thousands of victims all across the Wild West. This was the moment in which it would be decided whether or not the tomahawk of death would wreak havoc in this bitter way.

I took his hand and said:

"You should do, and you will do, whatever you want to do. But first, listen to my request. It may perhaps be the last one I make, and then you will hear the voice of your white friend and brother no more. Here lies Nsho-chi. You yourself say that she loved me and died with my name on her lips. She loved you, too—me as a friend, you as a brother—and you returned her love richly. So by these loves of ours, I ask you: wait to make your oath until the last stone has been laid on the grave of the noblest daughter of the Apaches. Do not make it now!"

He gave me a serious, dark look, and then lowered his gaze to the two dead bodies. His features became a little milder, and finally he turned back to me and said:

"My brother Old Shatterhand has a great influence on the hearts of all those he deals with. Nsho-chi would certainly have granted his wish, and so I will also. Only when these two bodies are buried and out of my sight shall it be decided if the Mississippi and all the rivers that feed it will carry the blood of the red and the white man to the sea. I have spoken. How!"

Thank God! I had succeeded, at least for a while, in averting a great disaster. I pressed his hand in thanks and spoke:

"My red brother will quickly see that I do not seek mercy for the guilty man. Let his punishment be as harsh and strong as he deserves. We have to make sure he doesn't have time to get away. We can't give him a head start. Let Winnetou say what we should do about him now."

"I cannot leave this place. Because I am so closely related to the dead, the customs of my people require me to stay with them until they are buried. Only then can I tread the path of revenge."

"And when will the burial take place?"

"I will discuss that with my warriors. Either we will bury them here, where they died, or we will take them back to the pueblo of their families. But even if they find their resting place here, many days will pass before the requirements have been sufficiently satisfied for the funeral of such a great chief."

"But then the murderer will get away for sure!"

"No. For although Winnetou cannot follow him, others can do what is necessary. Let my brother now tell me briefly how it happened that he came here."

Now that he was speaking of practical matters, he was as calm as ever. I told him what he wanted to know, and then there was a brief, thoughtful silence. Just then I heard a heavy sigh coming from one of the two rascals who I thought I had killed. Quickly, we went over to him. One of the men had been hit right in the heart. The other, though, had been hit in the chest like Nsho-chi. He was still alive and had just come to. He stared at us blankly and murmured words that I couldn't understand. I leaned down to him and shouted:

"Wake up, man! Do you know who we are?"

He was obviously struggling for consciousness. His eyes also cleared a bit, and I heard him whisper:

"Where is Santer?"

"Ran off," I answered, since I wasn't going to try to lie to a dying man, even if he was a murderer.

"Where to?"

"I don't know, but I hope to get a hint from you. Your other comrades are dead, and you have only seconds to live as well. You'll behave better on the brink of the grave than previously! Where does Santer come from?"

"Don't know."

"Is Santer really his name?"

"He's got many, many names."

"What is he really?"

"Don't know that either."

"Does he know anyone around here, maybe at one of the forts?"

"No."

"Where were you headed?"

"No place. Wherever there was gold."

"So you were professional thieves! Terrible! Where did you get the idea of ambushing the Apaches?"

"Nug . . . nuggets."

"But you couldn't have known about the nuggets."

"Wanted to go to. . ."

He stopped. It was extraordinarily difficult for him to answer. I guessed at what he wanted to say.

"You heard that these Apaches wanted to go East, and you figured that meant that they would be taking gold with them?"

He nodded.

"So you figured you'd ambush them, but you knew we'd be careful and observe you, so you rode a fair distance farther and you only turned back when you thought we were most likely reassured about your direction?"

He nodded again.

"And then you turned around and followed us. Did you spy on us at night?"

"Yes, Santer did."

"So it was Santer himself! Did he tell you what he heard?"

"Apaches. . . Nugget-tsil. . . Fetch nuggets in the morning."

"Just as I thought. Then you hid in the bushes and watched us from the trees. You wanted to discover the spot where the Apaches get their gold?"

He had closed his eyes and did not answer.

"Or were you just planning to ambush them on their return, so you could . . ."

Winnetou interrupted me:

"Let my brother ask no more questions. This paleface cannot answer any more; he is dead. These white dogs wanted to learn our secret, but they came too late. We were already on our way back when they heard us coming. They hid behind trees and shot at us. Inchu-chuna and Nsho-chi were shot down, but only my arm was grazed here. Then I shot at one, but he jumped behind a tree just as I fired, so I missed him. But my second bullet cut another one down. Then I hid behind this stone, but it wouldn't have saved my life if my brother Old Shatterhand had not come. Two of them kept me trapped on this side, and the other was circling around behind me, where I had no protection. His bullet would surely have gotten me. But then I heard the powerful voice of Old Shatterhand's bear-killer and I was saved. Now my white brother knows everthing, and he will learn how we must begin the task of catching Santer."

"Who will do this task?"

"Old Shatterhand will do it. He will certainly be able to follow Santer's tracks."

"Certainly. But much time will be lost while I search carefully for them."

"No. My brother does not need to search for them, for they will certainly lead to his horse, which he must now be going to find. There, where he spent the night with his people, there is grass, and so Old Shatterhand will easily see what direction he has taken."

"And then?"

"Then my brother will take ten warriors, to follow him and catch him. The other twenty warriors he will send to me here, to join me in singing the lament for the dead."

"So it will be. And I hope that I will justify the faith that my red brother is putting in me."

"I know that Old Shatterhand will do exactly what I would do in his place. How!"

He extended his hand to me, and I shook it. I bent once more over the faces of the two dead Indians, and then I left. At the edge of the clearing, I turned and looked back. Winnetou was just covering their faces and had begun the dull lamentation with which the Indians begin their funeral chant. How sad I felt, oh how sad! But I had been given a task, so I hurried back down the same trail by which I had come.

Chapter 36

I was inclined to agree that Winnetou's prediction about Santer's movements would prove true. But as I crossed over the ridge I mentioned earlier, another thought occurred to me.

Santer's top priority was to get as far as possible from us, as quickly as he could. But he would be doing the opposite of that if he went back down to his camp. He would only do that if he had to get a horse. But what if he found the one that I had ridden up on? He had fled down this same path, so he would have to have seen the horse.

This thought made me double my speed. I ran down the trail, anxious to find out if my horse was still there. But, reaching the spot, I was dismayed to see that it was gone! I paused only a moment, then flew more than ran down the canyon. Here, at least, I could hurry—the stony ground meant that time spent looking for tracks would have been futile. As I reached the main valley, I stopped to look carefully at the tracks. I wasn't immediately successful—the ground was very hard. But in ten minutes I was back on softer ground, which made it easier to recognize footprints and hoofprints.

But I was completely disappointed. I could peer and poke all I wanted, exercise my eyes and my skills to the fullest—it changed nothing. Santer had not passed by here. Farther up, where there were no tracks visible, he must have found a spot where he was able to leave the canyon. There was no other possibility.

So there I was. What should I do next? Should I go back and try to find Santer's escape route? That could take hours, and I couldn't afford that loss of time. It was better to hurry back down to our camp and get help.

That is what I did. It was a marathon run the like of which I had never done, but I survived it because I had been taught by Winnetou how to run so as not to run out of breath or to tire. The trick is to carry most of your body weight on just one leg and then, when it tires, to shift to the other. In this way, you can trot for hours without overly straining yourself. But you do need a good, healthy pair of lungs.

As I approached my destination, I turned first to Santer's camp. The three horses were still there among the bushes. I turned and untied them, mounted one, took the reigns of the other two, and rode to our camp. It was long past noon, and Sam called to me:

"Where have you been, Sir! You've missed your meal and I. . ." he caught his breath in the middle of his sentence, looked over at the horses in astonishment, and continued: "I'll be jiggered! You leave on foot and come back riding! Have you turned to stealing horses?"

"Not really. These horses are spoils of battle."

"Where did you get them?"

"Not very far from here."

"Who from?"

"Take a good look at them! I recognized them right away, and you've got good eyes too."

"Yes, I do. I immediately saw whose they were, but it didn't make any sense. These horses are the ones Santer and his men were riding. One is missing."

"We'll find that other one, and its rider too!"

"But how did you. . ."

"Hold on, Sam!" I interrupted him. "Something very important and very sad has happened. We must leave immediately."

"Leave? Why?"

Instead of answering, I called the Apaches together and shared the news of the death of Inchu-chuna and his daughter. When I had finished speaking, there was a deep silence. They couldn't believe what I was saying—my message was too horrible.

Then I repeated the story, with more details, and added: "Now, let my red brothers say who predicted the future better: Sam Hawkens or the medicine man! Inchu-chuna and Nsho-chi lost their lives because they left me, and it was I who saved Winnetou's life. So does my presence bring death or life?"

Now they could doubt no longer, and a great howl arose that must have been audible for miles around. The Indians ran around in a rage, waved their weapons, and made the most awful faces in giving expression to their fury. It was some time before I could make myself heard over their cries.

"Let the warriors of the Apache be silent," I requested. "Wailing leads to nothing. We must leave, to catch the murderer."

"Leave! Yes, Leave! Leave!" they cried, running to find their horses.

"Wait! Calm down!" I requested again. "My brothers don't yet know what they are supposed to do. I will tell them."

Now they crowded around me, so much so that I had to be careful not to be knocked down. If Santer had arrived at that moment, they would have ripped him to pieces. Hawkens, Stone, and Parker stood quietly together. The news had had a shattering impression on them. Now they came over to me, and Sam said:

"I feel like I've been hit in the head, and I still can't grasp it. Terrible! Outrageous! And the beautiful, sweet young lady! Always so friendly to me, and now she's dead! You know, Sir, the way it is with me. . ."

"However it is with you, Sam, better keep it to yourself!" I interrupted. "We have to set out after that murderer. Talking doesn't help."

"Well! I have to agree. But do you know where he went?"

"Not yet."

"I thought not. You couldn't find his tracks. And now we're supposed to find them? That seems unlikely, if not downright impossible."

"It's not so hard. In fact, it's easy."

"You think so? Hmm! I would have said we'd have to go looking up into that canyon, where he headed off to the side. We'll be looking a long time up there!"

"Forget about the canyon."

"Forget it? Well then, I'm very curious what your thoughts on the subject are. I know a greenhorn can have a good idea once in a while, but. . ."

"Enough of your "greenhorn" nonsense! I'm not in the mood for that kind of talk. My heart is grieving, so keep your jokes to yourself!"

"Jokes? Not a chance! Anyone who thinks I'm kidding around will get a kick in the pants that'll send him clear to California! I just don't see how you figure on finding Santer unless we go set our eyes on the spot where you lost his trail."

"Like you said, we'd spend a long time looking. And if we did find his trail, we'd have to follow it over hill and dale, through thick woods, and that wouldn't go fast. So I think we need to start elsewhere. Take a look at the mountains up there. They aren't really connected to each other. Each one is isolated."

"That's true enough. I know this area pretty well. There's plains on this side and plains on the far side of the mountains. These mountains aren't part of a range. They sit alone in the middle of the open prairie."

"Prairie? So there's grass?"

"Yes, grass all around, just like here."

"I was counting on that. Santer can ride up the mountain or between the mountains or wherever he likes. We don't need to worry about that. But as soon as he leaves them, he'll be in the open prairie and we'll find his tracks in the grass."

"What could be more obvious, Sir?"

"Wait, I'm not finished yet. Suppose we split into two groups and ride around the mountains—we four whites to the right, the ten Apaches Winnetou allocated to me to the left. We'll meet on the far side and we'll see whether either of the groups has found Santer's trail. I'm convinced we will find it, and then we'll follow it."

Little Sam gave me a sideways glance, made a not particularly edifying face, and cried out:

"Well, bless my soul! Who would have believed it! Why didn't I think of that? That's the simplest and surest approach. Any child could see that, if I'm not mistaken!"

"So you agree, Sam?"

"Completely, Sir, completely. Better go choose those ten Indians!"

"I'll pick the ones with the best horses. Who knows how long we'll be trailing this guy. We'll also need to pack plenty of provisions. You know the area reasonably well: how long will it take us to meet up on the other side of the mountains?"

"Even if we move fast, it'll be at least two hours."

"OK then, let's get going."

I picked out ten of the Apaches. They were glad to come, because they preferred to be out tracking the murderer rather than chanting funeral songs. I gave the other twenty precise instructions about how to find Winnetou, and they rode off.

Shortly after that, my ten headed off to the left around the mountains (circling them to the west). We were to circle the east side. Once we four were mounted, I led the others over to Santer's camp and found a spot where there was a good, clear print of the hoof of the horse I had ridden. I made a precise drawing of it on a piece of paper. Sam Hawkens shook his head and said, chuckling:

"Is that one of the skills of the surveyor, drawing horses' hooves?"

"No, but a frontiersman should know how to do it."

"A frontiersman? Why?"

"Because it might come in handy from time to time."

"In what way?"

"No doubt you'll see later. If I find a horse's hoofprint, I can compare it with this one."

"Ah! Hmm. Right. That's not half bad. Did you learn it in a book?"

"No."

"Where, then?"

"The thought just came to me."

"Really? There are really thoughts out there that enjoy coming to you? I wouldn't have thought it, hee-hee-hee!"

"Pshaw! They'd rather come to me than have to try to get through that wig of yours, Sam!"

"Right you are, right you are!" cried Dick Stone. "Don't you let him give you that stuff any more! Anyone can see how you've outstripped him, Sir!"

"Shut up!" Sam scolded him in mock anger. "What do you know about stripping, let alone outstripping! It's an insult, the way he always picks on my wig. I can't stand it any longer."

"What are you going to do about it?"

"I'll give it to you. Then I'll be rid of it, and you'll find out what kinds of thoughts accumulate under it. Anyway, I already admitted that our greenhorn's plan isn't so bad. But he should have given another nice drawing of a hoofprint to the ten Apaches who are riding around the other side of the mountain."

"I could have, but I thought it wasn't necessary," I replied.

"And why not?"

"Because I don't trust them to see the resemblance between a hoofprint and a drawing. They are wild people after all, and it would be useless to give them a drawing. And on top of that, I'm convinced that they won't encounter Santer's trail."

"And I hold the opposite opinion. We won't find it, they will. It's obvious that Santer will ride westward."

"It isn't so obvious to me."

"No? He was headed west when we first met him, and that's where he'll head now."

"Hardly. He's a crafty fellow, judging by the way he vanished without a trace. He'll figure out that we would expect him to head west, just like you said. So if he thinks we're going to look westward for him, he'll head some other direction—probably east. That's pretty clear to me."

"Well, when you put it that way, it makes sense. Let's hope you're right."

We spurred on our horses and galloped across the prairie, always keeping the fateful mountains to our left. We tried as much as possible to ride on soft ground, where Santer would have left clear prints if he had come through. We were looking down as we rode. The faster we went, the more carefully we had to pay attention—otherwise, we would miss the trail.

An hour passed in this way, and then half an hour more, and we had almost completed our half of the circle around the mountains, when we finally spotted a dark line through the grass, crossing our path. It was the track of a single rider—most likely, the one we were after. We dismounted, and I walked along it a bit, looking for a clear hoof impression. When I found one, I compared it with my drawing. They matched so completely that there could be no doubt that it was Santer.

"A drawing like that is extraordinarily useful," Sam allowed. "I'll make a note of it."

"Yes, do!" Parker concurred. "And you'd do well to note one other thing, too."

"What?"

"That things have gotten to the point where the teacher, which is what you were supposed to be, is learning from his student!"

"Are you trying to get a rise out of me, Will? It won't work, hee-hee-hee!" Sam laughed. "Why, it's an honor for a teacher to teach a pupil so well that the pupil ends up smarter and more skillful than the teacher. But with you, Will—forget about it. Think how many years I tried and tried to make a frontiersman out of you, but all for naught. At least, when you get old you won't forget anything—you never learned anything in the first place."

"Oh, don't I know it! You better start calling me a greenhorn. You can't go on calling Old Shatterhand a greenhorn, and you can't seem to live without that word."

"And what a greenhorn you are, too, and an old one at that! An old greenhorn being put to shame by a young one. The young one's already far superior, if I'm not mistaken."

Inspite of this battle of words, we all agreed that Santer's tracks were not much more than two hours old. We would have been happy to follow them immediately, but we had to wait for the ten Apaches. Unfortunately, this took another three-quarters of an hour. I sent one of them back to Winnetou, to let him know that we had found Santer's trail. We rode off to the East with the remaining nine Apaches.

It was late in the fall and the days were getting shorter. It was less than two hours to sundown, so we had to hurry. We wanted to cover as much territory as possible before dark. Then, we'd have to wait for morning—we couldn't ride if we couldn't see the tracks.

Unfortunately, Santer would be able to use the evening—and the night as well—to put distance between himself and us. He would certainly expect us to be following him. The next day, we would have a hard ride ahead of us, made harder and slower by the need to pay attention to the trail. He would have no such concerns. Fortunately, if he rode through the night, he would be tired in the morning and would have to indulge in a long rest stop, if not for himself, then for his horse. That would even things out somewhat.

The mountain that Winnetou and his father called "Nugget Mountain" disappeared rapidly behind us, and there was nothing but flat prairie in front of us, initially with some bushes, but subsequently just grass. The grass, green at first, gradually became more withered. It was easy enough to follow the tracks. Santer had ridden hard, and his horse's hooves had left obvious prints.

As it began to get dark, we dismounted and followed the trail on foot. It was easier to see that way. But finally we could no longer make it out. Fortunately, we were at a spot where the grass was a bit greener, and the horses could graze. We wrapped ourselves in our blankets and lay down for the night.

The night was very cool, and I observed that my companions were often awakened by it. I couldn't have slept in any case. The violent death of Inchu-chuna and his daughter kept me awake, and when I tried to close my eyes, I saw before me their bodies lying in a pool of blood and I heard Nsho-chi's last words. I asked myself whether I should have been friendlier toward her and whether I might have said something different in that conversation with her father. I almost felt as if that had somehow driven her to this death.

Toward morning, it got colder still, and I stood up to warm myself by moving back and forth. Sam Hawkens saw me and asked:

"Are you freezing, Sir? You should have brought a hot-water bottle along to the West. Greenhorns often to do that sort of thing. But I've got my old hunting jacket. No Indian arrow can get through it, and the cold can't either. Want to borrow it, hee-hee-hee?"

Chapter 37

Because of the uncomfortable cold, we were all up and about before dawn. By the time we could barely make out the trail, we were all in the saddle and off again. Our horses had rested, and they had been equally cold. They set out at a good pace, since that made them warmer, without needing any encouragement from us.

The prairie continued, now with rolling hills. On top of the hills, the grass was dry and stiff; in the valleys it was greener and softer. Now and then, we encountered a water hole, and we would stop and let our animals drink. The trail had taken us almost straight east, but around noon it turned a bit more to the south. When Hawkens saw this, he looked thoughtful. I asked him why, and got this answer:

"If it's the way I figure, all our efforts will be in vain."

"Why is that?"

"This fellow is clever. It looks like he's heading for the Kiowas."

"He wouldn't do that!"

"Why not? Should he do you a favor and stop in the middle of the prairie and let himself be grabbed by the hair? What do you think? He'll do what he can to save himself. He had his eyes open, so he know our horses are better than the one he has. So he must have figured that we'd catch up with him soon, and he hit on the idea of getting protection from the Kiowas."

"Do you think they'll take kindly to him?"

"No doubt about it. All he has to do is tell them how he shot Inchu-chuna and Nsho-chi, and he'll be the local hero. We better keep after him, and maybe we can reach him before evening."

"How old do you think these tracks are?"

"It's not important. These were made during the night. We'll have to see what we find when we reach the place where he camped. Then we'll see how old the new tracks are, that he made today.

The longer he rested, the sooner we'll catch up with him."

Around noon, we saw the signs of Santer's camp. You could see where his horse had lain down. It must have been very tired—we had already seen that from the tracks. Apparently he was just as exhausted, for we estimated the new tracks at under two hours old. He must have slept longer than he intended. The head-start that he got by riding at night had been lost. Indeed, we were at least half an hour closer now than when we started following him the previous day.

His trail turned still more to the south. He seemed to be leaving the watershed of the Cañada River and heading for the Red River. We only let our horses stop to catch their breath occasionally, since we had resolved to catch up with him before evening if at all possible.

In the afternoon, we had green prairie once more, and later we even encountered clumps of bushes. Careful examination of the tracks indicated that his lead was down to just half an hour. Ahead of us, the horizon was dark.

"That's forest," Sam explained. "I believe we're approaching a tributary of the North fork. I wish we had the prairie a bit longer— that would be safer for us."

It certainly would have been better. On the prairie, you can see what's ahead of you, but in the woods you can easily stumble into an ambush. And at the speed we were traveling, there was no possibility of scouting out the territory ahead before we reached it.

Sam was right. There was a small stream with no running water in it, just some pools here and there in low spots. There were bushes and trees near it, but no real forest—just various-sized groups of trees at irregular intervals along the banks.

Shortly before evening, we were so close to our quarry that he might at any moment have appeared before us. That made us even more eager than we had been. I was riding alone in front, since my chestnut had held up best and still had plenty of strength. Riding at the front, I too was obeying an inner drive. I had seen the murdered Indians lying before me, and I wanted to catch their murderer. It wasn't what you would describe as fury, as thirst for revenge, but rather an urgent longing to see the murderer punished.

We were riding through another of those clumps of trees that lay on the left bank of the stream. Riding ahead of the others, I reached the last of the trees and saw that the trail turned to the right, into the dry bed of the stream. I stopped for a moment, to let the rest know what I had found, and that was fortunate for us. For while I was waiting a few moments for the others to catch up, I let my eyes wander along the river bed and made a discovery that caused me to turn back into the trees and hide myself as quickly as possible.

Only five hundred paces from my clump of trees was another clump, over on the opposite bank. Near it, Indians were milling around on their horses. I saw poles stuck in the ground and bound together with leather strips, from which meat was hanging. If I had ridden one horse's length farther, the Indians would have seen me. I dismounted and indicated to the others what was ahead.

"Kiowas!" said one of the Apaches.

"Yes, Kiowas," Sam agreed. "The devil must be very fond of this Santer fellow. He always seems to find help at the last moment. I almost had him in my grasp. He will not escape us."

"It isn't a very large group of Kiowas," I noted.

"Hmm! We can only see the ones that are on this side of the trees. There are probably more on the other side. They are hunting and they stopped here to dry their meat."

"What do we do now, Sam? Turn around and stay as far away as possible?"

"Not a chance! We'll stay here."

"But that's dangerous!"

"Not at all."

"It would be so easy for an Indian to come over here."

"It won't occur to them. They're on the other bank, and it will soon be dark. They won't go far from camp in the dark."

"But the more careful we are, the better!"

"And the more scared you are, the more you're a greenhorn! I'm telling you, we're as safe from the Kiowas here as in New York. They're not thinking about coming over here, but we'll go over there. I must have this Santer, even if I have to drag him away from a thousand Kiowas!"

"Today you're being what you always accuse me of being: reckless!"

"What do you mean, reckless? Sam Hawkens reckless? Don't make me laugh, hee-hee-hee! No one has ever accused me of that before. Sir, you've never shown fear, and you even took on a grizzly with a knife. Why this sudden uneasiness?"

"It's not uneasiness. It's caution. We're too close to the enemy."

"Too close? You're joking! I think we'll even get closer. Just wait until it's dark."

Sam wasn't himself. The death of "that beautiful, friendly, good, red Miss" had outraged him so much that he longed for revenge. The Apaches thought he was right, and Parker and Stone agreed as well, so there was nothing I could do. We tethered our horses and sat down to wait for dusk.

I must admit that the Kiowas were moving around as if they felt completely secure. They rode and walked around in the open, called out to each other—in general, they behaved without inhibition almost as if they were at home in their secure and well-guarded Indian village.

"See how they're not worried a bit!" said Sam. "They are completely unsuspecting today."

"I hope you're right."

"Sam Hawkens is always right!"

"Pshaw. It could prove otherwise. I'm beginning to get the feeling they're putting on a show."

"Feeling! Old squaws have feelings, nobody else. Mark my words, Sir! What point would there be in putting on a show?"

"To entice us to come."

"That's completely unnecessary, since we're coming anyway without any enticements ."

"You figure that Santer is with them?"

"Naturally. When he reached this spot, he saw them and crossed the stream bed to meet them."

"And do you think he told them what happened and why he needed their protection?"

"What a question! It's obvious that he told them."

"Then he would also have told them that his pursuers were not far behind."

"He might have, sure."

"Then I'm surprised that they have made absolutely no precautions."

"Nothing surprising about that. They just don't think it's possible that we're so close. They probably don't expect us until tomorrow. As soon as it's dark enough, I'll sneak over there and see what the situation is. Then we'll figure out what to do. I must have this Santer!"

"Ok, then I'm coming along."

"That's not necessary."

"I think it is necessary."

"When Sam Hawkens goes out spying, he doesn't need any help. I'm not going to take you. I know you and your pointless humanitarian outlook. You probably want to save this murderer's life."

"I wouldn't dream of it!"

"Don't kid yourself!"

"I'm just telling you what I think. I want to catch Santer, too. I want to capture him alive, to bring him to Winnetou. Once I see that it's impossible, that I can't capture him alive, then I'll put a bullet through his head. You can depend on it."

"There you have it: a bullet through the head. You don't want him to be tortured. I'm against such executions myself, but in this case I believe with all my heart that the scoundrel deserves just such a painful death. We'll catch him and take him to Winnetou. First, though, we have to know how many Kiowas there are. We know there are more of them than us, that's for sure."

I decided to keep quiet. His words had made the Apaches suspicious of me. They knew that I had made an effort on behalf of Rattler, so they were inclined to think I might have something similar in mind here. So I pretended to go along with Sam's preference and I stretched out on the ground next to my horse.

The sun had long since disappeared, and twilight was setting in. The Kiowas had lit several fires over on the other bank, and their flames leaped high in the air. Indians are normally careful to avoid large fires, so I was more convinced than ever that they were trying to draw us in. We were supposed to believe that they knew nothing of our presence, and that would prompt us to attack them. If we did that, we would be delivering ourselves right into their hands.

While I was thinking about this, I thought I detected a noise that wasn't made by any of us. It was behind me, where no one else was lying—I had chosen the farthest spot. I listened, and heard the sound again. I heard it clearly and could distinguish it perfectly. It was a soft movement of a thick stalk on which dry leaves hung, something like the sound you make when you pull a few stalks out of a bundle of straw. It was not the movement of a smooth twig, but of a stalk, and it must have had stickers or thorns since the sound occurred in individual little jerks, generated by one sticker after another.

This told me immediately exactly where I could find the source of the sound. Behind me, between three trees that stood in a cluster, was a blackberry bush. Something must have brushed against a stalk of it. A small animal could be hiding there, but in our situation it was better to be safe. It could also be a person, and I had to check out that possibility. I had to see him.

See? In this darkness? Yes, indeed!

As I said, the Kiowas had lit huge fires on the other side. Their light didn't really illuminate anything on our side, but I could certainly see the silhouette of any object that was between me and the fires. I would be able to do this with the blackberry thicket if I could get to the other side of it, but I had to do this without being detected. I stood up and strolled off slowly, but not in the direction I really intended to go. Once I was far enough away, I turned around and approached the clump of trees from the appropriate side. As I got closer, I got down on the ground and crept very quietly toward the thicket, which I eventually reached, unnoticed even by my own people. It was right in front of me. I could even reach it with my hand, and in the same direction the fires on the far side of the streambed were still burning. There were a few places where I could see through it, but otherwise the thicket was too dense. There! Yes, there was the same noise again, and not in the middle of the thicket, but off at one side. I crept toward it and now saw clearly exactly what I had suspected.

A person, an Indian, had been hiding in the thicket and now wanted to leave. But that created little noises, so he had attempted to make small movements at varying intervals, and he was doing a masterful job of it. Instead of a single loud noise, there was only a soft, straw-like rustling from one minute to the next. I was the only one who had heard it, since I was lying the closest. He had almost succeeded in his difficult task. His whole body was in the open, and only his head, together with one shoulder and arm, were still under the thicket.

I crept up to him so that I was behind his back. He continued to gradually free himself. He got his shoulder free, then his neck, then his head, until only his arm was left. Then I raised myself up on my knees, grabbed his throat with my left hand and hit him two or three times in the head with my right, until he lay still.

"What was that?" Sam asked. "Do you hear anything?"

"Old Shatterhand's horse was stamping," answered Dick.

"He's gone. Where do you think he went? He better not do anything dumb!"

"Dumb? Him? He never did anything dumb yet, and he won't start now."

"Oh ho! He is certainly capable of dumb things. I bet he's seeking out the Kiowas in secret, to warn them and save Santer's life!"

"No, he won't do that. He'd rather strangle the murderer than see him go free. The two deaths affected him deeply. You must have noticed that."

"Could be. But I'm not taking him along when I go spying on the Kiowas. I wouldn't have any use for him. I just want to count them up and check out the area. Then we can figure out our plan of attack. He's generally pretty good as greenhorns go, but sneaking up on the Kiowa camp when they've got big fires like those—he wouldn't manage it. These fellows know we're coming, so they'll be careful and keep an ear cocked. Nobody but a veteran frontiersman would be able to get near. But I would be able to get close enough to see and hear everything."

At this, I stood up, went quickly over to him, and said: "You're wrong about that, Sam. You thought I was gone, but I'm here. So do I know how to sneak up on people or not?"

"I'll be jiggered!" he answered. "You're really here? We didn't notice you at all!"

"Well, that just proves that you're weak in exactly the area that you were claiming I was weak in. Not only that, but there are other people here besides me."

"Who, then? What are you talking about?"

"Go over to that blackberry bush over there, and you'll see him, Sam!"

He stood up and went where I had indicated. The others did the same.

"Holy Moses!" he cried. "There's a fellow lying here, an Indian! How did he get here?"

"Why don't you ask him?"

"But he's dead!"

"No. I just knocked him out."

"Where? Not here, surely? You were gone. You surprised him somewhere, gave him one of your punches, and brought him here."

"Don't believe it! He was hiding here in the thicket and I noticed him. As he was creeping out to get away, I knocked him out. I know you heard it: you asked about it and were told it was my horse stamping."

"I declare! That's true! So he really was hiding in the bush and heard everything we were talking about. Could have been a big problem for us if he had succeeded in getting away unnoticed. Sure am glad you knocked him out! Let's bind and gag him, if I'm not mistaken! But why didn't he stay over there with his people? What was he doing here? Do you suppose he got here before we did?"

"You ask questions like those and still have the nerve to call other people greenhorns? Those are real greenhorn questions. Of course he was he before we were. The Kiowas knew we were coming. They assumed we would be following Santer's tracks and would arrive here. They were planning a little reception for us, and they send out a scout to watch for us so they wouldn't miss the best opportunity. But because we rode so fast, or because he wasn't paying attention, or maybe because he arrived here just as we were arriving, we surprised him and he had to hide in the blackberries."

"But he could have fled back to his camp."

"He didn't have time. We would have seen him and realized that the Kiowas had been warned we were here. It is also possible that he had planned to hide here, to eavesdrop on us."

"Well, that's all possible. Be that as it may, it's a good thing that we discovered him. Now he'll have to confess to everything."

"He won't say a thing. You'll never get anything out of him."

"Could be. But we certainly don't owe him any special treatment. Anyway, now we know the situation. And what we don't know, I'll soon find out, because I'm heading over there now."

"Perhaps not to return?"

"Why?"

"Because the Kiowas will capture you. You said yourself that it's very difficult to sneak up on them with these big, bright fires everywhere."

"Sure, for you. But not for me. So like I said: I'm going over there, and you're staying here."

He said this with such an absolute, authoritarian voice that I felt I had to reply:

"What's wrong with you today, Sam? You don't think you can just tell me what to do, do you? "

"Of course I can."

"Well then, in a spirit of friendship I must tell you you're wrong. As a surveyor, I have authority over you—you were part of the group only to provide security. In addition, you know that I was declared a chief by Inchu-chuna with the agreement of the whole tribe. So you can look at your position any way you like, but I'm in charge and I'm the one who gives the orders."

"I don't take orders from any chief," he replied. "And furthermore, I'm an experienced frontiersman and you're a greenhorn, my student. And don't you forget it, if you don't want a reputation for being ungrateful. So I'm going, you're staying, and that's that!"

The Apaches murmured about him, and Stone also commented sullenly:

"He's not himself today. Accusing you of being ungrateful! We're the ones who should be grateful to you. We'd be dead if it weren't for you. Did he ever save your life?"

"Let him be," I replied. "He is a splendid little fellow, and even his demeanor today speaks well of him. It's just his anger about Inchu-chuna and Nsho-chi's death. But I won't obey him anyway.

I'm going too. In his present state of agitation, he could easily let himself get carried away and do something that he would normally avoid. Stay here until I get back, and even if you hear shots, don't move. If I need help, I'll call for you to come."

Chapter 38

I left my bear-killer behind, just as Sam had left his Liddy, and set off. I had noticed that Hawkens had gone directly across the stream bed. He planned to sneak up from the far bank. I thought that was the wrong approach, and decided to try to do better. The Kiowas knew that we were upstream from them, so that is where they would direct much of their attention. That was Sam's mistake, for he would be coming from that direction. I planned to approach from the opposite side. I went downstream on our side, far enough from the bank so that the light of the fires would not reach me, until I got to the end of the wooded area. No fires had been lit this far downstream, and the trees blocked the light from the other fires. It was so dark that I could slip down into the stream bed and back up the other side without being seen. Now I was among the trees. I lay down and crept forward. Eight fires were burning. That was more than necessary: I counted only about forty Indians. The fires had been set just to show us where the Kiowa camp was.

The Kiowas sat under the trees in scattered groups and had their guns in their hands, ready to shoot. Woe to us, if we had been so careless as to walk into the trap that had been set for us! And it was such an obvious and stupid trap, only inexperienced men would have fallen for it. I saw the Indians' horses grazing out on the prairie.

I wanted to eavesdrop on one of the groups, preferably the one with the leader in it, since I would be more likely to get the information I wanted there. But where was the leader? I told myself he would surely be in the group Santer was in, and so I slid from tree to tree, looking for Santer.

After searching a while, I found him. He was sitting with four Indians, none of whom, however, carried any sign of chief's status. But that wasn't necessary. By Indian custom, it would have to be the oldest of these four. Unfortunately, I couldn't get as close as I would have liked. There was no undergrowth to give me cover. But a few trees stood where their shadows gave me a limited amount of protection. Since there were eight fires, every tree had several shadows and half-shadows that danced around, giving the depths of the woods a ghostly appearance.

I was glad to find that the Indians were speaking loudly with each other. Their plan was not to be secretive: we were supposed to hear as well as see them. I reached the shadows of the trees and lay there, perhaps twelve paces from Santer's group. I was taking a significant chance, since it would be even easier for the other Indians to spot me than for this group.

Santer was doing all the talking. He told about the Nugget Mountain and urged the Indians to go there with him and dig up the treasure.

"Does my white brother know the spot where it can be found?" asked the oldest of the four Indians.

"No. We wanted to find it, but the Apaches came back too quickly. We thought they would stay long enough that we would be able to watch them."

"Then the search is useless. Ten times a hundred men could go there to look for it and they would not find it. The red man understands very well how to make such places hard to recognize. But since my brother has shot our greatest enemy and his daughter, we will do him the favor of riding there with him later and helping him to look. First we must catch your pursuers and then kill Winnetou."

"Winnetou? He's probably with them."

"No. He can't leave his dead, and he will keep the greater part of his warriors with him. A smaller group was sent after you, led by that white dog Old Shatterhand, who shattered the knees of our chief. We will overpower that group today."

"Then we'll ride to Nugget Mountain, kill Winnetou, and look for the gold!"

"That is not as easy as my brother thinks. Winnetou must bury his father and his sister, and we may not disturb him or the Great Spirit will never forgive us. But when he is finished, we will ambush him. Now he will not continue to the cities of the paleface. He will return home. Then we will set an ambush or lead him on as we are doing with Old Shatterhand today. He's sure to be among the pursuers. I'm only waiting for my scout, who is hidden over there, to return. And the guards, who I have placed widely around the camp, have not brought any information yet."

As I heard this, I shuddered. So there were guards beyond the group of trees. What if Sam Hawkens didn't see them and ended up between them! This thought had barely occurred to me when I heard a sharp cry from several voices. The leader jumped up and listened. All the other Kiowas went quiet and listened too.

A group of four Indians dragging a white man approached the camp. He resisted, but without success. He wasn't tied up, but was held in check by the four knives of his captors. The white man was the careless Sam! I made up my mind immediately: I would not leave him in the lurch, even if it meant risking my life.

"Sam Hawkens!" cried Santer, who recognized him. "Good evening, Sir! You probably didn't expect to meet me here."

"Scoundrel, robber, murderer!" answered the fearless little man, jumping forward and grabbing him by the throat. "Now I have you! You'll get your reward, if I'm not mistaken!"

Santer tried to defend himself. The Indians jumped in and pulled Sam away from him. A moment of chaos ensued, and I made use of it. I pulled both revolvers and jumped into the middle of the Indians.

"Old Shatterhand!" cried Santer, as he fled in fright.

I sent two bullets after him, which missed, and fired the remaining shots at the Indians, who retreated. I called to Sam:

"Come on, follow me! Stay close behind!"

It was as if horror had frozen the Indians in their tracks. They had stood still, even while I had shot at them (though I aimed to make my shots non-lethal). I grabbed Sam's arm and pulled him along with me, back into the trees, then down into the stream bed. It happened so quickly that from the moment of my attack barely a minute could have passed.

"Lord have mercy, that was in the nick of time!" Sam gasped once we had reached the stream bed. "These scoundrels. . ."

"Shut up and follow me," I interrupted, letting go of his arm and turning right to run downstream in the stream bed, for the immediate goal was to get outside of rifle range.

Now the Indians, who were completely dumbfounded and totally caught off guard, came to their senses. Their howls rang out behind us, so I couldn't hear Sam's footsteps any more. There were shrill cries, shots cracked, it was a hellish noise.

Why had I not run upstream, toward our camp, but rather downstream in the opposite direction? There was a very cogent reason. The Indians couldn't see us, since it was dark in the stream bed. So they would run upstream, thinking we were sure to flee in that direction. We could keep comparatively safe by running downstream, then circling back to camp.

When I thought I had run far enough, I stopped. I could still hear the howling of the Indians in the distance, but nothing stirred in my vicinity.

"Sam!" I called, in a low voice.

There was no answer.

"Sam, can you hear me?" I asked, a little louder.

Again there was no answer. Where could he be? Surely he had followed me. Had he perhaps stumbled and injured himself? The route had been through cracked, dried mud and deep puddles of water. I got bullets out of my belt, reloaded the revolvers, and started back slowly, looking for Sam.

The hellish noise that the Kiowas made continued, so I risked coming closer and closer until I was back at the spot in the woods where I had told Sam to follow me. I had not found him. He had had a different idea from mine and, ignoring my words, had climbed the opposite bank. But the light of the fire must have made him visible there, and he had exposed himself, not just to the eyes of the Kiowas, but also to their bullets. What thoughtlessness on the part of the little man, so obstinate that day. Now I was worried about him again. I crept away from the trees, until I was far enough not to be spotted, and then circled back to our camp.

Everyone was in a state of agitation. My colleagues, red and white, crowded around me, and Dick Stone cried reproachfully:

"Sir, why did tell us we couldn't come after you, even if we heard shots? We were sitting here, just waiting for your call. Thank God that you, at least, are back. And uninjured too, I see!"

"Where is Sam? Not here?" I inquired.

"Here? How can you ask that? Didn't you see what happened to him?"

"What happened?"

"After you left, we waited. After a long time, we heard an Indian cry out, then it was still again. Then suddenly we heard revolver shots, followed by horrible howling. Then we heard rifle shots and Sam appeared."

"Where?"

"Down by the trees, on this side of the stream bed."

"I thought so! I've never seen Sam as careless as he is today. Go on!"

"He came running toward us, but a whole bunch of Kiowas were right behind him. They caught up with him and captured him. We could see it clearly, since the fires were burning brightly, and we wanted to go to his aid. But before we could get there, they had already gotten him to the other side of the stream bed and disappeared into the trees. We wanted to follow and attack them, and free Sam, but we remembered your instructions and let it go."

"And that was wise of you. Eleven men wouldn't have accomplished anything. You all would have been killed."

"But what do we do now, Sir? Sam is captured!"

"Yes, unfortunately, and for the second time tonight!"

"The second time?" he cried, astonished.

"Yes. I rescued him the first time. All he had to do was follow me and he'd be standing right here now. But he's really pig-headed today."

I recounted the events in the Kiowa camp. Once I had finished, Will Parker said:

"That's no fault of yours, Sir! You did far more than anyone else would have attempted. Sam got himself into this fix, but still, we can't just leave him there!"

"No, we have to get him free. But it will be harder than it was the first time. We can be sure that the Kiowas will be twice as alert as last time."

"That's for sure. But it might still be possible to retrieve him again."

"Hmm. Anything is possible. But twelve men against fifty who are just waiting to be attacked! And yet, that looks like our only option. By daylight, we'd stand even less chance of making a raid on their camp."

"Well then, let's attack tonight!"

"Slow down, slow down. We need to think about this."

"Think about it, Sir, but in the meantime grant me permission to sneak over there and see how things stand."

"You can do that, but not just yet. Wait until they've calmed down a bit. Then both of us can go, and perhaps we'll take the whole group."

"Fine, very good, Sir! I accept that. Taking the rest along—that sounds a lot like an attack to me. We'll do our duty. I'll take on six or eight of the Kiowas myself, and Dick Stone can handle just as many, right, Dick?"

"Yes, you said it, Will," answered Stone. "A few more or a few less, it doesn't matter to me. Whatever it takes to get Sam free. He's normally a regular artful dodger, but today wasn't his day."

Yes, Sam had certainly shown his weak side that night. I silently pondered what the best way to free him might be. I would have risked my life for him, but was I justified in risking the Apaches' lives as well? Maybe a plan based on cunning would be better and less dangerous. We'd have to work that out later, after we had done a bit of spying over there. I wanted to take along the Apaches so as to be ready for anything. Perhaps it would turn out that a sudden attack would be advantageous, if we could do it without great risk.

For now, though, we waited. We saw that there was still a lot of activity on the other side. Soon it got quieter, and this quiet was broken only by loud tomahawk chops. The Indians were cutting wood, apparently with the idea of keeping the fires going full strength until morning.

Then the chopping stopped. The stars showed midnight, and I felt it was time to get to work. First, we made sure that the horses, which we had to leave behind, were well tethered and would not get loose, and I checked to be sure that our captured Kiowa was well bound and gagged. Then we left our camp and retraced the same route that I had used before to get to the stream bed.

Once we reached the stream bed below the area of trees, I told the Apaches to wait there under Dick Stone's command and to avoid all noise. Then Will Parker and I climbed softly up the bank to the trees. Upon reaching the top of the bank, we lay flat and listened. Everything was silent. We began to creep forwards. The eight fires were burning as high as ever. I saw that whole piles of branches had been thrown into them. That made me suspicious. We slid farther and farther forwards and saw not a single person. We finally convinced ourselves, still observing the greatest caution, that the woods were empty. There wasn't a single Kiowa there.

"They've left, just left, in secret!" said Parker, astonished. "And still they stirred up the fire like that!"

"To mask their retreat. As long as the fires were burning, we had to assume they were there."

"But where are they? Gone entirely?"

"I imagine so. Sam represents quite a prize for them, and they want to get him out of harm's way. But it's also possible that they're planning some trickery."

"What kind?"

"To attack us over there, just like we would have attacked them here."

"Bless my soul, that certainly is possible! We better turn around and get back as soon as possible, Sir!"

"Yes. We need to get back and secure our horses, even if it turns out later that it wasn't necessary. Better safe than sorry."

We rejoined the Apaches and hurried back to our camp, where nothing had been disturbed. But the Kiowas could still be coming later, so we saddled up and rode a good distance into the prairie, where we camped for the rest of the night. If the Kiowas should attack our old camp, they would discover we had gone and would have to wait for daylight to find us. Of course we took our prisoner along with us.

Now there was nothing to do but wait for morning. Those who could sleep, slept. The rest of us kept watch. Thus the night was passed, and at the first light of dawn, we mounted again and rode back to our previous camp. No one had been there, so it hadn't really been necessary to move, but there was no harm in it. Then we crossed the stream bed to the wooded area. The fires had burned out, and piles of ashes were the only evidence of the previous night's feverish activities.

We now examined the tracks. The tracks of the whole Kiowa group departed from the area where the horses had been grazing. They had ridden off in a southeasterly direction. It was clear they had given up on trying to fight us. They would gain nothing by it, since they no longer had the element of surprise on their side.

And Sam? They had taken him along, a fact that weighed very heavily on Dick Stone and Will Parker. I also really felt for the little man, and I would have been ready to try anything halfway sensible to free him.

"If we can't rescue him, they'll torture him at the stake," moaned Dick Stone.

"No," I reassured him. "We have a prisoner that we can trade for him."

"I wonder if they know that!"

"Certainly. Sam is smart enough to have told them. Anything they do to him, we'll do to our prisoner."

"But we have to ride after these Indians, no matter what!"

"No."

"What? You want to leave him in the lurch?"

"No again."

"But aren't you contradicting yourself? How can you combine both?"

"By not letting these Indians lead me around the prairie by the nose."

"By the nose? Sorry, but I can't understand you."

"Well, take a look at the tracks. How old would you say they are?"

"It looks to me like they left before midnight."

"I think so too. Close to ten hours have gone by since then. Do you think we could make up that head start today?"

"No."

"Or tomorrow?"

"Not tomorrow either."

"And where do you think they went?"

"Back to their villages."

"So they'll get there before we can catch up with them. Do you think that the twelve of us, in the middle of Kiowa territory, can attack one of their villages and free a prisoner?"

"That would be crazy."

"Right! So we agree: we won't ride after them."

Stone scratched himself behind his ear, and murmured hopelessly:

"But Sam, Sam, Sam! Our good old Sam, what happens to him?

We can't give up on him!"

"No, we won't do that. We'll rescue him."

"The devil take you, Sir! I'm not the man to solve puzzles like this. First you say we won't follow the Indians, and then you say we'll free their prisoner. You might as well call a donkey a camel and an ape in the same breath! Let someone else try to understand you—I can't!"

"It isn't like you think. Your comparison is a false one. The Kiowas aren't headed for their villages at all."

"No? Where do you think they're going?"

"You haven't figured it out?"

"No."

"Hmm! I would have expected more of an experienced frontiersman! Thank goodness for us greenhorns: we can wrestle a puzzle like this one to the ground without breaking a sweat! The Indians are actually headed for Nugget Mountain."

"Nugget Mountain? Do you really think so, Sir?"

"Absolutely. You can count on it."

"Are you convinced of that?"

"I'm not just convinced; I assert it with certainty."

"But they can't disturb the funeral ceremony!"

"And they don't plan to. They'll wait until it's over. They're no friends of ours or of the Apaches. They are itching for revenge. They welcomed Santer's arrival. They were very pleased to learn of the deaths of Inchu-chuna and his daughter. They would love for Winnetou and us to meet the same fate. When they learned we were following Santer, they came up with a plan to get us. But we were careful and, except for Sam, we avoided the trap. Now they'll try a different approach. They've ridden off as if they were heading for their villages. They think that will keep us from trying to follow them and we'll just return to Winnetou. But they'll just ride southeast for a while, picking up more warriors if they can, and then they'll turn around and head toward Nugget Mountain, where they figure they'll be able to make a surprise attack on us and slaughter us all."

"A pretty plan, yes indeed, a pretty plan! But we'll make sure it has a different outcome!"

"Yes we will. Probably Santer gave them this plan. He wants to use the opportunity to get himself some gold. Anyway, I'm completely convinced that what I just explained is what they have in mind. Now do you want to follow the Kiowas?"

"No chance. Your account seems a bit iffy to me, but for as long as I've known you, you've always been right. I imagine you'll probably turn out to be right this time, too. What do you think, Will?"

"I figure it's exactly like Old Shatterhand says. We need to get out of here, and quickly, to warn Winnetou in time. Do you agree, Sir?"

"Yes."

"And we take the prisoner along?"

"Of course. We'll tie him onto Sam's Mary, which might not necessarily be all that pleasant for him. As soon as we've done that, let's leave. But let's find a pool down in the stream bed where our horses can get a drink before we ride."

Half an hour later, we were on our way. We weren't happy about the success of our chase. Instead of capturing Santer, we lost Sam Hawkens, though it was his own fault. But if my assumptions were correct, we could confidently expect to free Sam and capture Santer before long.

When we had been on Santer's trail, we had to stay with his tracks even though it meant taking the long way around because he switched directions in the middle of his trip, making a blunt angle. I decided to cut off the angle, with the result that shortly before noon the next day we arrived at the canyon that led up to the clearing where the ambush and double murder had taken place.

We left the horses down in the valley in the care of one of the

Apaches, and began the climb up the canyon. A guard was stationed at the edge of the clearing. He greeted us with a silent movement of his hand. We immediately saw how industrious the twenty Apaches had been in preparing for the funeral of their chief and his daughter. I saw a pile of thin trees that had been cut down with tomahawks. They were intended for the scaffolding. Likewise, a great pile of stones had been carried over, and more were being brought. The Apaches that had come with me immediately joined in these tasks. I learned that the burial would take place the following day.

At one side, a temporary hut had been built in which the two bodies were kept. Winnetou was in the hut, and word was sent in to him that we had arrived. He walked out. What an appearance he made!

He had always been very serious, and you would rarely see a smile flit across his face. I never once heard him laugh out loud. But in spite of his earnestness, there was always an expression of goodness and good will on his handsome features, and on occasion his dark velvet eyes even had an expression of extraordinary friendliness. How often had they rested on me with a love and tenderness whose light one might normally expect only in a woman's eyes. Today, though, there wasn't a trace of all that. His face seemed to have become hard as stone, and his gaze turned somberly inwards. His movements were slow and heavy. He approached me, gave a dull, searching look around, shook my hand, looked at me with an expression that cut deep into my soul, and asked:

"When did my brother return?"

"Just now."

"Where's the murderer?"

"He escaped us."

Honesty requires me to admit that I looked at the ground when I gave this answer. I was almost ashamed to say these words.

"Did my brother lose the trail?"

"No, I'm on it even now."

"Let Old Shatterhand tell me about it!"

He sat down on a stone and I did the same. I gave him a precise and accurate report. He listened silently until the end, was quiet for a few moments more, and finally asked:

"My white brother is not sure whether the murderer was hit by the bullets from his revolver?"

"No, but I doubt that I even wounded him."

He nodded slightly, pressed my hand, and said:

"Let my brother forgive the question I asked before about losing the trail. Old Shatterhand did everything that he could, and in the end he acted very wisely. Sam Hawkens will regret very much his carelessness. We will forgive him and set him free. I agree with my brother: the Kiowas will come, but they will not find us as they expect to find us. The prisoner must not be badly treated, but let him be watched carefully. Tomorrow, the graves will be placed over Inchu-chuna and Nsho-chi. Does my brother want to be there?"

"I would be hurt if Winnetou did not permit me to come!"

"I don't permit you, I ask you to come. Your presence there will perhaps save the lives of many sons of palefaces. The law of blood requires the death of many white men, but your eyes are like the sun, whose warmth melts the hard ice and changes it to flowing water. You know who I have lost. Be a father to me, and a sister too. Please, Charley!"

A tear stood in his eye. He was ashamed of it, though it could not have been seen by anyone but me, and he hurried away, disappearing into the hut where the two bodies were laid out. That was the first time he ever called me by my first name, Karl, and from then on, that's how he always said it: "Charley."

At this point, I should describe the funeral, which was undertaken with the greatest possible Indian ceremony. While I know well that a detailed description of theses ceremonies would certainly be interesting, I feel such deep pain when I think about those sad hours, that even to this day it feels as if it happened yesterday. A description of it seems to me like a desecration — not a desecration of the memorial which we built for them both on Nugget Mountain, but of the monument to them that I erected in my heart, and that I have always been true to. Therefore, I know you will permit me to omit the description.

Inchu-chuna's body was tied to his horse, and the earth was piled over them both until the animal could no longer move. Then, the horse was shot through the head. The mound of earth was enlarged until it completely covered the rider, his weapons, and his medicine, and then it was covered with several layers of stones all the way to the top.

At my request, Nsho-chi was buried differently. I didn't want her to be in such direct contact with the earth. We set her against the trunk of a tree in a sitting position and then put stones all around her, making a hollow pyramid with the tree rising out of its peak.

I have returned to Nugget Mountain several times with Winnetou to visit the graves. We have always found them undamaged.

Chapter 39

You can imagine how Winnetou suffered from the loss of his father and sister. During the burial, he was permitted to express his sorrow, but afterwards he had to keep it locked up inside himself. This was partly due to Indian custom and partly because he would now need to focus all his attention on the expected arrival of the Kiowas. Now he was no longer the son and brother, nearly struck down with bitter loss. Now he was the leader of his band of warriors, to whom he had to explain his rejection of an attack on the enemy and his intention to capture the murderer Santer. He seemed to have the plan already thought out, for immediately after the burial, he told the Apaches to prepare to leave, and to bring the horses (which had been grazing in the valley below) up to the clearing.

"Why does my brother give this order?" I asked him. "The terrain is so rough that it will be very difficult to get the animals up here."

"I know that," he answered, "but we have to do it because I want to outsmart the Kiowas. They have protected the murderer and they will all have to die."

As he said this, his expression was one of resolution and threat. If he did as he said, the Kiowas were lost. My beliefs were milder than his. To be sure, the Kiowas were our enemies, but they weren't guilty of killing Inchu-chuna and his daughter. Should I try to change his mind? If I did, perhaps I would be inviting his anger, but this was the best opportunity I would have, since we were alone in the clearing. The Apaches had followed his orders and immediately moved out, and Stone and Parker had gone with them. No one would hear if, in his anger, he gave me an answer that would I would have to take as an insult if others were present. So I told him what I was thinking, and, to my surprise, the effect was not as I had feared. Though his eyes grew large and dark, he responded calmly:

"That is what I expected from my brother. He does not consider it a weakness to avoid the enemy."

"That's not how I meant it. There's no question of avoidance. I have even considered how we might take all of them prisoner. But what happened here is not their fault, and it would be unjust if they had to share in the punishment for it."

"They have sided with the murderer, and they are coming here to ambush us! Is that not reason enough to treat them without mercy?"

"No, it is not a reason, at least not for me. I am sorry to hear that my brother Winnetou wants to make the same mistake that has been the cause of the decline of all the red nations."

"What mistake does Old Shatterhand mean?"

"That the Indians tear each other limb from limb, rather than standing together against the common enemy. Permit me to speak honestly with you. In general, who do you think is smarter and more cunning, the red man or the paleface?"

"The paleface. I say this because it is the truth. The whites have more knowledge and more skillfulness than we do. They are superior to us in almost everything."

"That's right. We are often superior. But you are no ordinary Indian. The Great Spirit has given you gifts that white men rarely have, and you think differently from the typical red man. Your mind is sharp, and the eyes of your body and of your spirit see much farther than those of an ordinary warrior. How often the tomahawk of war is dug up among you! You must see that this is nothing but continuous, horrible suicide that the red man brings upon himself, and anyone who does that is participating in this suicide. Inchu-chuna and Nsho-chi were killed by whites, not Indians. One of the murderers fled to the Kiowas and persuaded them to attack you. Certainly, that is good reason to await them here and to fight them, but it doesn't justify shooting them down like caged wild dogs. They are your red brothers; think about it!"

I continued in this vein a little longer. He listened to me silently. When I was finished, he gave me his hand and said:

"Old Shatterhand is a true and honest friend of all red men, and he is right when he speaks of suicide. I will do as he says: I will capture the Kiowas, but then I will free them and keep only the murderer."

"Capture them? That will be difficult, since they will outnumber you. Or are you thinking of the same thing as I am?"

"What's that?"

"To lure the Kiowas into a place where they can't defend themselves."

"Yes, that is my plan."

"Mine too. You know the area here, and I was going to ask you if there was such a place nearby."

"There is one, and it is not far. It's an narrow gorge between cliffs, like a small canyon. I'll draw them into it."

"Do you think it will work?"

"Yes. When they are in this canyon, whose sides cannot be climbed, we will attack them at the front and the back. They will have to surrender or they will be shot down helplessly. I will give them their lives and be satisfied just to have Santer in my hands."

"Thank you! My brother Winnetou's heart always listens to a good word. Perhaps he will just as lenient about another matter."

"What does my brother Old Shatterhand mean?"

"You were going to swear revenge on all whites, and I asked you not to do it then, but to wait until after the funerals. Will you tell me what you have decided?"

He looked at the ground for a few seconds, then turned his gaze intently on me, pointed to the hut where the bodies had lain, and answered:

"I spent the night in there with my dead, battling with myself. For me, revenge was a great, bold idea. I wanted to call together the warriors of all the red nations and lead them against the palefaces. I knew I would be defeated. But in the battle with myself during the night, I was the victor."

"You let go of your great, bold thoughts?"

"Yes. I asked three people that I love, two dead and one living. They advised me to put aside this plan, and I decided to follow their advice."

I asked a question of him, not through words but through the expression on my face, and he continued:

"My brother does not know what people I speak of? I mean Kleki-petra, Nsho-chi, and you. In my thoughts, I asked you three, and three times I got the same answer."

"Yes, if both of them were alive and you could ask them, they would certainly say the same thing that I did. The plan you had in mind was a grand one, and you would be the right man to carry it out, but still. . ."

"Let my brother speak and think more modestly about me," he interrupted. "Even if a red chief succeeded in uniting the warriors of all the tribes, it could not happen as fast as I would like. It would take a long, difficult lifetime to achieve, and then it would be too late, at the end of life, to start the battle. One man alone, even the greatest and most famous red man, would not be able to complete this task, and after his death there would be no successor in a position to carry the work forward and bring it to its end."

"I'm glad my brother Winnetou came to this conclusion. It is the only correct one. One person is not enough, and it would be difficult to find a successor. And even if you could find one, the fight with the whites would have a sad ending for the red man."

"I know it. It would only make our downfall faster. Even if we win every battle, there are so many palefaces that they would continue to send new armies against us, while we would not be able to replace the warriors we lost. Victory would wipe us out just as surely as defeat, although more slowly. That is what I said to myself as I sat with my dead during the night. That is why I decided not to carry out my plan. I decided to be satisfied with catching the murderer and avenging myself against those who helped him ambush us. But my brother Old Shatterhand has convinced me not to do this either, so my revenge will be only to capture Santer and punish him. We will let the Kiowas go."

"Your words make me proud of the friendship that joins us. I will never forget them.

We are both convinced, though we can't know for sure, that the Kiowas will come. Now we need to know when."

"Today is the day they will arrive," he asserted as confidently as if he were talking of a completely established fact.

"How can you be so sure of that?"

"I conclude it from what you told me about your last ride. The Kiowas pretended to return to their villages, to lure you after them, but they really planned to come here. They couldn't have come straight here—otherwise they would have been able to arrive yesterday. They had to make other stops that slowed their trip here."

"Other stops? What do you mean?"

"Because of Sam Hawkens. They wouldn't bring him here. They would send him back to the tribe. They would have picked a suitable place for that. Or perhaps a good opportunity presented itself. Even then, it would be necessary to send off a messenger to warn of your approach."

"Oh, you mean the warriors from the village would ride out against us?"

"Yes. The warriors that you encountered at the dry riverbed tried to draw you after them. But they really want to come here, so they didn't take the time to fight with you. They would have sent one or two messengers back to their people so that a group from the villages could come out to fight you. These messengers would have taken Sam Hawkens with them. Then, the Kiowas would have changed direction and headed for Nugget-tsil. But they would want to hide this turning, so it would have to be done at a place where no tracks would be left. Such places are not common. You usually have to go out of your way to find them. That would add to the time lost. So the Kiowas could not have gotten here yesterday. They still have not arrived, but they will certainly come today."

"How do you know they haven't arrived yet?"

He pointed to the peak of the nearest mountain. A tall tree towered over the forest that covered it. That was the highest point of the Nugget Mountains, and anyone with a sharp eye sitting in that tree could observe all of the surrounding prairie.

"My brother does not know that I sent a warrior up there," he answered. "He has the eyes of a falcon, and he will watch for the Kiowas. As soon as he sees them coming, he will climb down and tell me."

"That's good. He hasn't come down yet, so they aren't here yet. But you are sure they will come today?"

"Yes. They can't wait any longer if they want to be sure of finding us here."

"But their plan was not to come all the way to Nugget-tsil, but to set an ambush for you on your return home."

"They might have been able to do that if they hadn't been overheard. But now that I know about it, I will lure them here. Our trip home would have taken us to the south, so that's where they would be waiting for us. But I will pretend to have gone north, and they will be drawn after me."

"But will they follow you?"

"Certainly. They will have to send a scout in any case, to make sure we're still here. We won't do anything to him. We will just let him return. Because of him, I gave the command to bring all the horses up here. There are more than thirty horses, so in spite of the hard ground and stony areas he'll surely find the tracks and he will follow them. We will head for the valley that will be the trap in which we will catch them. The spy won't follow us there. He'll only follow long enough to be sure that we have really left. Then he'll return quickly to tell his people that we went north, not south. Does my brother agree?"

"Yes. They will be forced to give up their idea of an ambush, and they are almost certain to come here and follow our trail."

"That is what they will do. I am sure of it. I must have Santer, and he will be in my hands yet today."

"What will you do with him?"

"My brother must not ask me about that. He will die; that is enough."

"Where? Here? Or will he be taken to the pueblo?"

"That has not been decided yet. I hope he is not a coward like Rattler, who we had to grant the quick death of a nasty coward. Listen! I hear the hooves of our horses. We will leave this place, and return to it later with our prisoners."

The horses appeared. My horse and Sam's Mary were among them. The terrain was so rough that we couldn't ride, so each man led his own horse by the bridle.

Winnetou led the way. It took us northwards out of the open and back into the woods, which dropped off fairly steeply. At the bottom there was an open meadow. We mounted our horses and rode across it towards a cliff that rose like a high, vertical wall of rock before us. It was split by a narrow opening. Winnetou pointed to it and said:

"That is the trap that I spoke of. We will ride through there."

The word "trap" fit this narrow passage very well. The walls on either side climbed almost vertically toward the sky, and there was no point at which they could be climbed. If the Kiowas were stupid enough to ride in here, and if we controlled both entrances of this canyon, it would be madness for them to try to fight back.

The path was not straight, but turned left at one moment, right at the next, and it took us a good quarter of an hour to reach the other end. There, we stopped and dismounted. We had hardly done so when the Apache lookout, who had been watching for the Kiowas from the tree, arrived.

"They have come," he reported. "I tried to count them but I could not. They were too far away and riding in a group."

"Did they ride toward the valley?" Winnetou enquired.

"No. They stopped out on the prairie, where they set up camp among the bushes. But then a single warrior left them on foot. He came toward the valley."

"That's the spy. We still have time to set the trap, so we can close it later. Let my brother Shatterhand take Stone, Parker, and twelve of my warriors and circle the mountain to the left from here. As soon as he sees a very strong and tall birch tree, he should turn and go into the forest. It will gradually go uphill, and then down again on the other side. When my brother gets there, he will find himself in the end of the valley that we climbed to reach Nugget-tsil. If he continues down the valley, he will come to the place where we left our horses. He knows the way from there. But he should not go into the open valley. He must keep himself hidden along the side of it. In this way, Old Shatterhand will hide on one side of the valley in the woods opposite the place where the canyon leads upwards. He will watch the Kiowa spy but will not hinder him. Then he will see the enemy coming and will let them enter the canyon."

"So that's the plan," I said, continuing with his idea. "You'll stay here, to occupy the exit of the trap, and I'll circle back, following the path you just described, to the foot of Nugget-tsil to await the enemy. I'll follow them secretly until they are inside the trap."

"Yes, that's what I have in mind. If my brother Old Shatterhand makes no mistakes, we will be sure to catch them."

"I will be as careful as possible. Does Winnetou have any other suggetions to give me?"

"No. I leave everything else to you."

"Who will negotiate with the Kiowas when we have succeeded in surrounding them?"

"I will. Old Shatterhand does not need to do anything except prevent them from leaving the canyon, when they see me and my warriors and try to turn around. But go quickly! The afternoon is almost over, and the Kiowas won't wait until morning to follow us. They will want to do it today, before it gets too dark."

The sun had, in fact, almost completed its daily arc. In not much more than an hour, evening would begin. So I set off with Dick,

Will, and the twelve Apaches. We went on foot, of course.

After barely a quarter of a hour, we saw the tall birch and headed into the woods. The area was exactly as Winnetou had described it, and on the other side we soon reached the part of the valley where our horses had grazed. Across from us was the opening of the side valley leading up to the clearing with the two graves. We found a spot where we could sit under the trees and watch for the Kiowas to come, without fear of being observed by them. We didn't expect them to come over to our side: they would head up the side valley opposite us.

The Apaches were silent, and Stone and Parker talked quietly to each other. They were convinced that the Kiowas, and Santer as well, would fall into our hands. I wasn't as sure of it as they were. We had at most twenty minutes of daylight left, and the Kiowas had not yet come. That led me to believe that the decisive moment would be postponed until the next morning. We hadn't even seen anything of the spy that the enemy had sent to the valley. It was rapidly getting dark where we sat, under the trees.

Parker and Stone had stopped whispering, a puff of air swept over the treetops, causing that rustling sound that is really more like steady, soft, deep sighing than rustling. It doesn't interfere with the recognition of any other sound, no matter how slight. That was the case now. It seemed as if something had flitted across the soft forest floor behind me. I listened closer: yes, something had moved. But what was it? No four-footed animal would have approached us so closely. A reptile? No, not that either. I turned around and lay flat on my stomach, to be able to see better above us. This happened just in time for me to see a dark figure that had been lying behind me and that was now slipping away between the trees. I jumped up and hurried after him. Like a dark splotch in the brighter half-shadow, I saw him and grabbed for him but found only a piece of cloth in my hand.

"Away!" cried a shocked voice, and the cloth was ripped from my hand. The shadow disappeared. I stood and listened, so as to at least hear him. But my companions had noticed my quick movements and had heard the cry. They jumped up and asked me what was happening.

"Quiet, be quiet!" I answered and listened again. There was nothing to be heard.

It was a man, who had been spying on us, a white man, to judge by his English cry, probably Santer himself. He was the only paleface among the Kiowas. I had to follow him, in spite of the darkness!

"Sit down and wait until I return!" I told my men, and I ran off.

There was no doubt about which direction to take. It would be toward the prairie, where the Kiowas were. The spy would be heading back to their camp and nowhere else. I needed to slow him down, and in order to do so, I had to frighten him. So I called out:

"Stop! Don't move or I'll shoot!"

A few seconds after this warning, I fired twice with my revolver. This was not a mistake, since our presence was no longer a secret. I could now assume that the spy would go deeper into the woods, where it was now completely dark, out of fear. I, on the other hand, hurried to the edge of the woods, where I could still see, and ran along it so that I could get ahead of him. I hoped to get down to the bottom of the valley this way, where I could hide. When the man came back down, he would have to go by me and I would be able to catch him.

While this was a good plan, I couldn't execute it. Just as I rounded one of the twists in the valley and came out from behind a clump of bushes, I saw men and horses ahead of me. I was barely able to throw myself backwards and slip into the trees without being noticed.

The Kiowas had made their camp here, behind the bushes. It was easy to see why.

They had initially stopped out on the prairie and sent out a scout. He did not have a difficult task, as I soon learned. Santer, who already knew the area, had ridden out ahead. He wanted to look around the area for us, so as to be able to report back to the Kiowas as soon as they arrived. But when they arrived, he had not returned, so they sent out a Indian scout to follow Santer's trail. He did not have to worry about any danger, since Santer would have come back to warn of any that he might encounter. So the scout went up the valley as far as he thought wise, found no enemies, and returned to report this. Since the valley provided a better camping place for the night than the open prairie, the Kiowas decided to leave the latter for the former. Santer could not miss them on his return, in spite of the fact that they were cautious enough not to light any fires.

Now it was certain that they would not fall into our hands that day, and probably not the next day either, assuming Santer had been clever enough to discover our plan. What to do? Should I return to my post and wait there to see if the Kiowas would head into the trap the next day after all? Or should I try to find Winnetou, to report our discovery and ask him for a new course of action? There was a third option, and this was a dangerous one for me: I could stay where I was. It would certainly be very valuable to us to learn what the Indians decided, once Santer told them what he had seen. If only I could eavesdrop on them! But I would be risking much—risking everything, in fact. Santer would surely say that I was following him, and that would almost certainly lead to my being discovered. Nevertheless, I decided to take the risk it if there was the slightest chance of success. The Indians had not made a fire, so that they would not be noticed. This circumstance, which protected them, provided me with some protection as well.

Scattered under the trees were large boulders, covered with moss and surrounded by ferns. Perhaps I could hide behind one of them.

The majority of the Indians were still occupied with the horses, which were being staked out so that they would not wander away and betray the camp. They other Indians were sitting or lying along the edge of the woods. From that area, I heard a hushed but commanding voice. That had to be the leader, and I imagined that he would remain in that location later. That's where I had to go, if it was even half possible!

Lying on the ground, I inched my way in that direction. I didn't have to worry too much about cover: it was completely dark, and most of the Indians were on the far side of the spot I wanted to reach. The only way I would be discovered now was if someone stumbled over me in the dark. Fortunately, that didn't happen and I successfully reached my goal. Nearby lay two boulders side by side, one long and high, the other lower. No one would be looking for a spy up there. I climbed from the lower to the higher one and stretched myself out on it. I lay more than two yards above them, in comparative security, for the Indians had no reason to climb up looking for me.

Chapter 40

The Indians who had been busy with the horses now returned and sat or lay down. From the area where I assumed the leader was came several hushed commands (which I didn't understand, since I hadn't learned the Kiowa language) and several Indians got up and left. They must have been guards, who had been given the first watch. I noticed that they took up posts on the valley side of the camp, but not in the forest. That was a fortunate situation for me, since it meant I would be able to get away later without worrying about running into one of them.

The Indians spoke with one another. To be sure, they kept their voices lowered, but still I could hear every word. Unfortunately, I couldn't understand any of it. How valuable it would have been to find out what they were saying! Again and again, during my expeditions across the West and in my travels to other lands, I have eavesdropped on camps and on the men occupying them. I can thank this habit for many of my successes, and often for saving my life. But those who read of this have no idea how difficult and dangerous this kind of spying is. And these are not just difficulties of physical skill, power, and endurance, but also (and more importantly), they are skills of mental conditioning and of developing the indispensable intelligence and knowledge that one must possess.

What's the point of being an expert at sneaking up on an Indian, Bedouin, or Kurdish camp, a Sudanese Seribah or a South American Gaucho village, without having mastered the appropriate language and without being able to understand what is being said? Usually, the substance of what is being said is more important than anything else that can be learned. That's why it has always been my first objective to learn the language of the men with whom I deal. Winnetou mastered sixteen Indian dialects, and he has been my greatest teacher in this area. Later on, I never had to spy on a camp without understanding what was being said.

After I had lain on the boulder for perhaps ten minutes, I heard a guard call out. The reply I had been hoping for followed:

"It's me, Santer. So you moved up here to the valley?"

"Yes. Let my white brother go a little further. He will see the red warriors."

I could understand these words. They were spoken in the mixture of English and Indian words that I had already learned. He came closer to me. The leader called him over and said:

"My white brother has been gone much longer than he first said. He must have an important reason for that."

"More important than you can imagine. How long have you been here?"

"For less time than the palefaces call half an hour."

"You found my horse?"

"Yes, and we followed your tracks. We stopped where you had left it tied. Then, when we rode here, we brought it along."

"You should have stayed out on the prairie! This place makes me uneasy."

"We didn't stay there because this was a better place to make camp. We thought that there would be no danger here. Otherwise, you would have come back quickly to warn us."

"It is just the opposite. I stayed away because we are in great danger here, and it took me a long time to find out what the danger was. Old Shatterhand is here."

"I thought so. Did my brother see him?"

"Yes."

"We will capture him and take him to our chief, whose legs he shattered. He will certainly die at the martyr's stake. Where is he?"

So the Kiowas had not wanted to lure us to their villages, but had assumed that we would return to Winnetou.

"It is still not certain whether we will be able to catch him," Santer answered.

"He will be caught. These dogs have only thirty warriors with them, but we have more than five times ten, and they don't know that we are here. We will take them completely by surprise."

"You are greatly mistaken. They know that we plan to come. They may even know that you are here, for they have sent spies to look for us."

"Ugh! They know?"

"Yes."

"Then we can't surprise them!"

"I'm afraid not."

"So it will come to a battle when we attack them. It will cost much blood: Winnetou and Old Shatterhand each count for ten warriors."

"Yes, they do. The death of Inchu-chuna and his daughter have surely filled Winnetou with rage. They are looking for revenge, and they will defend themselves like wild dogs, like enraged predators. But we must capture them. At the very least I must catch Winnetou."

"Why him?"

"Because of the nuggets. Now he's probably the only one left who knows where they are."

"And he will not reveal that to any man."

"Even if we capture him?"

"No."

"I will torture him until he reveals the secret."

"He will still be silent. This young Apache dog mocks all suffering. And if he knows we're coming, he will avoid falling into our hands."

"Oh, I know how we have to proceed in order to get our hands on him."

"If you know it, tell us!"

"We just have to be sly about using the trap they have set for us."

"They have set a trap? What is it?"

"They want to lure us into a narrow canyon where we have no room to defend ourselves, and then they plan to capture us."

"Ugh! Does my brother Santer know this for sure?"

"Yes."

"Does he know the canyon?"

"I have been in it."

"Tell me what you discovered!"

"I risked a great deal. If anyone had seen me, I would have faced the most gruesome death. I'm pleased as the devil that it went well. My success was thanks to the fact that I had gone to Nugget-tsil once before and I knew the area up there, where the graves are."

"The graves? So Winnetou buried his dead up there, as I expected."

"Yes. That was very fortunate for me, because the attention of the Apaches was distracted. I said to myself that they had to be up there in the clearing, so I was extra careful. I've done a lot in my time, and I can rightfully say I am not inexperienced as a frontiersman, but I have never been as careful as I was today. Naturally, I didn't go out into the open valley, but stayed in the woods at the back of it. At the place where the canyon goes off to the right, they had their horses. It was no small matter to get up there without going through the valley, but I managed it. Once I was up there, I had to redouble my caution. I decided it wasn't possible to advance up to the open area without being noticed. But the Apaches were paying attention only to the funeral, so I risked going as far as the cliffs on the edge of the clearing. From there I could observe everything."

"My white brother has been very bold. He is still alive only thanks to the funeral."

"I already admitted that! When the graves had been closed, Winnetou sent his men to get the horses."

"Up there? Isn't that difficult?"

"Very strenuous!"

"Then he must have had a reason for doing it!"

"Certainly. When we saw that they had taken their horses up there, we were supposed to follow with ours, follow their trail, and fall into their trap."

"Why do you suspect that?"

"I don't suspect it, I know it. I heard it."

"Who said it?"

"Winnetou. When he sent his people for the horses, he was alone with Old Shatterhand. They stood not far from my hiding place and I heard what they said to each other."

"Ugh! A great wonder has occurred! Winnetou has been spied on! That is only possible because his thoughts were not with us, but with his father and his sister."

"Oh, he was thinking about us all right. He sent a scout to the highest treetop, to watch for our arrival."

"Did he see us?"

"No. At least I didn't hear about it. You can see why it was a good idea for me to ride ahead by myself. As a lone rider, I escaped the notice of this scout."

"Yes, you were very clever. Tell us more."

"Once the horses had been brought, they didn't wait any longer. The left the clearing and descended into the valley on the far side of it. Once you cross that, you come to a very long, narrow canyon whose sides are impossible to climb. They planned to draw us into it."

"So Winnetou planned to close off and occupy the way in and the and way out of it?"

"Yes. But naturally he planned to wait until we were inside."

"Then he will have to divide his people. Half will ride through the canyon and wait at the end for us to come, while the other half will stay back so that they can follow behind us."

"That's what I thought too."

"Is the ground rocky or grassy there?"

"In the canyon it is rocky, but outside it, in the valley, it is grassy."

"Then the second group of Apaches will leave tracks when they hide, and we will find the tracks. So we will not fall into the trap."

"On the contrary! These fellows are more cunning than you think. The second group did not remain back. They rode through the canyon."

"Ugh! How do they plan to surround us from the front and back?"

"I asked myself that question. There was only one possible answer: that the second group would take another path to get behind us and follow us to the canyon."

"Once again my brother's thoughts are very clever. Have you discovered this other way?"

"Yes. I next went through the canyon myself. It was very dangerous, but I had to learn about it. Of course, I couldn't go all the way through since I would have run into the Apaches, who had occupied the other end of it. So I quickly turned around, but I was not yet out of the canyon when I heard rapid steps. Fortunately, there were several large boulders along the side, and I quickly ducked behind them. An Apache came by but didn't see me."

"Was that the scout from the mountain top?"

"Probably."

"So he saw us coming and hurried to tell Winnetou."

"Or maybe not. When Winnetou left the camp up near the graves, he sent word to the scout that he should rejoin the group."

"No. Then he would have been accompanied by the messenger who brought him this word. But he came alone. So it is as I thought: he saw us coming and hurried to tell Winnetou. How fortunate that you had enough time to hide! What did you do then?"

"I thought about it. If the enemy wanted to come at us from the rear, this would be easiest to do if they had a comfortable place to secretly wait for us. What place might that be? Certainly this valley here, that we're in right now, and probably the upper part of the valley, where the side canyon goes off to the right, leading up to the clearing. If the Apaches hid there on this side of the valley, under the trees, they would be able to see us coming without being noticed, and they could follow us to the trap and close it behind us. That is what I said to myself, and so I headed back down here and crept toward the area where I believed I would find them, if my calculations were correct."

"And did you find them?"

"Not right away, because I got there before they did. But I didn't have to wait long before they arrived."

"Who? Did you see them clearly and count them?"

"It was Old Shatterhand, the two other whites, and a few more than ten Indians."

"So Winnetou is commanding the other group, that is occupying the end of the narrow canyon."

"That's right. They are just sitting there. I had risked a great deal today and been successful. So I decided to take one more risk, to sneak up very close to them, to hear what they were saying to each other."

"What did they say?"

"Nothing. Before I was really close to them, the two other whites were talking to each other, but by the time I was close enough to understand, they were silent. The Apaches were silent, and Old Shatterhand didn't say a word. I was so close behind him that I could almost have touched him with my hand. Wouldn't he be angry if he knew!"

Santer was right about that. I was angry, and how! This man was just as clever as he was daring! To eavesdrop on Winnetou and me while we spoke alone near the graves! And then to follow us to the canyon, to discover our entire plan, and finally to wait for us right where Winnetou had sent us! He had been lying behind me, so close I could have caught him by the collar of his jacket! That was bad luck, as bad luck for us as his luck had been good today! If I had been able to get hold of him, things would have taken an entirely different turn for me, as I now know. Perhaps my whole life would have taken another direction. Thus it seems that the fate of men often hangs upon an instant, a single possibly insignificant deed or failure or occurrence. But this is only appearance, for the great force that guides the universe, without whose will the sun does not move and the butterfly does not flit from bloom to bloom, watches over every one of his children.

But along with my annoyance, there was at least a small satisfaction for me, because I had heard so much here, and Santer had learned nothing from us.

"You were that close to this dog?" cried the Kiowa. "Why didn't you stick your knife into his heart from the back?"

"I wouldn't think of doing that!"

"Why not?"

"Because that would have ruined everything. What an alarm there would have been! The Apaches would have run back to Winnetou, and he would have learned that his plan had been discovered. Then I wouldn't have been able to catch him, and how would I then get the nuggets, which I must have?"

"You won't get them anyway. Is Old Shatterhand still there where you found him?"

"I hope so."

"You only hope so? So it is possible that he has gone? I think he will wait for us!"

"That is what he planned to do, but now it is possible that he has given up that plan."

"What reason would he have to do that?"

"He knows that he has been observed."

"Ugh! How did he learn that?"

"From a hole, a cursed hole in the ground, probably made by an animal."

"Can holes speak?"

"In certain circumstances, yes. At least this one did. I wanted to sneak away and I turned around. As I did that, I had to put the whole weight of my body on my hands, and my right hand broke through the soft earth and into a hole that was just beneath the surface. It made a noise, and Old Shatterhand heard it. He turned around in an instant and he must have seen me. I jumped up quickly and tried to get away, but just as quickly, he was after me. He almost got me—he grabbed my jacket, but I tore it away and darted to the side. He called out for me to stop or he would shoot; but of course I didn't go for that nonsense. I headed deeper into the woods, where the darkness provided some protection. Then I sat down and waited until I could get away without danger."

"What did his men do?"

"They apparently wanted to look for me, but he told them not to. He instructed them to wait for his return, and then he continued looking for me. I heard his steps for a few more moments, and then it was quiet."

"He went away?"

"Yes."

"Where?"

"I don't know. He won't have gone far. He probably turned back once he recognized that he wasn't going to find me."

"Did he recognize you?"

"Not likely. It was too dark for that."

"Perhaps he came here and is hiding somewhere, watching us!"

"Impossible! He couldn't have seen where I went. Regardless, he must have returned to his men. Once I had waited long enough, I slipped away out of the woods and into the open, where I could travel faster. That's when your guard called out to me and I found out that you were here."

Now there was a long pause. The leader had learned what he wanted to know and seemed to be thinking it over. After a while, I heard him ask:

"What does my white brother intend to do next?"

"I will listen to what you decide."

"I have heard from you that it is now very different from what we thought. If we had succeeded in surprising the Apaches, they would have fallen into our hands, living or dead, without the cost of a lot of blood. But now, they are waiting for us. Old Shatterhand saw you, so he knows that his plan has been discovered and he will be very cautious. It is best for us to leave this place."

"Leave? You want to leave? What are you thinking of? Are you afraid of this handful of Apaches?"

"My white brother will not want to insult me! I am afraid of nothing. But if I can choose to have my enemy in my hands with or without spilling blood, I choose the second. Any smart warrior would do that, no matter how brave he is."

"Do you mean to say that by leaving this area we can actually catch these whites and the Apaches?"

"Yes."

"Oh ho! I'd like to know how!"

"They will follow us."

"That is not so certain."

"It is certain. Winnetou must avenge himself against you, and he knows that you are with us. He will be on our trail in an instant. We will intentionally make our trail so clear that it is easy to follow, and we will ride straight to our villages, where I sent Sam Hawkens, the white man we caught."

"And you think that the Apaches will follow us there?"

"Yes. They will follow us as fast as possible."

"I see! In order to catch me! Is that supposed to make me happy? Should I let them chase after me again, even though my best opportunity to get what I want is right here?"

"You will find nothing here, absolutely nothing, and you won't be in the slightest danger riding home with us."

"But if they catch up with us, I would be in the greatest possible danger!"

"They won't catch up with us. We will have a head start, and that will keep us safe. We will leave immediately, and they won't follow us until they notice we are gone. And that won't be until at least tomorrow noon."

"Leave now? Right now? I'm not in favor of that. What will your chief say when he learns that you gave up such a big advantage as you have right now, without being forced to? Think about that!"

The leader accepted this caution without giving an answer. Apparently it made an impression on him. Santer took notice of this and continued:

"Yes, we have an advantage right now which we wouldn't be able to match with your new plan. The only thing we need to do is to reverse the trap that they have set for us, and catch them in it."

"Ugh! How can we do that?"

"We will attack each of the two groups individually that are supposed to trap us in the canyon. That way, they won't be able to trap us."

"We would have to attack Old Shatterhand's group first. Is that what you mean?"

"Yes."

"Then we can go right by them in the morning as if we didn't know they were here."

"No. We don't need to wait that long. We can kill them all

today."

"Ugh! Let my white brother tell me how he plans to do that."

"It is so simple and obvious that it shouldn't be necessary to explain it. I know the exact spot where Old Shatterhand and his people are now, and I'll lead you there. The eyes of the Kiowa are used to the dark, and their movements are like the snake that cannot be heard as it glides through the moss in the woods. We will surround the Apaches and the three whites, and at a certain sign, we will attack them. None of them will be able to escape. We will wipe them out before they even realize they need to defend themselves."

"Ugh, ugh, ugh!" several of the listeners called out in agreement. They were clearly pleased with Santer's suggestion.

Their leader was not so quick to decide, but after thinking for a while, he said:

"It could succeed, if we proceed very carefully."

"It could succeed? It will succeed! The main thing is to completely surround them without making any noise, and that really isn't hard. Then, one powerful thrust of the knife and the deed is done. The booty that we capture from these fellows belongs to you—I don't want any of it. Then we'll head over to Winnetou's group."

"Still this very night?"

"No, in the morning. I'm so intent on capturing Winnetou alive that I must have my eyes on him when we attack. And I can't do that at night. We'll do what the Apaches did: we'll split into two groups. I will lead one half of our people into the canyon in which they planned to catch us. They will stay there until the first light of dawn, and then they will rush forward until they attack Winnetou at the other end. He will think that Old Shatterhand and his people are coming behind. I will take the other group and at dawn we will follow the path that Old Shatterhand used to return to this valley. I know I will be able to find it. I'm sure it goes straight through the woods and around the base of the mountain to the other entrance of the canyon where Winnetou is camped. He'll have all his attention focused on the battle inside the canyon and he'll be watching our first group. That is why he won't notice us approaching him from behind. He'll be surrounded, just as he planned to surround us, and since he can hardly have more than fifteen men, he will have to surrender if he doesn't want to be killed along with his men. That is my plan."

"If it can be carried out as my brother has described it, it is good."

"Then you agree?"

"Yes. The only thing I want is to capture Winnetou alive, to take him to the chief. This can be done as you have suggested, without waiting any longer."

"Then let us not delay in carrying out the plan!"

"To surround Old Shatterhand in the dark woods, without attracting his attention—that is difficult. I will pick out those of my warriors that have the sharpest eyes in the night and that are the best at spying."

He began naming these warriors, and I could see it was high time for me to get back to my people. Otherwise, if the Kiowas left quickly, I wouldn't be able to warn them in time. I slid from the high boulder to the lower one and from there to the ground and slipped away. When I reached the bushes at the corner of the valley, I went out into the open and ran up the valley by the light of the stars until I was opposite my people. Then I crossed over into the trees and found them waiting anxiously for me.

Chapter 41

"Who's there?" called Dick Stone, hearing my steps. "Is it you, Sir?"

"Yes," I answered.

"Where have you been all this time? There was someone there, wasn't there? Was it one of the Kiowas who happened upon us while he was out scouting?"

"No, it was Santer."

"Well, I'll be! Him? And we didn't catch him! This fellow runs right into our hands and we let him get away! You wouldn't think it was possible!"

"A lot more has happened than you would think was possible. I don't have time to tell you about it now because we have to get out of here. I'll tell you later."

"Leave here? Why?"

"The Kiowas are on their way to attack us right now."

"Are you serious, Sir?"

"Yes. I eavesdropped on them. They want to wipe us out here right now and then attack Winnetou at dawn. They know about our plan. Let's get out of here!"

"Where to?"

"Back to Winnetou."

"Right through the pitch-black woods? That will mean some nasty bumps on the head."

"Use your hands for eyes! Let's go!"

Going through the woods at night without a path is highly dangerous to the human face. Just as I had said, we had to 'use our hands for eyes', meaning that we depended far more on touch than vision. Two of our group led the way, feeling with their outstretched hands, and the others followed along, each one holding onto the man in front. It took us over an hour to put the forest behind us in this way. The hardest part was keeping in the right direction. Once we were out in the open, we could move more quickly and easily. We went around the foot of the mountain and up to the canyon where Winnetou was camped.

He had did not expect any enemy activity from this side, but he had placed a guard there anyway, who called out to us in a loud voice. I answered equally loudly. The Apaches knew my voice and sprang up from the ground.

"My brother Old Shatterhand has come?" asked Winnetou in a tone of mild surprise. "Something must have happened. We waited in vain for the Kiowas."

"They are planning to come tomorrow at dawn. Not through the canyon, but from this side. They plan to wipe you out."

"Ugh! If they wanted to do that, they would first have to conquer you, and they would have to know what we were planning."

"They know it all."

"Impossible!"

"They really do know. Santer was up by the graves and heard everything that you said to me when we were alone."

I couldn't see Winnetou's face, but he didn't answer me. This momentary pause betrayed the magnitude of his astonishment. Then he sat down and asked me to join him. He said:

"If you know this, you must have spied on him, the way he spied on us."

"Certainly."

"So all our plans are destroyed. Tell me what happened!"

I did as he requested. The Apaches gathered around so as not to miss a word. Now and then, an astonished "Ugh!" interrupted my story. But Winnetou was silent until I had finished. Then he asked:

"My brother Shatterhand thought it best to leave his post under these circumstances?"

"Yes. There were two things I might have done, and I wasn't certain enough that either one of them would have led to our goal."

"What were the two things?"

"First, we could have moved a small distance to avoid being attacked. We could have waited there until morning instead of coming all the way here right away."

"That would have been a mistake. In the morning, you would have been facing over fifty of the enemy, and our plan would have been thwarted. What was the second?"

"We could have stayed at our post. When I first thought about it, that is what I wanted to do. Santer was going to lead the Kiowas to us, so he would be at the front and would encounter us first. If I paid close attention, I would have heard him coming and could have knocked him out and carried him away."

"My brother is a bold warrior, but such daring would have certainly been ruinous for him. You would not have been able to travel fast enough carrying Santer, and you would have been overpowered and killed."

"That certainly could have happened. And I was not completely sure that Santer would be the very first. He might just have brought the Kiowas to the area and then stayed back, letting them do all the work. That's why I thought it best to coming looking for you."

"You did exactly the right thing. My brother always does what I would do if I were in his place."

"I also said to myself that it was advisable to come back to you so that we could discuss what to do next."

"What to do next? What does my brother Old Shatterhand suggest?"

"It really isn't possible to suggest anything until we find out what the Kiowas do after they find that we have left."

"Do we have to find this out? Can we perhaps deduce it? "

"Yes, we can deduce it, but deduction is never as safe as seeing and hearing, real observation. It's possible to make errors."

"Not in this case. The Kiowas are not children, but grown warriors. Of all the possibilities, they will choose the smartest, and in this situation that can only mean one thing."

"They will ride away? To their villages?"

"Yes. When they fail to find you, they will know that Santer's plan cannot be carried out, and the leader will go back to his previous idea. I am sure they will abandon the idea of attacking us here."

"Santer will try to convince them to do it anyway!"

"He certainly will, but no one will listen to him. They will leave."

"And what about us? What do we do? Do we ride after them, as they expect?"

"Or ride ahead of them!"

"Excellent! We can get out in front of them and surprise them."

"Yes, we could do that. But there is something much better. We must get Santer, and we must free Sam Hawkens. So we will have to go to Tangua's village, where Sam Hawkens is being held, but it doesn't have to be the same route that this group of Kiowas takes from here. We will have to avoid that path, because they will be looking for us there. If we take it, we will be observed. We can't allow that to happen if we want to achieve our goal."

"Does my brother Winnetou know Chief Tangua's village?"

"Yes."

"And does he know exactly where it lies?"

"As exactly as I know the position of my own pueblo. It lies on the Salt Fork of the North arm of the Red River."

"That's southeast from here?"

"Yes."

'Then they expect us to arrive from the northwest, so it will be easiest to approach from the opposite direction, the southeast."

"That is exactly what I want to do. My brother Shatterhand always thinks as I do. It is just as my father, Inchu-chuna, said when we drank the blood of brotherhood together: 'The soul lives in the blood. Let the souls of these two young warriors mingle with each other, to make a single soul. What Old Shatterhand thinks, let that be Winnetou's thought; and what Winnetou wants, let that also be the will of Old Shatterhand!' That is what he said, and so it has been. His eyes looked into our hearts and he could see our future. He will see us from the eternal hunting ground and be pleased, and because his prediction was so accurate, his happiness will be increased. How!"

He fell silent, and all the rest of us observed the same silence. It was a silent but eloquent expression of the reverence that the son dedicated to his dead father. It wasn't until a few minutes later that he cleared his throat as if embarrassed about the emotion that he had shown, and continued:

"Yes, we'll find our way to Tangua's village, but not by the shortest and straightest path, which the Kiowas will take. We will ride around the edge of his territory and come from the other side. That won't be guarded, and it will let us do what we need to do more easily. The only question is when we should depart from here. What does Old Shatterhand think about this?"

"We could leave immediately. The distance is great, and the sooner we get started, the sooner we will reach our goal. But I don't advise doing this."

"Why not?"

"Because we don't know when the Kiowas will leave this area."

"Probably this very evening."

"That seems likely to me, too, but it might not happen until tomorrow. I also am not completely certain that they will decide not to attack us. In any case, we can be sure that they will find and follow our tracks if we leave before they do. Then they might notice or discover what we are planning and prevent it."

"Once again, my brother speaks my own thoughts. We must stay here until they are gone. Then we can be sure that they can't hurt us. But we can't stay at this spot the rest of the night. We have to reckon with the possibility that they will come looking for us here, and we can't let that plan succeed."

"Then we must find ourselves a spot where we can still observe this entrance to the canyon, as soon as it gets light."

"I know of such a place. Let my brothers take their horses by the bridle and follow me!"

We got our horses, which were grazing nearby, and followed him out into the prairie. After a few hundred strides we came to a large group of trees behind which we stopped again. Here, we could camp without being found by the Kiowas, even if they had designs on us tonight. And when morning broke, the opening of the canyon would be right opposite us and it would be easy to observe anything that happened there.

The night was just as cold as the preceding night. I waited until my horse lay down, and then I lay down against its body so that it kept me warm. The animal lay as quietly as if it actually knew what service it was providing me, and I only woke up once during the night.

Once it was daylight, we remained where we were and observed the canyon for more than an hour. Nothing happened. We decided it would be wise to find out where the Kiowas were. Just in case they were around, we had to be very careful and approach them secretly, but this would be a slow process, so I made a suggestion:

"They arrived at Nugget-tsil from across the prairie, and they will leave the mountain on the same path. Why should we wear ourselves out looking for them? If we ride around the mountain to the place where our scout sighted them yesterday, we will surely see whether they have left or not. Why spend a lot of time on something that can be settled quickly and with little effort?"

"My brother has found the right plan. We will do as he says."

We mounted our horses and rode in a half-circle around the western and southern sides of the mountain. This was the same route, though backwards, that the Apaches had ridden when they were looking for Santer's tracks, after he had taken flight. As we reached the prairie lying to the south of Nugget-tsil, it turned out to be as I had thought. We saw two large, clear trails, one from yesterday leading into the valley, and one from today coming out. The Kiowas had left; there was no longer any doubt. All the same, we rode back into the valley and investigated the tracks we found until we were completely satisfied that the Kiowas were no longer there.

We now followed the new trail leading away from the Nuggest-tsil. It quickly merged with the previous one in the opposite direction, and it was so obvious that it was impossible to miss. They clearly wanted us to follow them, and they had even gone to the trouble of leaving obvious tracks in places where otherwise no trail would have been evident. A slight smile played around Winnetou's lips, and he said:

"These Kiowas ought to know us well enough by now that they should be trying to hide their tracks—although we would find them anyway. But they aren't, and that should be a warning to us. They are trying to be clever, but they manage to do the opposite, because they have no brains in their heads."

He said this loudly enough that the captured Kiowa (who, of course, we were still keeping with us) could hear it. Then, turning directly toward the Kiowa, he said:

"You will probably have to die. If Sam Hawkens is not set free, or if we find out that he has been tortured, we will kill you. But if we don't, and if we set you free, tell your warriors that they are behaving like little boys who know nothing and who are laughed at when they pretend to be grownups. We have no intention of following their tracks any further."

And, true to these words, he turned from the trail (which led to the southeast) and started off straight east. We were between the headwaters of the south branch of the Cañada River and the headwaters of the north arm of the Red River, and Winnetou intended to head for the latter.

The horses of the Apaches who had pursued Santer with me had gotten fairly worn out, and that meant they couldn't travel as fast as we would have liked. In addition, the provisions we had brought along were running low. Once they were gone, we realized we would have to start hunting, and that would be a big hindrance to the plan we were undertaking. First, we would lose time just when we didn't have a single hour to spare; and second, we wouldn't be able to take the necessary precautions while hunting. We would have to leave tracks, which we had otherwise avoided.

Fortunately, we encountered a small herd of bison in the late afternoon. These were the stragglers from the great buffalo herds that had already completed their migrations to the south. We shot two cows, and got enough meat from them to last a week. We could now concentrate on the actual objectives of our ride.

Chapter 42

On the next day, we reached the north arm of the Red River, which we followed downstream. There wasn't much water in it, but the banks were green, a change from the parched buffalo grass that we had been riding across. It made good fodder for our horses.

The Salt Fork comes out of the west and thus joins the Red River from the right side. In those days, the Chief Tangua's village lay in the angle formed by the convergence of the two rivers. We were on the other, or left, bank of the Red River, and so had a good chance of not being spotted. Even so, we made a wide detour away from the river when we reached the area where it joined the Salt Fork, coming back to the Red River only after a half-day's ride. As an additional precaution, we did that ride at night, and it wasn't until dawn that we saw the river before us once again. We were now in the desired position: on the side of the village opposite the direction from which they expected us. We sought out a protected spot to recover from the night-time ride. But there was no rest for Winnetou and me. He wanted to reconnoiter, and he asked me to accompany him.

While we had been traveling downstream until this point, our scouting mission required going upstream, and on the opposite side of the river. So we had to cross over (which would not have been very difficult even if there had been more water).

Naturally, we avoided crossing in the neighborhood of our camp, since that would have made the camp easy to find if someone had encountered our tracks and decided to follow them. Instead, we rode further downstream until we came to a creek that emptied into the Red River. We directed our horses into the water and rode upstream. That got rid of our tracks. After half an hour, we left the creek and turned back out into the prairie with the thought of reaching the Red River at a spot a few miles above our camp.

This detour to hide our tracks cost us a lot of time, but it very quickly proved to have been worthwhile. While we were still on the prairie, before we had even gotten back to the river, we saw two riders who were leading at least a dozen pack animals. They weren't coming toward us, but their direction of travel meant that they would cross in front of us. One of them rode in front and the other in back of the heavily-loaded mules. We were too far away to see their faces, but judging by their clothing, we suspected that they were whites.

They saw us and stopped. We would have made ourselves quite obvious if we had just ridden by them. On the other hand, we could potentially learn something useful from them, since they were evidently coming from the Kiowa village. It was unlikely that they could hurt us, and they would have no reason to follow our tracks to see where we had come from, since their direction would bring them to the creek far to the north of the place where we had left it. So I asked Winnetou:

"Shall we go over to them?"

"Yes," he answered. "It is palefaces, traders who have been bartering with the Kiowas. But they must not know who we are."

"Good! I'm an employee of an Indian agency, and my business takes me to the Kiowas. But since I don't understand their language, I have brought you along. You are a Pawnee Indian."

"That is good. Let my brother speak with these palefaces."

We rode up to them. They had raised their rifles, as one generally does during such encounters in the Wild West, and they looked expectantly at us.

"Put away your guns, Sirs," I requested when we drew near them. "We're not planning to bite you."

"It wouldn't work out well if you did," answered one of them. "We can bite too. We didn't raise our guns out of fear, but out of habit and because you looked suspicious to us."

"Suspcious? How so?"

"Well, when two gentlemen, one white and the other red, roam around the prairie alone like that, you can figure they're rascals. On top of that, you're wearing an Indian outfit. Frankly, I'd eat my hat if you were honest."

"Thank you for being so frank! It is always nice to know how you look to others. But I can assure you that you are mistaken."

"Possible. You don't have the look of a man ready for hanging, it's true. But it don't make a dime's worth of difference to me whether you hang now or later, as long as it's your neck and not mine. Perhaps you'd do us the favor of telling us where you're coming from."

"Gladly. We have no reason to be secretive about it. We've come from False Washita."

"I see. And where are you headed?"

"Into Kiowa territory."

"Which Kiowas?"

"We have business with Chief Tangua's tribe."

"That's not far from here."

"I know. The village is between the Red River and the Salt Fork."

"Right. But if you want my advice, you'll turn around now and not let a Kiowa see you."

"Why?"

"Because getting killed by Indians is a bad habit."

"Pshaw! I haven't made a habit of it yet, and I don't plan to."

"Nobody knows the future. I meant well with my warning, and I have sound reasons for it. We've just left Tangua. He's got the praiseworthy goal of wiping out every white man that falls into his hands. Every Indian, too, except for Kiowas."

"Then he's an exceptionally well-meaning gentleman! Did he tell you this himself?"

"Yes indeed, and more than once."

"What a joker!"

"On the contrary. He was dead serious about it."

"Serious? Really? How is it, then, that I have the pleasure of seeing you so lively and in good health before me? According to him, he wants to kill all the whites, and the Indians too. I would have sworn you were whites. Am I mistaken about that?"

"Enough of the dumb jokes! He didn't touch us. He made exceptions of us, since we're good, long-time friends of his. Like you probably guessed, we're traders, and honest traders too, not those rascals that trick the Indians with lousy goods and then disappear, never to be seen again. We're welcome anywhere. The Indians need our goods, and they're smart enough not to go for the scalp of an honest man that they can rely on and that is of use to them. But they'll give you a cold reception, you can count on it."

"Probably not that cold, since I too am honest with them and can be useful to them."

"Oh yeah? So who are you and what exactly is your business with them?"

"I belong to an agency."

"An agency? Listen, that's worse yet! Now don't take me wrong, but I have to tell you frankly that it's the agents especially that the Indians have the worst things to say about because. . . because"

He was reluctant to continue, so I finished his sentence for him:

"Because they have been deceived by agents so often. That's what you meant. And I admit you're right."

"Cheers me up no end, to hear you yourself admit that you agents are rascals!" he laughed. "The Kiowas themselves were shortchanged in the worst way with the last shipments. If you're in the mood for getting tortured to death, keep on riding. They'll accommodate you in a flash."

"I could do without that, Sir. I'm telling you, the Kiowas may not receive me well, but they'll be that much happier when they hear what I have to say, what I have in mind for them. I have arranged for the error that was made to be corrected. They will be getting the rest of the delivery, and I'm going to be telling them where they can pick up the goods."

"Bless my soul, aren't you a rare bird!" he cried in astonishment. "In that case I guess they won't do anything to you after all. But why do you have an Indian with you?"

"Because I don't understand the Kiowa dialect. He's my interpreter, a Pawnee who also knows Tangua."

"Well! Then everything should be fine, and my warning was unnecessary. But I had good reason for it. Tangua is not of a mind to tolerate anything that doesn't say 'Kiowa' right on it."

"Why not?"

"He's had a string of bad experiences lately. The Apaches came into his territory and stole a hundred horses. He chased after them, of course, but they had two or three times as many warriors and he got beat. Even though he was outnumbered, he would have won except the Apaches got help from a posse of white frontiersmen. One of them shot the chief in the legs and crippled him. They call him Old Shatterhand, this fellow, and he can knock down the strongest man with one blow of his fist. But it will end badly for him."

"Badly? Do the Indians want revenge?"

"Naturally. Tangua was shot through both knees. Terrible fate for a warrior chief! He's really seething with rage, and he won't rest until this Old Shatterhand and Winnetou are in his hands."

"Winnetou? Who's that?"

"A young Apache chief who was camped about two days' ride from here with a small band of warriors. The whites are with him. A group of Kiowas rode over there to try to draw these fellows back to their village."

"Hmm. Will these whites and Apaches be dumb enough to fall into the trap?"

"Probably. Tangua is convinced of it and has had the area that they'll have to come through occupied. Those people are goners. Actually, it's no concern of mine, but since there are whites among them, I figured it would be better to get right out of there. I would have preferred to stay a few more days with Tangua, but watching whites get tortured to death—that's not my cup of tea."

"Wouldn't you have been able to help them?"

"No, not even if I wanted to. But why should I stick my perfectly good hands in somebody else's fire, where they'd just get burned? I need them myself! You might say I'm a business associate of the Kiowas, and I would never consider hurting my reputation with them by sticking up for their enemies. I was kind-hearted enough to risk a small attempt, but I had to high-tail it out of there when Tangua started yelling at me like an angry watchdog."

"I can see what you mean, but it wasn't really the right time for you to stick up for the prisoners, seeing as they hadn't even been captured yet. You should have waited."

"Oh, they already captured one, a white man from Old Shatter-hand's people. A strange fellow who just kept laughing. He didn't behave like a man facing death."

"You saw him?"

"I saw them bring him and leave him lying, tied up, on the ground for an hour. Then they took him to the island."

"To the island? That's what they use for a prison?"

"Yes. It's in the Salt Fork, a short distance from the village and heavily guarded."

"Did you speak with the prisoner?"

"A few words. I asked him if maybe I could do something for him. He gave me a friendly smile and said he would love some buttermilk, and would I be willing to ride to Cincinnati and fetch him a glass. The fellow was insane. I told him his situation was no laughing matter, and he giggled at me again and told me I shouldn't worry about him, that other people were taking care of that. I pleaded with the chief for him, but he turned me away like a misbehaving dog. Anyway, he won't be mistreated since Old Shatterhand has a Kiowa as a hostage. Only Santer tries to make what little life he has left as miserable as possible."

"Santer? That sounds like the name of a white! Have other whites besides you been staying with the Kiowas?"

"Only the one. He calls himself Santer. I find the fellow disagreeable. He arrived yesterday with the Kiowas that were trying to lure Winnetou here, and he promptly tore into the prisoner. You'll soon meet him when you get to the village."

"Do you know what he wants with Tangua?"

"No. I met him, but I didn't pay him any mind after that. He didn't seem to care for me. I could have asked the Indians, but I didn't. If it's not my business, I don't want to hear about it. That's my policy, and it's served me well."

"Is this Santer staying with the chief, or does he have his own tent?"

"He was given one, an old leather one, down by the edge of the village. Guests that they welcome get tents right next to the chief. I figure he's not on the best of terms with the chief."

"Do you happen to know the white captive's name?"

"Sam Hawkens. He's pretty well known as a frontiersman in spite of his peculiarities. It's a shame he has to die, but I can't help him. Maybe the chief will be more willing to listen to you than he was to me, if you put in a good word for him."

"I'll give it a try. Can you tell me more precisely where Santer's tent is?"

"What for? You'll see it as soon as you get there. It's the fourth or fifth one, going up-river. I don't reckon you'll like the fellow much. He's got a face for the gallows. Watch out for him! In spite of your position, you're pretty young so I figure you won't take umbrage if an old man like me gives a bit of advice. Well, I've got to be moving on. Goodbye, and here's hoping you get out of there with your skin intact."

Should I have stopped him to try to learn more? Then I would have had to tell him who we were and what we wanted, and that seemed a bit risky to me. Winnetou was of the same opinion. He rode on a bit and then said, in a subdued voice:

"That is enough. Let my brother not ask any more questions. These people, who are friends of the Kiowas, would take notice."

"I agree. We've learned enough. We know fairly precisely where Hawkens is and where Santer is living, and we'll find both of them. How far shall we ride now?"

"Far enough to be out of the sight of these traders. Then we'll return to our camp. It was very lucky that we met them. Trying to learn what we learned from them by spying would have been very dangerous. Now we know what we are up against, and tonight we'll spy on the Kiowa village."

The two traders gradually disappeared from view. They had to ride slowly because they had so many pack animals. I learned later how fateful that would be for them. Likewise, I learned that they had exchanged a variety of pelts with the Kiowas. The one that had spoken with us was the actual trader. The other was his helper. Now that they were out of sight, we turned around and headed back as we had come, trying our best to hide our tracks.

Dick Stone and Will Parker were well satisfied with the success of our reconnoitering. They were especially pleased that Sam was doing well under the circumstances, and that he still had his irrepressible good spirits. They asked to come along on our spying mission, but Winnetou rejected this idea, explaining:

"Let my two white brothers stay here for today. We would have great difficulty in freeing Sam Hawkins on this trip. We probably can't do it until tomorrow, and you will be with us then."

Our camp was well-hidden under the circumstances, but we were in the middle of enemy territory, and the Kiowas might accidentally stumble on our camp by the river. So Winnetou suggested:

"I know of an island in the middle of the river, a little farther downstream. It has bushes and trees that will hide us. No one will come there. Let my brothers travel with me to this island."

We left our camp and rode downstream until we saw the island. The water was deep here and the bank was steep, but we made it across safely with our horses. Winnetou was right: the island was large, and there was enough foliage to hide us and our horses completely.

Chapter 43

I chose a spot between the bushes, lay down, and, figuring I wouldn't get to sleep that night, took a nap. Not that there wouldn't be time or opportunity for it, but I anticipated that I would be taking a swim, and sleep would be impossible after that.

Sam Hawkens was held prisoner on a small island, and I wanted to check it out. That meant going through the water. And before that, as we left camp, Winnetou and I would have to swim from our island to the riverbank, which meant we would get completely soaked. It was the middle of December, so the water was cold. Nobody would be able to sleep in the cold in wet clothes.

Once it was dark, we were wakened (Winnetou had been sleeping as well). It was time to head for the village. We removed all but the most essential clothes, and we left behind everything we had in our pockets. The only weapons we took were knives. Then we jumped into the water and swam to the right-hand bank, the side where we would find the mouth of the Salt Fork. We followed the river upstream, and in less than an hour we came to the place where the Salt Fork joined the Red River, and following the former a few hundred paces, we saw the fires of the village. It was on the left bank of the Salt Fork, whereas we were on the right bank. We would have to cross over.

We didn't do this immediately. First, we moved slowly up along the whole length of the village, but on the opposite side. By the word "village" I don't mean a group of solid buildings with gardens and fields. There was no hint of a garden or a field, and the houses were, at this time of year, tents of heavy leather. (In summer, the Indians lived in cloth tents.)

There was a fire in front of almost every tent. The residents were sitting by their fires, warming themselves and preparing their evening meal. The largest tent was roughly in the middle of the village. The entrance was decorated with spears on which eagle feathers and strangely shaped medicine bags were hung. Around its fire sat Tangua, the chief, with a young Indian, perhaps eighteen years old, and two boys who might have been fourteen and twelve.

"These three are his sons," said Winnetou. "The oldest is his favorite and will become a bold warrior. He runs so fast that he has been given the name Pida, which means stag."

We saw women going busily back and forth, but among the Indians, wives and daughters are not allowed to eat with the husbands and sons. They eat later and must be satisfied with what is left over, even though they perform all the work, including the hardest tasks.

I looked for the island. The clouded sky was completely black, with not a star to be seen. But by the light of the fires, we could see three islands which lay close to each other, near the river bank.

"Which one do you think Sam is on?" I asked.

"If my brother wants to know this, let him think about what the trader said," answered Winnetou.

"That the island was close to the bank? The first and third are closer to us, so it would have to be the middle one."

"Probably. And just to the right is the lower end of the village, where Santer lives in the fourth or fifth tent. Let's split up. I have my eye on the murderer of my father and my sister, and I will scout his tent. Sam is more your companion than mine, so you will look for him."

"And where will we meet afterwards?"

"Here, at the same place where we split up."

"If nothing exceptional happens, we can do that. But if one of us happens to be discovered, there will be a great uproar. In that case, we'll need another place, farther from the village."

"Our tasks are not easy. Yours is even harder than mine, since you'll have to swim to the island, and the guards will easily be able to see you. So you're more likely to be discovered than me. If they catch you, I will rush to your aid. But if you get free, go back to our island. But take the long way—we don't want them to know what direction you actually went."

"But they will find the tracks in the morning!"

"No, they won't. Rain is coming, and it will erase the tracks."

"Good! And if you run into trouble, I'll get you out of it."

"That won't happen, unless I run into bad luck. Look over there! No fire is burning in front of the fifth tent. That must be Santer's. I don't see him anywhere, so he's probably in there, asleep. It won't be hard to find out how things stand with him."

With these words he left, heading off downstream a bit, planning to swim across at a distance from the village and then to sneak back to the tents on the far side.

I had to proceed differently. My goal was illuminated by the firelight, which was unfortunate. I couldn't let myself be seen on the surface of the water, so I would have to reach the island by swimming underwater. But that would be very difficult to do directly. I could probably swim that far under water, but what if I surfaced right in front of a guard? No, first I had to get to the neighboring upstream island, which was apparently unoccupied. This island was about twenty yards from the second, middle island (my actual goal). I would probably be able to see what was happening on the second island from the first one.

I went a bit upstream and observed the upstream island as well as I could. There was not the slightest sign of movement, so probably no one was there. I let myself slowly into the water, dove under, and swam across. I arrived without incident. At first, I raised only my head out of the water, as far as my mouth, to catch my breath. I was at the upstream end of the first island, and I quickly saw that there was a better way then my original plan to accomplish my task.

The island I was next to was about twenty yards from the riverbank, where a row of perhaps twenty canoes were tied up. These boats could provide me with excellent cover. So I dived underwater again and swam toward the first canoe, from there to the second, the third, and so on, until I was hiding by the sixth canoe. It was so near the middle island that I could easily observe it.

It was nearer the land than the other two islands and was covered with low bushes over which two trees towered. I couldn't see any sign of the prisoner or his guards. I was just about to dive back underwater and swim over, when I heard a loud noise up on the riverbank. I looked up and saw an Indian coming down. It was Pida, the "stag," the chief's son. Fortunately, he came diagonally down the bank toward a canoe that was moored farther downstream, so he didn't see me. He jumped into the boat, cast off, and paddled to the middle island. I wouldn't be able to go there just yet. I waited.

I soon heard voices there, and recognized Sam's voice. I had to hear what they were saying, so I swam under water to the next canoe. There were so many that every independent villager must have had his own. When I surfaced, hidden behind this canoe, I could hear the son of the chief saying:

"Tangua, my father, wants to know it!"

"I have no intention of revealing it!" answered Sam.

"Then you will have to endure ten times the pain!"

"Don't make me laugh! Sam Hawkens and pain, hee-hee-hee! Your father wanted to have me tortured once before, with the Apaches on the Rio Pecos. And what was the result? Can you tell me that?"

"Old Shatterhand, the dog, made him a cripple!"

"Right. Something along those lines will happen here. You won't be able to harm me."

"If you are serious about what you say, then craziness has entered your head. We have caught you and you can't get away. You're tied up so that you can't move a muscle."

"Yes, I have good old Santer to thank for this bondage, and it's fine with me!"

"You're in pain, I know it, but you won't admit it. Besides the thongs that bind you, you are tied to the tree and four warriors are sitting here night and day, watching you. How could you escape?"

"That's my business, young man! I'm still enjoying it here right now. But wait until I feel like leaving. You won't be able to stop me."

"We will free you if you tell us where he is going."

"But I won't tell. I know what's happening. My good friend Santer was kind enough to tell me the story, to get me worried, but he didn't succeed. You rode to Nugget-tsil to capture Old Shatterhand and Winnetou. Laughable! To catch Old Shatterhand, my pupil, hee-hee-hee!"

"But you, his teacher, let yourself be caught?"

"Just to pass the time. I thought I'd like to spend a few days with you, since I'm so fond of you, if I'm not mistaken. So you made the trip to Nugget-tsil in vain, and now you hope that Winnetou, Old Shatterhand, and the Apaches will ride after you. I never heard of such a crazy idea! They didn't come, and now you don't know where they're hiding. So you want me to tell you where Old Shatterhand has ridden off to. You think I must know. And I must tell you frankly, I do know."

"Well, where?"

"Pshaw! You will soon find out without having to learn it from me, because . . ."

He was interrupted by a loud cry. Unfortunately, I couldn't understand the words, but it was the sort of cry that might have meant "Stop him, stop him!" And the name "Winnetou" was also shouted.

"Listen, there they are!" Hawkens cried with glee. "Where Winnetou is, there you'll find Old Shatterhand too. They're here! They're here!"

The yelling doubled in the village, and I heard the Indians running. They had seen Winnetou, although they hadn't caught him yet. That threw a monkey wrench into my plans. I saw the son of the chief stand up on the island and look over to the river bank. Then he jumped into his canoe and called to the guards:

"Take you guns in your hands and kill this paleface immediately if anyone comes to try to free him."

Then he paddled to the shore. I had wanted to rescue Sam today if there were any possibility of it, but now it was out of the question. Even if I had wanted to risk taking on the four Indians armed only with a knife, the result would have been instant death. They would have obeyed Pida and killed Hawkens.

But then another thought occurred to me, while Pida was still paddling over to the shore. He was the favorite son of the chief. If I could take him hostage, I could swap him for Sam. Admittedly, it was a crazy idea, but at that moment I wasn't worrying about that. I only wanted to capture the young chief without anyone seeing it.

I saw at a glance that the situation was favorable. Winnetou had been heading toward the Red River, off to the left, while our camp on the island was to the right, down-river. This was clever of him, since it led his pursuers away. A great cry could be heard from the direction he had gone, and the guards had turned in that direction. They were facing almost completely away from me, and no one else was nearby.

The chief's son reached the bank in his canoe, and began to tie it up. He was bent over. I surfaced near him, laid him out cold with a single blow, threw him in his canoe, jumped into it myself, and paddled upstream along the bank. The crazy scheme had worked. Up in the village, there was no one to take notice of me, and the guards were still looking the other way.

I put all my strength into the effort of getting away from the village as quickly as possible. Then, once the firelight no longer reached me, I paddled to the opposite bank of the Salt Fork, where I lay the unconscious Indian in the grass. Then I cut loose the leather thong that had been used to tie up the canoe, and bound the prisoner with that. I gave the canoe a push so that it floated out into the river. I didn't want its presence to give me away. Once I had bound Pida's arms fast to his body, I lifted him to my shoulders and made my way back to our island.

That was a tough job, not so much because my burden was too heavy, but because he was not willing to walk on his own, once he had come to. I frequently had to threaten him with my knife. Of course, I had taken his weapons.

"Who are you?" he finally growled. "A mangy paleface that my father, Tangua, will catch and destroy tomorrow!"

"Your father won't catch me. He can't even walk," I answered.

"But he has many warriors that he will send out after me!"

"Your warriors make me laugh. The same thing that happened to your father could easily happen to them, if they attempt to fight me."

"Ugh! You have fought with him?"

"Yes."

"Where?"

"Where he fell when my bullet went through both his legs."

"Ugh, ugh! So you are Old Shatterhand?" he asked, in shock.

"How can you ask such a thing? I knocked you out with my fist. Who else but Winnetou and Old Shatterhand would risk going right into your village and carrying away the chief's son?"

"Ugh! Then I must die, but you will not hear a sound of pain from my mouth."

"We won't kill you. We're not murderers like you are. If your father turns over the two palefaces to us, we will let you go."

"Santer and Hawkens?"

"Yes."

"He will give them to you. His son is worth more than ten Hawkens to him, and he doesn't care about Santer at all."

After this, he no longer resisted going with me. Winnetou's prediction proved correct, for it began to rain—so hard, in fact, that I couldn't find the spot on the bank that was opposite our island. So I sought out a protective tree where we could wait for either the end of the rain or the dawn.

That wait was a test of my patience. The rain kept falling and it seemed that the morning would never come. My only consolation was that I couldn't get any wetter than I already was—I was wet through and through—but it was so cold I periodically had to get up and do calisthenics to keep myself warm. I felt sorry for the young chief's son, who had to lie so still, but he was much more used to the cold than I was back then.

Finally, both my wishes were granted at the same time: the rain stopped, and the sky began to get gray. But a thick, heavy fog lay everywhere. Still, I didn't have much trouble finding the right spot on the river bank. I called out a loud "hello!"

"Hello!" Winnetou's voice answered immediately. "Is that my brother Shatterhand?"

"Yes."

"Come across! Why do you call out first? That is dangerous."

"I have a prisoner. Send over a good swimmer and some leather thongs!"

"I'll come myself."

How happy I was that he had not fallen into the hands of the Kiowas! Soon I saw his head appear between the fog and the water. As he came up the bank and saw the Indian, he said in astonishment:

"Ugh! Pida, the son of the chief! Where did my brother capture him?"

"On the river bank, not far from Hawkens' island."

"Did you see Hawkens?"

"No, but I heard him talking with this 'stag'. I would have spoken with him, and freed him too, but you were discovered and I had to leave."

"It was bad luck, which I couldn't avoid. I had almost reached Santer's tent when several Kiowas came along. I couldn't jump up, so I rolled to the side. They stopped and spoke to each other, and then one of them noticed me and walked over to me. Then I had to get up and run away. They saw me by the firelight and recognized me. I headed upstream instead of downstream, to lead them away from our camp. Then I swam across the river and got away. But I didn't see Santer."

"You'll see him soon. This young warrior has agreed to be exchanged for Santer and Sam Hawkens, and I am sure that the chief will agree to it."

"Ugh! That is good, very good! My brother Shatterhand was brave, maybe even foolhardy, in catching Pida; but it was the best thing that could possibly happen."

When I said that he would soon see Santer, I didn't realize how soon it would actually be. We tied the prisoner between us, so that his shoulders were bound to ours and his head was kept above water even though his arms were tied. He was able to help us swim with his feet. Pida offered no resistance. Indeed, once we were no longer touching the bottom, he kicked powerfully with his feet, in rhythm with us.

The fog lay so thick on the water that we couldn't see more than thirty feet ahead. But in the fog you can hear even better than usual. We weren't far from the bank when Winnetou said:

"Quiet! I heard something."

"What?"

"The sound of paddles dipping in the water, upriver from us."

"We'll stop here, then."

"Yes, listen!"

We made only the very minimum movements to keep our heads above water, and made no noise at all. Yes, Winnetou was right. Someone was paddling down-stream. He must be in a hurry, because in spite of the strong current here, he was paddling in addition.

He came rapidly closer. Should we let ourselves be seen or not? It could be an enemy spy. Perhaps it would be advantageous for us to know who it was. I gave Winnetou a questioning look. He understood and answered quietly:

"We'll stay here. I want to know who it is. He probably won't see us if we lie quietly in the water."

It was likely that we would not be noticed, since we had only our heads out of the water. So we did not swim back to the shore. Pida was as tense as we were. He could have called for help, but he didn't, knowing that his freedom was secure in any case.

Now the paddling was very close, and an Indian canoe emerged from the fog. Who sat in it? We had planned to stay quiet, but when Winnetou saw the man, he cried out:

"Santer! He's getting away!"

My friend, otherwise so quiet, was so incensed that he struck out powerfully with his arms and legs, trying to get to the canoe. But he was tied together with Pida and me, and that held him back.

"Ugh! I must get free, I must have him!" he cried, drawing his knife and cutting the thongs that tied Pida to him.

Of course Santer heard Winnetou's cry. He quickly looked over and saw us.

"What the devil?" he cried in shock. "Here are these. . ."

He stopped. An expression of malicious pleasure replaced the terror on his face. He recognized our situation, tossed the paddle into the canoe, grabbed his rifle, aimed it at us, and cried:

"Your last water game, you dogs!"

Fortunately, he pulled the trigger at exactly the moment that Winnetou freed himself from us and pushed off powerfully toward the boat. In doing so, he knocked Pida and me away from the spot where Santer had been aiming, and his bullet missed.

What I saw Winnetou do next was more like skimming over the water than swimming through it. He had taken his knife between his teeth and was heading for the enemy with huge surges, almost like a flat stone that one skips across the water. Santer still had his second barrel loaded. He pointed it at the Apache and cried out scornfully:

"Come on, you damn redskin! I'll send you to the devil!"

He thought that he had only to pull the trigger to make an easy shot of it. But he had misjudged Winnetou, who suddenly dove under water in order to come at the canoe from underneath and capsize it. If he could manage this, the rifle would be of no help to Santer, who would be thrown into the water where the two would have to fight it out hand-to-hand. The agile Apache would undoubtedly win if it came to that. Santer saw this, laid down his gun, and picked up his paddle. It was just in time: no sooner had he gotten the canoe moving again than Winnetou surfaced at the spot where he had just been. Santer gave up the attack and, with several powerful strokes of the paddle, moved himself out of the range of his angry enemy, crying:

"Thought you had me, dog? I'll keep my bullet for our next meeting!"

Winnetou swam with all his strength, but it was futile—he couldn't catch up with Santer. No swimmer, not even the world champion, can catch a canoe that is being paddled downstream in fast water.

Chapter 44

This whole episode took place in the space of barely half a minute. And yet, even as Santer disappeared into the fog, several Apaches had already jumped into the water to come to our aid. I called them to me, to help me get Pida back to the island. Once this had been done and I cut the Kiowa loose from me, Winnetou commanded his people:

"Let my red brothers get ready quickly! Santer just went down the river in a canoe, and we must follow him."

He was more agitated than I had ever seen him before.

"Yes, we must follow him," I agreed. "But what will happen to Sam Hawkens and our two prisoners?"

"I leave them to you," he answered.

"So I should stay here?"

"Yes. I must have Santer, the murderer of my father and sister. But your duty is to free Sam Hawkens, your comrade. We must part."

"For how long?"

He thought for only a moment and then said:

"I do not know when we will see each other again. That which men wish for and want is often not what the great spirit grants. I thought I would stay longer with my brother Shatterhand. But Manitou has suddenly spoken against it. His plan is different. Do you know why Santer left?"

"I can imagine. We weren't caught in the trap they set for us, and last night they saw you. So they know that we're here and that we won't rest until we capture Santer and free Hawkens. Santer got scared and took off."

"Yes. But it could also be another way. We appear and the chief's son disappears. Naturally the Kiowas think there is a connection. They assume he has fallen into our hands. Tangua is furious about this and he has taken out his anger on Santer, who is at fault for the whole matter, and chased him away."

"That is also likely. Santer must have heard that the Kiowas were not granting him protection any more."

"And why did he choose to leave by water and not riding his horse?"

"Because he feared us. He was worried that he would encounter us. And even if he didn't, we could have discovered his tracks and followed them. So he probably traded his horse for a canoe, and took off in it. Of course he had no idea that we were here on this island, and that we would learn of his escape precisely because he was trying to be so careful to avoid us. Now that he has seen us, he knows that we will follow him, and he'll paddle hard to get away as quickly as possible. Do you think you can catch up with him on horseback?"

"It is hard, but possible. We would have to cut across the turnings of the river."

"But that won't work. My brother Winnetou must see that that would be a mistake."

"Why?"

"Because he may well decide to leave the river and continue on land. That would give him a better chance of avoiding you. And since you don't know which side of the river he might decide to land on, you will have to divide into two groups and follow both banks of the Red River."

"My brother is right. We will do as he says."

"You will have to be very observant so that you don't miss the spot where he lands, and that will take time. And you won't be able to cut across the bends in the river. An inward bend on one bank is an outward bend on the other, and while one group cuts across a bend, the other will have an extra long distance to cover. You won't be able to keep the two groups together unless both follow along the bank."

"It is as my brother says. We are forced to follow the bends of the river. Now we cannot afford to waste a minute."

"How I would love to ride with you! But it really is my duty to help Sam Hawkens. I cannot abandon him."

"I would never want you to do anything that conflicts with your duty. You cannot. But if the Great Spirit wills it, we will see each other in a few days."

"Where?"

"When you ride from here, go toward the place where this river comes together with the Rio Bosco de Natchitoches. There, where the combined river begins, on the left bank, you will find one of my warriors, if a meeting is possible."

"And if I don't find a warrior there?"

"Then I am still following Santer and I don't know where he is going, so I can't tell you where to meet me. Then, you should travel with your three companions to St. Louis and the palefaces that want to build the road for the fire-horse. But I entreat you to return to us as soon as the good Manitou allows you to. You are always welcome in the pueblo on the Rio Pecos. And if I am not there, you will learn where to find me."

During our conversation, his Apaches had gotten ready to ride. He shook hands with Dick Stone and Will Parker and took his leave from them. Then he turned again to me:

"My brother knows how happy our hearts were as we began our ride from the Rio Pecos. But it brought death to Inchu-chuna and Nsho-chi. When you finally return to us, you will not hear the voice of the most beautiful daughter of the Apaches, who has gone to the land of the departed instead of the cities of the palefaces. Now, revenge takes me away from you, but love will bring you back to us again. I want very much to be able to report back to you at the mouth of the Rio Bosco, but if that is not possible please do not stay too long in the cities of the East. Come back to visit me very soon. You know who you must replace for me. Will you promise to return soon, my dear brother Charlie?"

"I promise. My heart goes with you, my dear brother Winnetou. You know what I promised Kleki-petra as he died. I will keep my promise."

"Then may the good Manitou lead your feet and protect you on all your travels. How!"

He embraced and kissed me, gave his people a brief command, mounted his horse, and rode it into the river. The effect of his command was that his Apaches split into two groups. One group followed Winnetou into the water toward the left bank, the other headed for the right bank. I watched Winnetou until he disappeared into the fog. It was as if a part of me was leaving, and I knew the departure was hard on him as well.

Stone and Parker recognized what a melancholy mood I was in. Stone said, in his steady, true-hearted way:

"Don't take it so hard, Sir! We will encounter the Apaches again soon. We'll be riding after them just as soon as Sam is free. So let's not waste any time; let's swap our prisoners. How do you think we should go about it?"

"You give me your opinion first, Dick. You have more experience than I."

He stroked his beard, flattered by this praise, and said:

"I figure it's easiest just to send the Kiowa prisoner back to Tangua right now. He can tell Tangua where his son can be found and under what conditions he will be freed. What do you say, Will?"

"Hmm," Parker grumbled. "That's about the dumbest idea you've ever had."

"Dumb? Me? Can you beat that? Why do you think it's dumb?"

"If we say where we are, Tangua will send his people here and they'll take Pida away without giving us Sam in exchange. I'd do it differently."

"How would you do it?"

"We head out into the prairie a good piece and find a stretch where we can see who's coming. Then we send the Kiowa prisoner back to the village. We specify the condition that two warriors, and no more, can bring Sam to us, and then we will turn Pida over to them. If we see more than two coming, we'll see them at a distance and we can get out of there. Don't you think that would be the best, Sir?"

"I'd rather be safer and not send a messenger," I answered.

"No messenger? But how will Tangua find out that his son. . ."

"Oh, he'll find out all right," I interrupted.

"From whom?"

"From me."

"From you? Are you thinking of going to the village yourself?"

"Yes."

"Forget it, Sir! That's too dangerous. They would take you prisoner immediately."

"I don't think so."

"Oh, absolutely!"

"Then Pida would be a goner. I'm not interested in sending one of our two prisoners as a messenger. That way, we lose a hostage."

"You're certainly right about that. But why do you want to go to the village? Let me do it!"

"I have no doubt that you are brave enough, but I think it's better if I speak with Tangua myself."

"But just think how much he hates you! If I go talk to him, he is more likely to accept our conditions than if he's upset by having to see you."

"That's exactly why I want to go myself. I want him to get mad. I want him to be furious that I would dare to come to him without him being able to harm me. If I send someone else, he may think I fear him, and I don't want any suspicions of that kind."

"Well then, do as you like, Sir! What do we do in the meantime? Stay here on the island? Or look for another, better spot?"

"There is no better spot."

"OK. But woe to our prisoners if anything happens to you in the village! We'll show no mercy. When do you plan to go?"

"Tonight."

"Not until then? Isn't that a bit late? If all goes well, we could work out the exchange by noon, and then ride after Winnetou."

"And the Kiowas would follow us en masse and wipe us out!"

"You think so?"

"Yes. Tangua will give us Sam in order to get his son back. But once his son is safe, he will put all his energy into getting his revenge on us. That's why the exchange has to be done at night. We'll ride out during the night, when they can't follow us, and get a good head start. Besides, waiting until evening is better because Tangua's anxiety about his son will grow the whole time. That will make him more compliant."

"That's true. But what if they discover us sooner, Mr. Shatterhand?"

"That's not so terrible either."

"They'll be searching for Pida, and they might come to the island."

"Not to the island, but if they come along the bank, we'll see them. They will find Winnetou's tracks, and they'll think we've gone off and taken Pida with us. And that will make Tangua even more anxious. Listen!"

We could hear voices ringing out. The fog was beginning to lift, and we could see the river bank. Several Kiowas were standing there, exchanging their views about the hoofprints they had just discovered. They quickly disappeared without having even glanced across at the island.

"They're gone, and it looks like they are in a hurry," Dick Stone said.

"Most likely they're headed back to the village, to report to Tangua about the tracks. He will send out a posse of riders right away to follow the tracks."

This prediction proved true. In less than two hours, a group of riders came down the riverbank, found the tracks, and set off along them. They would not catch up with Winnetou, since he would be riding at least as fast as they were.

We three had obviously been speaking quietly amongst ourselves. The prisoners had no need to hear what we were saying. They also had not seen what happened on the bank, since they were lying in the grass behind the bushes, tied up.

Before noon, the sun did us the favor of shining brightly on us. It not only dried out our camp, but us as well, and it increased the comfort in which we rested as we waited for the evening.

Shortly after noon, we saw an object floating toward us. It caught on one of the branches that hung into the water from the island. It was a canoe, with a paddle lying in it. The thongs with which the owner had tied it up had been cut. It had to be the canoe in which I had carried Pida off. It had drifted out of the Salt Fork and into the Red River. It must have gotten stuck somewhere along the way, accounting for the time it had taken to reach us. I was delighted to see it, and I pulled it up onto the island so that I would be able to use it in the evening. I would not have to get soaking wet again by swimming across to the shore.

As soon as it was dark, I shoved the canoe back in the water and paddled upstream. Stone and Parker had sent me off with their best wishes. I told them not to begin worrying about me unless I wasn't back by morning.

I made slow progress against the current. It took about an hour paddling up the Red River until I could finally turn up into the Salt Fork. Once I got fairly near the village, I paddled to the shore and tied the canoe to a tree, using a rope I had brought along.

Once again, I could see the fires burning, the men sitting, and the women going back and forth attending to them. I had thought the village would be heavily guarded, but I found that was not the case. The Kiowas had found the tracks of the Apaches and had sent the warriors to follow them. They assumed they were safe.

Tangua was once again seated in front of his tent, but had only the two younger sons with him. His head was bowed, and he stared glumly into the fire. I had landed on the left bank of the Salt Fork, where the village was. I crept off at a right angle to the river, then along behind the tents until I was right behind the chief's tent. I was lucky that there was no one in the area who might have discovered me. I got down on the ground and slid up to the back of the tent. From there, I could hear the chief's deep, monotonous song of mourning. In this Indian manner he lamented the loss of his favorite son. Now I crept around the tent, stood up, and suddenly appeared before the chief.

"Why does Tangua sing a sorrowful song?" I asked. "A bold warrior should have nothing to do with sounds of sorrow. Wailing is only for old squaws."

It is impossible to describe how stunned he was by my sudden appearance. He tried to speak, but no words came. He wanted to jump up, but thanks to his damaged knees, he had to remain seated. He stared at me as if I were a ghost, his eyes wide. Finally he stammered:

"Old. . . Old . . . Shat. . . Shat. . ugh, ugh, ugh! Where did you . . . You are still. . . Not gone?"

"As you see, I am still here. I have come because I want to talk with you."

"Old Shatterhand!" he finally managed to utter my name. When his two sons heard it, they ran into the tent.

"Old Shatterhand!" he repeated, still in a state of shock. Then his expression gradually turned to one of rage and he cried out some kind of command toward the other tents. I didn't understand it, since it was in his dialect, but it contained my name.

In an instant, a howl of rage arose in the village. The earth practically shook under my feet as all the warriors that remained came running with their weapons raised. I pulled out my knife and cried into Tangua's ear:

"Do you want Pida to die? He sent me to you!"

He understood me in spite of the howling of his people, and he raised his hand. The gesture was enough to bring quiet, but the Kiowas surrounded us. I could see from the looks they were giving me that it they had their way, I would not leave there alive. I sat down next to Tangua, looked calmly into his face (which bore an expression of astonishment for my audacity), and said:

"Tangua and I are deadly enemies. It is not my fault, but I accept it. It is all the same to me if my friends and I destroy one of his warriors or his whole tribe. If he wants to know whether I fear him, let him consider that I have appeared in the middle of his village to speak with him. Let's make it short: Pida is in our hands and will be hung from a tree if I do not return by a certain time."

No word, no movement of the Indians standing nearby (many of whom I recognized) revealed the impression made by my words. The chief's eyes glared angrily as he considered that he could not harm me without jeopardizing his son's life. Between his grinding teeth, he spit out the question:

"How did he fall into your hands?"

"Yesterday I was over there on the island when he spoke with Sam Hawkens, and I knocked him out and carried him away."

"Ugh! Old Shatterhand is the favorite of the evil spirits, who have protected him once again. Where is my son?"

"In a safe place that I will not tell you about yet. Later, he will be able to tell you about it himself. As you can tell from these words, I do not intend to kill Pida. We have another Kiowa with us as well, a prisoner that I pulled out of a thorn bush where he was spying on us. You will get him and your son back, if you give us San Hawkens."

"Ugh! You shall have him. First, you bring Pida and the other Kiowa warrior."

"Bring them? Not a chance! I know Tangua, and I know that he cannot be trusted. I am giving you two for one. That's an extraordinarily cheap and kind deal for you. For that, I must demand that you refrain from any hint of deceiving me."

"First prove to me that you really have Pida!"

"Prove? What are you thinking? I say it, and so it is true. Old

Shatterhand is no Tangua. Let me see Sam Hawkens! I doubt he's still down on the island, since you probably don't think it's safe any more. I want to speak with him."

"What do you want to talk about?"

"I want to hear from his own mouth how he has been treated. Then we'll work out the rest."

"First I must discuss it with my council of elders. Go over to the next tent and wait. We will tell you what we have decided."

"Good. But make it quick. If you delay me and I don't get back in time, Pida will hang."

Being hung is the most humiliating death for an Indian. You can imagine how furious Tangua was! I went to the next tent and sat down, still surrounded by warriors. Tangua called his councilors together and talked with them. In every glance directed at me, there was a fire that was kept from being venomous only out of concern for Pida. I noticed as well that my fearlessness was making a general impression.

After a while, the chief sent an Indian off. He disappeared into a tent and brought out Sam. I jumped up and went over to him. When he saw me, he cried:

"Hooray! Old Shatterhand! I always said you would come! You want your old Sam back?"

He held out his bound hands in my direction, to greet me.

"Yes," I answered, "the greenhorn has come to testify that you are a great master of spying, as you have now proved. Whatever anyone says to you, you always head the wrong way!"

"You can make your suggestions later, my most beloved Sir! But now tell me if my Mary is nearby."

"We have her with us."

"And my Liddy?"

"That old fire iron? We rescued that too."

"Then everything is fine, just fine, if I'm not mistaken. Come on, let's get out of here! I'm starting to get bored."

"Patience, patience, Sam! You behave as if there were nothing to it, as if it were child's play to come here and retrieve you."

"And child's play is exactly what it is, but only for you. I'd like to know if there's anything you can't do. You'd bring me back down from the moon if I happened to wander up there, hee-hee-hee!"

"Keep on laughing! It tells me that things weren't too awful for you."

"Awful? Where did you get that idea? It was fine, exceptionally good! Every Kiowa loved me like his own child. I was practically insane with all the caresses, hugs, and kisses. They fed me like a new bride, and if I wanted to sleep I didn't even have to lie down—I was always lying on my back anyway."

"They took your belongings?"

"Indeed. My pockets are empty."

"You'll get it all back, if it's still here. The council seems to have ended."

I told the chief that I couldn't wait any longer, if he wanted to see his son alive. Now, a short but energetic new set of negotiations began. I emerged the victor, since I was not willing to give an inch and the chief was worried about his son. The final agreement was that four armed warriors in two canoes would accompany Sam and me and would take possession of our two prisoners. I warned that Pida would die if more Kiowas secretly followed us.

It was really asking a lot for them to give Sam to me. I could certainly have put one over on the four Indians who accompanied us. But they believed what I said, and subsequently they always believed the words of Old Shatterhand. I didn't tell them where we would be paddling to. As soon as Sam was untied, he raised his short arms into the air and cried:

"Free, free again! I will never forget this, Sir! And never again will I run to the left when your blessed legs are running to the right."

As we prepared to leave, angry murmurs arose here and there. The Indians were mightily annoyed to have to let both the prisoner and me go, and Tangua hissed at me as we left:

"You are safe until my son gets back, but then the whole tribe will be after you, and they will hunt you down. We will find your tracks and we will capture you, even if you ride through the air!"

I didn't find it necessary to respond to this caustic threat. I led Sam and the four Kiowas to the river where we launched our three canoes, Sam with me and two Kiowas in each of the others. From the moment we left the bank, a great howling followed us until we were so far away that we couldn't hear it anymore.

As I paddled, I brought Sam up to date on the events that had occurred while he was a captive. He was disappointed that Winnetou had left, but he didn't complain too much about it because he had feared the reproaches of the Apaches.

In spite of the darkness, we landed safely on the island and were received with jubilation by Dick Stone and Will Parker. They hadn't realized until I had departed how big a risk I was taking.

We delivered the two captives, who said not a word of farewell to us, to the four warriors, and then we waited until we could no longer here the sound of their paddles. Then, we mounted our horses and struck out for the left bank of the river. We had to cover a lot of distance during the night, and it was good that Sam knew the area fairly well. He climbed into his Mary's saddle, raised his fist threateningly in the direction we had come, and said:

"Now they're putting their heads together back there, planning how they'll get their hands on us. They better think again! Sam Hawkens is not going to be dumb enough to get stuck in that kind of a hole once more, and have to get rescued by a greenhorn. No Kiowa will catch me again, if I'm not mistaken!"

THE END

Translator's note

As translating tasks go, translating Karl May's *Winnetou* is probably easier than most. The story is straightforward and clear, and there aren't a lot of subtle hidden meanings in it. In other words, many of the problems that give translators fits don't arise in this book.

On the other hand, *Winnetou* does present plenty of translation challenges. In resolving them, I have tried to keep two principles in mind. I have tried to deal with problems in a way (1) that Karl May would have approved of, and (2) that will not cause problems for the reader.

I imagine there are a few readers who are interested in translation, or who wonder how this translation differs from the German original. If you are one of them, read on. A few of the main translation and editing problems, and my solutions for them, are described below.

A tricky problem for the translator/editor appears on the very first page of the book, as the narrator is describing the meaning of the word "greenhorn." The main character's evolution from a "greenhorn" to an exceptionally competent "frontiersman" is a major theme of the book. The English word "greenhorn" (and never a German equivalent) is used throughout the German book. In my experience, far more Germans than Americans are familiar with the English word "greenhorn," and that is entirely due to the remarkable impact *Winnetou* has had on Germans for more than a century. So "greenhorn" is a key term in the book.

The problem comes when the narrator describes the origin of the word "greenhorn." He says it refers to the "feelers" with which a newcomer must explore new surroundings:

...and "horn" means "feeler." Thus, a greenhorn is a person who is still green (that is, inexperienced) and who has to carefully extend his feelers if he wants to avoid being laughed at.

Although Karl May researched the background for his books carefully, he made a mistake in this case. In reality, the word "greenhorn" comes from the appearance of the immature horns of a calf, not from "feelers." People who live in the cattle-breeding parts of the US still know this, and upon encountering the "feelers" passage on the very first page they might doubt whether the book they had just picked up was worth continuing to read. So, after a great deal of consideration, I decided not to translate the passage as written. I changed it to read:

Like a calf whose horns are still immature, he has a lot to learn before his comrades take him seriously.

This is the only place in the book where I have inserted a sentence of my own as a substitute for what was in the original. In doing so, I went beyond my role as a translator and even beyond what some would deem appropriate for an editor. I did it reluctantly, but I feel the change was necessary—and I think Karl May would have approved.

Along with the English word "greenhorn," the German word "Westmann" is a key term in the *Winnetou* saga, and it is not immediately obvious how "Westmann" should be translated into English. Karl May uses this word a lot (perhaps he even invented it), and it refers to a specific sort of rough-and-ready person with excellent survival skills who roamed the American West. The literal meaning is "westerner" (and this has been used in some translations) but I think that "westerner" fails to convey the "Wild West" sense that "Westmann" carries for May. After all, if you lived in a relatively civilized place like San Francisco back then, you would have called yourself a "westerner," but you might not have any of the traits that May thought a

"Westmann" should have.

"Scout" (which is also found in some translations) comes closer to conveying the meaning of "Westmann," but describes only one of the jobs a "Westmann" might do. Although the *Winnetou* books are sometimes described as "cowboy and Indian stories", the word "cowboy" doesn't work at all for "Westmann," because herding cattle is almost never part of the action in the *Winnetou* stories. "Mountain man" has the right sort of adventurous feeling, but it doesn't work as a translation because most of the action in the *Winnetou* books takes place on the plains, not in the mountains.

I eventually settled on "frontiersman" as the best translation for "Westmann." Every time Sam talks about being a "frontiersman" or Old Shatterhand thinks about what a good "frontiersman" would do, it is the German word "Westmann" that lies behind the passage.

Karl May has to be given a lot of credit for treating the good Indians in his books with great respect. (There are plenty of bad Indians too, of course, and they always get what they deserve.) On the whole, May's thinking about social topics like racial equality and spiritual diversity was far ahead of many of his nineteenth-century contemporaries. But Karl May was not entirely free of the stereotypes of his day, and *Winnetou* reflects that. I found it desirable to tone down some passages where May's preference for Christianity over other religions becomes overbearing, and others where he makes racist jokes at the expense of "Negroes." A literal translation of these passages, none of which is central to the story, would have resulted in a book that was arguably "more faithful" to the German, but also a book that some would find offensive. I decided to err on the side of not alienating potential readers. That, I believe, is how Karl May would have wanted it.

George Alexander, July 2008

Want to be notified of future books from Preposterous Press?

If you liked this book, wait until you see what else we're working on! We think we've found some terrific stories for young people, and we'll be publishing them over the coming months and years. Most will be chapter books for readers ages 9 to 13. If you would like to get an email letting you know when a new Preposterous Press book comes out, send us an email at:

george@changingoutlook.com

Just say "add me to your list" in the subject line. We promise not to share your email address with anyone else.

Printed in the United States
152937LV00007B/135/P